OXFORD WORLD'S CLASSICS

THE VICAR OF WAKEFIELD

OLIVER GOLDSMITH was born in 1730(?), the second son of Charles Goldsmith, curate of the parish of Kilkenny West in West Meath in Ireland. In 1745 he was admitted to Trinity College Dublin. He quickly dissipated his savings by gambling, which was to become an abiding interest. After periods at the Universities of Edinburgh and Leyden he spent 1755–6 travelling in Europe, where he is reputed to have eked out a living by playing the flute and disputing doctrinal points at monasteries and universities. Before embarking on a writing career he worked in London as an apothecary's assistant, a doctor, and a school usher. A combination of overwork, worry, and poor self-treatment hastened his death in 1774.

Goldsmith's ability and range as a professional writer were considerable. Best known perhaps for *The Vicar of Wakefield*, he was also the author of biographies, anthologies, translations, poems (*The Traveller*, 1764, and *The Deserted Village*, 1770), plays (*She Stoops to Conquer*, 1773), as well as numerous reviews and essays.

ARTHUR FRIEDMAN is the late distinguished Professor of English at the University of Chicago and editor of Goldsmith's *Collected Works*.

ROBERT L. MACK is a lecturer in the School of English at the University of Exeter. He has previously taught at Princeton University and Vanderbilt University, and is the editor of the *Arabian Nights' Entertainments* and *Oriental Tales* for Oxford World's Classics. His biography of the poet Thomas Gray was published by Yale University Press in 2000.

OXFORD WORLD'S CLASSICS

For over 100 years Oxford World's Classics have brought readers closer to the world's great literature. Now with over 700 titles—from the 4,000-year-old myths of Mesopotamia to the twentieth century's greatest novels—the series makes available lesser-known as well as celebrated writing.

The pocket-sized hardbacks of the early years contained introductions by Virginia Woolf, T. S. Eliot, Graham Greene, and other literary figures which enriched the experience of reading. Today the series is recognized for its fine scholarship and reliability in texts that span world literature, drama and poetry, religion, philosophy and politics. Each edition includes perceptive commentary and essential background information to meet the changing needs of readers.

OXFORD WORLD'S CLASSICS

OLIVER GOLDSMITH

The Vicar of Wakefield

Edited by
ARTHUR FRIEDMAN

With an Introduction and Notes by
ROBERT L. MACK

OXFORD
UNIVERSITY PRESS

OXFORD
UNIVERSITY PRESS

Great Clarendon Street, Oxford OX2 6DP

Oxford University Press is a department of the University of Oxford.
It furthers the University's objective of excellence in research, scholarship,
and education by publishing worldwide in

Oxford New York

Auckland Cape Town Dar es Salaam Hong Kong Karachi
Kuala Lumpur Madrid Melbourne Mexico City Nairobi
New Delhi Shanghai Taipei Toronto

With offices in

Argentina Austria Brazil Chile Czech Republic France Greece
Guatemala Hungary Italy Japan Poland Portugal Singapore
South Korea Switzerland Thailand Turkey Ukraine Vietnam

Oxford is a registered trade mark of Oxford University Press
in the UK and in certain other countries

Published in the United States
by Oxford University Press Inc., New York

First published as a World's Classics paperback 1981
Reissued as an Oxford World's Classics paperback 1999
New edition 2006
Reissued 2008

British Library Cataloguing in Publication Data

Data available

Library of Congress Cataloging in Publication Data

Data available

978-0-19-953754-9

15

Typeset in Ehrhardt
by RefineCatch Limited, Bungay, Suffolk
Printed in Great Britain by
Clays Ltd, Elcograf S.p.A.

CONTENTS

CONTENTS

INTRODUCTION

Composition, Publication, and Reception

The Vicar of Wakefield—Oliver Goldsmith's only novel—was first published on 27 March 1766. A second edition, in which Goldsmith made a great many stylistic revisions to the text, appeared on 31 May of that same year. Three further editions of the novel were to be published in the author's own lifetime, the last of which was dated 2 April 1774—just two days before Goldsmith's death.

The manner in which the manuscript of Goldsmith's novel first found its way into the hands of booksellers has become the stuff of literary legend. The most famous account first appeared in James Boswell's monumental *Life of Johnson* in 1791. Boswell reports Johnson as having recollected,

I received one morning a message from poor Goldsmith that he was in great distress, and, as it was not in his power to come to me, begging that I would come to him as soon as possible. I sent him a guinea, and promised to come to him directly. I accordingly went as soon as I was drest, and found that his landlady had arrested him for his rent, at which he was in a violent passion. I perceived that he had already changed my guinea, and had got a bottle Madeira and a glass before him. I put the cork into the bottle, desired he would be calm, and began to talk to him of the means by which he might be extricated. He then told me that he had a novel ready for the press, which he produced to me. I looked into it, and saw its merit; told the landlady I should soon return, and having gone to a bookseller, sold it for sixty pounds. I brought Goldsmith the money, and he discharged his rent, not without rating his landlady in a high tone for having used him so ill.[1]

Boswell was not alone in considering the anecdote worth preserving. Both Hester Lynch (Thrale) Piozzi and Sir John Hawkins

---

[1] James Boswell, *Life of Johnson* (Oxford: Oxford University Press, 1983), 294.

had included similar accounts in their own memoirs relating to Johnson (which appeared in 1786 and 1787, respectively), and still further details regarding the origin and history of Goldsmith's novel were to be forthcoming.[2] The inevitable contradictions between these several versions would extend to comprehend a wide range of disagreements regarding the actual date on which the transaction took place, the identity of the bookseller(s) involved, the precise amount of money that changed hands, and speculation as to where and when the work had been written or, indeed, if the novel had even been completed at the time of the sale. In whatever form one first encounters the story, however, its most striking feature remains the simple revelation that *The Vicar of Wakefield* is clearly among those works that finally reached the public only as a result of immediate financial need. Like Johnson's own *Rasselas* (1759)—said to have been written 'in the evenings of one week', and under the awful pressure of his mother's grave illness—*The Vicar of Wakefield*, for all its polite reputation as a genial and light-hearted work, was in actual fact the product of financial exigency.[3] In a manner similar to so many noteworthy novels of the period (among them not only the works of professional authors such as Eliza Haywood and Clara Reeve, but also the fictions of Frances Sheridan, Elizabeth Inchbald, and the later novels of Fanny Burney), Goldsmith's volume was written under conditions of considerable economic, emotional, and even physical stress. As an actual text, *The Vicar of Wakefield* was made available to a wider audience only as an impromptu means of last resort.

Goldsmith had already, even at this relatively early stage of his career in London, gained some reputation as one of the most prolific of the so-called 'Grub Street hacks'—that growing breed of writers-for-hire whose work was to fill the pages of an

[2] The accounts of Hawkins and Piozzi are included in E. H. Mikhail (ed.), *Goldsmith: Interviews and Recollections* (London: St Martin's Press, 1993), 30–4, 53–5; other versions of events can be found in several of the passages brought together in G. S. Rousseau (ed.), *Goldsmith: The Critical Heritage* (London: Routledge & Kegan Paul, 1974).

[3] Boswell, *Life of Johnson*, 240.

ever-increasing number of newspapers, journals, and magazines throughout the period. Since 1757 he had been turning out enormous amounts of material—translations, book reviews, short tales, and essays—writing at first for Ralph Griffiths's *Monthly Review*, and later for (among others) the *Critical Review*, the *British Magazine*, and the *Public Ledger*. He also found the time to see his own short-lived periodical—*The Bee* (1759)—through the press, and to publish his extended *Inquiry into the Present State of Polite Learning in Europe* (1759).

Given the rather chaotic circumstances under which the manuscript of Goldsmith's novel was sold in the autumn of 1762 and the difficult conditions under which it was written, it is all the more intriguing that his tale betrays in its telling what can only be described as a narrative pace of hasty leisure. In terms of its fictional stride, *The Vicar of Wakefield* falls somewhere between the ordered wanderings of Henry Fielding's *Tom Jones* (1749) and the more casual pilgrimage of Charlotte Lennox's *The Female Quixote* (1752). *The Vicar of Wakefield* remains a peculiarly odd generic hybrid that participates in modes as diverse as the picaresque novel, the French philosophical *conte*, the periodical essay, domestic conduct books, and the traditions of classical fabulists such as Aesop, while at the same time invoking the formal structures and arguments of everything from sermons and political pamphlets to the lyrics of the pleasure gardens and the popular ballads of the city streets. Assimilating such a wide variety of narrative voices, the novel moves at an expository speed that is at once both recognizable and unique; it is a notably short work possessed, if not of epic tropes and epic rhetoric, then at least of a certain degree of epic depth and resonance. An intimate, family story of fewer than two hundred pages that confines itself to what one chapter heading describes as 'The happiness of a country fire-side' (p. 27), Goldsmith's work has, nevertheless, routinely if paradoxically been regarded as little less than an iconic depiction of *national* identity. As the Victorian reader George Lillie Craik observed in 1845, *The Vicar of Wakefield* stands for many English readers as the 'first genuine novel of domestic life', and would continue for some considerable time to be looked upon as an achievement which—unlike the work of, say, Fielding or Sterne—furnished a balanced and historically specific 'representation of the common national mind and manners' and 'the broad general course of our English thinking and living'.[4] The character of an entire cultural point of view, in other words, was thought for generations to have been distilled in its pages to a perfect quintessence. Within the structural framework of what many would argue remains, essentially, little more than an extended fairy tale, *The Vicar of Wakefield* reaches towards—and at its most successful moments comes very near to articulating— the defining qualities normally to be found only in the most venerated of secular scriptures. Goldsmith's otherwise modest novel was a little book that had managed somehow to capture some very big ideas indeed.

At the time of the novel's first publication, Goldsmith himself, of course, had been far more anxious that his work prove an immediate financial success. If the text of the novel had in fact, as scholars now generally agree, been set down on paper sometime towards the middle of 1762, then Goldsmith would also have been looking to take full advantage of the vogue established by the recent popularity of Laurence Sterne's *Tristram Shandy*. The earliest volumes of Sterne's masterpiece had begun appearing to great acclaim in December 1759. Although he raged against Sterne both as a churchman and as a writer, Goldsmith would remain deeply envious of the tremendous financial success enjoyed by *Tristram Shandy*. His primary reason for writing an extended narrative fiction of his own in a vaguely similar manner was, in the straightforward words of one modern biographer, 'in the first place monetary'; Hester Piozzi shrewdly observed that Goldsmith 'fretted over the novel' because 'when done, [it was] to be his whole fortune'.[5] And although he clearly wrote the novel as a marketable property with the anxious dispatch of a working journalist, he had obviously been revolving certain elements of its

---

[4] George Lillie Craik, *Sketches of the History of Literature and Learning in England* (London: 1845), v. 160; repr. in Rousseau (ed.), *Goldsmith: Critical Heritage*, 303.
[5] See John Ginger, *The Singular Man: The Life and Times of Oliver Goldsmith* (London: Hamish Hamilton, 1977), 180–1.

plot and characterization over in his mind for many years. As matters so turned out, Goldsmith's publishers—John Newbery and his nephew, Francis—held on to the manuscript for a further three and a half years before seeing it into print. The reasons behind this delay remain unclear. Johnson himself suspected that the booksellers simply left the manuscript unpublished until Goldsmith had established a more financially viable reputation as a poet. Newbery, he noted practically, 'did not publish it till after the *Traveller* had appeared'. 'Then to be sure,' he added of the manuscript, 'it was actually worth some money'.[6]

Or so one would have thought. Despite Goldsmith's growing fame (in addition to the success of *The Traveller* (1764), referred to by Johnson above, the author had scored a series of hits with his 'Chinese Letters' of 1760–1 and a *Life of Richard Nash* in 1762, and had begun to make his mark as a writer of popular histories), *The Vicar of Wakefield* was surprisingly slow to find its audience. They may politely have admitted the broad and 'homely' appeal of his narrative, certainly, but none of Goldsmith's contemporaries could have foreseen that the work would in time assume its enviable position as one of the most genuinely beloved of our so-called English 'classics'. Though the novel had by 1774 passed through five authorized London editions, its sales were good yet by no means sensational; 'it seems doubtful', one biographer has speculated, 'if more than two thousand copies were sold in Goldsmith's lifetime'.[7] Only in the decades following its author's death, when it was championed by the likes of Sir Walter Scott, Byron, Schlegel, and Goethe, was *The Vicar of Wakefield* to demonstrate its peculiarly catholic appeal. William Hazlitt's 1821 judgement that 'if Goldsmith had never written anything but the two or three first chapters of *The Vicar of Wakefield* . . . they would have stamped him a genius' speaks for an entire generation of readers steeped in the conventions and expectations of European Romanticism, and singles out precisely those sorts of Rousseau-esque moments in the narrative they admired most.

---

[6] Boswell, *Life of Johnson*, 294.

[7] A. Lytton Sells, *Oliver Goldsmith: His Life and Works* (London: George Allen & Unwin Ltd., 1974), 112.

The editor William Spalding was to comment later in the century that Goldsmith's novel had 'been read, and liked, oftener than any other novel in any other European language'.[8] Influential readers throughout the Regency and early Victorian period—George Craik, Leigh Hunt, George Eliot, William Thackeray, and Thomas De Quincey among them—would repeatedly (if unvaryingly) echo such praise. Goldsmith's twentieth-century editor Arthur Friedman calculated that in the roughly twenty-five years after its author's death, twenty-three more London editions of the novel were published, and a further twenty-one editions in English were published elsewhere.[9] Throughout the nineteenth century—the early and middle decades of which saw the novel at the height of its popularity—Goldsmith's volume averaged two new editions each year in English alone. Figures for French and German translations were comparable. *The Vicar of Wakefield* is to this day one of only a small handful of English novels that can honestly lay a claim never to have passed out of print. It has even, to some extent, become a part of our everyday lives. Goldsmith's language is used to illustrate the meanings of hundreds of words in the second edition of the *Oxford English Dictionary* (1992); *The Vicar of Wakefield* is specifically cited in that work over seventy-five times. Readers are referred to the novel for illustrations of the usage of possibly unfamiliar expressions (e.g. 'blarney', 'monogamist', 'mouthed', 'muck', 'nightfall', 'overcivility'), as well as for those more specifically redolent of the eighteenth century ('elegist', 'entre nous', 'masquerade', 'necklace', 'palpitate'), and even for some of the most common words in the language ('may', 'mind', 'nicely').

The Plot of The Vicar of Wakefield *and the Book of Job*

The story that Goldsmith decided to tell in his novel strikes one even in its barest outlines deliberately to have been singled out

---

[8] William Spalding, in *The Complete Works of Oliver Goldsmith* (London: James Spalding, 1872), 7.

[9] See Arthur Friedman (ed.), *Collected Works of Oliver Goldsmith*, 5 vols. (Oxford, Clarendon Press, 1966), iv. 11.

for its potential mythic resonance. Even readers unaware of the circumstances under which the novel was actually written, as we have seen, might well be forgiven for supposing that the author had made a shrewd and calculated decision to write in a particular vein—and with an eye towards a very precise audience—purely in the interest of driving up sales. Narrated throughout by its central character, the Revd Dr Charles Primrose, the novel opens on a note of prelapsarian harmony. The Vicar of the novel's title, Dr Primrose, lives with his family in a state of modest comfort in the Edenic village of Wakefield. Benefiting from the income provided by the investment of a 'sufficient' private fortune, the Vicar is free to devote the profits of his living to the orphans and widows of the neighbourhood clergy. He keeps no curate, preferring to attend to all the necessary duties of the parish himself. He claims to have made it his business to become well acquainted with every man within his care. He exhorts the married members of his flock to temperance, and urges those who are yet bachelors to marry and establish households of their own. He confesses to derive a secret pleasure from having earned Wakefield its reputation as a town most noteworthy for three things: 'a parson wanting pride, young men wanting wives, and ale-houses wanting customers'. The even tenor of the Primrose household is troubled only occasionally by the Vicar's own obsession with a particularly obscure matter of church doctrine. One of his 'favourite topics', he tells us, is matrimony, further explaining that he values himself on being a 'strict monogamist' (p. 12); he has published several tracts arguing that it is illegal for any ordained minister of the Church of England to remarry after the death of his wife. The Vicar himself has for many years been happily married to the faithful if still independently minded Deborah Primrose. The couple's eldest son, George—the first of their six children—has just completed his studies at Oxford, and is about to be married to Miss Arabella Wilmot, the daughter of a neighbouring clergyman.

Within the space of only a few pages, however, the pastoral placidity of the Vicar's world is shattered. A series of misfortunes—precipitated by his own financial misjudgement in having placed the entire source of his private income in the hands of a local merchant, and further fuelled by his tactless adherence to his cherished doctrinal 'principles' in the face of a violent disagreement with the neighbour who was to be his son's father-in-law—soon compels the family to leave Wakefield altogether. The Vicar accepts a poorly paid curacy some seventy miles away. His prospects for marriage ruined, young George Primrose sets out alone to establish himself in a professional career, and hopefully to redeem the family's fortunes. As the rest of the family travels to the Vicar's new living, a fortuitous accident finds them introduced and indebted to Mr Burchell, a well-spoken and still youthful gentleman who, despite his handsome manners and appearance, seems currently to be possessed of little if any fortune himself. Happily familiar with the neighbourhood to which the Vicar is journeying, Burchell warns Primrose against the notorious reputation of the local Squire, a young man who, he confides, has been allowed to assume his current position though still dependent on his reclusive uncle, Sir William Thornhill. Young Squire Thornhill's libertine behaviour is all the more surprising because his uncle, who has withdrawn from the public eye, is known even to Primrose by reputation as an individual once widely praised throughout the kingdom for his highly developed sense of sympathy and benevolence.

No sooner has the family begun to establish itself with some degree of comfort in their newly reduced circumstances, but they receive a visit from the Squire himself. They find Thornhill to be quite unlike the haughty and disreputable figure Burchell's description had led them to expect, and decide that the latter was speaking merely and for some private motive out of envy or dislike. They look upon the Squire as a charming and quite dashing young man, and are flattered that he thinks nothing of condescending to pass much time with his new tenants. Primrose's two marriageable daughters—Olivia and Sophia—are overawed by the fact that the Squire should even think of spending his evenings in their humble company, and are soon caught up in their mother's ambitious vision of the possibilities of unlikely matches and wildly prosperous futures for either or both her girls. The Squire's further introduction of two apparently sophisticated

London ladies to the company, and their proposal that the Primrose girls accompany them back to town to experience the smartening effect of a proper social season, is greeted ecstatically in the Primrose household, although the Vicar professes still to have some reservations regarding such a scheme. Primrose is content to offer a generally rosy picture of their new way of life, however, and narrates with a wry amusement the several, harmless follies of his various family members. He wryly notes their attempts to ape the behaviour of their social betters, while at the same time looking down their noses on—and taking every possible opportunity themselves to impress—those near neighbours whose more suitable company the presence of the Squire and his retinue has instantly rendered beneath them.

Although throughout the first half of the novel the family thus appears to be adjusting to their situation with a minimum amount of dissatisfaction, the catastrophic second part of Goldsmith's tale reveals every one of the decisions taken up to that point to have been a disastrous mistake. The Vicar in particular, it turns out, has thoroughly misjudged the characters of the family's supposed friends and neighbours, to say nothing of their insidious and truly dangerous enemies. As a result, he has jeopardized their happiness, and remains generally ineffectual as they are each successively brought to the brink of tragedy. In a passage that was subsequently to become one of the best-known episodes in the novel, his young and pedantically affected son Moses is sent to the local market to sell one of the family's horses, only to be duped into swapping the animal for a gross of worthless green spectacles; the Vicar's attempts to remedy the situation by heading off to the market himself to sell their remaining horse find him similarly hoodwinked by the same man. Deborah, Olivia, and Sophia are so blinded by status and so hungry for social recognition that they ignore the warnings of Mr Burchell regarding the Squire's motives; indeed, they suspect Burchell himself of spreading false reports and slandering their reputation throughout the neighbourhood. When Olivia is glimpsed being driven away in a carriage in the company of two men, Primrose immediately suspects Burchell to be behind the abduction, and sets off in pursuit.

The narrative of his wanderings initiates a further catalogue of disasters. Primrose has no sooner begun to make progress in tracing his daughter's path, than he falls ill with a fever, and finds himself confined to his bed in a roadside alehouse for nearly three weeks. His return journey is interrupted by an encounter with a group of strolling players, in whose company he is fooled into being entertained at the home of a neighbourhood man, whom he takes to be—by his manners and bearing—nothing less than the local Member of Parliament. Their evening debate on the subject of politics and the best form of social order is interrupted by the unexpected return of the gentleman who turns out to be the true master of the house, and who reveals to those assembled around his table that their supposed 'host' was no better than his own butler, who 'in his master's absence, had a mind to cut a figure, and be for a while the gentleman himself' (p. 89). Primrose is further nonplussed to discover that this very same gentleman is the uncle to that same Miss Arabella Wilmot who was to have been married to his son George. He is even more shocked to find George himself—whom he thought to be making a respectable name for himself elsewhere in the world—revealed to be a member of the company of players.

The Vicar's own narrative is at this point interrupted by his son's account of his chequered fortunes as a 'philosophical vaga-bond' in and around the metropolis. Both father and son are surprised to learn that Arabella Wilmot has since their own departure from Wakefield become engaged to marry Squire Thornhill; Primrose is yet again taken aback when he stumbles upon Olivia herself on his way home, and discovers that it was the Squire and not Burchell who had run off with her and seduced her under the pretence of a false marriage. Realizing that she was to be treated as a common mistress, however, Olivia escaped and was also making her way home as best she could when accidentally discovered by her father. Only now does the Vicar realize that the Squire's recent and seemingly generous purchase of an army commission for his son George has merely served as an efficient means of getting him out of the country—and out of the way of his bride-to-be Arabella Wilmot—and so removing him from the picture altogether.

The tremendous events that greet the hopeful return of Primrose and Olivia to the family home initiate the final series of catastrophes in the novel, the mounting severity of which draw Primrose and his family further and further into a slough of misery and—for most readers—a vision of human behaviour that grotesquely resembles a universe not operating on any principles of benevolence, generosity, or fellow feeling, but motivated rather by a degree of selfish hypocrisy and a rank fetishism of power that would in all likelihood have driven even the likes of Thomas Hobbes to despair. The final ten chapters of *The Vicar of Wakefield* constitute the dark wonderland of Goldsmith's novel. We move increasingly in these pages within a night world of pain, penury, chains, and prisons—a world apparently abandoned by justice, and lit only sporadically by the fires of destruction.

The obvious narrative precedent for the headlong spectacle in these chapters of a righteous man confronted against his own will with the problem of evil and injustice in the world—a precedent for the presentation of the hero as 'victim', even—is the ancient legend that achieved its finest expression in the biblical Book of Job. It concerns a pious man of great virtue and integrity who is suddenly and without warning deprived of all the rewards of his labour and forced to undergo unspeakable trials. Despite the fact that he is subjected to great suffering and further loss, Job refuses, against the pressing advice of his friends and family, to renounce his God, but remains steadfast in his allegiance, and blesses his Lord even as before. His wife is among the first who fails to comprehend the depth of his enduring loyalty. 'Dost thou still retain thine integrity?', she asks scornfully, before advising him succinctly: 'curse God, and die' (Job 2: 9). Thanks in large part to the New Testament reminder in James 5: 11, to possess 'the patience of Job' has passed into our language as a proverbial expression applied to one who can with equanimity endure that which for any other individual would prove unendurable. The Job of the Old Testament, however, is far from passively 'patient' in the book that bears his name. He is angry, often furious, and decidedly *im*patient with a cosmos in which the wicked seem not only to go free but to flourish, and with a deity that remains unresponsive to his human demand for justice.

Goldsmith's Vicar recalls his biblical prototype in several important respects, but perhaps the strongest characteristic that links Dr Primrose to Job is the corresponding degree to which both tend to regard their own 'goodness'—their own practice of virtue and due deference—as 'money in the bank', as Stephen Mitchell puts it.[10] Fewer things, certainly, are likely to strike the reader upon repeated encounters with the eighteenth-century novel as forcefully as the underlying if deeply repressed anxiety of Dr Primrose himself with regard to the radical instability of this world. The rapid acceleration of catastrophes and events as the novel moves towards its conclusion in some respects represents nothing so accurately as the Vicar's escalating panic; his earlier attempts to present to his family—and to his readers—a face of serene acceptance when confronted with changes and disruptions are weakened to the point of absolute collapse with each devastating blow of fate. And the novel is to some extent a mere catalogue of instability—a recitation of catastrophes, many of them if not of biblical proportions, then at least of a biblical nature: marriages, promises, and trusts are broken, loyalties are betrayed, identities are disguised or thoroughly misapprehended, currency itself and 'values' of all kinds are in a constant state of flux, and the physical world of the novel is one that is visited without warning by outbreaks of fire and flood. The city may be the most obvious haunt of criminals and con men, but the natural world is hospitable only when tamed by the hand of man; even then it is subject always to whims of a seemingly amoral deity. Even the Vicar's obsession with the doctrines of William Whiston regarding the marriage of clergymen in certain circumstances can be read as a manifestation of his own fear that—should he ever find himself in such a position—he would be incapable of handling the disruption of any such change in circumstance. Primrose's repeated advocacy of his pet theories is an attempt to

---

[10] *The Book of Job*, trans. and introd. Stephen Mitchell (New York: Harper Collins, 1979), p. ix.

fortify himself against his own sense of weakness and inadequacy in the face of possible chaos.

Yet to whatever extent Goldsmith desired in his novel to recall to the minds of his readers the tribulations that beset even God's favourite, he is careful to avoid the most sombre aspects of his Old Testament model. Although *The Vicar of Wakefield* does arguably tackle a subject no less impressive than the ability and the moral strength of mankind to transcend human suffering, the author does not push his hero in any unconvincing way towards an achievement of bold and enlightened spiritual insight. Toward the end of his trials, Job regrets all that has been taken from him, and wishes only that he could exchange his present state for his past:

Oh that I were as in months past, as in the days when God preserved me;

When his candle shined upon my head, and when by his light I walked through darkness;

As I was in the days of my youth, when the secret of God was upon my tabernacle;

When the Almighty was yet with me, when my children were about me; . . .

When the ear heard me, then it blessed me; and when the eye saw me, it gave witness to me (Job 29: 2–5, 11)

Job's outburst markedly anticipates the words of Goldsmith's Vicar in his extremity. Yet whereas the lament of Job builds towards the end of his narrative to a bewildered cry of outrage against the comprehensive fact of human misery, the Vicar's more hysterical apostrophes are invariably thumped violently back to ground by the interruption of someone close to him who tells him essentially that he, of all people, ought to know better. As Dr Primrose approaches his lowest point, in prison and believing his daughter Olivia already to be dead, he is informed by his wife—who is herself nearly incoherent with grief and on the edge of collapse—that his younger daughter, Sophia, has also just been forcibly abducted by a 'well drest man' in a passing post-chaise. 'Now', the Vicar cries aloud to the prison cell, 'the sum of my misery is made up, nor is it in the power of any thing on earth to give me another pang. What! not one left! not to leave me one! the monster! the child that was next my heart! she had the beauty of an angel, and almost the wisdom of an angel. But support that woman [i.e., his wife, Deborah], nor let her fall. Not to leave me one!' (p. 139)

Deborah Primrose, however, unlike the wife of Job, is the one who more successfully resists the pressures of the moment, and serves herself as a model for her husband:

'Alas! my husband,' said my wife, 'you seem to want comfort even more than I. Our distresses are great; but I could bear this and more, if I saw you but easy. They may take away my children and all the world, if they leave me but you.' (pp. 139–40)

The Vicar manages to pull himself together and to regain some degree of composure, but the arrival of his son, George, bloody, wounded, and in fetters just two pages later proves to be too much for him. He is once again transformed into the accusing picture of angry despair. 'I tried to restrain my passions for a few minutes in silence,' he writes,

but I thought I should have died with the effort—'O my boy, my heart weeps to behold thee thus, and I cannot, cannot help it. In the moment that I thought thee blest, and prayed for thy safety, to behold thee thus again! Chained, wounded. And yet the death of the youthful is happy. But I am old, a very old man, and have lived to see this day. To see my children all untimely falling about me, while I continue a wretched survivor in the midst of ruin! May all the curses that ever sunk a soul fall heavy upon the murderer of my children. May he live, like me, to see—' (p. 142)

The Vicar is at this moment of mounting denunciation interrupted by no one other than his wounded, bloody son himself, who cries:

'Hold, Sir, . . . or I shall blush for thee. How, Sir, forgetful of your age, your holy calling, thus to arrogate the justice of heaven, and fling those curses upward that must soon descend to crush thy own grey head with destruction! No, Sir, let it be your care now to fit me for that vile death I must shortly suffer, to arm me with hope and resolution, to give me courage to drink of that bitterness which must shortly be my portion.' (p. 142)

The first-person account of Dr Primrose—a narrative voice that is throughout the novel skilfully interrupted and varied by what might be described as his own rhetorical 'encounters' with other forms of storytelling, versification, narration, sermonizing, representation, and debate—manages always to serve the same function that dramatic techniques such as discrepant awareness (whereby the audience can be reassured early in the action of a comedy that everything *will*, indeed, end happily) facilitate in the theatre. The narrative of Dr Primrose and his family is everywhere lightened by Goldsmith's own instinct for the sort of deft repetition that will come in time to characterize the comedy of the absurd.

Dr Primrose and his faith, by the end of the novel, may have been sorely tried, but at no point does the Vicar, like his Old Testament predecessor, achieve the sublime insight that leads to a gesture of wholehearted surrender or submission. Whereas the tone of Job's final words in the face of the Unnameable—the Voice that speaks to him from the Whirlwind—voices the serene transformation of bitterness to awe, that of the Vicar is merely, if appropriately, content. 'I know that thou canst do every thing, and that no thought can be withholden from thee', Job acknowledges before his God; 'Wherefore I abhor myself, and repent in dust and ashes' (Job 42: 2, 6). Dr Primrose finds final comfort not so much in any genuine repentance or comprehension of his own mortality, but in the renewal of familiar and comforting 'ceremonies'. The shadows that are increasingly visible throughout the thematic landscapes of Goldsmith's novel are shades cast only by momentary obstructions against a relatively constant background of light, however variable its intensity. If the first half of the novel had been bathed in the pastoral optimism and the possible attainment of a frugal, rural contentment, the second is a nightmare of cumulative disasters that is redeemed by an ending reminiscent of nothing so much as a late Shakespearian romance. The Vicar's pronouncement at the end of the novel seems in fact almost explicitly to recall the words not of the awe-stricken Job, but of Shakespeare's own Prospero, in the final moments of *The Tempest*. 'I had nothing now on this side of the grave to wish for,' runs the Vicar's concluding sentence in the novel, 'all my cares were over, my pleasure was unspeakable. It now only remained that my gratitude in good fortune should exceed my former submission in adversity' (p. 170).

Charm, Autobiography, and Sentiment

For many years the simple phenomenon of *The Vicar of Wakefield*'s sustained popularity appeared to be the main talking point for most criticism. The story itself—and Goldsmith's handling of it—seemed somehow beyond commentary. It is a testament not so much to any inherent excellence, but simply to the long-standing enigma of Goldsmith's novel, that Thomas Babington Macaulay's entry on the author, originally included in the 1856 (8th) edition of the *Encyclopaedia Britannica*, was to remain in print until as late as 1961. Some few critics paused to comment on what they thought to be the peculiarly arbitrary sequence of the novel's narrative 'incidents', but most were compelled merely to accept the work for the humorous and vaguely 'delightful' quality that formed the basis of its continued wide appeal.

Henry James best articulated the odd combination of approval and frustration the novel provoked within any individual determined to say something consequential or objective about its aesthetic achievement. He was driven to the point of distraction by Goldsmith's novel, memorably christening it 'the spoiled child of our literature', able to '[convert] everything it contains into a happy case of exemption and fascination. ... One admits the particulars [of *The Vicar of Wakefield*] with the sense that, as regards the place the thing has taken, it remains, by a strange little law of its own, quite undamaged—simply stands there smiling with impunity.'[11]

---

[11] Henry James, 'Introduction' to Oliver Goldsmith's *The Vicar of Wakefield* (New York, 1900); repr. in Rousseau (ed.), *Goldsmith: Critical Heritage*, 65–9, from which all quotations are taken.

In his final assessment of Goldsmith's work, James went as far as to suggest that—although singular—the novel so stretched the 'indulgence' of its readers, that it *must* on some level be judged a failure. 'Read as one of the masterpieces by a person not acquainted with our Literature,' he wrote, 'it might easily give the impression that this literature is not immense.' While tentatively suggesting that, in terms of Goldsmith's style, 'the frankness of his sweetness and the beautiful ease of his speech' is the quality that first appeals to Goldsmith's readers, confronted with its larger achievement, James concedes defeat: 'I am afraid I cannot go further than this in the way of speculation as to how a classic is grown,' he decides, wearily; 'In the open air is perhaps the most we can say. Goldsmith's style is the flower of what I have called its amenity, and [Goldsmith's own] amenity the making of that independence of almost everything by which *The Vicar* has triumphed.'

He concludes of the novel: 'the thing has succeeded by terms of its incomparable amenity', which reduces us to a point of critical helplessness, so that 'under its charm we resist the irritation of having to define [its] character'.

'Charm' and 'amenity' are not exactly the kinds of words that one is likely to find in any contemporary dictionary of critical terms. Yet until the most recent critics of Goldsmith's novel felt themselves free to pursue those apparently fragmented elements of the text that might be used as keys to unlock its relevance to specific issues of class, power, and politics, any more traditional interpretive approaches to the work seemed doomed to certain failure. Attempts to analyse Goldsmith's 'plot' invariably reached the same conclusions: the Vicar's narrative was poorly constructed, at once both dense and highly complicated, yet also stuttering in pace and lacking in proportion. Those few episodes in the first half of the novel that might with a more patient exposition have been developed into successful set pieces remained too confused and hurried; there was simply no excuse for the frenzied pace and unlikely reversals of the latter part of the work. Similarly, the 'calamities' that might otherwise have carried some emotional weight were so clumsily clustered together, and each followed so hard upon the next, that any impact they might otherwise have possessed was altogether dissipated. As for the 'realism' or sense of verisimilitude that one might with reason expect even from the simplest fairy story, the reader could only search in vain. Any comments on Goldsmith's plot, in other words, were invariably little more than echoes of Macaulay's observations of 1856, in which he dismissed the novel's 'fable' as not merely faulty, but 'one of the worst that ever was constructed'. 'It wants', Macaulay had sniffed, 'not merely the probability that ought to be found in a tale of common English life, but that consistency which ought to be found even in the wildest fiction about witches, giants, and fairies.'[12]

Hopeful suggestions that the novel was intended to be a spontaneous and self-consciously innovative attempt to break free from the increasing strictures imposed on novelistic fictions were no less quickly dispatched by the assertion that those very same aspects that struck new readers as unusual or at least well accomplished had simply been freely borrowed from existing works. Almost every narrative episode in the Vicar's account took its cue from or otherwise found its model not in lived human experience or behaviour, but had been drawn straight from the work of a contemporary or immediate predecessor. The narratives of seduction drew in almost every detail from novels such as Samuel Richardson's *Pamela* (1740–1) and *Clarissa* (1747–8); the prison scenes had already been 'done'—and to far better effect—by Henry Fielding in his *Amelia* (1751), and the picaresque adventures of Dr Primrose and his son owed more than a little of their colour to those of that same author's *Joseph Andrews* (1742); in tone, Goldsmith had failed in his obvious attempts to imitate the successful 'sensibility' of which Sterne continued to demonstrate himself a master, to capture the epigrammatic brilliance that Johnson had displayed to such fine effect in his *Rasselas*, or even to reproduce some of the anecdotal appeal of which he had demonstrated himself capable in his own 'Chinese Letters'.

---

[12] From Thomas Babington Macaulay's life of Goldsmith in *Encyclopaedia Britannica*, 8th edn. (1856), x. 705–9; repr. in Rousseau (ed.), *Goldsmith: Critical Heritage*, 349.

His 'characters', such as they were, amounted to little more than static, two-dimensional cut-outs of little if any emotional depth, and admitted no development.

The only quality for which *The Vicar of Wakefield* was likely to garner any positive critical attention at all, in fact, was its success-fully modest description—limited almost entirely to its earliest chapters—of an ideal of pastoral retirement and domestic harmony that was thought to be worthy of imitation. It was only when he limited himself to depictions of this nature, critics also suggested, that Goldsmith's style came close to suiting his subject. The opening lines of Chapter V provide an ideal example of such scenes. The Vicar is here describing the situation of his new living, and the manner in which the members of his family accommodated themselves to their fortunes:

At a small distance from the house my predecessors had made a seat, overshadowed by an hedge of hawthorn and honeysuckle. Here, when the weather was fine, and our labour soon finished, we usually sate together, to enjoy an extensive landscape [*sic*], in the calm of the evening. Here too we drank tea, which now was become an occasional banquet; and as we had it but seldom, it diffused a new joy, the prepar-ations for it being made with no small share of bustle and ceremony. On these occasions, our two little ones always read for us, and they were regularly served after we had done. Sometimes, to give a variety to our amusements, the girls sung to the guitar; and while they thus formed a little concert, my wife and I would stroll down the sloping field, that was embellished with blue bells and centaury, talk of our children with rapture, and enjoy the breeze that wafted both health and harmony (pp. 24–5).

Goldsmith was among those writers who, until recently, was often referred to as being in some way 'pre-Romantic'. The win-ning strengths of passages such as this, however, are those more accurately associated with the ethos of Augustan poetics; the Vicar's new home and pastimes are similar to those praised by poets earlier in the century (one thinks specifically of the ethos of John Pomfret's 'The Choice' (1700), for example, or the restrained environments and behaviour described in Alexander Pope's moral epistles). The language here is as cool and calm as

the activities are temperate; this is a landscape characterized by
the ideals of the beautiful and picturesque, not the vertiginous
ecstasy of the sublime, or the fantastic primitivism of any
Rousseau-esque 'natural world'.

The Vicar of Wakefield also owed much of its continued popularity—though it earned the respect of few critics—to its perceived value as a work of religious consolation. To whatever
extent readers as sympathetic as Johnson may have disparaged
the technical achievement of Goldsmith's novel when he dismissed it as 'a mere fanciful performance' that contained 'nothing
of real life . . . and very little of nature', for a great many members of Goldsmith's audience *The Vicar of Wakefield* seemed
absolutely to *insist* on being read for its morality and for its
reassuring spiritual message.[13] An early, unsigned notice that
appeared in Hugh Kelly's *Babler* shortly after the novel's publication simply took for granted that Goldsmith's primary reason
for presenting his readers with such a variety of calamitous circumstances was to provide 'a masterly vindication of that exterior
disparity in the dispensations of providence, at which our modern infidels seem to triumph with so unceasing a satisfaction'.
'And', the reviewer continued, 'it must undoubtedly yield a sublime consolation to the bosom of wretchedness to think, that if
the opulent are blessed with a continual round of temporal
felicity, they shall at least experience some moments of so
superior a rapture in the immediate presence of their God, as will
fully compensate for the seeming severity of their former situations.'[14] The spectacular series of denouements that closes the
novel, in other words, was thought to amount to a vindication of
the terminal justice and equity of the divine plan. Another early
reviewer, whose notice on the novel appeared in the *Monthly
Review* in May 1766, effaced any reservations he may have had
regarding the book's stylistic oddities to conclude:

---

[13] The judgement of Samuel Johnson noted here is recorded by Frances Burney in
The Diary and Letters of Madame D'Arblay, ed. Charlotte Barrett (Philadelphia, 1842),
38–9; repr. in Rousseau (ed.), *Goldsmith: Critical Heritage*, 189–90.
[14] Unsigned Review in Hugh Kelly's *Babler*, 77 (10 July 1776), 55–9; repr. in
Rousseau (ed.), *Goldsmith: Critical Heritage*, 54.

In brief, with all its faults, there is much rational entertainment to be met with in this very singular tale; but it deserves our warmer approbation for its moral tendency; particularly for the exemplary manner in which it recommends and enforces, the great obligations of universal BENEVOLENCE; the most amiable quality that can possibly distinguish and adorn the WORTHY MAN and the GOOD CHRISTIAN![15]

Well over a generation later, Goldsmith's biographer John Forster felt no need to apologize for similarly reading *The Vicar of Wakefield* as an attempt to justify the ways of God to man. Forster thought the novel had sprung from the 'sweet emotion' of Goldsmith's own 'chequered life', and concluded that the author's own experiences had merely been re-presented to the public so as 'to show us that patience in suffering, that persevering reliance on the providence of God ... are the easy and certain means of pleasure in this *world*, and of turning pain to noble uses'.[16]

Despite the dramatic shift in critical perspective within the last fifty years or more that has looked generally to separate the 'life' from the 'work', and which in its most extreme forms attempted to dispense with the role of the author in the task of textual interpretation altogether, biographically based readings of *The Vicar of Wakefield* have remained stubbornly popular well into the twenty-first century. Washington Irving's observation that Goldsmith's novel had simply offered readers its scenes and characters 'as seen through the medium of his own indulgent eye, and set ... forth with the colourings of his good head and heart' is in all likelihood liable to be no less acceptable a sentiment to the vast majority of today's readers than it would have been to those who first encountered it in 1825.[17] 'Any biographer who refused to read the family life of the Goldsmiths into the account of the Primrose family', as John Ginger confessed, 'would have to

---

[15] Unsigned notice, *in Monthly Review*, 34 (May 1766), 407; repr. in Rousseau (ed.), *Goldsmith: Critical Heritage*, 44.

[16] From John Forster's *Life of Oliver Goldsmith* (1848); portions of Forster's *Life* are included in George Lewes's review of that work, *British Quarterly*, 8 (1 Aug. 1848), 1–25; repr. in Rousseau (ed.), *Goldsmith: Critical Heritage*, 329.

[17] Washington Irving, *British Classics* (New York, 1825); repr. in Rousseau (ed.), *Goldsmith: Critical Heritage*, 265.

be made of stern stuff.'[18] George Rousseau was rather less understanding when he countered: 'At the heart of the problem—and
it *is* a problem—lies Goldsmith's life.' 'Goldsmith-the-man',
Rousseau with reason lamented, 'has interested critics more than
Goldsmith-the-writer.'[19]

Both Ginger and Rousseau, it must be conceded, make legit-
imate points; the briefest outline of Goldsmith's life *does* seem to
read like something straight out of his novel. Born into a modest
clerical family in rural Ireland, Goldsmith would often in his
work reimagine the fields and streams around his childhood home
of Lissoy to have constituted a veritable paradise; in the face of all
the economic and social realities of the time, for Goldsmith the
parsonage in which he had been raised, and the activities he was
always to associate with his young and relatively carefree existence there, were effortlessly resituated in his adult writing and
viewed through a haze that transformed them into a lost golden
age. Even his time at Trinity College Dublin, to which Goldsmith
was admitted in June 1745, emerges in most biographical
accounts as a challenging but by no means overstressful period in
his life. The only things most readers tend to remember about
Goldsmith's career as an undergraduate is that he was publicly
admonished and temporarily sent down for taking part in a student riot in 1747 (in which others were actually killed), became
addicted to gambling and other vices associated with 'low company', and began to display those traits what were eventually
to develop into lifelong habits of personal irresponsibility;
Goldsmith held the dubious distinction of actually having been
punched in his face by his own tutor. His wild misadventures
upon returning briefly to his mother's home (he attempted
unsuccessfully to be ordained into the Anglican Church, served
as a private tutor to a family in County Roscommon, and claimed
accidentally to have missed the boat that was to have carried him
as an emigrant to America), though matter enough for most men,

---

[18] John Ginger, *The Notable Man: The Life and Times of Oliver Goldsmith* (London:
Hamish Hamilton, 1977), 168.
[19] Ed.'s introd. in Rousseau (ed.), *Goldsmith: Critical Heritage*, 3.

served only as a kind of comic prelude to the more wide-ranging adventures he claimed to have experienced as a wandering traveller throughout Germany, Switzerland, France, and northern Italy some few years later, in 1755. His sporadic attempts to find a suitable occupation invariably led nowhere, although his time spent at Edinburgh University and then at Leyden from 1752 to 1754 would leave him with just enough knowledge later in life so as to pass himself off as a medical doctor. Prior to his first real success as a writer in his early thirties, Goldsmith lived a hand-to-mouth existence that resembled nothing so much as a series of Hogarth prints brought to life. He tried his hand at being an apothecary, an ad hoc physician, a proofreader, and an usher at a boys' school in Peckham; in 1758 he even applied (unsuccessfully) for a civilian position within the East India Company. He produced hundreds of pages of reviews and essays before the success of his verse-epistle *The Traveller* in December 1764 finally brought him some acclaim as an author of genuine merit. For a brief period, he enjoyed the intimate company of some of the period's finest writers, artists, and political thinkers. The further successes of *The Vicar of Wakefield* and of his 1770 poem *The Deserted Village*—along with his two comedies for the stage, *The Good-Natured Man* (1768) and *She Stoops to Conquer* (1773)—were no sooner to set him on a path to some degree of financial and personal stability than he died—of kidney disease—in April 1774, at the relatively young age of 43.

It is little wonder that readers have felt there to be important links between the story of Goldsmith's life and that of his novel. Almost all the elements that were to characterize his peculiar narrative romance are already present in his own personal history; many features needed hardly even to be transformed in any serious way. The pastoral settings within which the Revd Primrose and his family find themselves throughout much of the first half of the novel seem for many readers unequivocally to have been based on his own earliest experiences in Ireland (the area around Lissoy is today marketed to tourists as 'Goldsmith Country', despite the fact that the author was, after the age of 21, never again even to set foot in Ireland); the character of Primrose himself is routinely thought to embody the virtues of Goldsmith's own clergyman father; perhaps most significantly, entire extended sections in the second half of the novel relating to the adventures both of Primrose and of his son George were so inextricably linked to the author's own personal anecdotes and Continental adventures by Goldsmith's earliest biographers that it remains even today impossible to disentangle what is 'true' from what is purely fictitious.

Yet for a modern reader convincingly to maintain that in order to understand Goldsmith's novel, we must first gain a full appreciation of Goldsmith the man, is not merely unsustainable, but deeply misleading. Many critics, by contrast, treat *The Vicar of Wakefield* as an uncomplicated example of that peculiarly eighteenth-century literary kind, the 'sentimental novel'. Such novels were a narrative manifestation of the period's 'cult of feeling'. They gave expression to the new emphasis being placed on the significance of subjective experience. Readers—many of them women—were throughout the century increasingly drawn to works of fiction that exhibited the moving spectacle of 'virtue in distress'; one's own ability to empathize with the misfortunes of fictional others was looked upon as a measure of the strength of one's own 'heart' and of the vigour of those moral principles that in turn dictate the behaviour of our lives. Novels such as Samuel Richardson's *Pamela* and *Clarissa* simply paved the way for later works containing even more provocative displays of (usually female) suffering, all designed to draw forth from readers as highly sensitized and as actively sympathetic a response as possible. The period's obsession with such concepts as 'sentiment', 'sensibility', and 'melancholia' was thought to be witnessed everywhere in the literature of the era.

In order to read Goldsmith's novel in such a manner, readers must place no small degree of faith in the author's manipulation of the vicar himself as an effective narrator—one who is at once both dispassionate in the control he maintains over potentially disturbing emotions, yet also demurely impudent—and who manages successfully to record the events of the novel, as John Butt put it, 'briefly, even briskly, without being fundamentally unsettled by any of them'.[20] In presenting his tale through such an amiable and coherent figure, it might be argued, Goldsmith avoided those tendencies that would have rendered the work less successful in the hands of other contemporary practitioners in the form of the sentimental novel. Frances Sheridan, whose *Memoirs of Miss Sidney Bidulph* appeared in 1761, would have savoured the destitution of the characters. Similarly Henry Brooke, whose immensely popular *The Fool of Quality* (1766–72) first appeared in the same year as *The Vicar of Wakefield*, tended to display a feverish intensity and an 'uncontrolled vehemence' in his attempts to reconcile a world controlled by divine providence to the plight of helpless characters in positions of extreme distress in a hostile world. What some critics would argue to be the 'controlled spontaneity' of Goldsmith's narrator in *The Vicar of Wakefield* was complemented by the corresponding guidance he maintained over the structure of his narrative—a structure that modern readers are less likely to notice. Commentators have pointed out that the Vicar's story is perfectly divided into two halves—the first half being essentially a comedy, its episodes (apart from the initial expulsion from Wakefield) relatively minor and even comfortably domestic in nature. The second half of the novel, by contrast, is a quasi-tragedy rich in the pathos of multiple misfortunes and catastrophes. Goldsmith thrusts his characters into the world in a dramatic and distressing way—we move within the space of a few pages from financial discomfiture and minor mishaps to abductions, penury, destruction by fire, imprisonment, and a tone of near apocalyptic catastrophe. Whereas Goldsmith's narrative technique in the first part of the novel had been relatively limited, the second prominently includes a diversity of novelistic modes and voices, including traveller's tales, politics, discussions on philosophy and aesthetics, digressions on subjects including penal reform and the state of urban depravity, and even sermons. The symmetry of the entire novel is precise, and neatly reverses the sentiment of the

---

[20] See John Butt, *The Mid-Eighteenth Century*, ed. and completed by Geoffrey Carnell, Oxford History of English Literature, vol. viii. (Oxford: Clarendon Press, 1979), 473.

novel's epigraph: the happy family of the first part of the novel
should take heed in their felicity, much in the manner that they
should be sustained throughout the calamities of the second half
by the promise of Christian hope. The thirty-two chapters
are divided neatly into two halves of sixteen chapters each; further divisions can then be drawn that discern subsets of a pair of
eight chapters apiece. The three poems included in the novel
in each case punctuate crucial turning points of the narrative
action, contributing to subliminally perceived design that further
underscores the symmetrical effect of the novel as a whole.[21]

Sentiment versus Satire

If a great many readers of Goldsmith's work are still inclined to
look upon *The Vicar of Wakefield* primarily as a relatively
straightforward domestic fiction or sentimental romance of this
sort, professional critics have tended increasingly to agree that
the novel's seeming artlessness is in fact nothing more than a self-
conscious pose that has been assumed by the author—part of a
disingenuous attempt deliberately to trick his readers and to raise
false generic and narrative expectations. According to such a
view, Goldsmith superficially invokes various literary genres and
modes in the course of his tale only to subvert them. His apparently earnest narrative of sentiment is in fact an extended exer-
cise in irony. Such fundamental disagreements in approach have
ensured that certain passages in the novel thought by some to be
deeply felt and sincere are no less likely to be read by others as
rich with elements of parody and satire, and have raised a series of
critical questions that have yet to be fully answered. Just how far,
exactly, are we meant to trust the Revd Primrose's own narration

---

[21] See ibid. 475. The novel's structure is also addressed in Robert H. Hopkins's
influential reading of the novel as a satire in *The True Genius of Oliver Goldsmith*
(Baltimore: Johns Hopkins Press, 1974), 199–207; Sven Bäckman, *This Singular Tale: A
Study of the Vicar of Wakefield and Its Literary Background*, Lund Studies in English, 40
(Lund, Sweden: G. W. K. Gleerup, 1971); Arthur F. Kinney, *Oliver Goldsmith Revisited*
(Boston: Twayne, 1991), 76–7; Ricardo Quintana, *Oliver Goldsmith: A Georgian Study*
(London: Weidenfeld and Nicolson, 1967), 109–12.

of his 'tale' when, even from the opening pages of the volume, he reveals himself to be wildly inconsistent, illogical, and, at worst, completely hypocritical? To what extent could readers ever accept Goldsmith's fiction as somehow true to life or at least relevant to their lived experience, much less autobiographical, when it is so clearly a work that on every page—and increasingly throughout the text—bears the traces of its deliberate confusion of almost every literary 'type' that flourished in the period? Did Goldsmith in fact set out actually to write a satire on the vogue for sentimental fiction or 'sensibility' in general (as he was more obviously to do in his theatrical comedies), yet allow his narrative in this instance to spin so wildly out of control as to lose all authority over his own plot and characters? As the critic Ricardo Quintana sometime ago observed, for all its apparent simplicity and innocence, *The Vicar of Wakefield* has given rise to 'more questions and presents greater difficulties of interpretation than any of Goldsmith's other compositions'.[22]

Those novels that participate most successfully in the traditions of satire in English tend usually to alert their audiences from the very outset that they will need always to be vigilant; they insist that their readers be aware of the fragile seam of irony that divides the perceived appearance of things from the fictional 'reality' of the novelistic world. *The Vicar of Wakefield* may not fail completely to alert readers to its possible parodic or satiric agendas. Yet Goldsmith's particular blend of irony and sincerity in the novel has posed no end of questions for generations of readers. Upon closer examination, we soon discover that nothing about *The Vicar of Wakefield* is ever as simple as it first appears to be. The text of the novel—indeed, even the language with which the work introduces itself to its audience and announces its supposed intentions—initiates a complicated and occasionally coy strategy of linguistic play. The novel also contains an astounding number of characters who disguise themselves or participate in some sort of 'masquerade'. Many tend effortlessly to assume

---

[22] See Quintana, *Oliver Goldsmith: A Georgian Study*, Masters of World Literature series (London: Weidenfeld and Nicolson, 1969), 99–100.

different identities and to 'play' the roles of others in a romantic or dramatic manner.

The Vicar of Wakefield even begins, like some vexed and impish *Hamlet*, not by answering questions, but by asking them. The original title page pointedly characterizes the narrative as 'a Tale, supposed to have been written by himself'.[23] Modern readers are unfortunately unlikely to pay much if any attention to the specific designation of the fiction they hold in their hands as a 'Tale'. The extended subtitles of most eighteenth-century novels, however, alerted readers to important claims of authenticity and provenance—they called attention to the balance of tradition and innovation, of authority and licence. Narratives designated to be tales tended to feature an intrusive and slightly wayward narrative persona, and were often marked by a tendency towards digression and generic inclusivity. Goldsmith's further qualification that his is a tale 'supposed to have been written by [the Vicar of Wakefield]' is perhaps even more peculiar—particularly in his use of that troubling '*supposed*'. Is Goldsmith (or an otherwise unnamed and unidentified 'editor') asking us here to believe that the Vicar's narrative is true? Is the subtitle working to highlight the nature of the Vicar's story *as* fiction? Or is it merely an assumption on the part of an 'editor'? At the very least, the uncertainty reflected in this seemingly straightforward phrase anticipates Goldsmith's manipulation of what will remain an enigmatic and at times even wildly inconsistent narrative voice throughout the novel itself.

It is further typical of *The Vicar of Wakefield* that even the central title of the novel is deliberately misleading. How many of Goldsmith's readers over the years must have wondered why it is that the Vicar is so prominently described as being 'of Wakefield', when he in fact *leaves* Wakefield for ever in the opening pages of his story (Dr Primrose inhabits the village of the novel's title for less than ten pages of a narrative that remains in any modern edition close to 190 pages long)? Why, for that matter, does

---

[23] For some further consideration of the ambiguities of Goldsmith's title, see Hopkins, *True Genius of Oliver Goldsmith*, 173.

Goldsmith allow the location of the curacy in the gift of Sir William Thornhill that the Vicar subsequently takes on—the setting for most the novel's action—itself to remain nameless? Some readers may not even notice that the man who is 'supposed' to be relating the autobiographical 'tale' of the designated 'Vicar of Wakefield' is, oddly, for the better part of the narrative technically *not* the Vicar of Wakefield at all. The levels of narrative awareness that are supposed to filter the story first from the original teller of the tale to any assumed listeners, and only thence from an editor to the printer or bookseller, further obscure the veracity of the final product.

In any event, the unnamed community depicted in the novel to which the Vicar and his family remove is emphatically *not* the idyllic, pastoral 'Wakefield' that has established itself in the popular imagination, but rather, as the Vicar himself describes it, an isolated living in a 'little neighbourhood' of farmers attached to a nearby town that is a straggling place consisting of 'a few mean houses, having lost all its former opulence, and retaining no marks of its ancient superiority but the gaol'. This same 'ancient superiority' yet attaches itself to the town in a lingering manner primarily because of its fortress-like prison—a building, we are informed, that had 'formerly been built for the purposes of war' (p. 124). The Vicar imagined by so many readers as inhabiting a bucolic world of easy contentment that is disrupted by the unexpected intrusion of the kinds of external forces more typically confined to the city and the urban environment, in actual fact lives near the run-down and economically depressed remnant of a military community—a town the only distinction of which remains the fortress that serves simultaneously as a monument to its foundation as a bulwark against the bellicose instability of its former inhabitants and near-neighbours, and a living testimony, as a prison, to the ineradicable poverty and depravity of human nature.

Not merely 'Wakefield' but all the names in the novel would appear carefully to have been designed just to provoke confusion. Goldsmith's specific designation of the town of Wakefield has prompted many readers to wonder how it came about that he should ever have desired to associate his novel with the actual town of Wakefield, in Yorkshire (to which Goldsmith's fictional community bears little if any resemblance) or perhaps to another, smaller village of that same name closer to London. The fact that the author pointedly draws attention to the connotations of names and naming throughout the work would seem to encourage readers to pursue such matters; proper names *do* carry significant connotations in the work. The Vicar's speculation early in the novel, for example, that the naming of his daughters was influenced by his wife's weakness for romantic fiction may itself be the stuff of old wives' tales, yet the names finally chosen for the two girls do indeed carry appropriately 'romantic' and classical connotations. Olivia, deriving from Latin and related to the masculine Oliver, literally means 'of the olive tree', and so, metaphorically, 'peace'; it entered English after it was prominently used by Shakespeare in his *Twelfth Night* (1601), where it was associated with misguided romantic infatuation. Sophia is from the Greek, and means 'wisdom' (often traditionally connoting 'holy wisdom'). In the Christian tradition, the name is associated with the mythical saint who is said to have died of grief after witnessing the martyrdom of her three daughters. Both names are consequently of ancient origin, and both would be appropriate designations for the heroines of popular—and, in the eyes of the Vicar, unfortunately 'feminine'—romantic fictions; both are likewise obscurely related to the perceived feminine activities of loss and suffering. In stark contrast, the female name most favoured by the Vicar, 'Grissel', is suitably mundane and emphatically Anglo-Saxon, being derived from the Germanic *gris* or 'grey', and *hild*, meaning 'battle'. In contrast to the names chosen by Deborah Primrose, Griselda, for example, is the name given to a patient wife in one of Chaucer's *Canterbury Tales* (1400).

Goldsmith's novel of course includes names that are 'realistic' (e.g. 'Wilmot', 'Cripse'); yet it does so alongside names that are in some way descriptive or potentially symbolic ('Primrose', 'Grogram', 'Pinwire'), or that are resonant of other literary characters ('Burchell', 'Arnold'), as well as those that quite specifically call to mind recent and contemporary political figures

('Wilkinson', 'Thornhill'). *The Vicar of Wakefield*, in other words, appears to combine a number of converging trends in this area, much in the manner that it brings together related, developing trends in genre and literary modes. Returning to the village named in the novel's title, it is more than possible that an eighteenth-century audience would still have been aware of the origins of such a place name to designate, quite literally, the field in which the rural parish community held its annual 'wake' or festival—a celebration that originally fell on a Sunday or the feast day of a saint, and was an occasional holiday that featured dancing, village sports, and other amusements. In a very real sense, Dr Primrose is following in the footsteps of his island forebears no less clearly than he is being subjected to the trials of the biblical Job—ranging from Piers Plowman and Colin Cloute to John Bunyan's Christian in his *Pilgrim's Progress* (1678). As Oswald Doughty observed some time ago, 'the Vicar of Wakefield *is* Christian in the mid-eighteenth century'.[24]

If Goldsmith's novel is to be read as a satire rather than a sincere work of 'sentimental fiction', one needs to remain very much alive to the subtle inconsistencies and illogicalities of the Vicar's narration. Critics such as Robert Hopkins have convincingly demonstrated the intricate manner in which Goldsmith manipulates Primrose's voice throughout the text to reveal his own shortcomings, and his manifestations of often petty vindictiveness and pride. The several instances of bathos in the novel— moments when an attempt at the sublime is suddenly undercut by the revelation of the questionable perceptions and judgements of a deeply flawed humanity—simply must be taken into account in any coherent reading of the novel. Whether or not one would wish to go so far as Hopkins himself in arguing that the novel is not merely a playful parody, but an intense and calculated satire, is another question altogether. Henry James may himself, finally, have been not so far from articulating a certain kind of truth

[24] Oswald Doughty, 'Introduction' to Oliver Goldsmith, *The Vicar of Wakefield* (London: Scholartis Press, 1928), p. xli.

when he confronted what he characterized as the novel's unfailing 'charm' and 'amenity'. John Trusler, writing on the meaning of specific words and terminology shortly after *The Vicar of Wakefield* was published,[25] emphasized the notion that charm—much like any related spell or enchantment—is a quality only naturally averse to reason; 'charm' is an attribute or feature, as dictionary definitions tend to stress even to this day, that exerts some kind of fascinating or attractive *influence* that excites admiration or love despite its being contrary to all the more sensible arguments against it. For all the sophistication of the analyses that have subsequently been brought to bear on the novel, James's suggestion that the enduring qualities of *The Vicar of Wakefield* are rooted firmly in its ability continually to charm its readers suggests no small achievement on Goldsmith's part after all.

[25] John Trusler's *The Difference, Between Words, Esteemed Synonymous*, . . . 2 vols. (Dublin, 1776), i. 36.

NOTE ON THE TEXT

Most writers on Goldsmith would today agree that *The Vicar of Wakefield* was probably written at Goldsmith's lodgings in Wine Office Court in late 1761 or in 1762. Internal evidence supports the supposition that the manuscript was sold sometime near the end of 1762. For reasons that have not been satisfactorily explained the novel was not published until some three and a half years later, on 27 March 1766, when it appeared in two volumes with the imprint: 'SALISBURY: Printed by B. COLLINS, For F. Newbery in Pater-Noster-Row, London'. Two other authorized editions appeared in 1766, the second edition (with many stylistic revisions) on 31 May, and the third on 27 August. The fourth authorized edition, dated 1770, was published on 9 December 1769 and the fifth, dated 1773, on 2 April 1774, two days before Goldsmith's death. By 1820, at least 111 editions had appeared.

The text of the present edition is substantially that established for Arthur Friedman's *Collected Works of Oliver Goldsmith* (Oxford, 1966), volume iv. It is the text of the first edition modified by the new readings of the second edition for which Goldsmith appears to have been responsible. Friedman accepted as authoritative no new readings from editions after the second; verbal variants from the third, fourth, and fifth editions can be found in *Collected Works*, iv. 185.

SELECT BIBLIOGRAPHY

Editions

The Collected Letters of Oliver Goldsmith, ed. Katherine C. Balderston (Cambridge: Cambridge University Press, 1928); includes the recollections of Goldsmith's sister, Mrs Catherine Hudson, as appendix III.

Collected Works of Oliver Goldsmith, ed. Arthur Friedman, 5 vols. (Oxford: Clarendon Press, 1966); Friedman's carefully edited text of the novel is printed in vol. iv, with a brief but excellent introduction detailing its composition, sale, and publication.

Goldsmith: Selected Works, ed. Richard Garnett, the Reynard Library (London: Rupert Hart-Davis, 1967).

The Miscellaneous Works of Oliver Goldsmith, ed. James Prior (London, 1801).

The Plays of Oliver Goldsmith together with The Vicar of Wakefield, ed. C.E. Doble and G. Ostler (Oxford: Oxford University Press, 1909).

The Poems of Gray, Collins, and Goldsmith, ed. Roger Lonsdale, Annotated English Poets (London: Longman, 1969).

The Vicar of Wakefield, ed. Oswald Doughty (London: Scholartis Press, 1928).

The Vicar of Wakefield and Other Writings, ed. Frederick W. Hilles (New York: The Modern Library, 1955).

The Works of Oliver Goldsmith, ed. Peter Cunningham, 4 vols. (London, 1854).

Biography, Biographical Sources, and Bibliographies

Black, William, *Goldsmith*, English Men of Letters (London, 1878).

Dobson, Austin, *Life and Writings of Oliver Goldsmith*, Great Writers (London, n.d. [1889]).

Dussinger, John A., 'Goldsmith, Oliver (1728?–1774)', in Colin Matthew and Brian Harrison (eds.), *Oxford Dictionary of National Biography* (Oxford: Oxford University Press, 2004).

Forster, John, *The Life and Times of Oliver Goldsmith*, 2 vols. (1848; 6th edn., London: Bickerson and Son, 1877).

Friedman, Arthur, 'Oliver Goldsmith', in George Watson (ed.),

The New Cambridge Bibliography of English Literature, 5 vols. (Cambridge: Cambridge University Press, 1971), ii. 1191–1210.

Ginger, John, *The Notable Man: The Life and Times of Oliver Goldsmith* (London: Hamish Hamilton, 1977).

Irving, Washington, *Oliver Goldsmith* (1844; 2nd edn., New York: 1849) (revised from 1st edn. of Forster, *Life and Times*, above).

Jefferes, A. Norman, *Oliver Goldsmith*, Writers and Their Work (London, 1959).

Lytton Sells, A., *Oliver Goldsmith: His Life and Works* (London: George Allen & Unwin Ltd., 1974).

Mikhail, E. H., *Goldsmith: Interviews and Recollections* (New York: St Martin's Press, 1993).

Percy, Thomas, 'The Life of Dr Oliver Goldsmith', in *The Miscellaneous Works of Oliver Goldsmith*, vol. i (London, 1801), i. 1–118.

Prior, James, *The Life of Oliver Goldsmith, M.B.*, 4 vols. (London, 1837).

Quintana, Ricardo, *Oliver Goldsmith: A Georgian Study*, Masters of World Literature series (London: Weidenfeld and Nicolson, 1969).

Sherwin, Oscar, *Goldy: The Life and Times of Oliver Goldsmith* (New York: Twayne, 1961).

Wardle, Ralph M., *Oliver Goldsmith* (London: Constable & Co., 1957).

Woods, Samuel H., *Oliver Goldsmith: A Reference Guide* (Boston: G. K. Hall, 1982).

Critical Studies of Sensibility and Sentimentalism

Bredvold, Louis I., *The Natural History of Sensibility* (Detroit: Wayne State University Press, 1962).

Braudy, Leo, 'The Form of the Sentimental Novel', *Novel*, 7 (Fall 1973), 5–13.

Brissenden, R. F., *Virtue in Distress: Studies in the Novel of Sentiment from Richardson to Sade* (London: Hutchinson, 1974).

Conger, Sydney McMillan (ed.), *Sensibility in Transformation: Creative Resistance to Sentiment from the Augustans to the Romantics; Essays in Honour of Jean H. Hagstrum* (Rutherford, NJ: Farleigh Dickinson University Press, 1990).

Crane, R. S., 'Suggestions toward a Genealogy of the "Man of Feeling" ', *ELH* 1 (1934), 205–30.

Ellis, Markman, *The Politics of Sensibility: Race, Gender, and Commerce in the Sentimental Novel* (Cambridge: Cambridge University Press, 1996).

Friedman, Arthur, 'Aspects of Sentimentalism in Eighteenth-Century Literature', in H. K. Miller, Eric Rothstein, and G. S. Rousseau (eds.) *The Augustan Milieu: Essays Presented to Louis A. Landa* (Oxford: Clarendon Press, 1970).

Knox, Ronald, *Enthusiasm: A Chapter in the History of Religion* (Oxford: Clarendon Press, 1950).

Mason, John, *Gentlefolk in the Making, 1531–1774* (Philadelphia: University of Pennsylvania Press, 1935).

Mullan, John, *Sentiment and Sociability: The Language of Feeling in the Eighteenth Century* (Oxford: Clarendon Press, 1988).

Rawson, Claude, *Satire and Sentiment, 1660–1830* (Cambridge: Cambridge University Press, 1933).

Starr, G. A., 'Sentimental Novels of the Later Eighteenth Century' in John Richetti, John Bender, Deidre David, and Michael Seidel, (eds.), *The Columbia History of the British Novel* (New York: Columbia University Press, 1994), 181–98.

Todd, Janet, *Sensibility: An Introduction* (London: Methuen, 1987).

Van Sant, Ann Jessie, *Eighteenth-Century Sensibility and the Novel: The Senses in Social Context*, Cambridge Studies in Eighteenth-Century English Literature and Thought (Cambridge: Cambridge University Press, 1993).

Critical Studies of Goldsmith and The Vicar of Wakefield

Bäckman, Sven, *This Singular Tale: A Study of 'The Vicar of Wakefield' and Its Literary Background*, Lund Studies in English, 40 (Lund: C. W. K. Gleerup, 1971).

Bataille, Robert A., 'City and Country in *The Vicar of Wakefield*', *Eighteenth-Century Life*, 3 (1977), 112–14.

Battestin, Martin, 'Goldsmith: The Comedy of Job', in *The Providence of Wit: Aspects of Form in Augustan Literature and the Arts* (Oxford: Clarendon Press, 1974), 193–214.

Bender, John, 'Prison Reform and the Sentence of Narration in *The Vicar of Wakefield*', in Felicity Nussbaum and Laura Browns (eds.), *The New Eighteenth Century* (New York: Methuen, 1987), 168–88.

Carson, James P., ' "The Little Republic" of the Family: Goldsmith's Politics of Nostalgia', *Eighteenth-Century Fiction*, 16/2 (Jan. 2004), 174–96.

Dixon, Peter, *Oliver Goldsmith Revisited* (Boston: Twayne Publishers, 1991).

Durant, David, 'The Vicar of Wakefield and the Sentimental Novel', *Studies in English Literature, 1500–1900*, 17 (1977), 477–91.

Dussinger, John A., 'The Vicar of Wakefield: "Sickly Sensibility" and the Rewards of Fortune', in *The Discourse of the Mind in Eighteenth-Century Fiction* (The Hague and Paris: Mouton, 1974), 148–72.

Dykstal, Timothy, 'The Story of O: Politics and Pleasure in *The Vicar of Wakefield*', *ELH* 62 (1995), 329–46.

Ferguson, Oliver W. 'Goldsmith as Ironist', *Studies in Philology*, 81/2 (1984), 212–28.

—— 'Goldsmith, *The Vicar of Wakefield*, and the Periodicals', *Journal of English and Germanic Philology*, 76 (1977), 525–36.

Golden, Morris, 'The Time of Writing of *The Vicar of Wakefield*' *Bulletin of the New York Public Library* (Sept. 1961), 442–50.

Harkin, Maureen, 'Goldsmith on Authorship in *The Vicar of Wakefield*', *Eighteenth-Century Fiction*, 14/3–4 (2002), 325–44.

Hilliard, Raymond F. 'The Redemption of Fatherhood in *The Vicar of Wakefield*', *Studies in English Literature*, 23 (1983), 465–80.

Hopkins, Robert H., *The True Genius of Oliver Goldsmith* (Baltimore: The Johns Hopkins Press, 1969).

—— 'Matrimony in *The Vicar of Wakefield* and the Marriage Act of 1753', *Studies in Philology*, 74 (1977), 322–39.

Jaarsma, Richard J., 'Satiric Intent in *The Vicar of Wakefield*', *Studies in Short Fiction*, 5 (1967–68), 331–41.

Jaffares, Norman A., 'The Vicar of Wakefield' in Seàn Lucy (ed.), *Goldsmith: The Gentle Master* (Cork: Cork University Press, 1984).

Mullan, John, *Sentiment and Sociability: The Language of Feeling in the Eighteenth Century* (Oxford: Clarendon Press, 1988).

Murray, David, 'From Patrimony to Paternity in *The Vicar of Wakefield*', in *Eighteenth-Century Fiction*, 9/3 (Apr. 1997), 327–36.

Pierce, Robert B., 'Moral Education in the Novel of the 1750s', *Philological Quarterly*, 44 (1965), 73–83.

Quintana, Ricardo, 'The Vicar of Wakefield: The Problem of Critical Approach', *Modern Philology*, 71 (1973), 59–65.

Rogers, Henry N., 'God's Implausible Plot: The Providential Design of *The Vicar of Wakefield*', *Philological Review*, 28/1 (2002), 5–17.

Rothstein, Eric, and Weinbrot, Howard, 'The Vicar of Wakefield, Mr Wilmot, and the "Whitsonean Controversy"', *Philological Quarterly*, 55 (1976), 225–40.

Rousseau, G. S. (ed.), *Goldsmith: The Critical Heritage*, Critical Heritage series (gen. ed. Brian C. Southam) (London and Boston: Routledge & Kegan Paul, 1974).

Swarbrick, Andrew (ed.), *The Art of Oliver Goldsmith* (London: Vision Press, 1984).

Taylor, Richard C., 'Goldsmith's First Vicar', *Review of English Studies*, 41/162 (1990), 191–9.

Further Reading in Oxford World's Classics

Austen, Jane, *Catharine and Other Writings*, ed. Margaret Anne Doody and Douglas Murray.

—— *Sense and Sensibility*, ed. James Kinsley, Margaret Anne Doody and Claire Lamont.

Boswell, James, *Life of Johnson*, ed. Pat Rogers and R. W. Chapman.

Burke, Edmund, *A Philosophical Enquiry into the Origin of Our Ideas of the Sublime and Beautiful*, ed. Adam Phillips.

Burney, Fanny, *Evelina*, ed. Edward A. Bloom and Vivien Jones.

Defoe, Daniel, *Robinson Crusoe*, ed. J. Donald Crowley.

Fielding, Henry, *Joseph Andrews* and *Shamela*, ed. Thomas Keymer.

—— *Tom Jones*, ed. John Bender and Simon Stern.

Hume, David, *Selected Essays*, ed. Stephen Copley and Andrew Edgar.

Johnson, Samuel, *The History of Rasselas, Prince of Abissinia*, ed. J. P. Hardy.

Mackenzie, Henry, *The Man of Feeling*, ed. Brian Vickers, Stephen Bending, and Stephen Bygrave.

Sterne, Laurence, *A Sentimental Journey and Other Writings*, ed. Ian Jack and Tim Parnell.

—— *The Life and Opinions of Tristram Shandy, Gentleman*, ed. Ian Campbell Ross.

A CHRONOLOGY OF OLIVER GOLDSMITH

1730? (10 November) born, either at Pallas, County Longford, or at Ardnagowan—his grandmother's house—near Elphin, the second son and fifth child of the Revd Charles Goldsmith and his wife Ann (née James). The family soon moves to Lissoy, where Goldsmith spends his childhood. James Thomson completes *The Seasons*.

1735–45 Attends school at Lissoy, the Diocesan School at Elphin, and schools in Athlone and Edgeworthstown, County Longford.

1745 (11 June) admitted as a sizar to Trinity College Dublin. Death of Jonathan Swift.

1747 (21 May) death of father; Goldsmith takes part in a student riot for which he received a 'public admonishment'. Samuel Richardson's *Clarissa* (to 1748).

1749 Henry Fielding's *Tom Jones*.

1750 Receives AB degree. Samuel Johnson begins *The Rambler*.

1750–2 Attempts unsuccessfully to be ordained into the Anglican Church. Returns to his mother's home near Athlone, and entertains the possibility of emigrating to America (from Cork) and studying law in London. He is engaged for a short time as a private tutor to a family in County Roscommon.

1751 Tobias Smollett's *Peregrine Pickle*; Henry Fielding's *Amelia*.

1752 Charlotte Lennox's *The Female Quixote*.

1752–4 Studies medicine at Edinburgh.

1753 Elected to the Medical Society at Edinburgh University.

1754 Leaves Edinburgh and attends medical lectures at Leyden. Death of Henry Fielding.

1755–6 Travels across the Continent, often on foot, visiting Germany, Switzerland, France, and northern Italy.

1755 Samuel Johnson's *Dictionary of the English Language*.

1756 (1 February) returns to England; settles in London.

1756–7 Engaged in various odd jobs in and around London, including positions as an apothecary, physician, proofreader, and an usher in a boys' school in Peckham. May have applied for and received his medical degree from Trinity College Dublin.

1757   Begins reviewing for the *Monthly Review*, while lodging with its editor, Ralph Griffiths.

1759   Begins contributing to Tobias Smollett's *Critical Review*; (2 April) publishes *An Inquiry into the Present State of Polite Learning in Europe*; also contributes essays and reviews to *The Busy Body*, *The British Magazine*, and *The Lady's Magazine*; (6 October–25 November) writes the periodical paper *The Bee*.

1760–1 Publishes his 'Chinese Letters' in the *Public Ledger* and continues to write for other magazines.

1761   (31 May) first visited by Dr Samuel Johnson.

1762   The 'Chinese Letters' collected and republished as *The Citizen of the World*; publishes *The Life of Richard Nash*; effects his release from arrest for debt by selling a third share in *The Vicar of Wakefield* on 28 October.

1764   *An History of England, in a Series of Letters from a Nobleman to his Son* and (19 December) *The Traveller, or A Prospect of Society*.

1765   *Essays by Mr. Goldsmith*; private edition of *Edwin and Angelina*.

1766   (27 March) *The Vicar of Wakefield*; (31 May) second edition; (27 August) third edition.

1767   (April) two-volume anthology, *The Beauties of English Poesy*.

1768   (29 January) *The Good Natur'd Man* acted at Covent Garden and published; death of his brother Henry, to whom he had dedicated *The Traveller*. Death of Laurence Sterne and publication of *A Sentimental Journey Through France and Italy*.

1769   (18 May) publishes *The Roman History*; (December) appointed professor of Ancient History in the Royal Academy. (9 December) fourth authorized edition of *The Vicar of Wakefield*; David Garrick's Shakespeare Jubilee in Stratford-Upon-Avon; John Wilkes expelled from the House of Commons.

1770   (26 May) publishes *The Deserted Village*.

1771   Henry Mackenzie's *The Man of Feeling*.

1772 Performance of his *Threnodia Augustalis*; falls ill in the late summer with a serious bladder infection.

1773 *She Stoops to Conquer* produced at Covent Garden and published; contributes essays to the *Westminster Magazine*.

1774 (2 April) fifth authorized edition of *The Vicar of Wakefield*; *Retaliation* and *An History of the Earth, and Animated Nature*; (4 April) dies in his chambers in the Middle Temple.

1776 Monument to Goldsmith erected in Westminster Abbey. *The Haunch of Venison* published posthumously. Edward Gibbon's *Decline and Fall of the Roman Empire* (vol. i); Adam Smith's *The Wealth of Nations*; American Declaration of Independence.

THE VICAR OF WAKEFIELD*

A Tale

Supposed to be written by himself

*Sperate miseri, cavete fælices**

ADVERTISEMENT*

THERE are an hundred faults in this Thing, and an hundred things might be said to prove them beauties. But it is needless. A book may be amusing with numerous errors, or it may be very dull without a single absurdity. The hero of this piece unites in himself the three greatest characters upon earth; he is a priest, an husbandman, and the father of a family. He is drawn as ready to teach, and ready to obey, as simple in affluence, and majestic in adversity. In this age of opulence and refinement whom can such a character please? Such as are fond of high life, will turn with disdain from the simplicity of his country fire-side. Such as mistake ribaldry for humour, will find no wit in his harmless conversation; and such as have been taught to deride religion, will laugh at one whose chief stores of comfort are drawn from futurity.

OLIVER GOLDSMITH

CONTENTS

CHAPTER I

The description of the family of Wakefield; in which a kindred likeness prevails as well of minds as of persons

I was ever of opinion, that the honest man who married and brought up a large family, did more service than he who continued single, and only talked of population. For this motive, I had scarce taken orders a year before I began to think seriously of matrimony, and chose my wife as she did her wedding gown, not for a fine glossy surface, but such qualities as would wear well. To do her justice, she was a good-natured notable woman; and as for breeding, there were few country ladies who could shew more. She could read any English book without much spelling, but for pickling, preserving, and cookery, none could excel her. She prided herself also upon being an excellent contriver in housekeeping; tho' I could never find that we grew richer with all her contrivances.

However, we loved each other tenderly, and our fondness encreased as we grew old. There was in fact nothing that could make us angry with the world or each other. We had an elegant house, situated in a fine country, and a good neighbourhood. The year was spent in moral or rural amusements; in visiting our rich neighbours, and relieving such as were poor. We had no revolutions to fear, nor fatigues to undergo; all our adventures were by the fire-side, and all our migrations from the blue bed to the brown.*

As we lived near the road, we often had the traveller or stranger visit us to taste our gooseberry wine, for which we had great reputation; and I profess with the veracity of an historian, that I never knew one of them find fault with it. Our cousins too, even to the fortieth remove, all remembered their affinity, without any help from the Herald's office,* and came very frequently to see us. Some of them did us no great honour by these claims of kindred; as we had the blind, the maimed, and the halt amongst the number. However, my wife always insisted that as they were the same *flesh and blood*, they should sit with us at the same table. So that if we had not very rich, we generally had very happy friends about us; for this remark will hold good thro' life, that the poorer the guest, the better pleased he ever is with being treated: and as some men gaze with admiration at the colours of a tulip, or the wing of a butterfly, so I was by nature an admirer of happy human faces. However, when any one of our relations was found to be a person of very bad character, a troublesome guest, or one we desired to get rid of, upon his leaving my house, I ever took care to lend him a riding coat, or a pair of boots, or sometimes an horse of small value, and I always had the satisfaction of finding he never came back to return them. By this the house was cleared of such as we did not like; but never was the family of Wakefield known to turn the traveller or the poor dependant out of doors.

Thus we lived several years in a state of much happiness, not but that we sometimes had those little rubs which Providence sends to enhance the value of its favours. My orchard was often robbed by school-boys, and my wife's custards plundered by the cats or the children. The 'Squire would sometimes fall asleep in the most pathetic* parts of my sermon, or his lady return my wife's civilities at church with a mutilated curtesy. But we soon got over the uneasiness caused by such accidents, and usually in three or four days began to wonder how they vext us.

My children, the offspring of temperance, as they were educated without softness, so they were at once well formed and healthy; my sons hardy and active, my daughters beautiful and blooming. When I stood in the midst of the little circle, which promised to be the supports of my declining age, I could not avoid repeating the famous story of Count Abensberg,* who, in Henry II's progress through Germany, while other courtiers came with their treasures, brought his thirty-two children, and presented them to his sovereign as the most valuable offering he had to bestow. In this manner, though I had but six, I considered them as a very valuable present made to my country, and consequently looked upon it as my debtor. Our eldest son was named George, after his uncle, who left us ten thousand pounds. Our second child, a girl, I intended to call after her aunt Grissel; but my wife, who during her pregnancy had been reading romances, insisted upon her being called Olivia. In less than another year we had another daughter, and now I was determined that Grissel should be her name; but a rich relation taking a fancy to stand godmother, the girl was, by her directions, called Sophia; so that we had two romantic names in the family;* but I solemnly protest I had no hand in it. Moses was our next, and after an interval of twelve years, we had two sons more.

It would be fruitless to deny my exultation when I saw my little ones about me; but the vanity and the satisfaction of my wife were even greater than mine. When our visitors would say, 'Well, upon my word, Mrs. Primrose, you have the finest children in the whole country.'—'Ay, neighbour,' she would answer, 'they are as heaven made them, handsome enough, if they be good enough; for handsome is that handsome does.'* And then she would bid the girls hold up their heads; who, to conceal nothing, were certainly very handsome. Mere outside is so very trifling a circumstance with me, that I should scarce have remembered to mention it, had it not been a general topic of conversation in the country. Olivia, now about eighteen, had that luxuriancy of beauty with which painters generally draw Hebe;* open, sprightly, and commanding. Sophia's features were not so striking at first; but often did more certain execution; for they were soft, modest, and alluring. The one vanquished by a single blow, the other by efforts successfully repeated.

The temper of a woman is generally formed from the turn of her features, at least it was so with my daughters. Olivia wished for many lovers, Sophia to secure one. Olivia was often affected from too great a desire to please. Sophia even represt excellence from her fears to offend. The one entertained me with her vivacity when I was gay, the other with her sense when I was serious. But these qualities were never carried to excess in either, and I have often seen them exchange characters for a whole day together. A suit of mourning has transformed my coquet into a prude, and a new set of ribbands* has given her younger sister more than natural vivacity. My eldest son George was bred at

Oxford, as I intended him for one of the learned professions.* My second boy Moses, whom I designed for business, received a sort of a miscellaneous education at home. But it is needless to attempt describing the particular characters of young people that had seen but very little of the world. In short, a family likeness prevailed through all, and properly speaking, they had but one character, that of being all equally generous, credulous,* simple, and inoffensive.

CHAPTER II

Family misfortunes. The loss of fortune only serves to encrease the pride of the worthy

THE temporal concerns of our family were chiefly committed to my wife's management, as to the spiritual I took them entirely under my own direction. The profits of my living, which amounted to but thirty-five pounds a year,* I made over to the orphans and widows of the clergy of our diocese;* for having a sufficient fortune of my own, I was careless of temporalities, and felt a secret pleasure in doing my duty without reward. I also set a resolution of keeping no curate,* and of being acquainted with every man in the parish, exhorting the married men to temperance and the bachelors to matrimony; so that in a few years it was a common saying, that there were three strange wants at Wakefield, a parson wanting pride, young men wanting wives, and ale-houses wanting customers.

Matrimony was always one of my favourite topics, and I wrote several sermons to prove its happiness: but there was a peculiar tenet which I made a point of supporting; for I maintained with Whiston,* that it was unlawful for a priest of the church of England, after the death of his first wife, to take a second, or to express it in one word, I valued myself upon being a strict monogamist.

I was early innitiated into this important dispute, on which so many laborious volumes have been written. I published some tracts upon the subject myself, which, as they never sold, I have the consolation of thinking are read only by the happy *Few*. Some of my friends called this my weak side; but alas! they had not like me made it the subject of long contemplation. The more I reflected upon it, the more important it appeared. I even went a step beyond Whiston in displaying my principles: as he had engraven upon his wife's tomb that she was the *only* wife of William Whiston; so I wrote a similar epitaph for my wife, though still living, in which I extolled her prudence, œconomy, and obedience till death; and having got it copied fair, with an elegant frame, it was placed over the chimney-piece, where it answered several very useful purposes. It admonished my wife of her duty to me, and my fidelity to her; it inspired her with a passion for fame, and constantly put her in mind of her end.

It was thus, perhaps, from hearing marriage so often recommended, that my eldest son, just upon leaving college, fixed his affections upon the daughter of a neighbouring clergyman, who was a dignitary in the church, and in circumstances to give her a large fortune: but fortune was her smallest accomplishment. Miss Arabella Wilmot was allowed by all, except my two daughters, to be completely pretty. Her youth, health, and innocence, were still heightened by a complexion so transparent,* and such an happy sensibility of look, as even age could not gaze on with indifference. As Mr. Wilmot knew that I could make a very handsome settlement on my son, he was not averse to the match; so both families lived together in all that harmony which generally precedes an expected alliance. Being convinced by experience that the days of courtship are the most happy of our lives, I was willing enough to lengthen the period; and the various amusements which the young couple every day shared in each other's company, seemed to encrease their passion. We were generally awaked in the morning by music, and on fine days rode a hunting. The hours between breakfast and dinner the ladies devoted to dress and study: they usually read a page, and then gazed at themselves in the glass, which even philosophers might own often presented the page of greatest beauty. At dinner my wife took the lead; for as she always insisted upon carving every thing herself, it being her mother's way, she gave us upon these occasions the history of every dish. When we had dined, to prevent the ladies leaving us,* I generally ordered the table to be removed; and sometimes, with the music master's assistance, the girls would give us a very agreeable concert. Walking out, drinking tea, country dances, and forfeits,* shortened the rest of the day, without the assistance of cards, as I hated all manner of gaming, except backgammon, at which my old friend and I sometimes took a twopenny hit.* Nor can I here pass over an ominous circumstance that happened the last time we played together: I only wanted to fling a quatre, and yet I threw deuce ace* five times running.

Some months were elapsed in this manner, till at last it was thought convenient to fix a day for the nuptials of the young couple, who seemed earnestly to desire it. During the preparations for the wedding, I need not describe the busy importance of my wife, nor the sly looks of my daughters: in fact, my attention was fixed on another object, the completing a tract which I intended shortly to publish in defence of my favourite principle. As I looked upon this as a master-piece both for argument and style, I could not in the pride of my heart avoid shewing it to my old friend Mr. Wilmot, as I made no doubt of receiving his approbation; but not till too late I discovered that he was most violently attached to the contrary opinion, and with good reason; for he was at that time actually courting a fourth wife.* This, as may be expected, produced a dispute attended with some acrimony, which threatened to interrupt our intended alliance: but on the day before that appointed for the ceremony, we agreed to discuss the subject at large.

It was managed with proper spirit on both sides: he asserted that I was heterodox, I retorted the charge: he replied, and I rejoined. In the mean time, while the controversy was hottest, I was called out by one of my relations, who, with a face of concern, advised me to give up the dispute, at least till my son's wedding was over. 'How,' cried I, 'relinquish the cause of truth, and let him be an husband, already driven to the very verge of absurdity. You might as well advise me to give up my fortune as my argument.' 'Your fortune,' returned my friend, 'I am now sorry to inform you, is almost nothing. The merchant in town, in whose hands your money was lodged, has gone off, to avoid a statute of bankruptcy,* and is thought not to have left a shilling in the pound. I was unwilling to shock you or the family with the account till after the wedding: but now it may serve to moderate your warmth in the argument; for, I suppose, your own prudence will enforce the necessity of dissembling at least till your son has the young lady's fortune secure.'*—'Well,' returned I, 'if what you tell me be true, and if I am to be a beggar, it shall never make me a rascal, or induce me to disavow my principles. I'll go this moment and inform the company of my circumstances; and as for the argument, I even here retract my former concessions in the old gentleman's favour, nor will I allow him now to be an husband in any sense of the expression.'

It would be endless to describe the different sensations of both families when I divulged the news of our misfortune; but what others felt was slight to what the lovers appeared to endure. Mr. Wilmot, who seemed before sufficiently inclined to break off the match, was by this blow soon determined: one virtue he had in perfection, which was prudence,* too often the only one that is left us at seventy-two.

CHAPTER III

A migration. The fortunate circumstances of our lives are generally found at last to be of our own procuring

THE only hope of our family now was, that the report of our misfortunes might be malicious or premature: but a letter from my agent in town soon came with a confirmation of every particular. The loss of fortune to myself alone would have been trifling; the only uneasiness I felt was for my family, who were to be humble without an education to render them callous to contempt.

Near a fortnight had passed before I attempted to restrain their affliction; for premature consolation is but the remembrancer of

Note

sorrow. During this interval, my thoughts were employed on some future means of supporting them; and at last a small Cure* of fifteen pounds a year was offered me in a distant neighbourhood, where I could still enjoy my principles without molestation.* With this proposal I joyfully closed, having determined to encrease my salary by managing a little farm.

Having taken this resolution, my next care was to get together the wrecks of my fortune; and all debts collected and paid, out of fourteen thousand pounds we had but four hundred remaining. My chief attention therefore was now to bring down the pride of my family to their circumstances; for I well knew that aspiring beggary is wretchedness itself. 'You can't be ignorant, my children,' cried I, 'that no prudence of ours could have prevented our late misfortune; but prudence may do much in disappointing its effects. We are now poor, my fondlings, and wisdom bids us

Note

conform to our humble situation. Let us then, without repining, give up those splendours with which numbers are wretched, and seek in humbler circumstances that peace with which all may be happy. The poor live pleasantly without our help, why then should not we learn to live without theirs. No, my children, let us from this moment give up all pretensions to gentility; we have still enough left for happiness if we are wise, and let us draw upon content for the deficiencies of fortune.'

As my eldest son was bred a scholar, I determined to send him to town, where his abilities might contribute to our support and his own. The separation of friends and families is, perhaps, one of the most distressful circumstances attendant on penury. The day soon arrived on which we were to disperse for the first time. My son, after taking leave of his mother and the rest, who mingled their tears with their kisses, came to ask a blessing from me. This I gave him from my heart, and which, added to five guineas, was all the patrimony I had now to bestow. 'You are going, my boy,' cried I, 'to London on foot, in the manner Hooker, your great ancestor, travelled there before you. Take from me the same horse that was given him by the good bishop Jewel, this staff,* and take this book too, it will be your comfort on the way: these two lines in it are worth a million, *I have been young, and now am old; yet* *never saw I the righteous man forsaken, or his seed begging their bread.** Let this be your consolation as you travel on. Go, my boy, whatever be thy fortune let me see thee once a year; still keep a good heart, and farewell.' As he was possest of integrity and honour, I was under no apprehensions from throwing him naked into the amphitheatre of life,* for I knew he would act a good part whether vanquished or victorious.

His departure only prepared the way for our own, which arrived a few days afterwards. The leaving a neighbourhood in which we had enjoyed so many hours of tranquility, was not without a tear, which scarce fortitude itself could suppress. Besides, a journey of seventy miles to a family that had hitherto never been above ten from home, filled us with apprehension, and the cries of the poor, who followed us for some miles, contributed to encrease it. The first day's journey brought us in safety within thirty miles of our future retreat, and we put up for the night at an obscure inn in a village by the way. When we were shewn a room, I desired the landlord, in my usual way, to let us have his company, with which he complied, as what he drank would encrease the bill next morning. He knew, however, the whole neighbourhood to which I was removing, particularly 'Squire Thornhill, who was to be my landlord, and who lived within a few miles of the place. This gentleman he described as one who desired to know little more of the world than its pleasures, being particularly remarkable for his attachment to the fair sex. He observed that no virtue was able to resist his arts and assiduity, and that scarce a farmer's daughter within ten miles round but what had found him successful and faithless. Though this account gave me some pain, it had a very different effect upon my daughters, whose features seemed to brighten with the expect- ation of an approaching triumph, nor was my wife less pleased and confident of their allurements and virtue. While our thoughts were thus employed, the hostess entered the room to inform her husband, that the strange gentleman, who had been two days in the house, wanted money, and could not satisfy them for his reckoning. 'Want money!' replied the host, 'that must be impos- sible; for it was no later than yesterday he paid three guineas to our beadle to spare an old broken soldier that was to be whipped through the town for dog-stealing.* The hostess, however, still persisting in her first assertion, he was preparing to leave the room, swearing that he would be satisfied one way or another, when I begged the landlord would introduce me to a stranger of so much charity as he described. With this he complied, shewing in a gentleman who seemed to be about thirty, drest in cloaths that once were laced.* His person was well formed, and his face marked with the lines of thinking. He had something short and dry in his address, and seemed not to understand ceremony, or to despise it. Upon the landlord's leaving the room, I could not avoid expressing my concern to the stranger at seeing a gentleman in such circumstances, and offered him my purse to satisfy the present demand. 'I take it with all my heart, Sir,' replied he, 'and am glad that a late oversight in giving what money I had about me, has shewn me that there are still some men like you. I must, however, previously entreat being informed of the name and residence of my benefactor, in order to repay him as soon as possible.' In this I satisfied him fully, not only mentioning my name and late misfortunes, but the place to which I was going to remove. 'This,' cried he, 'happens still more luckily than I hoped for, as I am going the same way myself, having been detained here two days by the floods, which, I hope, by to-morrow will be found passable.' I testified the pleasure I should have in his company, and my wife and daughters joining in entreaty, he was prevailed upon to stay supper. The stranger's conversation, which was at once pleasing and instructive, induced me to wish for a continuance of it; but it was now high time to retire and take refreshment against the fatigues of the following day.

The next morning we all set forward together: my family on horseback, while Mr. Burchell, our new companion,* walked along the foot-path by the road-side, observing, with a smile, that as we were ill mounted, he would be too generous to attempt leaving us behind. As the floods were not yet subsided, we were obliged to hire a guide, who trotted on before, Mr. Burchell and I bringing up the rear. We lightened the fatigues of the road with philosophical disputes, which he seemed to understand perfectly. But what surprised me most was, that though he was a money-borrower, he defended his opinions with as much obstinacy as if he had been my patron. He now and then also informed me to whom the different seats belonged that lay in our view as we travelled the road. 'That,' cried he, pointing to a very magnificent house which stood at some distance, 'belongs to Mr. Thornhill, a young gentleman who enjoys a large fortune, though entirely dependant on the will of his uncle, Sir William Thornhill, a gentleman, who content with a little himself, permits his nephew to enjoy the rest, and chiefly resides in town.' 'What!' cried I, 'is my young landlord then the nephew of a man whose virtues, generosity, and singularities are so universally known? I have heard Sir William Thornhill represented as one of the most generous, yet whimsical, men in the kingdom; a man of consummate benevolence'—'Something, perhaps, too much so,' replied Mr. Burchell, 'at least he carried benevolence to an excess* when young; for his passions were then strong, and as they all were upon the side of virtue, they led it up to a romantic extreme. He early began to aim at the qualifications of the soldier and scholar; was soon distinguished in the army, and had some reputation among men of learning. Adulation ever follows the ambitious; for such alone receive most pleasure from flattery. He was surrounded with crowds, who shewed him only one side of their character; so that he began to lose a regard for private interest in universal sympathy. He loved all mankind; for fortune prevented him from knowing that there were rascals. Physicians tell us of a disorder in which the whole body is so exquisitely sensible, that the slightest touch gives pain: what some have thus suffered in their persons, this gentleman felt in his mind.* The slightest distress, whether real or fictitious, touched him to the quick, and his soul laboured under a sickly sensibility of the miseries of others. Thus disposed to relieve, it will be easily conjectured, he found numbers disposed to solicit: his profusions began to impair his fortune, but not his good-nature; that, indeed, was seen to encrease as the other seemed to decay: he grew improvident as he grew poor; and though he talked like a man of sense, his actions were those of a fool. Still, however, being surrounded

Note

with importunity, and no longer able to satisfy every request that was made him, instead of *money* he gave *promises*. They were all he had to bestow, and he had not resolution enough to give any man pain by a denial. By this he drew round him crowds of dependants, whom he was sure to disappoint; yet wished to relieve. These hung upon him for a time, and left him with merited reproaches and contempt. But in proportion as he became contemptible to others, he became despicable to himself. His mind had leaned upon their adulation, and that support taken away, he could find no pleasure in the applause of his heart, which he had never learnt to reverence. The world now began to wear a different aspect; the flattery of his friends began to dwindle into simple approbation. Approbation soon took the more friendly form of advice, and advice when rejected produced their reproaches. He now therefore found that such friends as benefits had gathered round him, were little estimable: he now found that a man's own heart must be ever given to gain that of another. I now found, that—that—I forget what I was going to observe:* in short, sir, he resolved to respect himself, and laid down a plan of restoring his falling fortune. For this purpose, in his own whimsical manner he travelled through Europe on foot, and now, though he has scarce attained the age of thirty, his circumstances are more affluent than ever. At present, his bounties are more rational and moderate than before; but still he preserves the character of an humourist, and finds most pleasure in eccentric virtues.'

My attention was so much taken up by Mr. Burchell's account, that I scarce looked forward as we went along, till we were alarmed by the cries of my family, when turning, I perceived my youngest daughter in the midst of a rapid stream, thrown from her horse, and struggling with the torrent. She had sunk twice, nor was it in my power to disengage myself in time to bring her relief. My sensations were even too violent to permit my attempting her rescue: she must have certainly perished had not my companion, perceiving her danger, instantly plunged in to her relief, and, with some difficulty, brought her in safety to the opposite shore. By taking the current a little farther up, the rest of the family got safely over; where we had an opportunity of joining our acknowledgments to her's. Her gratitude may be more readily imagined than described: she thanked her deliverer more with looks than words, and continued to lean upon his arm, as if still willing to receive assistance. My wife also hoped one day to have the pleasure of returning his kindness at her own house. Thus, after we were refreshed at the next inn, and had dined together, as Mr. Burchell was going to a different part of the country, he took leave; and we pursued our journey. My wife observing as we went, that she liked him extremely, and protesting, that if he had birth and fortune to entitle him to match into such a family as our's, she knew no man she would sooner fix upon. I could not but smile to hear her talk in this lofty strain: but I was never much displeased with those harmless delusions that tend to make us more happy.

CHAPTER IV

A proof that even the humblest fortune may grant
happiness, which depends not on circumstance, but
constitution

THE place of our retreat was in a little neighbourhood, consisting of farmers, who tilled their own grounds, and were equal strangers to opulence and poverty. As they had almost all the conveniencies of life within themselves, they seldom visited towns or cities in search of superfluity. Remote from the polite,* they still retained the primæval simplicity of manners, and frugal by habit, they scarce knew that temperance was a virtue. They wrought with chearfulness on days of labour; but observed festivals as intervals of idleness and pleasure. They kept up the Christmas carol, sent true love-knots on Valentine morning, eat pancakes on Shrove-tide, shewed their wit on the first of April, and religiously cracked nuts on Michaelmas eve.* Being apprized of our approach, the whole neighbourhood came out to meet their minister, drest in their finest cloaths, and preceded by a pipe and tabor: A feast also was provided for our reception, at which we sat chearfully down; and what the conversation wanted in wit, was made up in laughter.

Our little habitation was situated at the foot of a sloping hill, sheltered with a beautiful underwood behind, and a pratling river before; on one side a meadow, on the other a green. My farm consisted of about twenty acres of excellent land, having given an hundred pound for my predecessor's good-will. Nothing could exceed the neatness of my little enclosures:* the elms and hedge rows appearing with inexpressible beauty. My house consisted of but one story, and was covered with thatch, which gave it an air of great snugness; the walls on the inside were nicely white-washed, and my daughters undertook to adorn them with pictures of their own designing. Though the same room served us for parlour and kitchen, that only made it the warmer. Besides, as it was kept with the utmost neatness, the dishes, plates, and coppers, being well scoured, and all disposed in bright rows on the shelves, the eye was agreeably relieved, and did not want richer furniture. There were three other apartments, one for my wife and me, another for our two daughters, within our own, and the third, with two beds, for the rest of the children.

The little republic to which I gave laws,* was regulated in the following manner: by sun-rise we all assembled in our common appartment; the fire being previously kindled by the servant. After we had saluted each other with proper ceremony, for I always thought fit to keep up some mechanical forms of good breeding, without which freedom ever destroys friendship, we all bent in gratitude to that Being who gave us another day. This duty being performed, my son and I went to pursue our usual industry abroad, while my wife and daughters employed themselves in providing breakfast, which was always ready at a certain time. I allowed half an hour for this meal, and an hour for dinner; which time was taken up in innocent mirth between my wife and daughters, and in philosophical arguments between my son and me.

As we rose with the sun, so we never pursued our labours after it was gone down, but returned home to the expecting family; where smiling looks, a neat hearth, and pleasant fire, were prepared for our reception. Nor were we without guests: sometimes farmer Flamborough, our talkative neighbour, and often the blind piper,* would pay us a visit, and taste our gooseberry wine; for the making of which we had lost neither the receipt nor the reputation. These harmless people had several ways of being good company, while one played, the other would sing some soothing ballad, Johnny Armstrong's last good night, or the cruelty of Barbara Allen.* The night was concluded in the manner we began the morning, my youngest boys being appointed to read the lessons of the day, and he that read loudest, distinctest, and best, was to have an half-penny on Sunday to put in the poor's box.

When Sunday came, it was indeed a day of finery, which all my sumptuary edicts* could not restrain. How well so ever I fancied my lectures against pride had conquered the vanity of my daughters; yet I still found them secretly attached to all their former finery: they still loved laces, ribbands, bugles and catgut,* my wife herself retained a passion for her crimson paduasoy,* because I formerly happened to say it became her.

The first Sunday in particular their behaviour served to mortify me: I had desired my girls the preceding night to be drest early the next day; for I always loved to be at church a good while before the rest of the congregation. They punctually obeyed my directions; but when we were to assemble in the morning at breakfast, down came my wife and daughters, drest out in all their former splendour; their hair plaistered up with pomatum, their faces patched* to taste, their trains bundled up into an heap behind, and rustling at every motion. I could not help smiling at their vanity, particularly that of my wife, from whom I expected more discretion. In this exigence, therefore, my only resource was to order my son, with an important air, to call our coach. The girls were amazed at the command; but I repeated it with more solemnity than before.—'Surely, my dear, you jest,' cried my wife, 'we can walk it perfectly well: we want no coach to carry us now.' 'You mistake, child,' returned I, 'we do want a coach; for if we walk to church in this trim, the very children in the parish will hoot after us.'—'Indeed,' replied my wife, 'I always imagined that my Charles was fond of seeing his children neat and handsome about him.'—'You may be as neat as you please,' interrupted I, 'and I shall love you the better for it; but all this is not neatness, but frippery. These rufflings, and pinkings,* and patchings, will only make us hated by all the wives of all our neighbours. No, my children,' continued I, more gravely, 'those gowns may be altered into something of a plainer cut; for finery is very unbecoming in us, who want the means of decency. I don't know whether such flouncing and shredding* is becoming even in the rich, if we consider, upon a moderate calculation, that the naked-ness of the indigent world may be cloathed from the trimmings of the vain.'*

This remonstrance had the proper effect; they went with great composure, that very instant, to change their dress; and the next day I had the satisfaction of finding my daughters, at their own request employed in cutting up their trains into Sunday waist-coats for Dick and Bill, the two little ones, and what was still more satisfactory, the gowns seemed improved by this curtailing.

CHAPTER V

A new and great acquaintance introduced. What we place most hopes upon, generally proves most fatal

At a small distance from the house my predecessor had made a seat, overshaded by an hedge of hawthorn and honeysuckle. Here, when the weather was fine, and our labour soon finished, we usually sate together, to enjoy an extensive landscape, in the calm of the evening. Here too we drank tea, which now was become an occasional banquet; and as we had it but seldom, it diffused a new joy, the preparations for it being made with no small share of bustle and ceremony. On these occasions, our two little ones always read for us, and they were regularly served after we had done. Sometimes, to give a variety to our amusements, the girls sung to the guitar; and while they thus formed a little con-cert, my wife and I would stroll down the sloping field, that was embellished with blue bells and centaury,* talk of our children with rapture, and enjoy the breeze that wafted both health and harmony.

In this manner we began to find that every situation in life might bring its own peculiar pleasures: every morning waked us to a repetition of toil; but the evening repaid it with vacant* hilarity.

It was about the beginning of autumn, on a holiday, for I kept such as intervals of relaxation from labour, that I had drawn out my family to our usual place of amusement, and our young musicians began their usual concert. As we were thus engaged, we saw a stag bound nimbly by, within about twenty paces of where we were sitting, and by its panting, it seemed prest by the hunters. We had not much time to reflect upon the poor animal's distress, when we perceived the dogs and horsemen come sweeping along at some distance behind, and making the very path it had taken. I was instantly for returning in with my family; but either curiosity or surprize, or some more hidden motive, held my wife and daughters to their seats. The huntsman, who rode foremost, past us with great swiftness, followed by four or five persons more, who seemed in equal haste. At last, a young gentleman of a more genteel appearance than the rest, came forward, and for a while regarding us, instead of pursuing the chace, stopt short, and giving his horse to a servant who attended, approached us with a careless superior air. He seemed to want no introduction, but was going to salute my daughters* as one certain of a kind reception; but they had early learnt the lesson of looking presumption out of countenance. Upon which he let us know that his name was Thornhill, and that he was owner of the estate that lay for some extent round us. He again, therefore, offered to salute the female part of the family, and such was the power of fortune and fine cloaths, that he found no second repulse. As his address, though confident, was easy, we soon became more familiar; and perceiving musical instruments lying near, he begged to be favoured with a song. As I did not approve of such disproportioned acquaintances,* I winked upon my daughters in order to prevent their compliance; but my hint was counteracted by one from their mother; so that with a chearful air they gave us a favourite song of Dryden's.* Mr. Thornhill seemed highly delighted with their performance and choice, and then took up the guitar himself. He played but very indifferently; however, my eldest daughter repaid his former applause with interest, and assured him that his tones were louder than even those of her master. At this compliment he bowed, which she returned with a curtesy. He praised her taste, and she commended his understanding: an age could not have made them better acquainted. While the fond mother too, equally happy, insisted upon her landlord's stepping in, and tasting a glass of her gooseberry. The whole family seemed earnest to please him: my girls attempted to entertain him with topics they thought most modern, while Moses, on the contrary, gave him a question or two from the ancients, for which he had the satisfaction of being laughed at:* my little ones were no less busy, and fondly stuck close to the stranger. All my endeavours could scarce keep their dirty fingers from handling and tarnishing the lace on his cloaths, and lifting up the flaps of his pocket holes, to see what was there. At the approach of evening he took leave; but not till he had requested permission to renew his visit, which, as he was our landlord, we most readily agreed to.

As soon as he was gone, my wife called a council on the conduct of the day. She was of opinion, that it was a most fortunate hit; for that she had known even stranger things at last brought to bear. She hoped again to see the day in which we might hold up our heads with the best of them; and concluded, she protested she could see no reason why the two Miss Wrinklers should marry great fortunes, and her children get none. As this last argument was directed to me, I protested I could see no reason for it neither, nor why Mr. Simpkins got the ten thousand pound prize in the lottery, and we sate down with a blank:* 'I protest, Charles,' cried my wife, 'this is the way you always damp my girls and me when we are in Spirits. Tell me, Sophy, my dear, what do you think of our new visitor? Don't you think he seemed to be good-natured?'—'Immensely so, indeed, Mamma,' replied she. 'I think he has a great deal to say upon every thing, and is never at a loss; and the more trifling the subject, the more he has to say.'—'Yes,' cried Olivia, 'he is well enough for a man; but for my part, I don't much like him, he is so extremely impudent and familiar; but on the guitar he is shocking.' These two last speeches I interpreted by contraries. I found by this, that Sophia internally despised, as much as Olivia secretly admired him.—— 'Whatever may be your opinions of him, my children,' cried I, 'to confess a truth, he has not prepossest me in his favour. Disproportioned friendships ever terminate in disgust; and I thought, notwithstanding all his ease, that he seemed perfectly sensible of the distance between us. Let us keep to companions of our own rank. There is no character more contemptible than a man that is a fortune-hunter, and I can see no reason why fortune-hunting women should not be contemptible too. Thus, at best, we shall be contemptible if his views be honourable; but if they be otherwise! I should shudder but to think of that! It is true I have no apprehensions from the conduct of my children, but I think there are some from his character.'—I would have proceeded, but for the interruption of a servant from the 'Squire, who, with his compliments, sent us a side of venison, and a promise to dine with us some days after. This well-timed present pleaded more powerfully in his favour, than any thing I had to say could obviate. I therefore continued silent, satisfied with just having pointed out danger, and leaving it to their own discretion to avoid it. That virtue which requires to be ever guarded, is scarce worth the centinel.

CHAPTER VI

The happiness of a country fire-side

As we carried on the former dispute with some degree of warmth, in order to accommodate matters, it was universally agreed, that we should have a part of the venison for supper, and the girls undertook the task with alacrity. 'I am sorry,' cried I, 'that we have no neighbour or stranger to take a part in this good cheer: feasts of this kind acquire a double relish from hospitality.'—'Bless me,' cried my wife, 'here comes our good friend

Mr. Burchell, that saved our Sophia, and that run you down fairly in the argument.'—'Confute me in argument, child!' cried I. 'You mistake there, my dear. I believe there are but few that can do that: I never dispute your abilities at making a goose-pye, and I beg you'll leave argument to me.'—As I spoke, poor Mr. Burchell entered the house, and was welcomed by the family, who shook him heartily by the hand, while little Dick officiously reached him a chair.

I was pleased with the poor man's friendship for two reasons; because I knew that he wanted mine, and I knew him to be friendly as far as he was able. He was known in our neighbourhood by the character of the poor Gentleman that would do no good when he was young, though he was not yet thirty. He would at intervals talk with great good sense; but in general he was fondest of the company of children, whom he used to call harmless little men. He was famous, I found, for singing them ballads, and telling them stories; and seldom went out without something in his pockets for them, a piece of ginger-bread, or an halfpenny whistle.* He generally came for a few days into our neighbourhood once a year, and lived upon the neighbours hospitality. He sate down to supper among us, and my wife was not sparing of her gooseberry wine. The tale went round; he sung us old songs, and gave the children the story of the Buck of Beverland, with the history of Patient Grissel, the adventures of Catskin, and then Fair Rosamond's bower.* Our cock, which always crew at eleven, now told us it was time for repose; but an unforeseen difficulty started about lodging the stranger: all our beds were already taken up, and it was too late to send him to the next alehouse. In this dilemma, little Dick offered him his part of the bed, if his brother Moses would let him lie with him; 'And I,' cried Bill, 'will give Mr. Burchell my part, if my sisters will take me to theirs.'—'Well done, my good children,' cried I, 'hospitality is one of the first christian duties. The beast retires to its shelter, and the bird flies to its nest; but helpless man can only find refuge from his fellow creature. The greatest stranger in this world, was he that came to save it.* He never had an house, as if willing to see what hospitality was left remaining amongst us. Deborah, my dear,' cried I, to my wife, 'give those boys a lump of sugar each, and let Dick's be the largest, because he spoke first.'

In the morning early I called out my whole family to help at saving an after-growth of hay,* and our guest offering his assistance, he was accepted among the number. Our labours went on lightly, we turned the swath to the wind, I went foremost, and the rest followed in due succession. I could not avoid, however, observing the assiduity of Mr. Burchell in assisting my daughter Sophia in her part of the task. When he had finished his own, he would join in her's, and enter into a close conversation: but I had too good an opinion of Sophia's understanding, and was too well convinced of her ambition, to be under any uneasiness from a man of broken fortune. When we were finished for the day, Mr. Burchell was invited as on the night before; but he refused, as he was to lie that night at a neighbour's, to whose child he was carrying a whistle. When gone, our conversation at supper turned upon our late unfortunate guest. 'What a strong instance,' said I, 'is that poor man of the miseries attending a youth of levity and extravagance. He by no means wants sense, which only serves to aggravate his former folly. Poor forlorn creature, where are now the revellers, the flatterers, that he could once inspire and command! Gone, perhaps, to attend the bagnio pander,* grown rich by his extravagance. They once praised him, and now they applaud the pander: their former raptures at his wit, are now converted into sarcasms at his folly: he is poor, and perhaps deserves poverty; for he has neither the ambition to be independent, nor the skill to be useful.' Prompted, perhaps, by some secret reasons, I delivered this observation with too much acrimony, which my Sophia gently reproved. 'Whatsoever his former conduct may be, pappa, his circumstances should exempt him from censure now. His present indigence is a sufficient punishment for former folly; and I have heard my pappa himself say, that we should never strike our unnecessary blow at a victim over whom providence holds the scourge of its resentment.'—'You are right, Sophy,' cried my son Moses, 'and one of the ancients finely represents so malicious a conduct, by the attempts of a rustic to flay Mar whose skin, the fable tells us, had been wholly strip

another.* Besides, I don't know if this poor man's situation be so
bad as my father would represent it. We are not to judge of the
feelings of others by what we might feel if in their place. However
dark the habitation of the mole to our eyes, yet the animal itself
finds the apartment sufficiently lightsome.* And to confess a truth,
this man's mind seems fitted to his station; for I never heard any
one more sprightly than he was to-day, when he conversed with
you.'—This was said without the least design, however it excited
a blush, which she strove to cover by an affected laugh, assuring
him, that she scarce took any notice of what he said to her; but
that she believed he might once have been a very fine gentleman.
The readiness with which she undertook to vindicate herself, and
her blushing, were symptoms I did not internally approve; but I
represt my suspicions.

As we expected our landlord the next day, my wife went to
make the venison pasty; Moses sate reading, while I taught the
little ones: my daughters seemed equally busy with the rest; and I
observed them for a good while cooking something over the fire. I
at first supposed they were assisting their mother; but little Dick
informed me in a whisper, that they were making a *wash** for the
face. Washes of all kinds I had a natural antipathy to; for I knew
that instead of mending the complexion they spoiled it. I therefore approached my chair by sly degrees to the fire, and grasping
the poker, as if it wanted mending, seemingly by accident, over-
turned the whole composition, and it was too late to begin another.

CHAPTER VII

A town wit described. The dullest fellows may learn to be
comical for a night or two

WHEN the morning arrived on which we were to entertain our
young landlord, it may be easily supposed what provisions were
exhausted to make an appearance. It may also be conjectured that
my wife and daughters expanded their gayest plumage upon
this occasion. Mr. Thornhill came with a couple of friends, his

chaplain and feeder.* The servants, who were numerous, he politely ordered to the next ale-house: but my wife, in the triumph of her heart, insisted on entertaining them all; for which, by the bye, our family was pinched for three weeks after. As Mr. Burchell had hinted to us the day before, that he was making some proposals of marriage to Miss Wilmot, my son George's former mistress, this a good deal damped the heartiness of his reception: but accident, in some measure, relieved our embarrassment; for one of the company happening to mention her name, Mr. Thornhill observed with an oath, that he never knew any thing more absurd than calling such a fright a beauty: 'For strike me ugly,' continued he, 'if I should not find as much pleasure in choosing my mistress by the information of a lamp under the clock at St. Dunstan's.* At this he laughed, and so did we:—the jests of the rich are ever successful. Olivia too could not avoid whispering, loud enough to be heard, that he had an infinite fund of humour.

After dinner, I began with my usual toast, the Church; for this I was thanked by the chaplain, as he said the church was the only mistress of his affections.—'Come tell us honestly, Frank,' said the 'Squire, with his usual archness, 'suppose the church, your present mistress, drest in lawn sleeves,* on one hand, and Miss Sophia, with no lawn about her, on the other, which would you be for?' 'For both, to be sure,' cried the chaplain.—'Right Frank,' cried the 'Squire; 'for may this glass suffocate me but a fine girl is worth all the priestcraft in the creation. For what are tythes and tricks but an imposition,* all a confounded imposture, and I can prove it.'—'I wish you would,' cried my son Moses, 'and I think,' continued he, 'that I should be able to answer you.'—'Very well, Sir,' cried the 'Squire, who immediately smoaked him,* and winking on the rest of the company, to prepare us for the sport, 'if you are for a cool argument upon that subject, I am ready to accept the challenge. And first, whether are you for managing it analogically, or dialogically?' 'I am for managing it rationally,' cried Moses, quite happy at being permitted to dispute. 'Good again,' cried the 'Squire, 'and firstly, of the first. I hope you'll not deny that whatever is is. If you don't grant me that, I can go no further.' —

'Why,' returned Moses, 'I think I may grant that, and make the best of it.'—'I hope too,' returned the other, 'you'll grant that a part is less than the whole.' 'I grant that too,' cried Moses, 'it is but just and reasonable.'—'I hope,' cried the 'Squire, 'you will not deny, that the two angles of a triangle are equal to two right ones.'—'Nothing can be plainer,' returned t'other, and looked round with his usual importance.—'Very well,' cried the 'Squire, speaking very quick, 'the premises being thus settled, I proceed to observe, that the concatanation of self existences, proceeding in a reciprocal duplicate ratio, naturally produce a problematical dialogism, which in some measure proves that the essence of spirituality may be referred to the second predicable'—'Hold, hold,' cried the other, 'I deny that: Do you think I can thus tamely submit to such heterodox doctrines?'—'What,' replied the 'Squire, as if in a passion, 'not submit! Answer me one plain question: Do you think Aristotle right when he says, that relatives are related?' 'Undoubtedly,' replied the other.—'If so then,' cried the 'Squire, 'answer me directly to what I propose: Whether do you judge the analytical investigation of the first part of my enthymem deficient secundum quoad, or quoad minus, and give me your reasons: give me your reasons, I say, directly.'—'I protest,' cried Moses, 'I don't rightly comprehend the force of your reasoning; but if it be reduced to one simple proposition, I fancy it may then have an answer.'—'O, sir,' cried the 'Squire, 'I am your most humble servant, I find you want me to furnish you with argument and intellects too. No, sir, there I protest you are too hard for me.' This effectually raised the laugh against poor Moses, who sate the only dismal figure in a groupe of merry faces: nor did he offer a single syllable more during the whole entertainment.

But though all this gave me no pleasure, it had a very different effect upon Olivia, who mistook it for humour, though but a mere act of the memory. She thought him therefore a very fine gentle-man; and such as consider what powerful ingredients a good figure, fine cloaths, and fortune, are in that character, will easily forgive her. Mr. Thornhill, notwithstanding his real ignorance, talked with ease, and could expatiate upon the common topics of conversation with fluency. It is not surprising then that such talents should win the affections of a girl, who by education was taught to value an appearance in herself, and consequently to set a value upon it in another.

Upon his departure, we again entered into a debate upon the merits of our young landlord. As he directed his looks and conversation to Olivia, it was no longer doubted but that she was the object that induced him to be our visitor. Nor did she seem to be much displeased at the innocent raillery of her brother and sister upon this occasion. Even Deborah herself seemed to share the glory of the day, and exulted in her daughter's victory as if it were her own. 'And now, my dear,' cried she to me, 'I'll fairly own, that it was I that instructed my girls to encourage our landlord's addresses. I had always some ambition, and you now see that I was right; for who knows how this may end?' 'Ay, who knows that indeed,' answered I, with a groan: 'for my part I don't much like it; and I could have been better pleased with one that was poor and honest, than this fine gentleman with his fortune and infidelity; for depend on't, if he be what I suspect him, no free-thinker shall ever have a child of mine.'

'Sure, father,' cried Moses, 'you are too severe in this; for heaven will never arraign him for what he thinks, but for what he does. Every man has a thousand vicious thoughts, which arise without his power to suppress. Thinking freely of religion, may be involuntary with this gentleman: so that allowing his sentiments to be wrong, yet as he is purely passive in his assent, he is no more to be blamed for his errors than the governor of a city without walls for the shelter he is obliged to afford an invading enemy.'

'True, my son,' cried I; 'but if the governor invites the enemy, there he is justly culpable. And such is always the case with those who embrace error. The vice does not lie in assenting to the proofs they see; but in being blind to many of the proofs that offer. So that, though our erroneous opinions be involuntary when formed, yet as we have been wilfully corrupt, or very negligent in forming them, we deserve punishment for our vice, or contempt for our folly.'

My wife now kept up the conversation, though not the argument: she observed, that several very prudent men of our acquaintance were free-thinkers,* and made very good husbands; and she knew some sensible girls that had skill enough to make converts of their spouses: 'And who knows, my dear,' continued she, 'what Olivia may be able to do. The girl has a great deal to say upon every subject, and to my knowledge is very well skilled in controversy.'

'Why, my dear, what controversy can she have read?' cried I. 'It does not occur to me that I ever put such books into her hands: you certainly over-rate her merit.' 'Indeed, pappa,' replied Olivia, 'she does not: I have read a great deal of controversy. I have read the disputes between Thwackum and Square;* the controversy between Robinson Crusoe and Friday the savage,* and I am now employed in reading the controversy in Religious courtship.'*— 'Very well,' cried I, 'that's a good girl, I find you are perfectly qualified for making converts, and so go help your mother to make the gooseberry-pye.'

CHAPTER VIII

An amour, which promises little good fortune, yet may be
productive of much

THE next morning we were again visited by Mr. Burchell, though I began, for certain reasons, to be displeased with the frequency of his return; but I could not refuse him my company and fireside. It is true his labour more than requited his entertainment; for he wrought among us with vigour, and either in the meadow or at the hay-rick put himself foremost. Besides, he had always something amusing to say that lessened our toil, and was at once so out of the way, and yet so sensible, that I loved, laughed at, and pitied him. My only dislike arose from an attachment he discovered to my daughter: he would, in a jesting manner, call her his little mistress, and when he bought each of the girls a set of ribbands, hers was the finest. I knew not how, but he every day seemed to become more amiable, his wit to improve, and his simplicity to assume the superior airs of wisdom.

Our family dined in the field, and we sate, or rather reclined, round a temperate repast, our cloth spread upon the hay, while Mr. Burchell gave chearfulness to the feast. To heighten our satisfaction two blackbirds answered each other from opposite hedges, the familiar redbreast came and pecked the crumbs from our hands, and every sound seemed but the echo of tranquillity. 'I never sit thus,' says Sophia, 'but I think of the two lovers, so sweetly described by Mr. Gay,* who were struck dead in each other's arms. There is something so pathetic in the description, that I have read it an hundred times with new rapture.'—'In my opinion,' cried my son, 'the finest strokes in that description are much below those in the Acis and Galatea of Ovid.* The Roman poet understands the use of *contrast* better, and upon that figure artfully managed all strength in the pathetic depends.'—'It is remarkable,' cried Mr. Burchell, 'that both the poets you mention have equally contributed to introduce a false taste into their respective countries, by loading all their lines with epithet. Men of little genius found them most easily imitated in their defects, and English poetry, like that in the latter empire of Rome, is nothing at present but a combination of luxuriant images, without plot or connexion; a string of epithets that improve the sound, without carrying on the sense.* But perhaps, madam, while I thus reprehend others, you'll think it just that I should give them an opportunity to retaliate, and indeed I have made this remark only to have an opportunity of introducing to the company a ballad, which, whatever be its other defects, is I think at least free from those I have mentioned.'

A BALLAD*

'TURN, gentle hermit of the dale,
    And guide my lonely way,
To where yon taper cheers the vale,
    With hospitable ray.

'For here forlorn and lost I tread,
　　With fainting steps and slow;
Where wilds immeasurably spread,
　　Seem lengthening as I go.'

'Forbear, my son,' the hermit cries,
　　'To tempt the dangerous gloom;
For yonder faithless phantom flies
　　To lure thee to thy doom.

'Here to the houseless child of want,
　　My door is open still;
And tho' my portion is but scant,
　　I give it with good will.

'Then turn to-night, and freely share
　　Whate'er my cell bestows;
My rushy couch, and frugal fare,
　　My blessing and repose.

'No flocks that range the valley free,
　　To slaughter I condemn:
Taught by that power that pities me,
　　I learn to pity them.

'But from the mountain's grassy side,
　　A guiltless feast I bring;
A scrip with herbs and fruits supply'd,
　　And water from the spring.

'Then, pilgrim, turn, thy cares forego;
　　All earth-born cares are wrong:
Man wants but little here below,
　　Nor wants that little long.'

Soft as the dew from heav'n descends,
　　His gentle accents fell:
The modest stranger lowly bends,
　　And follows to the cell.

Far in a wilderness obscure
　　The lonely mansion lay;

A refuge to the neighbouring poor,
 And strangers led astray

No stores beneath its humble thatch
 Requir'd a master's care;
The wicket opening with a latch,
 Receiv'd the harmless pair.

And now when busy crowds retire
 To take their evening rest,
The hermit trimm'd his little fire,
 And cheer'd his pensive guest:

And spread his vegetable store,
 And gayly prest, and smil'd;
And skill'd in legendary lore,
 The lingering hours beguil'd.

Around in sympathetic mirth
 Its tricks the kitten tries,
The cricket chirrups in the hearth;
 The crackling faggot flies.

But nothing could a charm impart
 To sooth the stranger's woe;
For grief was heavy at his heart,
 And tears began to flow.

His rising cares the hermit spy'd,
 With answering care opprest:
'And whence, unhappy youth,' he cry'd,
 'The sorrows of thy breast?

'From better habitations spurn'd,
 Reluctant dost thou rove;
Or grieve for friendship unreturn'd,
 Or unregarded love?

'Alas! the joys that fortune brings,
 Are trifling and decay;
And those who prize the paltry things,
 More trifling still than they.

'And what is friendship but a name,
      A charm that lulls to sleep;
A shade that follows wealth or fame,
      But leaves the wretch to weep?

'And love is still an emptier sound,
      The modern fair one's jest:
On earth unseen, or only found
      To warm the turtle's nest.

'For shame fond youth thy sorrows hush,
      And spurn the sex,' he said:
But while he spoke a rising blush
      His love-lorn guest betray'd.

Surpriz'd he sees new beauties rise,
      Swift mantling to the view;
Like colours o'er the morning skies,
      As bright, as transient too.

The bashful look, the rising breast,
      Alternate spread alarms:
The lovely stranger stands confest
      A maid in all her charms.

'And, ah, forgive a stranger rude,
      A wretch forlorn,' she cry'd;
'Whose feet unhallowed thus intrude
      Where heaven and you reside.

'But let a maid thy pity share,
      Whom love has taught to stray;
Who seeks for rest, but finds despair
      Companion of her way.

'My father liv'd beside the Tyne,
      A wealthy Lord was he;
And all his wealth was mark'd as mine,
      He had but only me.

'To win me from his tender arms,
      Unnumber'd suitors came;

Who prais'd me for imputed charms,
    And felt or feign'd a flame.

'Each hour a mercenary crowd,
    With richest proffers strove:
Among the rest young Edwin bow'd,
    But never talk'd of love.

'In humble simplest habit clad,
    No wealth nor power had he;
Wisdom and worth were all he had,
    But these were all to me.

'The blossom opening to the day,
    The dews of heaven refin'd,
Could nought of purity display,
    To emulate his mind.

'The dew, the blossom on the tree,
    With charms inconstant shine;
Their charms were his, but woe to me,
    Their constancy was mine.

'For still I try'd each fickle art,
    Importunate and vain;
And while his passion touch'd my heart,
    I triumph'd in his pain.

'Till quite dejected with my scorn,
    He left me to my pride;
And sought a solitude forlorn,
    In secret where he died.

'But mine the sorrow, mine the fault,
    And well my life shall pay;
I'll seek the solitude he sought,
    And stretch me where he lay.

'And there forlorn despairing hid,
    I'll lay me down and die:
'Twas so for me that Edwin did,
    And so for him will I.'

'Forbid it heaven!' the hermit cry'd,
    And clasp'd her to his breast:
The wondering fair one turn'd to chide,
    'Twas Edwin's self that prest.

'Turn, Angelina, ever dear,
    My charmer, turn to see,
Thy own, thy long-lost Edwin here,
    Restor'd to love and thee.

'Thus let me hold thee to my heart,
    And ev'ry care resign:
And shall we never, never part,
    My life,—my all that's mine.

'No, never, from this hour to part,
    We'll live and love so true;
The sigh that rends thy constant heart,
    Shall break thy Edwin's too.'

While this ballad was reading, Sophia seemed to mix an air of tenderness with her approbation. But our tranquillity was soon disturbed by the report of a gun just by us, and immediately after a man was seen bursting through the hedge, to take up the game he had killed. This sportsman was the 'Squire's chaplain, who had shot one of the blackbirds that so agreeably entertained us. So loud a report, and so near, startled my daughters; and I could perceive that Sophia in the fright had thrown herself into Mr. Burchell's arms for protection. The gentleman came up, and asked pardon for having disturbed us, affirming that he was ignorant of our being so near. He therefore sate down by my youngest daughter, and, sportsman like, offered her what he had killed that morning. She was going to refuse, but a private look from her mother soon induced her to correct the mistake, and accept his present, though with some reluctance. My wife, as usual, discovered her pride in a whisper, observing, that Sophy had made a conquest of the chaplain, as well as her sister had of the 'Squire. I suspected, however, with more probability, that her affections were placed upon a different object. The chaplain's errand was to inform us, that Mr. Thornhill had provided music and refreshments, and intended that night giving the young ladies a ball by moon-light, on the grass-plot before our door. 'Nor can I deny,' continued he, 'but I have an interest in being first to deliver this message, as I expect for my reward to be honoured with miss Sophy's hand as a partner.' To this my girl replied, that she should have no objection, if she could do it with honour: 'But here,' continued she, 'is a gentleman,' looking at Mr. Burchell, 'who has been my companion in the task for the day, and it is fit he should share in its amusements.' Mr. Burchell returned her a compliment for her intentions; but resigned her up to the chaplain, adding that he was to go that night five miles, being invited to an harvest supper. His refusal appeared to me a little extraordinary, nor could I conceive how so sensible a girl as my youngest, could thus prefer a man of broken fortune to one whose expectations were much greater. But as men are most capable of distinguishing merit in women, so the ladies often form the truest judgments of us. The two sexes seem placed as spies upon each other, and are furnished with different abilities, adapted for mutual inspection.

CHAPTER IX

Two ladies of great distinction introduced. Superior finery
ever seems to confer superior breeding

MR. BURCHELL had scarce taken leave, and Sophia consented to dance with the chaplain, when my little ones came running out to tell us that the 'Squire was come, with a crowd of company. Upon our return, we found our landlord, with a couple of under gentlemen and two young ladies richly drest, whom he introduced as women of very great distinction and fashion from town.* We happened not to have chairs enough for the whole company; but Mr. Thornhill immediately proposed that every gentleman should sit in a lady's lap. This I positively objected to, notwithstanding a look of disapprobation from my wife. Moses was therefore dispatched to borrow a couple of chairs; and as we were in want of ladies to make up a set at country dances, the two gentlemen went with him in quest of a couple of partners. Chairs and partners were soon provided. The gentlemen returned with my neighbour Flamborough's rosy daughters, flaunting with red top-knots,* but an unlucky circumstance was not adverted to; though the Miss Flamboroughs were reckoned the very best dancers in the parish, and understood the jig and the round-about to perfection; yet they were totally unacquainted with country dances.* This at first discomposed us: however, after a little shoving and dragging, they at last went merrily on. Our music consisted of two fiddles, with a pipe and tabor. The moon shone bright, Mr. Thornhill and my eldest daughter led up the ball, to the great delight of the spectators; for the neighbours hearing what was going forward, came flocking about us. My girl moved with so much grace and vivacity, that my wife could not avoid discovering the pride of her heart, by assuring me, that though the little chit* did it so cleverly, all the steps were stolen from herself. The ladies of the town strove hard to be equally easy, but without success. They swam, sprawled, languished, and frisked; but all would not do: the gazers indeed owned that it was fine; but neighbour Flamborough observed, that Miss Livy's feet seemed as pat to the music as its echo. After the dance had continued about an hour, the two ladies, who were apprehensive of catching cold, moved to break up the ball. One of them, I thought, expressed her sentiments upon this occasion in a very coarse manner, when she observed, that by the *living jingo*, she was all of a muck of sweat.* Upon our return to the house, we found a very elegant cold supper, which Mr. Thornhill had ordered to be brought with him. The conversation at this time was more reserved than before. The two ladies threw my girls quite into the shade; for they would talk of nothing but high life, and high lived company; with other fashionable topics, such as pictures, taste, Shakespear, and the musical glasses.* 'Tis true they once or twice mortified us sensibly by slipping out an oath; but that appeared to me as the surest symptom of their distinc-tion, (tho' I am since informed that swearing is perfectly unfashionable.) Their finery, however, threw a veil over any grossness in their conversation. My daughters seemed to regard their superior accomplishments with envy; and what appeared amiss was ascribed to tip-top quality breeding. But the condescension of the ladies was still superior to their other accomplishments. One of them observed, that had miss Olivia seen a little more of the world, it would greatly improve her. To which the other added, that a single winter in town* would make her little Sophia quite another thing. My wife warmly assented to both; adding, that there was nothing she more ardently wished than to give her girls a single winter's polishing. To this I could not help replying, that their breeding was already superior to their fortune; and that greater refinement would only serve to make their poverty ridiculous, and give them a taste for pleasures they had no right to possess.—'And what pleasures,' cried Mr. Thornhill, 'do they not deserve to possess, who have so much in their power to bestow? As for my part,' continued he, 'my fortune is pretty large, love, liberty, and pleasure, are my maxims; but curse me if a settlement of half my estate could give my charming Olivia pleasure, it should be hers; and the only favour I would ask in return would be to add myself to the benefit.' I was not such a stranger to the world as to be ignorant that this was the fashionable cant to disguise the insolence of the basest proposal; but I made an effort to suppress my resentment. 'Sir,' cried I, 'the family which you now condescend to favour with your company, has been bred with as nice a sense of honour as you. Any attempts to injure that, may be attended with very dangerous consequences. Honour, Sir, is our only possession at present, and of that last treasure we must be particularly careful.'—I was soon sorry for the warmth with which I had spoken this, when the young gentleman, grasping my hand, swore he commended my spirit, though he disapproved my suspicions. 'As to your present hint,' continued he, 'I protest nothing was farther from my heart than such a thought. No, by all that's tempting, the virtue that will stand a regular siege was never to my taste; for all my amours are carried by a coup de main.'*

The two ladies, who affected to be ignorant of the rest, seemed highly displeased with this last stroke of freedom, and began a very discreet and serious dialogue upon virtue: in this my wife, the chaplain, and I, soon joined; and the 'Squire himself was at last brought to confess a sense of sorrow for his former excesses. We talked of the pleasures of temperance, and of the sun-shine in the mind unpolluted with guilt. I was so well pleased, that my little ones were kept up beyond the usual time to be edified by so much good conversation. Mr. Thornhill even went beyond me, and demanded if I had any objection to giving prayers. I joyfully embraced the proposal, and in this manner the night was passed in a most comfortable way, till at last the company began to think of returning. The ladies seemed very unwilling to part with my daughters; for whom they had conceived a particular affection, and joined in a request to have the pleasure of their company home. The 'Squire seconded the proposal, and my wife added her entreaties: the girls too looked upon me as if they wished to go. In this perplexity I made two or three excuses, which my daughters as readily removed; so that at last I was obliged to give a peremptory refusal; for which we had nothing but sullen looks and short answers the whole day ensuing.

CHAPTER X

The family endeavours to cope with their betters. The miseries of the poor when they attempt to appear above their circumstances

I NOW began to find that all my long and painful lectures upon temperance, simplicity, and contentment, were entirely disregarded. The distinctions lately paid us by our betters awaked that pride which I had laid asleep, but not removed. Our windows again, as formerly, were filled with washes for the neck and face. The sun was dreaded as an enemy to the skin without doors, and the fire as a spoiler of the complexion within. My wife observed, that rising too early would hurt her daughters eyes, that working after dinner would redden their noses, and she convinced me that the hands never looked so white as when they did nothing. Instead therefore of finishing George's shirts, we now had them new modelling their old gauzes, or flourishing upon catgut.* The poor Miss Flamboroughs, their former gay companions, were cast off as mean acquaintance, and the whole conversation ran upon high life and high lived company, with pictures, taste, Shakespear, and the musical glasses.

But we could have borne all this, had not a fortune-telling gypsey come to raise us into perfect sublimity. The tawny sybil no sooner appeared, than my girls came running to me for a shilling a piece to cross her hand with silver. To say the truth, I was tired of being always wise, and could not help gratifying their request, because I loved to see them happy. I gave each of them a shilling; though, for the honour of the family, it must be observed, that they never went without money themselves, as my wife always generously let them have a guinea each, to keep in their pockets; but with strict injunctions never to change it. After they had been closetted up with the fortune-teller for some time, I knew by their looks, upon their returning, that they had been promised something great.—'Well, my girls, how have you sped? Tell me, Livy, has the fortune-teller given thee a pennyworth?'—'I protest, pappa,' says the girl, 'I believe she deals with some body that's not right; for she positively declared, that I am to be married to a 'Squire in less than a twelvemonth?'—'Well now, Sophy, my child,' said I, 'and what sort of a husband are you to have?' 'Sir,' replied she, 'I am to have a Lord soon after my sister has married the 'Squire.'—'How,' cried I, 'is that all you are to have for your two shillings! Only a Lord and a 'Squire for two shillings! You fools, I could have promised you a Prince and a Nabob* for half the money.'

This curiosity of theirs, however, was attended with very serious effects: we now began to think ourselves designed by the stars for something exalted, and already anticipated our future grandeur.

It has been a thousand times observed, and I must observe it once more, that the hours we pass with happy prospects in view, are more pleasing than those crowned with fruition. In the first case we cook the dish to our own appetite; in the latter nature cooks it for us. It is impossible to repeat the train of agreeable reveries we called up for our entertainment. We looked upon our fortunes as once more rising; and as the whole parish asserted that the 'Squire was in love with my daughter, she was actually so with him; for they persuaded her into the passion. In this agreeable interval, my wife had the most lucky dreams in the world, which she took care to tell us every morning, with great solemnity and exactness. It was one night a coffin and cross bones, the sign of an approaching wedding: at another time she imagined her daughters pockets filled with farthings, a certain sign of their being shortly stuffed with gold. The girls themselves had their omens. They felt strange kisses on their lips; they saw rings in the candle, purses bounced from the fire,* and true love-knots lurked in the bottom of every tea-cup.

Towards the end of the week we received a card from the town ladies; in which, with their compliments, they hoped to see all our family at church the Sunday following. All Saturday morning I could perceive, in consequence of this, my wife and daughters in close conference together, and now and then glancing at me with looks that betrayed a latent plot. To be sincere, I had strong suspicions that some absurd proposal was preparing for appearing with splendor the next day. In the evening they began their operations in a very regular manner, and my wife undertook to conduct the siege. After tea, when I seemed in spirits, she began thus.—'I fancy, Charles, my dear, we shall have a great deal of good company at our church to-morrow.'—'Perhaps we may, my dear,' returned I; 'though you need be under no uneasiness about that, you shall have a sermon whether there be or not.'—'That is what I expect,' returned she; 'but I think, my dear, we ought to appear there as decently as possible, for who knows what may happen?' 'Your precautions,' replied I, 'are highly commendable. A decent behaviour and appearance in church is what charms me. We should be devout and humble, chearful and serene.'—'Yes,' cried she, 'I know that; but I mean we should go there in as proper a manner as possible; not altogether like the scrubs* about us.' 'You are quite right, my dear,' returned I, 'and I was going to make the very same proposal. The proper manner of going is, to go there as early as possible, to have time for meditation before the service begins.'—'Phoo, Charles,' interrupted she, 'all that is very true; but not what I would be at. I mean, we should go there genteelly. You know the church is two miles off, and I protest I don't like to see my daughters trudging up to their pew all blowzed and red with walking, and looking for all the world as if they had been winners at a smock race.* Now, my dear, my proposal is this: there are our two plow horses, the Colt that has been in our family these nine years, and his companion Blackberry, that have scarce done an earthly thing for this month past. They are both grown fat and lazy. Why should not they do something as well as we? And let me tell you, when Moses has trimmed them a little, they will cut a very tolerable figure.'

To this proposal I objected, that walking would be twenty times more genteel than such a paltry conveyance, as Blackberry was wall-eyed, and the Colt wanted a tail: that they had never been broke to the rein; but had an hundred vicious tricks; and that we had but one saddle and pillion in the whole house. All these objections, however, were over-ruled; so that I was obliged to comply. The next morning I perceived them not a little busy in collecting such materials as might be necessary for the expedition; but as I found it would be a business of time, I walked on to the church before, and they promised speedily to follow. I waited near an hour in the reading desk for their arrival; but not finding them come as expected, I was obliged to begin, and went through the service, not without some uneasiness at finding them absent. This was encreased when all was finished, and no appearance of the family. I therefore walked back by the horse-way, which was five miles round, tho' the foot-way was but two, and when got about half way home, perceived the procession marching slowly forward towards the church; my son, my wife, and the two little ones exalted upon one horse, and my two daughters upon the other. I demanded the cause of their delay; but I soon found by their looks they had met with a thousand misfortunes on the road. The horses had at first refused to move from the door, till Mr. Burchell was kind enough to beat them forward for about two hundred yards with his cudgel. Next the straps of my wife's pillion* broke down, and they were obliged to stop to repair them before they could proceed. After that, one of the horses took it into his head to stand still, and neither blows nor entreaties could prevail with him to proceed. It was just recovering from this dismal situation that I found them; but perceiving every thing safe, I own their present mortification did not much displease me, as it would give me many opportunities of future triumph, and teach my daughters more humility.

CHAPTER XI

The family still resolve to hold up their heads

MICHAELMAS eve happening on the next day,* we were invited to burn nuts and play tricks at neighbour Flamborough's. Our late mortifications had humbled us a little, or it is probable we might have rejected such an invitation with contempt: however, we suffered ourselves to be happy. Our honest neighbour's goose and dumplings were fine, and the lamb's-wool,* even in the opinion of my wife, who was a connoiseur, was excellent. It is true, his manner of telling stories was not quite so well. They were very long, and very dull, and all about himself, and we had laughed at them ten times before: however, we were kind enough to laugh at them once more.

Mr. Burchell, who was of the party, was always fond of seeing some innocent amusement going forward, and set the boys and girls to blind man's buff. My wife too was persuaded to join in the diversion, and it gave me pleasure to think she was not yet too old. In the mean time, my neighbour and I looked on, laughed at every feat, and praised our own dexterity when we were young. Hot cockles* succeeded next, questions and commands followed that, and last of all, they sate down to hunt the slipper. As every person may not be acquainted with this primæval pastime, it may be necessary to observe, that the company at this play plant themselves in a ring upon the ground, all, except one who stands in the middle, whose business it is to catch a shoe, which the company shove about under their hams from one to another, something like a weaver's shuttle. As it is impossible, in this case, for the lady who is up to face all the company at once, the great beauty of the play lies in hitting her a thump with the heel of the shoe on that side least capable of making a defence. It was in this manner that my eldest daughter was hemmed in, and thumped about, all blowzed, in spirits, and bawling for fair play, fair play, with a voice that might deafen a ballad singer, when confusion on confusion, who should enter the room but our two great acquaintances from town, Lady Blarney and Miss Carolina Wilelmina Amelia Skeggs! Description would but beggar, therefore it is unnecessary to describe this new mortification. Death! To be seen by ladies of such high breeding in such vulgar attitudes! Nothing better could ensue from such a vulgar play of Mr. Flamborough's proposing. We seemed stuck to the ground for some time, as if actually petrified with amazement.

The two ladies had been at our house to see us, and finding us from home, came after us hither, as they were uneasy to know what accident could have kept us from church the day before. Olivia undertook to be our prolocutor,* and delivered the whole in a summary way, only saying, 'We were thrown from our horses.' At which account the ladies were greatly concerned; but being told the family received no hurt, they were extremely glad: but being informed that we were almost killed by the fright, they were vastly sorry; but hearing that we had a very good night, they were extremely glad again. Nothing could exceed their complaisance to my daughters; their professions the last evening were warm, but now they were ardent. They protested a desire of having a more lasting acquaintance. Lady Blarney was particularly attached to Olivia; Miss Carolina Wilelmina Amelia Skeggs (I love to give the whole name) took a greater fancy to her sister. They supported the conversation between themselves, while my daughters sate silent, admiring their exalted breeding. But as every reader, however beggarly himself, is fond of high-lived dialogues, with anecdotes of Lords, Ladies, and Knights of the Garter, I must beg leave to give him the concluding part of the present conversation.

'All that I know of the matter,' cried Miss Skeggs, 'is this, that it may be true, or it may not be true: but this I can assure your Ladyship, that the whole rout was in amaze; his Lordship turned all manner of colours, my Lady fell into a sound;* but Sir Tomkyn, drawing his sword, swore he was her's to the last drop of his blood.'

'Well,' replied our Peeress, 'this I can say, that the Dutchess never told me a syllable of the matter, and I believe her Grace would keep nothing a secret from me. This you may depend upon as fact, that the next morning my Lord Duke cried out three times to his valet de chambre, Jernigan, Jernigan, Jernigan, bring me my garters.'

But previously I should have mentioned the very impolite behaviour of Mr. Burchell, who, during this discourse, sate with his face turned to the fire, and at the conclusion of every sentence would cry out *fudge*, an expression which displeased us all, and in some measure damped the rising spirit of the conversation.*

'Besides, my dear Skeggs,' continued our Peeress, 'there is nothing of this in the copy of verses that Dr. Burdock made upon the occasion.' *Fudge!*

'I am surprised at that,' cried Miss Skeggs; 'for he seldom leaves any thing out, as he writes only for his own amusement. But can your Ladyship favour me with a sight of them?' *Fudge!*

'My dear creature,' replied our Peeress, 'do you think I carry such things about me? Though they are very fine to be sure, and I think myself something of a judge; at least I know what pleases myself. Indeed I was ever an admirer of all Doctor Burdock's little pieces; for except what he does, and our dear Countess at Hanover-Square, there's nothing comes out but the most lowest stuff in nature; not a bit of high life among them.' *Fudge!*

'Your Ladyship should except,' says t'other, 'your own things in the Lady's Magazine.* I hope you'll say there's nothing low lived there? But I suppose we are to have no more from that quarter?' *Fudge!*

'Why, my dear,' says the Lady, 'you know my reader and companion has left me, to be married to Captain Roach, and as my poor eyes won't suffer me to write myself, I have been for some time looking out for another. A proper person is no easy matter to find, and to be sure thirty pounds a year is a small stipend for a well-bred girl of character, that can read, write, and behave in company; as for the chits about town, there is no bearing them about one.' *Fudge!*

'That I know,' cried Miss Skeggs, 'by experience. For of the three companions I had this last half year, one of them refused to do plain-work* an hour in the day, another thought twenty-five guineas a year too small a salary, and I was obliged to send away the third, because I suspected an intrigue with the chaplain. Virtue, my dear Lady Blarney, virtue is worth any price; but where is that to be found?' *Fudge!*

My wife had been for a long time all attention to this discourse; but was particularly struck with the latter part of it. Thirty pounds and twenty-five guineas a year made fifty-six pounds five shillings English money, all which was in a manner going a-begging, and might easily be secured in the family. She for a moment studied my looks for approbation; and, to own a truth, I was of opinion, that two such places would fit our two daughters exactly. Besides, if the 'Squire had any real affection for my eldest daughter, this would be the way to make her every way qualified for her fortune. My wife therefore was resolved that we should not be deprived of such advantages for want of assurance, and undertook to harangue for the family. 'I hope,' cried she, 'your Ladyships will pardon my present presumption. It is true, we have no right to pretend to such favours; but yet it is natural for me to wish putting my children forward in the world. And I will be bold to say my two girls have had a pretty good education, and capacity, at least the country can't shew better. They can read, write, and cast accompts; they understand their needle, breadstitch, cross and change, and all manner of plain-work; they can pink, point, and frill; and know something of music; they can do up small cloaths, work upon catgut; my eldest can cut paper,* and my youngest has a very pretty manner of telling fortunes upon the cards.' *Fudge!*

When she had delivered this pretty piece of eloquence, the two ladies looked at each other a few minutes in silence, with an air of doubt and importance. At last, Miss Carolina Wilelmina Amelia Skeggs condescended to observe, that the young ladies, from the opinion she could form of them from so slight an acquaintance, seemed very fit for such employments: 'But a thing of this kind, Madam,' cried she, addressing my spouse, 'requires a thorough examination into characters, and a more perfect knowledge of each other. Not, Madam,' continued she, 'that I in the least suspect the young ladies virtue, prudence and discretion; but there is a form in these things, Madam, there is a form.'

My wife approved her suspicions very much, observing, that she was very apt to be suspicious herself; but referred her to all the neighbours for a character: but this our Peeress declined as unnecessary, alledging that her cousin Thornhill's recommendation would be sufficient, and upon this we rested our petition.

CHAPTER XII

Fortune seems resolved to humble the family of Wakefield.
Mortifications are often more painful than real calamities

WHEN we were returned home, the night was dedicated to schemes of future conquest. Deborah exerted much sagacity in conjecturing which of the two girls was likely to have the best place, and most opportunities of seeing good company. The only obstacle to our preferment was in obtaining the 'Squire's recommendation; but he had already shewn us too many instances of his friendship to doubt of it now. Even in bed my wife kept up the usual theme: 'Well, faith, my dear Charles, between ourselves, I think we have made an excellent day's work of it.'—'Pretty well,' cried I, not knowing what to say.—'What only pretty well!' returned she. 'I think it is very well. Suppose the girls should come to make acquaintances of taste in town! This I am assured of, that London is the only place in the world for all manner of husbands. Besides, my dear, stranger things happen every day:

and as ladies of quality are so taken with my daughters, what will not men of quality be! Entre nous, I protest I like my Lady Blarney vastly, so very obliging. However, Miss Carolina Wilelmina Amelia Skeggs has my warm heart. But yet, when they came to talk of places in town, you saw at once how I nailed them. Tell me, my dear, don't you think I did for my children there?'— 'Ay,' returned I, not knowing well what to think of the matter, 'heaven grant they may be both the better for it this day three months!' This was one of those observations I usually made to impress my wife with an opinion of my sagacity; for if the girls succeeded, then it was a pious wish fulfilled; but if any thing unfortunate ensued, then it might be looked upon as a prophecy. All this conversation, however, was only preparatory to another scheme, and indeed I dreaded as much. This was nothing less than, that as we were now to hold up our heads a little higher in the world, it would be proper to sell the Colt, which was grown old, at a neighbouring fair, and buy us an horse that would carry single or double upon an occasion, and make a pretty appearance at church or upon a visit. This at first I opposed stoutly; but it was as stoutly defended. However, as I weakened, my antagonist gained strength, till at last it was resolved to part with him.

As the fair happened on the following day, I had intentions of going myself; but my wife persuaded me that I had got a cold, and nothing could prevail upon her to permit me from home. 'No, my dear,' said she, 'our son Moses is a discreet boy, and can buy and sell to very good advantage; you know all our great bargains are of his purchasing. He always stands out and higgles,* and actually tires them till he gets a bargain.'

As I had some opinion of my son's prudence, I was willing enough to entrust him with this commission; and the next morning I perceived his sisters mighty busy in fitting out Moses for the fair; trimming his hair, brushing his buckles, and cocking his hat with pins.* The business of the toilet being over, we had at last the satisfaction of seeing him mounted upon the Colt, with a deal box before him to bring home groceries in. He had on a coat made of that cloth they call thunder and lightning,* which, though grown too short, was much too good to be thrown away. His waistcoat

was of gosling green,* and his sisters had tied his hair with a broad
black ribband. We all followed him several paces from the door,
bawling after him good luck, good luck, till we could see him no
longer.

He was scarce gone, when Mr. Thornhill's butler came to congratulate us upon our good fortune, saying, that he overheard his
young master mention our names with great commendation.

Good fortune seemed resolved not to come alone. Another
footman from the same family followed, with a card for my
daughters, importing, that the two ladies had received such pleasing accounts from Mr. Thornhill of us all, that, after a few previous enquiries, they hoped to be perfectly satisfied. 'Ay,' cried my
wife, 'I now see it is no easy matter to get into the families of the
great; but when one once gets in, then, as Moses says, one may
go sleep.' To this piece of humour, for she intended it for wit,
my daughters assented with a loud laugh of pleasure. In short,
such was her satisfaction at this message, that she actually put
her hand in her pocket, and gave the messenger seven-pence
halfpenny.

This was to be our visiting-day. The next that came was
Mr. Burchell, who had been at the fair. He brought my little ones
a pennyworth of gingerbread each, which my wife undertook to
keep for them, and give them by letters at a time.* He brought my
daughters also a couple of boxes, in which they might keep
wafers, snuff, patches, or even money,* when they got it. My wife
was usually fond of a weesel skin purse,* as being the most lucky;
but this by the bye. We had still a regard for Mr. Burchell, though
his late rude behaviour was in some measure displeasing; nor
could we now avoid communicating our happiness to him, and
asking his advice: although we seldom followed advice, we were
all ready enough to ask it. When he read the note from the two
ladies, he shook his head, and observed, that an affair of this sort
demanded the utmost circumspection.—This air of diffidence
highly displeased my wife. 'I never doubted, Sir,' cried she, 'your
readiness to be against my daughters and me. You have more
circumspection than is wanted. However, I fancy when we come
to ask advice, we will apply to persons who seem to have made use

of it themselves.'—'Whatever my own conduct may have been, madam,' replied he, 'is not the present question; tho' as I have made no use of advice myself, I should in conscience give it to those that will.'—As I was apprehensive this answer might draw on a repartee, making up by abuse what it wanted in wit, I changed the subject, by seeming to wonder what could keep our son so long at the fair, as it was now almost night-fall.—'Never mind our son,' cried my wife, 'depend upon it he knows what he is about. I'll warrant we'll never see him sell his hen of a rainy day.* I have seen him buy such bargains as would amaze one. I'll tell you a good story about that, that will make you split your sides with laughing—But as I live, yonder comes Moses, without an horse, and the box at his back.'

As she spoke, Moses came slowly on foot, and sweating under the deal box, which he had strapt round his shoulders like a pedlar.—'Welcome, welcome, Moses; well, my boy, what have you brought us from the fair?'—'I have brought you myself,' cried Moses, with a sly look, and resting the box on the dresser.—'Ay, Moses,' cried my wife, 'that we know, but where is the horse?' 'I have sold him,' cried Moses, 'for three pounds five shillings and two-pence.'—'Well done, my good boy,' returned she, 'I knew you would touch them off. Between ourselves, three pounds five shillings and two-pence is no bad day's work. Come, let us have it then.'—'I have brought back no money,' cried Moses again. 'I have laid it all out in a bargain, and here it is,' pulling out a bundle from his breast: 'here they are; a groce of green spectacles, with silver rims and shagreen* cases.'—'A groce of green spectacles!' repeated my wife in a faint voice. 'And you have parted with the Colt, and brought us back nothing but a groce of green paltry spectacles!'—'Dear mother,' cried the boy, 'why won't you listen to reason? I had them a dead bargain, or I should not have bought them. The silver rims alone will sell for double the money.'—'A fig for the silver rims,' cried my wife, in a passion: 'I dare swear they won't sell for above half the money at the rate of broken silver, five shillings an ounce.'—'You need be under no uneasiness,' cried I, 'about selling the rims; for they are not worth six-pence, for I perceive they are only copper varnished over.'—'What,' cried my wife, 'not silver, the rims not silver!' 'No,' cried I, 'no more silver than your sauce-pan.'—'And so,' returned she, 'we have parted with the Colt, and have only got a groce of green spectacles, with copper rims and shagreen cases! A murrain take such trumpery.* The blockhead has been imposed upon, and should have known his company better.'—'There, my dear,' cried I, 'you are wrong, he should not have known them at all.'—'Marry, hang the ideot,' returned she, 'to bring me such stuff, if I had them, I would throw them in the fire.' 'There again you are wrong, my dear,' cried I; 'for though they be copper, we will keep them by us, as copper spectacles, you know, are better than nothing.'

By this time the unfortunate Moses was undeceived. He now saw that he had indeed been imposed upon by a prowling sharper,* who, observing his figure, had marked him for an easy prey. I therefore asked the circumstances of his deception. He sold the horse, it seems, and walked the fair in search of another. A reverend looking man brought him to a tent, under pretence of having one to sell. 'Here,' continued Moses, 'we met another man, very well drest, who desired to borrow twenty pounds upon these, saying, that he wanted money, and would dispose of them for a third of the value. The first gentleman, who pretended to be my friend, whispered me to buy them, and cautioned me not to let so good an offer pass. I sent for Mr. Flamborough, and they talked him up as finely as they did me, and so at last we were persuaded to buy the two groce between us.'

CHAPTER XIII

Mr. Burchell is found to be an enemy; for he has the confidence to give disagreeable advice

OUR family had now made several attempts to be fine; but some unforeseen disaster demolished each as soon as projected. I endeavoured to take the advantage of every disappointment, to improve their good sense in proportion as they were frustrated in ambition. 'You see, my children,' cried I, 'how little is to be got by attempts to impose upon the world, in coping with our betters. Such as are poor and will associate with none but the rich, are hated by those they avoid, and despised by these they follow. Unequal combinations are always disadvantageous to the weaker side: the rich having the pleasure, and the poor the inconveniencies that result from them. But come, Dick, my boy, and repeat the fable that you were reading to-day, for the good of the company.'

'Once upon a time,' cried the child, 'a Giant and a Dwarf were friends, and kept together. They made a bargain that they would never forsake each other, but go seek adventures. The first battle they fought was with two Saracens, and the Dwarf, who was very courageous, dealt one of the champions a most angry blow. It did the Saracen but very little injury, who lifting up his sword, fairly struck off the poor Dwarf's arm. He was now in a woeful plight; but the Giant coming to his assistance, in a short time left the two Saracens dead on the plain, and the Dwarf cut off the dead man's head out of spite. They then travelled on to another adventure. This was against three bloody-minded Satyrs, who were carrying away a damsel in distress. The Dwarf was not quite so fierce now as before; but for all that, struck the first blow, which was returned by another, that knocked out his eye: but the Giant was soon up with them, and had they not fled, would certainly have killed them every one. They were all very joyful for this victory, and the damsel who was relieved fell in love with the Giant, and married him. They now travelled far, and farther than I can tell, till they met with a company of robbers. The Giant, for the first time, was foremost now; but the Dwarf was not far behind. The battle was stout and long. Wherever the Giant came all fell before him; but the Dwarf had like to have been killed more than once. At last the victory declared for the two adventurers; but the Dwarf lost his leg. The Dwarf was now without an arm, a leg, and an eye, while the Giant was without a single wound. Upon which he cried out to his little companion, My little heroe, this is glorious sport; let us get one victory more, and then we shall have honour for ever. No, cries the Dwarf, who was by this time grown wiser, no, I declare off; I'll fight no more: for I find in every battle that you get all the honour and rewards, but all the blows fall upon me.'

I was going to moralize this fable, when our attention was called off to a warm dispute between my wife and Mr. Burchell, upon my daughters intended expedition to town. My wife very strenuously insisted upon the advantages that would result from it. Mr. Burchell, on the contrary, dissuaded her with great ardor, and I stood neuter.* His present dissuasions seemed but the second part of those which were received with so ill a grace in the morning. The dispute grew high, while poor Deborah, instead of reasoning stronger, talked louder, and at last was obliged to take shelter from a defeat in clamour. The conclusion of her harangue, however, was highly displeasing to us all: she knew, she said, of some who had their own secret reasons for what they advised; but, for her part, she wished such to stay away from her house for the future.—'Madam,' cried Burchell, with looks of great composure, which tended to enflame her the more, 'as for secret reasons, you are right: I have secret reasons, which I forbear to mention, because you are not able to answer those of which I make no secret: but I find my visits here are become troublesome; I'll take my leave therefore now, and perhaps come once more to take a final farewell when I am quitting the country.' Thus saying, he took up his hat, nor could the attempts of Sophia, whose looks seemed to upbraid his precipitancy, prevent his going.

When gone, we all regarded each other for some minutes with confusion. My wife, who knew herself to be the cause, strove to hide her concern with a forced smile, and an air of assurance, which I was willing to reprove: 'How, woman,' cried I to her, 'is it thus we treat strangers? Is it thus we return their kindness? Be assured, my dear, that these were the harshest words, and to me the most unpleasing that ever escaped your lips!'—'Why would he provoke me then,' replied she; 'but I know the motives of his advice perfectly well. He would prevent my girls from going to town, that he may have the pleasure of my youngest daughter's company here at home. But whatever happens, she shall chuse better company than such low-lived fellows as he.'—'Low-lived, my dear, do you call him,' cried I, 'it is very possible we may mistake this man's character: for he seems upon some occasions the most finished gentleman I ever knew.—Tell me, Sophia, my girl, has he ever given you any secret instances of his attachment?'—'His conversation with me, sir,' replied my daughter, 'has ever been sensible, modest, and pleasing. As to aught else, no, never. Once, indeed, I remember to have heard him say he never knew a woman who could find merit in a man that seemed poor.' 'Such, my dear,' cried I, 'is the common cant of all the unfortunate or idle. But I hope you have been taught to judge properly of such men, and that it would be even madness to expect happiness from one who has been so very bad an œconomist of his own. Your mother and I have now better prospects for you. The next winter, which you will probably spend in town, will give you opportunities of making a more prudent choice.'

What Sophia's reflections were upon this occasion, I can't pretend to determine; but I was not displeased at the bottom that we were rid of a guest from whom I had much to fear. Our breach of hospitality went to my conscience a little: but I quickly silenced that monitor by two or three specious reasons, which served to satisfy and reconcile me to myself. The pain which conscience gives the man who has already done wrong, is soon got over. Conscience is a coward, and those faults it has not strength enough to prevent, it seldom has justice enough to accuse.

CHAPTER XIV

Fresh mortifications, or a demonstration that seeming calamities may be real blessings

THE journey of my daughters to town was now resolved upon, Mr. Thornhill having kindly promised to inspect their conduct himself, and inform us by letter of their behaviour. But it was thought indispensably necessary that their appearance should equal the greatness of their expectations, which could not be done without expence. We debated therefore in full council what were the easiest methods of raising money, or, more properly speaking, what we could most conveniently sell. The deliberation was soon finished, it was found that our remaining horse was utterly useless for the plow, without his companion, and equally unfit for the road, as wanting an eye, it was therefore determined that we should dispose of him for the purposes above-mentioned, at the neighbouring fair, and, to prevent imposition, that I should go with him myself. Though this was one of the first mercantile transactions of my life, yet I had no doubt about acquitting myself with reputation. The opinion a man forms of his own prudence is measured by that of the company he keeps, and as mine was mostly in the family way, I had conceived no unfavourable sentiments of my worldly wisdom. My wife, however, next morning, at parting, after I had got some paces from the door, called me back, to advise me, in a whisper, to have all my eyes about me.

I had, in the usual forms, when I came to the fair, put my horse through all his paces; but for some time had no bidders. At last a chapman approached, and, after he had for a good while examined the horse round, finding him blind of one eye, he would have nothing to say to him: a second came up; but observing he had a spavin, declared he would not take him for the driving home: a third perceived he had a wind-gall, and would bid no money: a fourth knew by his eye that he had the botts: a fifth, wondered what a plague I could do at the fair with a blind, spavined, galled hack,* that was only fit to be cut up for a dog kennel. By this time I began to have a most hearty contempt for the poor animal myself, and was almost ashamed at the approach of every customer; for though I did not entirely believe all the fellows told me; yet I reflected that the number of witnesses was a strong presumption they were right, and St. Gregory, upon good works, professes himself to be of the same opinion.*

I was in this mortifying situation, when a brother clergyman, an old acquaintance, who had also business to the fair, came up, and shaking me by the hand, proposed adjourning to a public-house and taking a glass of whatever we could get. I readily closed with the offer, and entering an ale-house, we were shewn into a little back room, where there was only a venerable old man, who sat wholly intent over a large book, which he was reading. I never in my life saw a figure that pre-possessed me more favourably. His locks of silver grey venerably shaded his temples, and his green old age seemed to be the result of health and benevolence. However, his presence did not interrupt our conversation; my friend and I discoursed on the various turns of fortune we had met: the Whistonean controversy, my last pamphlet, the archdeacon's reply, and the hard measure that was dealt me.* But our attention was in a short time taken off by the appearance of a youth, who, entering the room, respectfully said something softly to the old stranger. 'Make no apologies, my child,' said the old man, 'to do good is a duty we owe to all our fellow creatures: take this, I wish it were more; but five pounds will relieve your distress, and you are welcome.' The modest youth shed tears of gratitude, and yet his gratitude was scarce equal to mine. I could have hugged the good old man in my arms, his benevolence pleased me so. He continued to read, and we resumed our conversation, until my companion, after some time, recollecting that he had business to transact in the fair, promised to be soon back; adding, that he always desired to have as much of Dr. Primrose's company as possible. The old gentleman, hearing my name mentioned, seemed to look at me with attention, for some time, and when my friend was gone, most respectfully demanded if I was any way related to the great Primrose, that couragious monogamist, who had been the bulwark of the church. Never did my heart feel sincerer rapture than at that moment. 'Sir,' cried I, 'the applause of so good a man, as I am sure you are, adds to that happiness in my breast which your benevolence has already excited. You behold before you, Sir, that Doctor Primrose, the monogamist, whom you have been pleased to call great. You here see that unfortunate Divine, who has so long, and it would ill become me to say, successfully, fought against the deuterogamy of the age.' 'Sir,' cried the stranger, struck with awe, 'I fear I have been too familiar; but you'll forgive my curiosity, Sir: I beg pardon.' 'Sir,' cried I, grasping his hand, 'you are so far from displeasing me by your familiarity, that I must beg you'll accept my friendship, as you already have my esteem.'—'Then with gratitude I accept the offer,' cried he, squeezing me by the hand, 'thou glorious pillar of

unshaken orthodoxy; and do I behold—' I here interrupted what
he was going to say; for tho', as an author, I could digest no small
share of flattery, yet now my modesty would permit no more.
However, no lovers in romance ever cemented a more instantaneous friendship. We talked upon several subjects: at first I
thought he seemed rather devout than learned, and began to
think he despised all human doctrines* as dross. Yet this no way
lessened him in my esteem; for I had for some time begun privately to harbour such an opinion myself. I therefore took occasion to observe, that the world in general began to be blameably
indifferent as to doctrinal matters, and followed human speculations too much—'Ay, Sir,' replied he, as if he had reserved all his
learning to that moment, 'Ay, Sir, the world is in its dotage, and
yet the cosmogony or creation of the world has puzzled philosophers of all ages. What a medly of opinions have they not broached
upon the creation of the world? Sanconiathon, Manetho, Berosus,*
and Ocellus Lucanus, have all attempted it in vain. The latter has
these words, *Anarchon ara kai atelutaion to pan,** which imply that
all things have neither beginning nor end. Manetho also, who
lived about the time of Nebuchadon-Asser, Asser being a Syriac
word usually applied as a sirname to the kings of that country, as
Teglat Phael-Asser, Nabon-Asser, he, I say, formed a conjecture
equally absurd; for as we usually say *ek to biblion kubernetes,** which
implies that books will never teach the world; so he attempted to
investigate—But, Sir, I ask pardon, I am straying from the question.'—That he actually was; nor could I for my life see how the
creation of the world had any thing to do with the business I was
talking of; but it was sufficient to shew me that he was a man of
letters, and I now reverenced him the more. I was resolved therefore to bring him to the touch-stone; but he was too mild and too
gentle to contend for victory. Whenever I made any observation
that looked like a challenge to controversy, he would smile, shake
his head, and say nothing; by which I understood he could say
much, if he thought proper. The subject therefore insensibly
changed from the business of antiquity to that which brought us
both to the fair; mine I told him was to sell an horse, and very
luckily, indeed, his was to buy one for one of his tenants. My horse

was soon produced, and in fine we struck a bargain. Nothing now remained but to pay me, and he accordingly pulled out a thirty pound note,* and bid me change it. Not being in a capacity of complying with his demand, he ordered his footman to be called up, who made his appearance in a very genteel livery. 'Here, Abraham,' cried he, 'go and get gold for this; you'll do it at neighbour Jackson's, or any where.' While the fellow was gone, he entertained me with a pathetic harangue on the great scarcity of silver,* which I undertook to improve, by deploring also the great scarcity of gold; so that by the time Abraham returned, we had both agreed that money was never so hard to be come at as now. Abraham returned to inform us, that he had been over the whole fair and could not get change, tho' he had offered half a crown for doing it. This was a very great disappointment to us all; but the old gentleman having paused a little, asked me if I knew one Solomon Flamborough in my part of the country: upon replying that he was my next door neighbour, 'If that be the case then,' returned he, 'I believe we shall deal. You shall have a draught upon him, payable at sight;* and let me tell you he is as warm a man as any within five miles round him. Honest Solomon and I have been acquainted for many years together. I remember I always beat him at three jumps; but he could hop upon one leg farther than I.' A draught upon my neighbour was to me the same as money; for I was sufficiently convinced of his ability: the draught was signed and put into my hands, and Mr. Jenkinson, the old gentleman, his man Abraham, and my horse, old Blackberry, trotted off very well pleased with each other.

After a short interval being left to reflection, I began to recollect that I had done wrong in taking a draught from a stranger, and so prudently resolved upon following the purchaser, and having back my horse. But this was now too late: I therefore made directly homewards, resolving to get the draught changed into money at my friend's as fast as possible. I found my honest neighbour smoking his pipe at his own door, and informing him that I had a small bill upon him, he read it twice over. 'You can read the name, I suppose,' cried I, 'Ephraim Jenkinson.' 'Yes,' returned he, 'the name is written plain enough, and I know the gentleman too, the greatest rascal under the canopy of heaven. This is the very same rogue who sold us the spectacles. Was he not, a venerable looking man, with grey hair, and no flaps to his pocket-holes? And did he not talk a long string of learning about Greek and cosmogony, and the world?' To this I replied with a groan. 'Aye,' continued he, 'he has but that one piece of learning in the world, and he always talks it away whenever he finds a scholar in company; but I know the rogue, and will catch him yet.'

Though I was already sufficiently mortified, my greatest struggle was to come, in facing my wife and daughters. No truant was ever more afraid of returning to school, there to behold the master's visage, than I was of going home. I was determined, however, to anticipate their fury, by first falling into a passion myself.

But, alas! upon entering, I found the family no way disposed for battle. My wife and girls were all in tears, Mr. Thornhill having been there that day to inform them, that their journey to town was entirely over. The two ladies having heard reports of us from some malicious person about us, were that day set out for London. He could neither discover the tendency, nor the author of these, but whatever they might be, or whoever might have broached them, he continued to assure our family of his friendship and protection. I found, therefore, that they bore my disappointment with great resignation, as it was eclipsed in the greatness of their own. But what perplexed us most was to think who could be so base as to asperse the character of a family so harmless as ours, too humble to excite envy, and too inoffensive to create disgust.

CHAPTER XV

All Mr. Burchell's villainy at once detected. The folly of being over-wise

THAT evening and a part of the following day was employed in fruitless attempts to discover our enemies: scarce a family in the neighbourhood but incurred our suspicions, and each of us had reasons for our opinion best known to ourselves. As we were in this perplexity, one of our little boys, who had been playing abroad, brought in a letter-case,* which he found on the green. It was quickly known to belong to Mr. Burchell, with whom it had been seen, and, upon examination, contained some hints upon different subjects; but what particularly engaged our attention was a sealed note, superscribed, *the copy of a letter to be sent to the two ladies at Thornhill-castle*. It instantly occurred that he was the base informer, and we deliberated whether the note should not be broke open. I was against it; but Sophia, who said she was sure that of all men he would be the last to be guilty of so much baseness, insisted upon its being read. In this she was seconded by the rest of the family, and, at their joint solicitation, I read as follows:

'LADIES,

'THE bearer will sufficiently satisfy you as to the person from whom this comes: one at least the friend of innocence, and ready to prevent its being seduced. I am informed for a truth, that you have some intention of bringing two young ladies to town, whom I have some knowledge of, under the character of companions. As I would neither have simplicity imposed upon, nor virtue contaminated, I must offer it as my opinion, that the impropriety of such a step will be attended with dangerous consequences. It has never been my way to treat the infamous or the lewd with severity; nor should I now have taken this method of explaining myself, or reproving folly, did it not aim at guilt. Take therefore the admonition of a friend, and seriously reflect on the consequences

of introducing infamy and vice into retreats where peace and
innocence have hitherto resided.'

Our doubts were now at an end. There seemed indeed something applicable to both sides in this letter, and its censures might
as well be referred to those to whom it was written, as to us; but
the malicious meaning was obvious, and we went no farther. My
wife had scarce patience to hear me to the end, but railed at the
writer with unrestrained resentment. Olivia was equally severe,
and Sophia seemed perfectly amazed at his baseness. As for my
part, it appeared to me one of the vilest instances of unprovoked
ingratitude I had met with. Nor could I account for it in any other
manner than by imputing it to his desire of detaining my youngest daughter in the country, to have the more frequent opportunities of an interview. In this manner we all state ruminating upon
schemes of vengeance, when our other little boy came running in
to tell us that Mr. Burchell was approaching at the other end of
the field. It is easier to conceive than describe the complicated
sensations which are felt from the pain of a recent injury, and the
pleasure of approaching vengeance. Tho' our intentions were
only to upbraid him with his ingratitude; yet it was resolved to do
it in a manner that would be perfectly cutting. For this purpose
we agreed to meet him with our usual smiles, to chat in the
beginning with more than ordinary kindness, to amuse him a
little; and then in the midst of the flattering calm to burst upon
him like an earthquake, and overwhelm him with the sense of his
own baseness. This being resolved upon, my wife undertook to
manage the business herself, as she really had some talents for
such an undertaking. We saw him approach, he entered, drew a
chair, and sate down.—'A fine day, Mr. Burchell.'—'A very fine
day, Doctor; though I fancy we shall have some rain by the shooting of my corns.'*—'The shooting of your horns,' cried my wife,
in a loud fit of laughter, and then asked pardon for being fond of a
joke.—'Dear madam,' replied he, 'I pardon you with all my heart;
for I protest I should not have thought it a joke had you not told
me.'—'Perhaps not, Sir,' cried my wife, winking at us, 'and yet I
dare say you can tell us how many jokes go to an ounce.'—'I

fancy, madam,' returned Burchell, 'you have been reading a jest book* this morning, that ounce of jokes is so very good a conceit; and yet, madam, I had rather see half an ounce of understanding.'—'I believe you might,' cried my wife, still smiling at us, though the laugh was against her; 'and yet I have seen some men pretend to understanding that have very little.'—'And no doubt,' replied her antagonist, 'you have known ladies set up for wit that had none.'—I quickly began to find that my wife was likely to gain but little at this business; so I resolved to treat him in a stile of more severity myself. 'Both wit and understanding,' cried I, 'are trifles, without integrity: it is that which gives value to every character. The ignorant peasant, without fault, is greater than the philosopher with many; for what is genius or courage without an heart? *An honest man is the noblest work of God*.'*

'I always held that hackney'd maxim of Pope,' returned Mr. Burchell, 'as very unworthy a man of genius, and a base desertion of his own superiority. As the reputation of books is raised not by their freedom from defect, but the greatness of their beauties; so should that of men be prized not for their exemption from fault, but the size of those virtues they are possessed of. The scholar may want prudence, the statesman may have pride, and the champion ferocity; but shall we prefer to these the low mechanic, who laboriously plods on through life, without censure or applause? We might as well prefer the tame correct paintings of the Flemish school to the erroneous, but sublime animations of the Roman pencil.'*

'Sir,' replied I, 'your present observation is just, when there are shining virtues and minute defects; but when it appears that great vices are opposed in the same mind to as extraordinary virtues, such a character deserves contempt.'

'Perhaps,' cried he, 'there may be some such monsters as you describe, of great vices joined to great virtues; yet in my progress through life, I never yet found one instance of their existence: on the contrary, I have ever perceived, that where the mind was capacious, the affections were good. And indeed Providence seems kindly our friend in this particular, thus to debilitate the understanding where the heart is corrupt, and diminish the power where there is the will to do mischief. This rule seems to extend even to other animals: the little vermin race are ever treacherous, cruel, and cowardly, whilst those endowed with strength and power are generous, brave, and gentle.'

'These observations sound well,' returned I, 'and yet it would be easy this moment to point out a man,' and I fixed my eye stedfastly upon him, 'whose head and heart form a most detestable contrast. Ay, Sir,' continued I, raising my voice, 'and I am glad to have this opportunity of detecting him in the midst of his fancied security. Do you know this, Sir, this pocket-book?'—'Yes, Sir,' returned he, with a face of impenetrable assurance, 'that pocket-book is mine, and I am glad you have found it.'—'And do you know,' cried I, 'this letter? Nay, never falter man; but look me full in the face: I say, do you know this letter?'—'That letter,' returned he, 'yes, it was I that wrote that letter.'—'And how could you,' said I, 'so basely, so ungratefully presume to write this letter?'—'And how came you,' replied he, with looks of unparalleled effrontery, 'so basely to presume to break open this letter? Don't you know, now, I could hang you all for this? All that I have to do, is to swear at the next justice's, that you have been guilty of breaking open the lock of my pocket-book, and so hang you all up at his door.* This piece of unexpected insolence raised me to such a pitch, that I could scarce govern my passion. 'Ungrateful wretch, begone, and no longer pollute my dwelling with thy baseness. Begone, and never let me see thee again: go from my doors, and the only punishment I wish thee is an allarmed conscience, which will be a sufficient tormentor!' So saying, I threw him his pocket-book, which he took up with a smile, and shutting the clasps with the utmost composure, left us, quite astonished at the serenity of his assurance. My wife was particularly enraged that nothing could make him angry, or make him seem ashamed of his villainies. 'My dear,' cried I, willing to calm those passions that had been raised too high among us, 'we are not to be surprised that bad men want shame; they only blush at being detected in doing good, but glory in their vices.

'Guilt and shame, says the allegory, were at first companions, and in the beginning of their journey inseparably kept together.

But their union was soon found to be disagreeable and inconveni-
ent to both; guilt gave shame frequent uneasiness, and shame
often betrayed the secret conspiracies of guilt. After long disagreement, therefore, they at length consented to part for ever.
Guilt boldly walked forward alone, to overtake fate, that went
before in the shape of an executioner: but shame being naturally
timorous, returned back to keep company with virtue, which, in
the beginning of their journey, they had left behind. Thus, my
children, after men have travelled through a few stages in vice,
shame forsakes them, and returns back to wait upon the few
virtues they have still remaining.'

CHAPTER XVI

The family use art, which is opposed with still greater

WHATEVER might have been Sophia's sensations, the rest of the
family was easily consoled for Mr. Burchell's absence by the
company of our landlord, whose visits now became more frequent
and longer. Though he had been disappointed in procuring my
daughters the amusements of the town, as he designed, he took
every opportunity of supplying them with those little recreations
which our retirement would admit of. He usually came in the
morning, and while my son and I followed our occupations
abroad, he sat with the family at home, and amused them by
describing the town, with every part of which he was particularly
acquainted. He could repeat all the observations that were
retailed in the atmosphere of the playhouses, and had all the good
things of the high wits by rote long before they made way into the
jest-books. The intervals between conversation were employed in
teaching my daughters piquet.* or sometimes in setting my two
little ones to box to make them *sharp*,* as he called it: but the hopes
of having him for a son-in-law, in some measure blinded us to all
his imperfections. It must be owned that my wife laid a thousand
schemes to entrap him, or, to speak it more tenderly, used every
art to magnify the merit of her daughter. If the cakes at tea eat

short and crisp, they were made by Olivia: if the gooseberry wine was well knit,* the gooseberries were of her gathering: it was her fingers which gave the pickles their peculiar green; and in the composition of a pudding, it was her judgment that mix'd the ingredients. Then the poor woman would sometimes tell the 'Squire, that she thought him and Olivia extremely of a size, and would bid both stand up to see which was tallest. These instances of cunning, which she thought impenetrable, yet which every body saw through, were very pleasing to our benefactor, who gave every day some new proofs of his passion, which though they had not arisen to proposals of marriage, yet we thought fell but little short of it; and his slowness was attributed sometimes to native bashfulness, and sometimes to his fear of offending his uncle. An occurrence, however, which happened soon after, put it beyond a doubt that he designed to become one of our family, my wife even regarded it as an absolute promise.

My wife and daughters happening to return a visit to neighbour Flamborough's, found that family had lately got their pictures drawn by a limner,* who travelled the country, and took likenesses for fifteen shillings a head. As this family and ours had long a sort of rivalry in point of taste, our spirit took the alarm at this stolen march upon us, and notwithstanding all I could say, and I said much, it was resolved that we should have our pictures done too. Having, therefore, engaged the limner, for what could I do? our next deliberation was to shew the superiority of our taste in the attitudes. As for our neighbour's family, there were seven of them, and they were drawn with seven oranges,* a thing quite out of taste, no variety in life, no composition in the world. We desired to have something in a brighter style, and, after many debates, at length came to an unanimous resolution of being drawn together, in one large historical family piece.* This would be cheaper, since one frame would serve for all, and it would be infinitely more genteel; for all families of any taste were now drawn in the same manner. As we did not immediately recollect an historical subject to hit us, we were contented each with being drawn as independent historical figures. My wife desired to be represented as Venus, and the painter was desired not to be too

frugal of his diamonds in her stomacher* and hair. Her two little
ones were to be as Cupids by her side, while I, in my gown and
band, was to present her with my books on the Whistonian controversy. Olivia would be drawn as an Amazon,* sitting upon a
bank of flowers, drest in a green joseph, richly laced with gold,*
and a whip in her hand. Sophia was to be a shepherdess, with as
many sheep as the painter could put in for nothing; and Moses
was to be drest out with an hat and white feather. Our taste so
much pleased the 'Squire, that he insisted on being put in as one
of the family in the character of Alexander the great, at Olivia's
feet. This was considered by us all as an indication of his desire to
be introduced into the family, nor could we refuse his request.
The painter was therefore set to work, and as he wrought with
assiduity and expedition, in less than four days the whole was
compleated. The piece was large, and it must be owned he did not
spare his colours; for which my wife gave him great encomiums.*
We were all perfectly satisfied with his performance; but an
unfortunate circumstance had not occurred till the picture was
finished, which now struck us with dismay. It was so very large
that we had no place in the house to fix it. How we all came to
disregard so material a point is inconceivable; but certain it is, we
had been all greatly remiss. The picture, therefore, instead of
gratifying our vanity, as we hoped, leaned, in a most mortifying
manner, against the kitchen wall, where the canvas was stretched
and painted, much too large to be got through any of the doors,
and the jest of all our neighbours. One compared it to Robinson
Crusoe's long-boat, too large to be removed;* another thought it
more resembled a reel in a bottle;* some wondered how it could be
got out, but still more were amazed how it ever got in.

But though it excited the ridicule of some, it effectually raised
more malicious suggestions in many. The 'Squire's portrait being
found united with ours, was an honour too great to escape envy.
Scandalous whispers began to circulate at our expence, and our
tranquility was continually disturbed by persons who came as
friends to tell us what was said of us by enemies. These reports
we always resented with becoming spirit; but scandal ever
improves by opposition.

We once again therefore entered into a consultation upon obviating the malice of our enemies, and at last came to a resolution which had too much cunning to give me entire satisfaction. It was this: as our principal object was to discover the honour of Mr. Thornhill's addresses, my wife undertook to sound him, by pretending to ask his advice in the choice of an husband for her eldest daughter. If this was not found sufficient to induce him to a declaration, it was then resolved to terrify him with a rival. To this last step, however, I would by no means give my consent, till Olivia gave me the most solemn assurances that she would marry the person provided to rival him upon this occasion, if he did not prevent it, by taking her himself. Such was the scheme laid, which though I did not strenuously oppose, I did not entirely approve.

The next time, therefore, that Mr. Thornhill came to see us, my girls took care to be out of the way, in order to give their mamma an opportunity of putting her scheme in execution; but they only retired to the next room, from whence they could overhear the whole conversation: My wife artfully introduced it, by observing, that one of the Miss Flamboroughs was like to have a very good match of it in Mr. Spanker. To this the 'Squire assenting, she proceeded to remark, that they who had warm* fortunes were always sure of getting good husbands: 'But heaven help,' continued she, 'the girls that have none. What signifies beauty, Mr. Thornhill? or what signifies all the virtue, and all the qualifications in the world, in this age of self-interest? It is not, what is she? but what has she? is all the cry.'

'Madam,' returned he, 'I highly approve the justice, as well as the novelty, of your remarks, and if I were a king, it should be otherwise. It should then, indeed, be fine times with the girls without fortunes: our two young ladies should be the first for whom I would provide.'

'Ah, Sir!' returned my wife, 'you are pleased to be facetious: but I wish I were a queen, and then I know where my eldest daughter should look for an husband. But now, that you have put it into my head, seriously Mr. Thornhill, can't you recommend me a proper husband for her? She is now nineteen years old, well grown and well educated, and, in my humble opinion, does not want for parts.'

'Madam,' replied he, 'if I were to chuse, I would find out a person possessed of every accomplishment that can make an angel happy. One with prudence, fortune, taste, and sincerity, such, madam, would be, in my opinion, the proper husband.' 'Ay, Sir,' said she, 'but do you know of any such person?'—'No, madam,' returned he, 'it is impossible to know any person that deserves to be her husband: she's too great a treasure for one man's possession: she's a goddess. Upon my soul, I speak what I think, she's an angel.'—'Ah, Mr. Thornhill, you only flatter my poor girl: but we have been thinking of marrying her to one of your tenants, whose mother is lately dead, and who wants a manager: you know whom I mean, farmer Williams; a warm man, Mr. Thornhill, able to give her good bread; and who has several times made her proposals: (which was actually the case) but, Sir,' concluded she, 'I should be glad to have your approbation of our choice.'—'How, madam,' replied he, 'my approbation! My approbation of such a choice! Never. What! Sacrifice so much beauty, and sense, and goodness, to a creature insensible of the blessing! Excuse me, I can never approve of such a piece of injustice! And I have my reasons!'—'Indeed, Sir,' cried Deborah, 'if you have your reasons, that's another affair; but I should be glad to know those reasons.'—'Excuse me, madam,' returned he, 'they lie too deep for discovery: (laying his hand upon his bosom) they remain buried, rivetted here.'

After he was gone, upon general consultation, we could not tell what to make of these fine sentiments. Olivia considered them as instances of the most exalted passion; but I was not quite so sanguine: it seemed to me pretty plain, that they had more of love than matrimony in them: yet, whatever they might portend, it was resolved to prosecute the scheme of farmer Williams, who, from my daughter's first appearance in the country, had paid her his addresses.

CHAPTER XVII

Scarce any virtue found to resist the power of long and
pleasing temptation

As I only studied my child's real happiness, the assiduity of
Mr. Williams pleased me, as he was in easy circumstances, prudent, and sincere. It required but very little encouragement to
revive his former passion; so that in an evening or two he and
Mr. Thornhill met at our house, and surveyed each other for
some time with looks of anger: but Williams owed his landlord no
rent, and little regarded his indignation. Olivia, on her side, acted
the coquet to perfection, if that might be called acting which was
her real character, pretending to lavish all her tenderness on her
new lover. Mr. Thornhill appeared quite dejected at this preference, and with a pensive air took leave, though I own it puzzled
me to find him so much in pain as he appeared to be, when he had
it in his power so easily to remove the cause, by declaring an
honourable passion. But whatever uneasiness he seemed to
endure, it could easily be perceived that Olivia's anguish was still
greater. After any of these interviews between her lovers, of
which there were several, she usually retired to solitude, and
there indulged her grief. It was in such a situation I found her one
evening, after she had been for some time supporting a fictitious
gayety.—'You now see, my child,' said I, 'that your confidence in
Mr. Thornhill's passion was all a dream: he permits the rivalry of
another, every way his inferior, though he knows it lies in his
power to secure you to himself by a candid declaration.'—'Yes,
pappa,' returned she, 'but he has his reasons for this delay: I
know he has. The sincerity of his looks and words convince me of
his real esteem. A short time, I hope, will discover the generosity
of his sentiments, and convince you that my opinion of him has
been more just than yours.'—'Olivia, my darling,' returned I,
'every scheme that has been hitherto pursued to compel him to a
declaration, has been proposed and planned by yourself, nor can
you in the least say that I have constrained you. But you must not

suppose, my dear, that I will ever be instrumental in suffering his honest rival to be the dupe of your ill-placed passion. Whatever time you require to bring your fancied admirer to an explanation shall be granted; but at the expiration of that term, if he is still regardless, I must absolutely insist that honest Mr. Williams shall be rewarded for his fidelity. The character which I have hitherto supported in life demands this from me, and my tenderness, as a parent, shall never influence my integrity as a man. Name then your day, let it be as distant as you think proper, and in the mean time take care to let Mr. Thornhill know the exact time on which I design delivering you up to another. If he really loves you, his own good sense will readily suggest that there is but one method alone to prevent his losing you for ever.'—This proposal, which she could not avoid considering as perfectly just, was readily agreed to. She again renewed her most positive promise of marrying Mr. Williams, in case of the other's insensibility; and at the next opportunity, in Mr. Thornhill's presence, that day month was fixed upon for her nuptials with his rival.

Such vigorous proceedings seemed to redouble Mr. Thornhill's anxiety: but what Olivia really felt gave me some uneasiness. In this struggle between prudence and passion, her vivacity quite forsook her, and every opportunity of solitude was sought, and spent in tears. One week passed away; but Mr. Thornhill made no efforts to restrain her nuptials. The succeeding week he was still assiduous; but not more open. On the third he discontinued his visits entirely, and instead of my daughter testifying any impatience, as I expected, she seemed to retain a pensive tranquillity, which I looked upon as resignation. For my own part, I was now sincerely pleased with thinking that my child was going to be secured in a continuance of competence and peace, and frequently applauded her resolution, in preferring happiness to ostentation. It was within about four days of her intended nuptials, that my little family at night were gathered round a charming fire, telling stories of the past, and laying schemes for the future. Busied in forming a thousand projects, and laughing at whatever folly came uppermost, 'Well, Moses,' cried I, 'we shall soon, my boy, have a wedding in the family, what is your opinion of matters and things in general?'—'My opinion, father, is, that all things go on very well; and I was just now thinking, that when sister Livy is married to farmer Williams, we shall then have the loan of his cyder-press and brewing tubs for nothing.'—'That we shall, Moses,' cried I, 'and he will sing us Death and the Lady,* to raise our spirits into the bargain.'—'He has taught that song to our Dick,' cried Moses; 'and I think he goes thro' it very prettily.'—'Does he so,' cried I, 'then let us have it: where's little Dick? let him up with it boldly.'—'My brother Dick,' cried Bill my youngest, 'is just gone out with sister Livy; but Mr. Williams has taught me two songs, and I'll sing them for you, pappa. Which song do you chuse, *the Dying Swan,** or the *Elegy on the death of a mad dog?*' 'The elegy, child, by all means,' said I, 'I never heard that yet; and Deborah, my life, grief you know is dry, let us have a bottle of the best gooseberry wine, to keep up our spirits. I have wept so much at all sorts of elegies of late, that without an enlivening glass I am sure this will overcome me; and Sophy, love, take your guitar, and thrum in with the boy a little.'

An ELEGY on the Death of a Mad Dog*

GOOD people all, of every sort,
  Give ear unto my song;
And if you find it wond'rous short,
  It cannot hold you long.

In Isling town there was a man,
  Of whom the world might say,
That still a godly race he ran,
  Whene'er he went to pray.

A kind and gentle heart he had,
  To comfort friends and foes;
The naked every day he clad,
  When he put on his cloaths.

And in that town a dog was found,
  As many dogs there be,

Both mungrel, puppy, whelp, and hound,
    And curs of low degree.

This dog and man at first were friends;
    But when a pique began,
The dog, to gain some private ends,
    Went mad and bit the man.

Around from all the neighbouring streets,
    The wondering neighbours ran,
And swore the dog had lost his wits,
    To bite so good a man.

The wound it seem'd both sore and sad,
    To every christian eye;
And while they swore the dog was mad,
    They swore the man would die.

But soon a wonder came to light,
    That shew'd the rogues they lied,
The man recovered of the bite,
    The dog it was that dy'd.

'A very good boy, Bill, upon my word, and an elegy that may truly be called tragical. Come, my children, here's Bill's health, and may he one day be a bishop.'

'With all my heart,' cried my wife; 'and if he but preaches as well as he sings, I make no doubt of him. The most of his family, by the mother's side, could sing a good song: it was a common saying in our country, that the family of the Blenkinsops could never look strait before them, nor the Huginsons blow out a candle; that there were none of the Grograms* but could sing a song, or of the Marjorams but could tell a story.'—'However that be,' cried I, 'the most vulgar ballad of them all generally pleases me better than the fine modern odes, and things that petrify us in a single stanza; productions that we at once detest and praise. Put the glass to your brother, Moses.* The great fault of these elegiasts is, that they are in despair for griefs that give the sensible part of mankind very little pain. A lady loses her muff, her fan, or her lap-dog, and so the silly poet runs home to versify the disaster.'

'That may be the mode,' cried Moses, 'in sublimer compositions; but the Ranelagh* songs that come down to us are perfectly familiar, and all cast in the same mold: Colin meets Dolly, and they hold a dialogue together; he gives her a fairing to put in her hair, and she presents him with a nosegay; and then they go together to church, where they give good advice to young nymphs and swains to get married as fast as they can.'*

'And very good advice too,' cried I, 'and I am told there is not a place in the world where advice can be given with so much propriety as there; for, as it persuades us to marry, it also furnishes us with a wife; and surely that must be an excellent market, my boy, where we are told what we want, and supplied with it when wanting.'

'Yes, Sir,' returned Moses, 'and I know but of two such markets for wives in Europe, Ranelagh in England, and Fontarabia* in Spain. The Spanish market is open once a year, but our English wives are saleable every night.'

'You are right, my boy,' cried his mother, 'Old England is the only place in the world for husbands to get wives.'—'And for wives to manage their husbands,' interrupted I. 'It is a proverb abroad, that if a bridge were built across the sea, all the ladies of the Continent would come over* to take pattern from ours; for there are no such wives in Europe as our own.

'But let us have one bottle more, Deborah, my life, and Moses give us a good song. What thanks do we not owe to heaven for thus bestowing tranquillity, health, and competence. I think myself happier now than the greatest monarch upon earth. He has no such fire-side, nor such pleasant faces about it. Yes, Deborah, we are now growing old; but the evening of our life is likely to be happy. We are descended from ancestors that knew no stain, and we shall leave a good and virtuous race of children behind us. While we live they will be our support and our pleasure here, and when we die they will transmit our honour untainted to posterity. Come, my son, we wait for a song: let us have a chorus. But where is my darling Olivia? That little cherub's voice is always sweetest in the concert.'—Just as I spoke Dick came running in. 'O pappa, pappa, she is gone from us, she is gone from us, my sister Livy is gone from us for ever'—'Gone, child'—'Yes, she is gone off with two gentlemen in a post chaise,* and one of them kissed her, and said he would die for her; and she cried very much, and was for coming back; but he persuaded her again, and she went into the chaise, and said, O what will my poor pappa do when he knows I am undone!' —'Now then,' cried I, 'my children, go and be miserable; for we shall never enjoy one hour more. And O may heaven's everlasting fury light upon him and his! Thus to rob me of my child! And sure it will, for taking back my sweet innocent that I was leading up to heaven. Such sincerity as my child was possest of. But all our earthly happiness is now over! Go, my children, go, and be miserable and infamous; for my heart is broken within me!'—'Father,' cried my son, 'is this your fortitude?'—'Fortitude, child! Yes, he shall see I have fortitude! Bring me my pistols. I'll pursue the traitor. While he is on earth I'll pursue him. Old as I am, he shall find I can sting him yet. The villain! The perfidious villain!'—I had by this time reached down my pistols, when my poor wife, whose passions were not so strong as mine, caught me in her arms. 'My dearest, dearest husband,' cried she, 'the bible is the only weapon that is fit for your old hands now. Open that, my love, and read our anguish into patience, for she has vilely deceived us.'—'Indeed, Sir,' resumed my son, after a pause, 'your rage is too violent and unbecoming. You should be my mother's comforter, and you encrease her pain. It ill suited you and your reverend character thus to curse your greatest enemy: you should not have curst him, villain as he is.'— 'I did not curse him, child, did I?'—'Indeed, Sir, you did; you curst him twice.'—'Then may heaven forgive me and him if I did. And now, my son, I see it was more than human benevolence that first taught us to bless our enemies! Blest be his holy name for all the good he hath given, and for all that he hath taken away. But it is not, it is not, a small distress that can wring tears from these old eyes, that have not wept for so many years. My Child!— To undo my darling! May confusion seize! Heaven forgive me, what am I about to say! You may remember, my love, how good

she was, and how charming; till this vile moment all her care was
to make us happy. Had she but died! But she is gone, the honour
of our family contaminated, and I must look out for happiness in
other worlds than here. But my child, you saw them go off: perhaps he forced her away? If he forced her, she may yet be innocent.'—'Ah no, Sir!' cried the child; 'he only kissed her, and
called her his angel, and she wept very much, and leaned upon his
arm, and they drove off very fast.'—'She's an ungrateful creature,' cried my wife, who could scarce speak for weeping, 'to use
us thus. She never had the least constraint put upon her affections. The vile strumpet has basely deserted her parents without
any provocation, thus to bring your grey hairs to the grave, and I
must shortly follow.'

In this manner that night, the first of our real misfortunes,
was spent in the bitterness of complaint, and ill supported sallies
of enthusiasm. I determined, however, to find out our betrayer,
wherever he was, and reproach his baseness. The next morning
we missed our wretched child at breakfast, where she used to give
life and chearfulness to us all. My wife, as before, attempted to
ease her heart by reproaches. 'Never,' cried she, 'shall that vilest
stain of our family again darken those harmless doors. I will never
call her daughter more. No, let the strumpet live with her vile
seducer: she may bring us to shame, but she shall never more
deceive us.'

'Wife,' said I, 'do not talk thus hardly: my detestation of her
guilt is as great as yours; but ever shall this house and this heart
be open to a poor returning repentant sinner. The sooner she
returns from her transgression, the more welcome shall she be to
me. For the first time the very best may err; art may persuade,
and novelty spread out its charm. The first fault is the child of
simplicity; but every other the offspring of guilt. Yes, the wretched
creature shall be welcome to this heart and this house, tho'
stained with ten thousand vices. I will again hearken to the music
of her voice, again will I hang fondly on her bosom, if I find but
repentance there. My son, bring hither my bible and my staff; I
will pursue her, wherever she is, and tho' I cannot save her from
shame, I may prevent the continuance of iniquity.'

CHAPTER XVIII

The pursuit of a father to reclaim a lost child to virtue

THO' the child could not describe the gentleman's person who handed his sister into the post-chaise, yet my suspicions fell entirely upon our young landlord, whose character for such intrigues was but too well known. I therefore directed my steps towards Thornhill-castle, resolving to upbraid him, and, if possible, to bring back my daughter: but before I had reached his seat, I was met by one of my parishioners, who said he saw a young lady resembling my daughter in a post-chaise with a gentleman, whom, by the description, I could only guess to be Mr. Burchell, and that they drove very fast. This information, however, did by no means satisfy me. I therefore went to the young 'Squire's, and though it was yet early, insisted upon seeing him immediately: he soon appeared with the most open familiar air, and seemed perfectly amazed at my daughter's elopement, protesting upon his honour that he was quite a stranger to it. I now therefore condemned my former suspicions, and could turn them only on Mr. Burchell, who I recollected had of late several private conferences with her: but the appearance of another witness left me no room to doubt of his villainy, who averred, that he and my daughter were actually gone towards the wells, about thirty miles off, where there was a great deal of company. Being driven to that state of mind in which we are more ready to act precipitately than to reason right, I never debated with myself, whether these accounts might not have been given by persons purposely placed in my way, to mislead me, but resolved to pursue my daughter and her fancied deluder thither. I walked along with earnestness, and enquired of several by the way; but received no accounts, till entering the town, I was met by a person on horseback, whom I remembered to have seen at the 'Squire's, and he assured me that if I followed them to the races,* which were but thirty miles farther, I might depend upon overtaking them; for he had seen them dance there the night before, and the whole assembly seemed charmed with my daughter's performance. Early the next day I walked forward to the races, and about four in the afternoon I came upon the course. The company made a very brilliant appearance, all earnestly employed in one pursuit, that of pleasure; how different from mine, that of reclaiming a lost child to virtue! I thought I perceived Mr. Burchell at some distance from me; but, as if he dreaded an interview, upon my approaching him, he mixed among a crowd, and I saw him no more. I now reflected that it would be to no purpose to continue my pursuit farther, and resolved to return home to an innocent family, who wanted my assistance. But the agitations of my mind, and the fatigues I had undergone, threw me into a fever, the symptoms of which I perceived before I came off the course. This was another unexpected stroke, as I was more than seventy miles distant from home: however, I retired to a little ale-house by the road-side, and in this place, the usual retreat of indigence and frugality, I laid me down patiently to wait the issue of my disorder. I languished here for near three weeks; but at last my constitution prevailed, though I was unprovided with money to defray the expences of my entertainment. It is possible the anxiety from this last circumstance alone might have brought on a relapse, had I not been supplied by a traveller, who stopt to take a cursory refreshment. This person was no other than the philanthropic bookseller in St. Paul's church-yard,* who has written so many little books for children: he called himself their friend; but he was the friend of all mankind. He was no sooner alighted, but he was in haste to be gone; for he was ever on business of the utmost importance, and was at that time actually compiling materials for the history of one Mr. Thomas Trip.* I immediately recollected this good-natured man's red pimpled face; for he had published for me against the Deuterogamists* of the age, and from him I borrowed a few pieces, to be paid at my return. Leaving the inn, therefore, as I was yet but weak, I resolved to return home by easy journies of ten miles a day. My health and usual tranquillity were almost restored, and I now condemned that pride which had made me refractory to the hand of correction. Man little knows what calamities are beyond his patience to bear till he tries them; as in ascending the heights of ambition, which look bright from below, every step we rise shews us some new and gloomy prospect of hidden disappointment; so in our descent from the summits of pleasure, though the vale of misery below may appear at first dark and gloomy, yet the busy mind, still attentive to its own amusement, finds as we descend something to flatter and to please. Still as we approach, the darkest objects appear to brighten, and the mental eye becomes adapted to its gloomy situation.

I now proceeded forward, and had walked about two hours, when I perceived what appeared at a distance like a waggon, which I was resolved to overtake; but when I came up with it, found it to be a strolling company's cart, that was carrying their scenes and other theatrical furniture to the next village, where they were to exhibit. The cart was attended only by the person who drove it, and one of the company, as the rest of the players were to follow the ensuring day. Good company upon the road, says the proverb, is the shortest cut, I therefore entered into conversation with the poor player; and as I once had some theatrical powers myself, I disserted on such topics with my usual freedom: but as I was pretty much unacquainted with the present state of the stage, I demanded who were the present theatrical writers in vogue, who the Drydens and Otways of the day.*—'I fancy, Sir,' cried the player, 'few of our modern dramatists would think themselves much honoured by being compared to the writers you mention. Dryden and Row's manner, Sir, are quite out of fashion; our taste has gone back a whole century, Fletcher, Ben Johnson,* and all the plays of Shakespear, are the only things that go down.'—'How,' cried I, 'is it possible the present age can be pleased with that antiquated dialect, that obsolete humour, those over-charged characters, which abound in the works you mention?'—'Sir,' returned my companion, 'the public think nothing about dialect, or humour, or character; for that is none of their business, they only go to be amused, and find themselves happy when they can enjoy a pantomime, under the sanction of Johnson's or Shakespear's name.'—'So then, I suppose,' cried I, 'that our modern dramatists are rather imitators of Shakespear than of nature.'—'To say the truth,' returned my companion, 'I don't know that they imitate any thing at all; nor indeed does the public require it of them: it is not the composition of the piece, but the number of starts and attitudes that may be introduced into it that elicits applause. I have known a piece, with not one jest in the whole, shrugged into popularity, and another saved by the poet's throwing in a fit of the gripes. No, Sir, the works of Congreve and Farquhar have too much wit in them for the present taste; our modern dialect is much more natural.'*

By this time the equipage of the strolling company was arrived at the village, which, it seems, had been apprised of our approach, and was come out to gaze at us; for my companion observed, that strollers always have more spectators without doors than within. I did not consider the impropriety of my being in such company till I saw a mob gather about me. I therefore took shelter, as fast as possible, in the first ale-house that offered, and being shewn into the common room, was accosted by a very well-drest gentleman, who demanded whether I was the real chaplain of the company, or whether it was only to be my masquerade character in the play. Upon informing him of the truth, and that I did not belong in any sort to the company, he was condescending enough to desire me and the player to partake in a bowl of punch, over which he discussed modern politics with great earnestness and interest. I set him down in my mind for nothing less than a parliament-man at least; but was almost confirmed in my conjectures, when upon my asking what there was in the house for supper, he insisted that the player and I should sup with him at his house, with which request, after some entreaties, we were prevailed on to comply.

CHAPTER XIX

The description of a person discontented with the present government, and apprehensive of the loss of our liberties

THE house where we were to be entertained, lying at a small distance from the village, our inviter observed, that as the coach was not ready, he would conduct us on foot, and we soon arrived at one of the most magnificent mansions I had seen in that part of the country. The apartment into which we were shewn was perfectly elegant and modern; he went to give orders for supper, while the player, with a wink, observed that we were perfectly in luck. Our entertainer soon returned, an elegant supper was brought in, two or three ladies, in an easy deshabille,* were introduced, and the conversation began with some sprightliness. Politics, however, was the subject on which our entertainer chiefly expatiated; for he asserted that liberty was at once his boast and his terror. After the cloth was removed, he asked me if I had seen the last Monitor, to which replying in the negative, 'What, nor the Auditor,* I suppose?' cried he. 'Neither, Sir,' returned I. 'That's strange, very strange,' replied my entertainer. 'Now, I read all the politics that come out. The Daily, the Public, the Ledger, the Chronicle, the London Evening, the White-hall Evening,* the seventeen magazines, and the two reviews,* and though they hate each other, I love them all. Liberty, Sir, liberty is the Briton's boast, and by all my coal mines in Cornwall,* I reverence its guardians.' 'Then it is to be hoped,' cried I, 'you reverence the king.' 'Yes,' returned my entertainer, 'when he does what we would have him; but if he goes on as he has done of late, I'll never trouble myself more with his matters. I say nothing. I think only. I could have directed some things better. I don't think there has been a sufficient number of advisers: he should advise with every person willing to give him advice, and then we should have things done in anotherguess manner.'*

'I wish,' cried I, 'that such intruding advisers were fixed in the pillory. It should be the duty of honest men to assist the weaker side of our constitution, that sacred power that has for some years been every day declining, and losing its due share of influence in the state. But these ignorants still continue the cry of liberty, and if they have any weight basely throw it into the subsiding scale.'

'How,' cried one of the ladies, 'do I live to see one so base, so sordid, as to be an enemy to liberty, and a defender of tyrants? Liberty, that sacred gift of heaven, that glorious privilege of Britons!'

'Can it be possible,' cried our entertainer, 'that there should be any found at present advocates for slavery? Any who are for meanly giving up the privileges of Britons? Can any, Sir, be so abject?'

'No, Sir,' replied I, 'I am for liberty, that attribute of Gods! Glorious liberty! that theme of modern declamation. I would have all men kings. I would be a king myself. We have all naturally an equal right to the throne: we are all originally equal. This is my opinion, and was once the opinion of a set of honest men who were called Levellers.* They tried to erect themselves into a community, where all should be equally free. But, alas! it would never answer; for there were some among them stronger, and some more cunning than others, and these became masters of the rest; for as sure as your groom rides your horses, because he is a cunninger animal than they, so surely will the animal that is cunninger or stronger than he, sit upon his shoulders in turn. Since then it is entailed upon humanity to submit, and some are born to command, and others to obey, the question is, as there must be tyrants, whether it is better to have them in the same house with us, or in the same village, or still farther off, in the metropolis. Now, Sir, for my own part, as I naturally hate the face of a tyrant, the farther off he is removed from me, the better pleased am I. The generality of mankind also are of my way of thinking, and have unanimously created one king, whose election at once diminishes the number of tyrants, and puts tyranny at the greatest distance from the greatest number of people. Now the great who were tyrants themselves before the election of one tyrant, are naturally averse to a power raised over them, and whose weight must ever lean heaviest on the subordinate orders. It is the interest of the great, therefore, to diminish kingly power as much as possible; because whatever they take from that is naturally restored to themselves; and all they have to do in the state, is to undermine the single tyrant, by which they resume their primæval authority. Now, the state may be so circumstanced, or its laws may be so disposed, or its men of opulence so minded, as all to conspire in carrying on this business of undermining monarchy. For, in the first place, if the circumstances of our state be such, as to favour the accumulation of wealth, and make the opulent still more rich, this will encrease their ambition. An accumulation of wealth, however, must necessarily be the consequence, when as at present more riches flow in from external commerce, than arise from internal industry: for external commerce can only be managed to advantage by the rich, and they have also at the same time all the emoluments arising from internal industry: so that the rich, with us, have two sources of wealth, whereas the poor have but one. For this reason, wealth in all commercial states is found to accumulate, and all such have hitherto in time become aristocratical. Again, the very laws also of this country may contribute to the accumulation of wealth; as when by their means the natural ties that bind the rich and poor together are broken, and it is ordained that the rich shall only marry with the rich; or when the learned are held unqualified to serve their country as counsellors merely from a defect of opulence, and wealth is thus made the object of a wise man's ambition; by these means I say, and such means as these, riches will accumulate. Now the possessor of accumulated wealth, when furnished with the necessaries and pleasures of life, has no other method to employ the superfluity of his fortune but in purchasing power. That is, differently speaking, in making dependants, by purchasing the liberty of the needy or the venal, of men who are willing to bear the mortification of contiguous tyranny for bread. Thus each very opulent man generally gathers round him a circle of the poorest of the people; and the polity abounding in accumulated wealth, may be compared to a Cartesian system, each orb with a vortex of its own.* Those, however, who are willing to move in a great man's vortex, are only such as must be slaves, the rabble of mankind, whose souls and whose education are adapted to servitude, and who know nothing of liberty except the name. But there must still be a large number of the people without the sphere of the opulent man's influence, namely, that order of men which subsists between the very rich and the very rabble; those men who are possest of too large fortunes to submit to the neighbouring man in power, and yet are too poor to set up for tyranny themselves. In this middle order of mankind are generally to be found all the arts, wisdom, and virtues of society. This order alone is known to be the true preserver of freedom, and may be called the People. Now it may happen that this middle order of mankind may lose all its influence in a state; and its voice be in a manner drowned in that of the rabble: for if the fortune sufficient for qualifying a person at present to give his voice in state affairs, be ten times less than was judged sufficient upon forming the constitution, it is evident that greater numbers of the rabble will thus be introduced into the political system, and they ever moving in the vortex of the great, will follow where greatness shall direct. In such a state, therefore, all that the middle order has left, is to preserve the prerogative and privileges of the one principal governor with the most sacred circumspection. For he divides the power of the rich, and calls off the great from falling with tenfold weight on the middle order placed beneath them. The middle order may be compared to a town of which the opulent are forming the siege, and which the governor from without is hastening the relief. While the besiegers are in dread of an enemy over them, it is but natural to offer the townsmen the most specious terms; to flatter them with sounds, and amuse them with privileges: but if they once defeat the governor from behind, the walls of the town will be but a small defence to its inhabitants. What they may then expect, may be seen by turning our eyes to Holland, Genoa, or Venice, where the laws govern the poor, and the rich govern the law. I am then for, and would die for, monarchy, sacred monarchy; for if there be any thing sacred amongst men, it must be the anointed sovereign of his people, and every diminution of his power in war, or in peace, is an infringement upon the real liberties of the subject. The sounds of liberty, patriotism, and Britons, have already done *much*, it is to be hoped that the true sons of freedom will prevent their ever doing more. I have known many of those pretended champions for liberty in my time, yet do I not remember one that was not in his heart and in his family a tyrant.*

My warmth I found had lengthened this harangue beyond the rules of good breeding: but the impatience of my entertainer, who often strove to interrupt it, could be restrained no longer. 'What,' cried he, 'then I have been all this while entertaining a Jesuit in parson's cloaths; but by all the coal mines of Cornwall, out he shall pack, if my name be Wilkinson.* I now found I had gone too far, and asked pardon for the warmth with which I had spoken. 'Pardon,' returned he in a fury: 'I think such principles demand ten thousand pardons. What, give up liberty, property, and, as the Gazetteer says, lie down to be saddled with wooden shoes!* Sir, I insist upon your marching out of this house immediately, to prevent worse consequences, Sir, I insist upon it.' I was going to repeat my remonstrances; but just then we heard a footman's rap at the door, and the two ladies cried out, 'As sure as death there is our master and mistress come home.' It seems my entertainer was all this while only the butler, who, in his master's absence, had a mind to cut a figure, and be for a while the gentleman himself; and, to say the truth, he talked politics as well as most country gentlemen do. But nothing could now exceed my confusion upon seeing the gentleman, and his lady, enter, nor was their surprize, at finding such company and good cheer, less than ours. 'Gentlemen,' cried the real master of the house, to me and my companion, 'my wife and I are your most humble servants; but I protest this is so unexpected a favour, that we almost sink under the obligation.' However unexpected our company might be to them, theirs, I am sure, was still more so to us, and I was struck dumb with the apprehensions of my own absurdity, when whom should I next see enter the room but my dear miss Arabella Wilmot, who was formerly designed to be married to my son George; but whose match was broken off, as already related. As soon as she saw me, she flew to my arms with the utmost joy. 'My dear sir,' cried she, 'to what happy accident is it that we owe so unexpected a visit? I am sure my uncle and aunt will be in raptures when they find they have the good Dr. Primrose for their guest.' Upon hearing my name, the old gentleman and lady very politely stept up, and welcomed me with most cordial hospitality. Nor could they forbear smiling upon being informed of the nature of my present visit: but the unfortunate butler, whom they at first seemed disposed to turn away, was, at my intercession, forgiven.

Mr. Arnold and his lady, to whom the house belonged, now insisted upon having the pleasure of my stay for some days, and as their niece, my charming pupil, whose mind, in some measure, had been formed under my own instructions, joined in their entreaties, I complied. That night I was shewn to a magnificent chamber, and the next morning early Miss Wilmot desired to walk with me in the garden, which was decorated in the modern manner.* After some time spent in pointing out the beauties of the place, she enquired with seeming unconcern, when last I had heard from my son George. 'Alas! Madam,' cried I, 'he has now been near three years absent,* without ever writing to his friends or me. Where he is I know not; perhaps I shall never see him or happiness more. No, my dear Madam, we shall never more see such pleasing hours as were once spent by our fire-side at Wakefield. My little family are now dispersing very fast, and poverty has brought not only want, but infamy upon us.' The good-natured girl let fall a tear at this account; but as I saw her possessed of too much sensibility, I forbore a more minute detail of our sufferings. It was, however, some consolation to me to find that time had made no alteration in her affections, and that she had rejected several matches that had been made her since our leaving her part of the country. She led me round all the extensive improvements of the place, pointing to the several walks and arbours, and at the same time catching from every object a hint for some new question relative to my son. In this manner we spent the forenoon, till the bell summoned us in to dinner, where we found the manager of the strolling company that I mentioned before, who was come to dispose of tickets for the Fair Penitent, which was to be acted that evening, the part of Horatio* by a young gentleman who had never appeared on any stage. He seemed to be very warm in the praises of the new performer, and averred, that he never saw any who bid so fair for excellence. Acting, he observed, was not learned in a day; 'But this gentleman,' continued he, 'seems born to tread the stage. His voice, his figure, and attitudes, are all admirable. We caught him up accidentally in our journey down.' This account, in some measure, excited our curiosity, and, at the entreaty of the ladies, I was prevailed upon to accompany them to the play-house, which was no other than a barn. As the company with which I went was incontestably the chief of the place, we were received with the greatest respect, and placed in the front seat of the theatre; where we sate for some time with no small impatience to see Horatio make his appearance. The new performer advanced at last, and let parents think of my sensations by their own, when I found it was my unfortunate son. He was going to begin, when, turning his eyes upon the audience, he perceived Miss Wilmot and me, and stood at once speechless and immoveable. The actors behind the scene, who ascribed this pause to his natural timidity, attempted to encourage him; but instead of going on, he burst into a flood of tears, and retired off the stage. I don't know what were my feelings on this occasion; for they succeeded with too much rapidity for description: but I was soon awaked from this disagreeable reverie by Miss Wilmot, who, pale and with a trembling voice, desired me to conduct her back to her uncle's. When got home, Mr. Arnold, who was as yet a stranger to our extraordinary behaviour, being informed that the new performer was my son, sent his coach, and an invitation, for him; and as he persisted in his refusal to appear again upon the stage, the players put another in his place, and we soon had him with us. Mr. Arnold gave him the kindest reception, and I received him with my usual transport; for I could never counterfeit false resentment. Miss Wilmot's reception was mixed with seeming neglect, and yet I could perceive she acted a studied part. The tumult in her mind seemed not yet abated; she said twenty giddy things that looked like joy, and then laughed loud at her own want of meaning. At intervals she would take a sly peep at the glass, as if happy in the consciousness of unresisting beauty, and often would ask questions, without giving any manner of attention to the answers.

CHAPTER XX

The history of a philosophic vagabond, pursuing novelty,
but losing content

AFTER we had supped, Mrs. Arnold politely offered to send a couple of her footmen for my son's baggage, which he at first seemed to decline; but upon her pressing the request, he was obliged to inform her, that a stick and a wallet were all the moveable things upon this earth that he could boast of. 'Why, aye my son,' cried I, 'you left me but poor, and poor I find you are come back; and yet I make no doubt you have seen a great deal of the world.'—'Yes, Sir,' replied my son, 'but travelling after fortune, is not the way to secure her; and, indeed, of late, I have desisted from the pursuit.'—'I fancy, Sir,' cried Mrs. Arnold, 'that the account of your adventures would be amusing: the first part of them I have often heard from my niece; but could the company prevail for the rest, it would be an additional obligation.'— 'Madam,' replied my son, 'I promise you the pleasure you have in hearing, will not be half so great as my vanity in repeating them; and yet in the whole narrative I can scarce promise you one adventure, as my account is rather of what I saw than what I did. The first misfortune of my life, which you all know, was great; but tho' it distrest, it could not sink me. No person ever had a better knack at hoping than I. The less kind I found fortune at one time, the more I expected from her another, and being now at the bottom of her wheel, every new revolution might lift, but could not depress me. I proceeded, therefore, towards London in a fine morning, no way uneasy about to-morrow, but chearful as the birds that caroll'd by the road, and comforted myself with reflecting, that London was the mart where abilities of every kind were sure of meeting distinction and reward.

'Upon my arrival in town, Sir, my first care was to deliver your letter of recommendation to our cousin, who was himself in little better circumstances than I. My first scheme, you know, Sir, was to be usher at an academy,* and I asked his advice on the affair.

Our cousin received the proposal with a true Sardonic grin. Aye, cried he, this is indeed a very pretty career, that has been chalked out for you. I have been an usher at a boarding school myself; and may I die by an anodyne necklace,* but I had rather be an under turnkey in Newgate. I was up early and late: I was brow-beat by the master, hated for my ugly face by the mistress, worried by the boys within, and never permitted to stir out to meet civility abroad. But are you sure you are fit for a school? Let me examine you a little. Have you been bred apprentice to the business? No. Then you won't do for a school. Can you dress the boys hair? No. Then you won't do for a school. Have you had the small-pox? No. Then you won't do for a school. Can you lie three in a bed? No. Then you will never do for a school. Have you got a good stomach? Yes. Then you will by no means do for a school. No, Sir, if you are for a genteel easy profession, bind yourself seven years as an apprentice to turn a cutler's wheel; but avoid a school by any means. Yet come, continued he, I see you are a lad of spirit and some learning, what do you think of commencing author, like me? You have read in books, no doubt, of men of genius starving at the trade: At present I'll shew you forty very dull fellows about town that live by it in opulence. All honest jogg trot men,* who go on smoothly and dully, and write history and politics, and are praised; men, Sir, who, had they been bred coblers, would all their lives have only mended shoes, but never made them.

'Finding that there was no great degree of gentility affixed to the character of an usher, I resolved to accept his proposal; and having the highest respect for literature, hailed the antiqua mater of Grub-street with reverence. I thought it my glory to pursue a track which Dryden and Otway trod before me. I considered the goddess of this region as the parent of excellence; and however an intercourse with the world might give us good sense, the poverty she granted I supposed to be the nurse of genius! Big with these reflections, I sate down, and finding that the best things remained to be said on the wrong side, I resolved to write a book that should be wholly new. I therefore drest up three paradoxes with some ingenuity. They were false, indeed, but they were new.

The jewels of truth have been so often imported by others, that nothing was left for me to import but some splendid things that at a distance looked every bit as well. Witness you powers what fancied importance sate perched upon my quill while I was writing. The whole learned world, I made no doubt, would rise to oppose my systems; but then I was prepared to oppose the whole learned world. Like the porcupine I sate self collected, with a quill pointed against every opposer.'

'Well said, my boy,' cried I, 'and what subject did you treat upon? I hope you did not pass over the importance of Monogamy. But I interrupt, go on; you published your paradoxes; well, and what did the learned world say to your paradoxes?'

'Sir,' replied my son, 'the learned world said nothing to my paradoxes; nothing at all, Sir. Every man of them was employed in praising his friends and himself, or condemning his enemies; and unfortunately, as I had neither, I suffered the cruellest mortification, neglect.

'As I was meditating one day in a coffee-house on the fate of my paradoxes, a little man happening to enter the room, placed himself in the box before me, and after some preliminary discourse, finding me to be a scholar, drew out a bundle of proposals, begging me to subscribe to a new edition he was going to give the world of Propertius,* with notes. This demand necessarily produced a reply that I had no money; and that concession led him to enquire into the nature of my expectations. Finding that my expectations were just as great as my purse, I see, cried he, you are unacquainted with the town, I'll teach you a part of it. Look at these proposals, upon these very proposals I have subsisted very comfortably for twelve years. The moment a nobleman returns from his travels, a Creolian arrives from Jamaica,* or a dowager from her country seat, I strike for a subscription. I first besiege their hearts with flattery, and then pour in my proposals at the breach. If they subscribe readily the first time, I renew my request to beg a dedication fee.* If they let me have that, I smite them once more for engraving their coat of arms at the top. Thus, continued he, I live by vanity, and laugh at it. But between ourselves, I am now too well known, I should be glad to borrow your face a bit: a nobleman of distinction has just returned from Italy; my face is familiar to his porter; but if you bring this copy of verses, my life for it you succeed, and we divide the spoil.'

'Bless us, George,' cried I, 'and is this the employment of poets now! Do men of their exalted talents thus stoop to beggary! Can they so far disgrace their calling, as to make a vile traffic of praise for bread?'

'O no, Sir,' returned he, 'a true poet can never be so base; for wherever there is genius there is pride. The creatures I now describe are only beggars in rhyme. The real poet, as he braves every hardship for fame, so he is equally a coward to contempt, and none but those who are unworthy protection condescend to solicit it.

'Having a mind too proud to stoop to such indignities, and yet a fortune too humble to hazard a second attempt for fame, I was now obliged to take a middle course, and write for bread. But I was unqualified for a profession where mere industry alone was to ensure success. I could not suppress my lurking passion for applause; but usually consumed that time in efforts after excellence which takes up but little room, when it should have been more advantageously employed in the diffusive productions of fruitful mediocrity. My little piece would therefore come forth in the mist of periodical publication, unnoticed and unknown. The public were more importantly employed, than to observe the easy simplicity of my style, or the harmony of my periods. Sheet after sheet was thrown off to oblivion. My essays were buried among the essays upon liberty, eastern tales, and cures for the bite of a mad dog; while Philautos, Philalethes, Philelutheros, and Philanthropos,* all wrote better, because they wrote faster, than I.

'Now, therefore, I began to associate with none but disappointed authors, like myself, who praised, deplored, and despised each other. The satisfaction we found in every celebrated writer's attempts, was inversely as their merits. I found that no genius in another could please me. My unfortunate paradoxes had entirely dried up that source of comfort. I could neither read nor write with satisfaction; for excellence in another was my aversion, and writing was my trade.

'In the midst of these gloomy reflections, as I was one day sitting on a bench in St. James's park, a young gentleman of distinction, who had been my intimate acquaintance at the university, approached me. We saluted each other with some hesitation, he almost ashamed of being known to one who made so shabby an appearance, and I afraid of a repulse. But my suspicions soon vanished; for Ned Thornhill was at the bottom a very good-natured fellow.'

'What did you say, George?' interrupted I. 'Thornhill, was not that his name? It can certainly be no other than my landlord.'—'Bless me,' cried Mrs. Arnold, 'is Mr. Thornhill so near a neighbour of yours? He has long been a friend in our family, and we expect a visit from him shortly.'

'My friend's first care,' continued my son, 'was to alter my appearance by a very fine suit of his own cloaths, and then I was admitted to his table upon the footing of half-friend, half-underling. My business was to attend him at auctions, to put him in spirits when he sate for his picture, to take the left hand in his chariot when not filled by another, and to assist at tattering a kip,* as the phrase was, when we had a mind for a frolic. Beside this, I had twenty other little employments in the family. I was to do many small things without bidding; to carry the cork screw; to stand godfather to all the butler's children; to sing when I was bid; to be never out of humour; always to be humble, and, if I could, to be very happy.

'In this honourable post, however, I was not without a rival. A captain of marines, who was formed for the place by nature, opposed me in my patron's affections. His mother had been laundress to a man of quality, and thus he early acquired a taste for pimping and pedigree. As this gentleman made it the study of his life to be acquainted with lords, though he was dismissed from several for his stupidity; yet he found many of them who were as dull as himself, that permitted his assiduities. As flattery was his trade, he practised it with the easiest address imaginable; but it came aukward and stiff from me; and as every day my patron's desire of flattery encreased, so every hour being better acquainted with his defects, I became more unwilling to give it. Thus I was once more fairly going to give up the field to the captain, when my friend found occasion for my assistance. This was nothing less than to fight a duel for him, with a gentleman whose sister it was pretended he had used ill. I readily complied with his request, and tho' I see you are displeased at my conduct, yet as it was a debt indispensably due to friendship, I could not refuse. I undertook the affair, disarmed my antagonist, and soon after had the pleasure of finding that the lady was only a woman of the town, and the fellow her bully and a sharper.* This piece of service was repaid with the warmest professions of gratitude; but as my friend was to leave town in a few days, he knew no other method of serving me, but by recommending me to his uncle Sir William Thornhill, and another nobleman of great distinction, who enjoyed a post under the government. When he was gone, my first care was to carry his recommendatory letter to his uncle, a man whose character for every virtue was universal, yet just. I was received by his servants with the most hospitable smiles; for the looks of the domestics ever transmit their master's benevolence. Being shewn into a grand apartment, where Sir William soon came to me, I delivered my message and letter, which he read, and after pausing some minutes, Pray, Sir, cried he, inform me what you have done for my kinsman, to deserve this warm recommendation? But I suppose, Sir, I guess your merits, you have fought for him; and so you would expect a reward from me, for being the instrument of his vices. I wish, sincerely wish, that my present refusal may be some punishment for your guilt; but still more, that it may be some inducement to your repentance.— The severity of this rebuke I bore patiently, because I knew it was just. My whole expectations now, therefore, lay in my letter to the great man. As the doors of the nobility are almost ever beset with beggars, all ready to thrust in some sly petition, I found it no easy matter to gain admittance. However, after bribing the servants with half my worldly fortune, I was at last shewn into a spacious apartment, my letter being previously sent up for his lordship's inspection. During this anxious interval I had full time to look round me. Every thing was grand, and of happy contrivance: the paintings, the furniture, the gildings, petrified me with awe, and raised my idea of the owner. Ah, thought I to myself, how very great must the possessor of all these things be, who carries in his head the business of the state, and whose house displays half the wealth of a kingdom: sure his genius must be unfathomable! During these awful reflections I heard a step come heavily forward. Ah, this is the great man himself! No, it was only a chambermaid. Another foot was heard soon after. This must be He! No, it was only the great man's valet de chambre. At last his lordship actually made his appearance. Are you, cried he, the bearer of this here letter? I answered with a bow. I learn by this, continued he, as how that—But just at that instant a servant delivered him a card, and without taking farther notice, he went out of the room, and left me to digest my own happiness at leisure. I saw no more of him, till told by a footman that his lordship was going to his coach at the door. Down I immediately followed, and joined my voice to that of three or four more, who came, like me, to petition for favours. His lordship, however, went too fast for us, and was gaining his Chariot door with large strides, when I hallowed out to know if I was to have any reply. He was by this time got in, and muttered an answer, half of which only I heard, the other half was lost in the rattling of his chariot wheels. I stood for some time with my neck stretched out, in the posture of one that was listening to catch the glorious sounds, till looking round me, I found myself alone at his lordship's gate.*

'My patience, continued my son, 'was now quite exhausted: stung with the thousand indignities I had met with, I was willing to cast myself away, and only wanted the gulph to receive me. I regarded myself as one of those vile things that nature designed should be thrown by into her lumber room,* there to perish in obscurity. I had still, however, half a guinea left, and of that I thought fortune herself should not deprive me: but in order to be sure of this, I was resolved to go instantly and spend it while I had it, and then trust to occurrences for the rest. As I was going along with this resolution, it happened that Mr. Cripse's office* seemed invitingly open to give me a welcome reception. In this office Mr. Cripse kindly offers all his majesty's subjects a generous promise of 30 l. a year, for which promise all they give in return is their liberty for life, and permission to let him transport them to America as slaves. I was happy at finding a place where I could lose my fears in desperation, and entered this cell, for it had the appearance of one, with the devotion of a monastic. Here I found a number of poor creatures, all in circumstances like myself, expecting the arrival of Mr. Cripse, presenting a true epitome of English impatience. Each untractable soul at variance with fortune, wreaked her injuries on their own hearts: but Mr. Cripse at last came down, and all our murmurs were hushed. He deigned to regard me with an air of peculiar approbation, and indeed he was the first man who for a month past talked to me with smiles. After a few questions, he found I was fit for every thing in the world. He paused a while upon the properest means of providing for me, and slapping his forehead, as if he had found it, assured me, that there was at that time an embassy talked of from the synod of Pensylvania to the Chickasaw Indians, and that he would use his interest to get me made secretary. I knew in my own heart that the fellow lied, and yet his promise gave me pleasure, there was something so magnificent in the sound. I fairly, therefore, divided my half guinea, one half of which went to be added to his thirty thousand pound, and with the other half I resolved to go to the next tavern, to be there more happy than he.

'As I was going out with that resolution, I was met at the door by the captain of a ship, with whom I had formerly some little acquaintance, and he agreed to be my companion over a bowl of punch. As I never chose to make a secret of my circumstances, he assured me that I was upon the very point of ruin, in listening to the office-keeper's promises; for that he only designed to sell me to the plantations. But, continued he, I fancy you might, by a much shorter voyage, be very easily put into a genteel way of bread. Take my advice. My ship sails to-morrow for Amsterdam; What if you go in her as a passenger? The moment you land all you have to do is to teach the Dutchmen English, and I'll warrant you'll get pupils and money enough. I suppose you understand English, added he, by this time, or the deuce is in it. I confidently assured him of that; but expressed a doubt whether the Dutch would be willing to learn English. He affirmed with an oath that they were fond of it to distraction; and upon that affirmation I agreed with his proposal, and embarked the next day to teach the Dutch English in Holland. The wind was fair, our voyage short, and after having paid my passage with half my moveables, I found myself, fallen as from the skies, a stranger in one of the principal streets of Amsterdam. In this situation I was unwilling to let any time pass unemployed in teaching. I addressed myself therefore to two or three of those I met, whose appearance seemed most promising; but it was impossible to make ourselves mutually understood. It was not till this very moment I recollected, that in order to teach Dutchmen English, it was necessary that they should first teach me Dutch. How I came to overlook so obvious an objection, is to me amazing; but certain it is I overlooked it.

'This scheme thus blown up, I had some thoughts of fairly shipping back to England again; but happening into company with an Irish student, who was returning from Louvain,* our conversation turning upon topics of literature, (for by the way it may be observed, that I always forgot the meanness of my circumstances when I could converse upon such subjects) from him I learned that there were not two men in his whole university who understood Greek. This amazed me. I instantly resolved to travel to Louvain, and there live by teaching Greek; and in this design I was heartened by my brother student, who threw out some hints that a fortune might be got by it.

'I set boldly forward the next morning. Every day lessened the burthen of my moveables, like Æsop and his basket of bread;* for I paid them for my lodgings to the Dutch as I travelled on. When I came to Louvain, I was resolved not to go sneaking to the lower professors, but openly tendered my talents to the principal himself. I went, had admittance, and offered him my service as a master of the Greek language, which I had been told was a desideratum in his university. The *principal* seemed at first to doubt of my abilities; but of these I offered to convince him, by turning a part of any Greek author he should fix upon into Latin. Finding me perfectly earnest in my proposal, he addressed me thus: You see me, young man, continued he, I never learned Greek, and I don't find that I have ever missed it. I have had a doctor's cap and gown without Greek: I have ten thousand florins a year without Greek; I eat heartily without Greek, and in short, continued he, as I don't know Greek, I do not believe there is any good in it.

'I was now too far from home to think of returning; so I resolved to go forward.* I had some knowledge of music, with a tolerable voice, and now turned what was once my amusement into a present means of subsistence. I passed among the harmless peasants of Flanders, and among such of the French as were poor enough to be very merry; for I ever found them sprightly in proportion to their wants. Whenever I approached a peasant's house towards night-fall, I played one of my most merry tunes, and that procured me not only a lodging, but subsistence for the next day. I once or twice attempted to play for people of fashion; but they always thought my performance odious, and never rewarded me even with a trifle. This was to me the more extraordinary, as whenever I used in better days to play for company, when playing was my amusement, my music never failed to throw them into raptures, and the ladies especially; but as it was now my only means, it was received with contempt: a proof how ready the world is to under rate those talents by which a man is supported.

'In this manner I proceeded to Paris, with no design but just to look about me, and then to go forward. The people of Paris are much fonder of strangers that have money, than of those that have wit. As I could not boast much of either, I was no great favourite. After walking about the town four or five days, and seeing the outsides of the best houses, I was preparing to leave this retreat of venal hospitality, when passing through one of the principal streets, whom should I meet but our cousin, to whom you first recommended me. This meeting was very agreeable to me, and I believe not displeasing to him. He enquired into the nature of my journey to Paris, and informed me of his own business there, which was to collect pictures, medals, intaglios,* and antiques of all kinds, for a gentleman in London, who had just stept into taste and a large fortune. I was the more surprised at seeing our cousin pitched upon for this office, as he himself had often assured me he knew nothing of the matter. Upon my asking how he had been taught the art of a connoscento* so very suddenly, he assured me that nothing was more easy. The whole secret consisted in a strict adherence to two rules: the one always to observe, that the picture might have been better if the painter had taken more pains; and the other, to praise the works of Pietro Perugino.* But, says he, as I once taught you how to be an author in London, I'll now undertake to instruct you in the art of picture buying at Paris.

'With this proposal I very readily closed, as it was a living, and now all my ambition was to live. I went therefore to his lodgings, improved my dress by his assistance, and after some time, accompanied him to auctions of pictures, where the English gentry were expected to be purchasers. I was not a little surprised at his intimacy with people of the best fashion, who referred themselves to his judgment upon every picture or medal, as to an unerring standard of taste. He made very good use of my assistance upon these occasions; for when asked his opinion, he would gravely take me aside, and ask mine, shrug, look wise, return, and assure the company, that he could give no opinion upon an affair of so much importance. Yet there was sometimes an occasion for a more supported assurance. I remember to have seen him, after giving his opinion that the colouring of a picture was not mellow enough, very deliberately take a brush with brown varnish, that was accidentally lying by, and rub it over the piece with great composure before all the company, and then ask if he had not improved the tints.

'When he had finished his commission in Paris, he left me strongly recommended to several men of distinction, as a person very proper for a travelling tutor; and after some time I was employed in that capacity by a gentleman who brought his ward to Paris, in order to set him forward on his tour through Europe. I was to be the young gentleman's governor, but with a proviso that he should always be permitted to govern himself. My pupil in fact understood the art of guiding in money concerns much better than I. He was heir to a fortune of about two hundred thousand pounds, left him by an uncle in the West Indies; and his guardians, to qualify him for the management of it, had bound him apprentice to an attorney. Thus avarice was his prevailing passion: all his questions on the road were how money might be saved, which was the least expensive course of travel; whether any thing could be bought that would turn to account when disposed of again in London. Such curiosities on the way as could be seen for nothing he was ready enough to look at; but if the sight of them was to be paid for, he usually asserted that he had been told they were not worth seeing. He never paid a bill, that he would not observe, how amazingly expensive travelling was, and all this though he was not yet twenty-one. When arrived at Leghorn, as we took a walk to look at the port and shipping, he enquired the expence of the passage by sea home to England. This he was informed was but a trifle, compared to his returning by land, he was therefore unable to withstand the temptation; so paying me the small part of my salary that was due, he took leave, and embarked with only one attendant for London.

'I now therefore was left once more upon the world at large, but then it was a thing I was used to. However my skill in music could avail me nothing in a country where every peasant was a better musician than I; but by this time I had acquired another talent, which answered my purpose as well, and this was a skill in disputation. In all the foreign universities and convents, there are upon certain days philosophical theses maintained against every adventitious disputant; for which, if the champion opposes with any dexterity, he can claim a gratuity in money, a dinner, and a bed for one night. In this manner therefore I fought my way towards England, walked along from city to city, examined mankind more nearly, and, if I may so express it, saw both sides of the picture. My remarks, however, are but few: I found that monarchy was the best government for the poor to live in, and commonwealths for the rich. I found that riches in general were in every country another name for freedom; and that no man is so fond of liberty himself as not to be desirous of subjecting the will of some individuals in society to his own.

'Upon my arrival in England, I resolved to pay my respects first to you, and then to enlist as a volunteer in the first expedition that was going forward; but on my journey down my resolutions were changed, by meeting an old acquaintance, who I found belonged to a company of comedians, that were going to make a summer campaign in the country. The company seemed not much to disapprove of me for an associate. They all, however, apprized me of the importance of the task at which I aimed; that the public was a many headed monster, and that only such as had very good heads could please it: that acting was not to be learnt in a day; and that without some traditional shrugs, which had been on the stage, and only on the stage, these hundred years, I could never pretend to please. The next difficulty was in fitting me with parts, as almost every character was in keeping. I was driven for some time from one character to another, till at last Horatio was fixed upon, which the presence of the present company has happily hindered me from acting.'

CHAPTER XXI

The short continuance of friendship amongst the vicious,
which is coeval only with mutual satisfaction

MY son's account was too long to be delivered at once, the first part of it was begun that night, and he was concluding the rest after dinner the next day, when the appearance of Mr. Thornhill's equipage at the door seemed to make a pause in the general satisfaction. The butler, who was now become my friend in the family, informed me with a whisper, that the 'Squire had already made some overtures to Miss Wilmot, and that her aunt and uncle seemed highly to approve the match. Upon Mr. Thornhill's entering, he seemed, at seeing my son and me, to start back; but I readily imputed that to surprize, and not displeasure. However, upon our advancing to salute him, he returned our greeting with the most apparent candour; and after a short time, his presence served only to encrease the general good humour.

After tea he called me aside, to enquire after my daughter; but upon my informing him that my enquiry was unsuccessful, he seemed greatly surprised; adding, that he had been since frequently at my house, in order to comfort the rest of my family, whom he left perfectly well. He then asked if I had communicated her misfortune to Miss Wilmot, or my son; and upon my replying that I had not told them as yet, he greatly approved my prudence and precaution, desiring me by all means to keep it a secret: 'For at best,' cried he, 'it is but divulging one's own infamy; and perhaps Miss Livy may not be so guilty as we all imagine.' We were here interrupted by a servant, who came to ask the 'Squire in, to stand up at country dances; so that he left me quite pleased with the interest he seemed to take in my concerns. His addresses, however, to Miss Wilmot, were too obvious to be mistaken; and yet she seemed not perfectly pleased, but bore them rather in compliance to the will of her aunt, than from real inclination. I had even the satisfaction to see her lavish some kind looks upon my unfortunate son, which the other could neither extort by his fortune nor assiduity. Mr. Thornhill's seeming composure, however, not a little surprised me: we had now continued here a week, at the pressing instances of Mr. Arnold; but each day the more tenderness Miss Wilmot shewed my son, Mr. Thornhill's friendship seemed proportionably to encrease for him.

He had formerly made us the most kind assurances of using his interest to serve the family; but now his generosity was not confined to promises alone: the morning I designed for my departure, Mr. Thornhill came to me with looks of real pleasure to inform me of a piece of service he had done for his friend George. This was nothing less than his having procured him an ensign's commission in one of the regiments that was going to the West Indies,* for which he had promised but one hundred pounds, his interest having been sufficient to get an abatement of the other two. 'As for this trifling piece of service,' continued the young gentleman, 'I desire no other reward but the pleasure of having served my friend; and as for the hundred pound to be paid, if you are unable to raise it yourselves, I will advance it, and you shall repay me at your leisure.' This was a favour we wanted words to express our sense of: I readily therefore gave my bond for the money, and testified as much gratitude as if I never intended to pay.

George was to depart for town the next day to secure his commission, in pursuance of his generous patron's directions, who judged it highly expedient to use dispatch, lest in the mean time another should step in with more advantageous proposals. The next morning, therefore, our young soldier was early prepared for his departure, and seemed the only person among us that was not affected by it. Neither the fatigues and dangers he was going to encounter, nor the friends and mistress, for Miss Wilmot actually loved him, he was leaving behind, any way damped his spirits. After he had taken leave of the rest of the company, I gave him all I had, my blessing. 'And now, my boy,' cried I, 'thou art going to fight for thy country, remember how thy brave grandfather fought for his sacred king, when loyalty among Britons was a virtue. Go, my boy, and immitate him in all but his misfortunes, if it was a misfortune to die with Lord Falkland.* Go, my boy, and if you fall, tho' distant, exposed and unwept by those that love you, the most precious tears are those with which heaven bedews the unburied head of a soldier.'

The next morning I took leave of the good family, that had been kind enough to entertain me so long, not without several expressions of gratitude to Mr. Thornhill for his late bounty. I left them in the enjoyment of all that happiness which affluence and good breeding procure, and returned towards home, despairing of ever finding my daughter more, but sending a sigh to heaven to spare and to forgive her. I was now come within about twenty miles of home, having hired an horse to carry me, as I was yet but weak, and comforted myself with the hopes of soon seeing all I held dearest upon earth. But the night coming on, I put up at a little public-house by the road-side, and asked for the landlord's company over a pint of wine. We sate beside his kitchen fire, which was the best room in the house, and chatted on politics and the news of the country. We happened, among other topics, to talk of young 'Squire Thornhill, who the host assured me was hated as much as his uncle Sir William, who sometimes came down to the country, was loved. He went on to observe, that he made it his whole study to betray the daughters of such as received him to their houses, and after a fortnight or three weeks possession, turned them out unrewarded and abandoned to the world. As we continued our discourse in this manner, his wife, who had been out to get change, returned, and perceiving that her husband was enjoying a pleasure in which she was not a sharer, she asked him, in an angry tone, what he did there, to which he only replied in an ironical way, by drinking her health. 'Mr. Symmonds,' cried she, 'you use me very ill, and I'll bear it no longer. Here three parts of the business is left for me to do, and the fourth left unfinished; while you do nothing but soak with the guests all day long, whereas if a spoonful of liquor were to cure me of a fever, I never touch a drop.' I now found what she would be at, and immediately poured her out a glass, which she received with a curtesy, and drinking towards my good health, 'Sir,' resumed she, 'it is not so much for the value of the liquor I am angry, but one cannot help it, when the house is going out of the windows.* If the customers or guests are to be dunned, all the burthen lies upon my back, he'd as lief eat that glass as budge after them himself. There now above stairs, we have a young woman who has come to take up her lodgings here, and I don't believe she has got any money by her over-civility. I am certain she is very slow of payment, and I wish she were put in mind of it.'—'What signifies minding her,' cried the host, 'if she be slow, she is sure.'—'I don't know that,' replied the wife; 'but I know that I am sure she has been here a fortnight, and we have not yet seen the cross of her money.'—'I suppose, my dear,' cried he, 'we shall have it all in a lump.'—'In a lump!' cried the other, 'I hope we may get it any way; and that I am resolved we will this very night, or out she tramps, bag and baggage.'—'Consider, my dear,' cried the husband, 'she is a gentlewoman, and deserves more respect.' —'As for the matter of that,' returned the hostess, 'gentle or simple, out she shall pack with a sassarara.* Gentry may be good things where they take; but for my part I never saw much good of them at the sign of the Harrow.'—Thus saying, she ran up a narrow flight of stairs, that went from the kitchen to a room over-head, and I soon perceived by the loudness of her voice, and the bitterness of her reproaches, that no money was to be had from her lodger. I could hear her remonstrances very distinctly: 'Out I say, pack out this moment, tramp thou infamous strumpet, or I'll give thee a mark thou won't be the better for this three

months. What! you trumpery, to come and take up an honest
house, without cross or coin to bless yourself with; come along I
say.'—'O dear madam,' cried the stranger, 'pity me, pity a poor
abandoned creature for one night, and death will soon do the
rest.'—I instantly knew the voice of my poor ruined child Olivia.
I flew to her rescue, while the woman was dragging her along by
the hair, and I caught the dear forlorn wretch in my arms.—
'Welcome, any way welcome, my dearest lost one, my treasure, to
your poor old father's bosom. Tho' the vicious forsake thee, there
is yet one in the world that will never forsake thee; tho' thou hadst
ten thousand crimes to answer for, he will forget them all.'—'O
my own dear'—for minutes she could no more—'my own dearest
good papa! Could angels be kinder! How do I deserve so much!
The villain, I hate him and myself, to be a reproach to such
goodness. You can't forgive me. I know you cannot.'—'Yes, my
child, from my heart I do forgive thee! Only repent, and we both
shall yet be happy. We shall see many pleasant days yet, my
Olivia!'—'Ah! never, sir, never. The rest of my wretched life must
be infamy abroad and shame at home. But, alas! papa, you look
much paler than you used to do. Could such a thing as I am give
you so much uneasiness? Sure you have too much wisdom to take
the miseries of my guilt upon yourself.'—'Our wisdom, young
woman,' replied I.—'Ah, why so cold a name, papa?' cried she.
'This is the first time you ever called me by so cold a name.'—'I
ask pardon, my darling,' returned I; 'but I was going to observe,
that wisdom makes but a slow defence against trouble, though at
last a sure one.'

The landlady now returned to know if we did not chuse a
more genteel apartment, to which assenting, we were shewn a
room, where we could converse more freely. After we had talked
ourselves into some degree of tranquility, I could not avoid
desiring some account of the gradations that led to her present
wretched situation. 'That villain, sir,' said she, 'from the first
day of our meeting made me honourable, though private,
proposals.'

'Villain indeed,' cried I; 'and yet it in some measure surprises
me, how a person of Mr. Burchell's good sense and seeming

honour could be guilty of such deliberate baseness, and thus step into a family to undo it.'

'My dear papa,' returned my daughter, 'you labour under a strange mistake, Mr. Burchell never attempted to deceive me. Instead of that he took every opportunity of privately admonishing me against the artifices of Mr. Thornhill, who I now find was even worse than he represented him.'—'Mr. Thornhill,' interrupted I, 'can it be?'—'Yes, Sir,' returned she, 'it was Mr. Thornhill who seduced me, who employed the two ladies, as he called them, but who, in fact, were abandoned women of the town, without breeding or pity, to decoy us up to London. Their artifices, you may remember would have certainly succeeded, but for Mr. Burchell's letter, who directed those reproaches at them, which we all applied to ourselves. How he came to have so much influence as to defeat their intentions, still remains a secret to me; but I am convinced he was ever our warmest sincerest friend.'

'You amaze me, my dear,' cried I; 'but now I find my first suspicions of Mr. Thornhill's baseness were too well grounded: but he can triumph in security; for he is rich and we are poor. But tell me, my child, sure it was no small temptation that could thus obliterate all the impressions of such an education, and so virtuous a disposition as thine.'

'Indeed, Sir,' replied she, 'he owes all his triumph to the desire I had of making him, and not myself, happy. I knew that the ceremony of our marriage, which was privately performed by a popish priest, was no way binding, and that I had nothing to trust to but his honour.' 'What,' interrupted I, 'and were you indeed married by a priest, and in orders?'—'Indeed, Sir, we were,' replied she, 'though we were both sworn to conceal his name.'— 'Why then, my child, come to my arms again, and now you are a thousand times more welcome than before; for you are now his wife to all intents and purposes; nor can all the laws of man, tho' written upon tables of adamant, lessen the force of that sacred connexion.'

'Alas, Papa,' replied she, 'you are but little acquainted with his villainies: he has been married already, by the same priest, to six or eight wives more, whom, like me, he has deceived and abandoned.'

'Has he so?' cried I, 'then we must hang the priest, and you shall inform against him to-morrow.'* 'But Sir,' returned she, 'will that be right, when I am sworn to secrecy?'—'My dear,' I replied, 'if you have made such a promise, I cannot, nor will I tempt you to break it. Even tho' it may benefit the public, you must not inform against him. In all human institutions a smaller evil is allowed to procure a greater good; as in politics, a province may be given away to secure a kingdom; in medicine, a limb may be lopt off, to preserve the body. But in religion the law is written, and inflexible, *never* to do evil. And this law, my child, is right: for otherwise, if we commit a smaller evil, to procure a greater good, certain guilt would be thus incurred, in expectation of contingent advantage. And though the advantage should certainly follow, yet the interval between commission and advantage, which is allowed to be guilty, may be that in which we are called away to answer for the things we have done, and the volume of human actions is closed for ever. But I interrupt you, my dear, go on.'

'The very next morning,' continued she, 'I found what little expectations I was to have from his sincerity. That very morning he introduced me to two unhappy women more, whom, like me, he had deceived, but who lived in contented prostitution. I loved him too tenderly to bear such rivals in his affections, and strove to forget my infamy in a tumult of pleasures. With this view, I danced, dressed, and talked; but still was unhappy. The gentlemen who visited there told me every moment of the power of my charms, and this only contributed to encrease my melancholy, as I had thrown all their power quite away. Thus each day I grew more pensive, and he more insolent, till at last the monster had the assurance to offer me to a young Baronet of his acquaintance. Need I describe, Sir, how his ingratitude stung me. My answer to this proposal was almost madness. I desired to part. As I was going he offered me a purse; but I flung it at him with indignation, and burst from him in a rage, that for a while kept me insensible of the miseries of my situation. But I soon looked round me, and saw myself a vile, abject, guilty thing, without one friend in the world to apply to.

'Just in that interval, a stage-coach happening to pass by, I took a place, it being my only aim to be driven at a distance from a wretch I despised and detested. I was set down here, where, since my arrival, my own anxiety, and this woman's unkindness, have been my only companions. The hours of pleasure that I have passed with my mamma and sister, now grow painful to me. Their sorrows are much; but mine is greater than theirs; for mine are mixed with guilt and infamy.'

'Have patience, my child,' cried I, 'and I hope things will yet be better. Take some repose to-night, and to-morrow I'll carry you home to your mother and the rest of the family, from whom you will receive a kind reception. Poor woman, this has gone to her heart: but she loves you still, Olivia, and will forget it.'

CHAPTER XXII

Offences are easily pardoned where there is love at bottom

THE next morning I took my daughter behind me, and set out on my return home. As we travelled along, I strove, by every persuasion, to calm her sorrows and fears, and to arm her with resolution to bear the presence of her offended mother. I took every opportunity, from the prospect of a fine country, through which we passed, to observe how much kinder heaven was to us, than we to each other, and that the misfortunes of nature's making were very few. I assured her, that she should never perceive any change in my affections, and that during my life, which yet might be long, she might depend upon a guardian and an instructor. I armed her against the censures of the world, shewed her that books were sweet unreproaching companions to the miserable, and that if they could not bring us to enjoy life, they would at least teach us to endure it.

The hired horse that we rode was to be put up that night at an inn by the way, within about five miles from my house, and as I was willing to prepare my family for my daughter's reception, I determined to leave her that night at the inn, and to return for her, accompanied by my daughter Sophia, early the next morning. It was night before we reached our appointed stage: however, after seeing her provided with a decent apartment, and having ordered the hostess to prepare proper refreshments, I kissed her, and proceeded towards home. And now my heart caught new sensations of pleasure the nearer I approached that peaceful mansion. As a bird that had been frighted from its nest, my affections out-went my haste, and hovered round my little fire-side, with all the rapture of expectation. I called up the many fond things I had to say, and anticipated the welcome I was to receive. I already felt my wife's tender embrace, and smiled at the joy of my little ones. As I walked but slowly, the night wained apace. The labourers of the day were all retired to rest; the lights were out in every cottage; no sounds were heard but of the shrilling cock, and the deep-mouthed watch-dog, at hollow distance. I approached my little abode of pleasure, and before I was within a furlong of the place, our honest mastiff came running to welcome me.

It was now near mid-night that I came to knock at my door: all was still and silent: my heart dilated with unutterable happiness, when, to my amazement, I saw the house bursting out in a blaze of fire, and every apperture red with conflagration! I gave a loud convulsive outcry, and fell upon the pavement insensible. This alarmed my son, who had till this been asleep, and he perceiving the flames, instantly waked my wife and daughter, and all running out, naked, and wild with apprehension, recalled me to life with their anguish. But it was only to objects of new terror; for the flames had, by this time, caught the roof of our dwelling, part after part continuing to fall in, while the family stood, with silent agony, looking on, as if they enjoyed the blaze. I gazed upon them and upon it by turns, and then looked round me for my two little ones; but they were not to be seen. O misery! 'Where,' cried I, 'where are my little ones?'—'They are burnt to death in the flames,' says my wife calmly, 'and I will die with them.'—That moment I heard the cry of the babes within, who were just awaked by the fire, and nothing could have stopped me. 'Where, where, are my children?' cried I, rushing through the flames, and bursting the door of the chamber in which they were confined, 'Where are my little ones?'—'Here, dear papa, here we are,' cried they together, while the flames were just catching the bed where they lay. I caught them both in my arms, and snatched them through the fire as fast as possible, while just as I was got out, the roof sunk in. 'Now,' cried I, holding up my children, 'now let the flames burn on, and all my possessions perish. Here they are, I have saved my treasure. Here, my dearest, here are our treasures, and we shall yet be happy.' We kissed our little darlings a thousand times, they clasped us round the neck, and seemed to share our transports, while their mother laughed and wept by turns.

I now stood a calm spectator of the flames, and after some time, began to perceive that my arm to the shoulder was scorched in a terrible manner. It was therefore out of my power to give my son any assistance, either in attempting to save our goods, or preventing the flames spreading to our corn. By this time, the neighbours were alarmed, and came running to our assistance; but all they could do was to stand, like us, spectators of the calamity. My goods, among which were the notes I had reserved for my daughters fortunes, were entirely consumed, except a box, with some papers, that stood in the kitchen, and two or three things more of little consequence, which my son brought away in the beginning. The neighbours contributed, however, what they could to lighten our distress. They brought us cloaths, and furnished one of our out-houses with kitchen utensils; so that by daylight we had another, tho' a wretched, dwelling to retire to. My honest next neighbour, and his children, were not the least assiduous in providing us with every thing necessary, and offering what ever consolation untutored benevolence could suggest.

When the fears of my family had subsided, curiosity to know the cause of my long stay began to take place; having therefore informed them of every particular, I proceeded to prepare them for the reception of our lost one, and tho' we had nothing but wretchedness now to impart, I was willing to procure her a welcome to what we had. This task would have been more difficult but for our recent calamity, which had humbled my wife's pride, and blunted it by more poignant afflictions. Being unable to go for my poor child myself, as my arm grew very painful, I sent my son and daughter, who soon returned, supporting the wretched delinquent, who had not the courage to look up at her mother, whom no instructions of mine could persuade to a perfect reconciliation; for women have a much stronger sense of female error than men. 'Ah, madam,' cried her mother, 'this is but a poor place you are come to after so much finery. My daughter Sophy and I can afford but little entertainment to persons who have kept company only with people of distinction. Yes, Miss Livy, your poor father and I have suffered very much of late; but I hope heaven will forgive you.'—During this reception, the unhappy victim stood pale and trembling, unable to weep or to reply; but I could not continue a silent spectator of her distress, wherefore assuming a degree of severity in my voice and manner, which was ever followed with instant submission, 'I entreat, woman, that my words may be now marked once for all: I have here brought you back a poor deluded wanderer; her return to duty demands the revival of our tenderness. The real hardships of life are now coming fast upon us, let us not therefore encrease them by dissention among each other. If we live harmoniously together, we may yet be contented, as there are enough of us to shut out the censuring world, and keep each other in countenance. The kindness of heaven is promised to the penitent, and let ours be directed by the example. Heaven, we are assured, is much more pleased to view a repentant sinner, than ninety nine persons who have supported a course of undeviating rectitude.* And this is right; for that single effort by which we stop short in the down-hill path to perdition, is itself a greater exertion of virtue, than an hundred acts of justice.'

CHAPTER XXIII

None but the guilty can be long and completely miserable

SOME assiduity was now required to make our present abode as convenient as possible, and we were soon again qualified to enjoy our former serenity. Being disabled myself from assisting my son in our usual occupations, I read to my family from the few books that were saved, and particularly from such, as, by amusing the imagination, contributed to ease the heart. Our good neighbours too came every day with the kindest condolence, and fixed a time in which they were all to assist at repairing my former dwelling. Honest farmer Williams was not last among these visitors; but heartily offered his friendship. He would even have renewed his addresses to my daughter; but she rejected them in such a manner as totally repress his future solicitations. Her grief seemed formed for continuing, and she was the only person of our little society that a week did not restore to chearfulness. She now lost that unblushing innocence which once taught her to respect herself, and to seek pleasure by pleasing. Anxiety now had taken strong possession of her mind, her beauty began to be impaired with her constitution, and neglect still more contributed to diminish it. Every tender epithet bestowed on her sister brought a pang to her heart and a tear to her eye; and as one vice, tho' cured, ever plants others where it has been, so her former guilt, tho' driven out by repentance, left jealousy and envy behind. I strove a thousand ways to lessen her care, and even forgot my own pain in a concern for her's, collecting such amusing passages of history, as a strong memory and some reading could suggest. 'Our happiness, my dear,' I would say, 'is in the power of one who can bring it about a thousand unforeseen ways, that mock our foresight. If example be necessary to prove this, I'll give you a story, my child, told us by a grave, tho' sometimes a romancing, historian.

'Matilda was married very young to a Neapolitan nobleman of the first quality, and found herself a widow and a mother at the age of fifteen. As she stood one day caressing her infant son in the open window of an apartment, which hung over the river Volturna, the child, with a sudden spring, leaped from her arms into the flood below, and disappeared in a moment. The mother, struck with instant surprize, and making an effort to save him, plunged in after; but, far from being able to assist the infant, she herself with great difficulty escaped to the opposite shore, just when some French soldiers were plundering the country on that side, who immediately made her their prisoner.

'As the war was then carried on between the French and Italians with the utmost inhumanity, they were going at once to perpetrate those two extremes, suggested by appetite and cruelty. This base resolution, however, was opposed by a young officer, who, tho' their retreat required the utmost expedition, placed her behind him, and brought her in safety to his native city. Her beauty at first caught his eye, her merit soon after his heart. They were married; he rose to the highest posts; they lived long together, and were happy. But the felicity of a soldier can never be called permanent: after an interval of several years, the troops which he commanded having met with a repulse, he was obliged to take shelter in the city where he had lived with his wife. Here they suffered a siege, and the city at length was taken. Few histories can produce more various instances of cruelty, than those which the French and Italians at that time exercised upon each other. It was resolved by the victors, upon this occasion, to put all the French prisoners to death; but particularly the husband of the unfortunate Matilda, as he was principally instrumental in protracting the siege. Their determinations were, in general, executed almost as soon as resolved upon. The captive soldier was led forth, and the executioner, with his sword, stood ready, while the spectators in gloomy silence awaited the fatal blow, which was only suspended till the general, who presided as judge, should give the signal. It was in this interval of anguish and expectation, that Matilda came to take her last farewell of her husband and deliverer, deploring her wretched situation, and the cruelty of fate, that had saved her from perishing by a premature death in the river Volturna, to be the spectator of still greater calamities. The general, who was a young man, was struck with surprize

at her beauty, and pity at her distress; but with still stronger
emotions when he heard her mention her former dangers. He was
her son, the infant for whom she had encounter'd so much danger. He acknowledged her at once as his mother, and fell at her
feet. The rest may be easily supposed: the captive was set free,
and all the happiness that love, friendship, and duty could confer
on each, were united.'

In this manner I would attempt to amuse my daughter; but she
listened with divided attention; for her own misfortunes engrossed
all the pity she once had for those of another, and nothing gave
her ease. In company she dreaded contempt; and in solitude she
only found anxiety. Such was the colour of her wretchedness,
when we received certain information, that Mr. Thornhill was
going to be married to Miss Wilmot, for whom I always suspected
he had a real passion, tho' he took every opportunity before me to
express his contempt both of her person and fortune. This news
only served to encrease poor Olivia's affliction; such a flagrant
breach of fidelity, was more than her courage could support. I was
resolved, however, to get more certain information, and to defeat,
if possible, the completion of his designs, by sending my son to old
Mr. Wilmot's, with instructions to know the truth of the report,
and to deliver Miss Wilmot a letter, intimating Mr. Thornhill's
conduct in my family. My son went, in pursuance of my directions, and in three days returned, assuring us of the truth of the
account; but that he had found it impossible to deliver the letter,
which he was therefore obliged to leave, as Mr. Thornhill and
Miss Wilmot were visiting round the country. They were to be
married, he said, in a few days, having appeared together at church
the Sunday before he was there, in great splendour, the bride
attended by six young ladies, and he by as many gentlemen. Their
approaching nuptials filled the whole country with rejoicing, and
they usually rode out together in the grandest equipage that had
been seen in the country for many years. All the friends of
both families, he said, were there, particularly the 'Squire's
uncle, Sir William Thornhill, who bore so good a character. He
added, that nothing but mirth and feasting were going forward;
that all the country praised the young bride's beauty, and the

bridegroom's fine person, and that they were immensely fond of each other; concluding, that he could not help thinking Mr. Thornhill one of the most happy men in the world.

'Why let him if he can,' returned I: 'but, my son, observe this bed of straw, and unsheltering roof; those mouldering walls, and humid floor; my wretched body thus disabled by fire, and my children weeping round me for bread; you have come home, my child, to all this, yet here, even here, you see a man that would not for a thousand worlds exchange situations. O, my children, if you could but learn to commune with your own hearts, and know what noble company you can make them, you would little regard the elegance and splendours of the worthless. Almost all men have been taught to call life a passage, and themselves the travellers. The similitude still may be improved when we observe that the good are joyful and serene, like travellers that are going towards home; the wicked but by intervals happy, like travellers that are going into exile.'

My compassion for my poor daughter, overpowered by this new disaster, interrupted what I had farther to observe. I bade her mother support her, and after a short time she recovered. She appeared from that time more calm, and I imagined had gained a new degree of resolution: but appearances deceived me; for her tranquility was the langour of over-wrought resentment. A supply of provisions, charitably sent us by my kind parishioners, seemed to diffuse new chearfulness amongst the rest of the family, nor was I displeased at seeing them once more sprightly and at ease. It would have been unjust to damp their satisfactions, merely to condole with resolute melancholy, or to burthen them with a sadness they did not feel. Thus, once more, the tale went round and the song was demanded, and chearfulness condescended to hover round our little habitation.

CHAPTER XXIV

Fresh calamities

THE next morning the sun rose with peculiar warmth for the season; so that we agreed to breakfast together on the honey-suckle bank: where, while we sate, my youngest daughter, at my request, joined her voice to the concert on the trees about us. It was in this place my poor Olivia first met her seducer, and every object served to recall her sadness. But that melancholy, which is excited by objects of pleasure, or inspired by sounds of harmony, sooths the heart instead of corroding it. Her mother too, upon this occasion, felt a pleasing distress, and wept, and loved her daughter as before. 'Do, my pretty Olivia,' cried she, 'let us have that little melancholy air your pappa was so fond of, your sister Sophy has already obliged us. Do child, it will please your old father.' She complied in a manner so exquisitely pathetic as moved me.

> WHEN lovely woman stoops to folly,*
> And finds too late that men betray,
> What charm can sooth her melancholy,
> What art can wash her guilt away?
>
> The only art her guilt to cover,
> To hide her shame from every eye,
> To give repentance to her lover,
> And wring his bosom—is to die.

As she was concluding the last stanza, to which an interruption in her voice from sorrow gave peculiar softness, the appearance of Mr. Thornhill's equipage at a distance alarmed us all, but particularly encreased the uneasiness of my eldest daughter, who, desirous of shunning her betrayer, returned to the house with her sister. In a few minutes he was alighted from his chariot, and making up to the place where I was still sitting, enquired after my health with his usual air of familiarity. 'Sir,' replied I, 'your present assurance only serves to aggravate the baseness of your character; and there was a time when I would have chastised your insolence, for presuming thus to appear before me. But now you are safe; for age has cooled my passions, and my calling restrains them.'

'I vow, my dear sir,' returned he, 'I am amazed at all this; nor can I understand what it means! I hope you don't think your daughter's late excursion with me had any thing criminal in it.'

'Go,' cried I, 'thou art a wretch, a poor pitiful wretch, and every way a lyar; but your meanness secures you from my anger! Yet sir, I am descended from a family that would not have borne this! And so, thou vile thing, to gratify a momentary passion, thou hast made one poor creature wretched for life, and polluted a family that had nothing but honour for their portion.'

'If she or you,' returned he, 'are resolved to be miserable, I cannot help it. But you may still be happy; and whatever opinion you may have formed of me, you shall ever find me ready to contribute to it. We can marry her to another in a short time, and what is more, she may keep her lover beside; for I protest I shall ever continue to have a true regard for her.'

I found all my passions alarmed at this new degrading proposal; for though the mind may often be calm under great injuries, little villainy can at any time get within the soul, and sting it into rage.—'Avoid my sight, thou reptile,' cried I, 'nor continue to insult me with thy presence. Were my brave son at home, he would not suffer this; but I am old, and disabled, and every way undone.'

'I find,' cried he, 'you are bent upon obliging me to talk in an harsher manner than I intended. But as I have shewn you what may be hoped from my friendship, it may not be improper to represent what may be the consequences of my resentment. My attorney, to whom your late bond has been transferred, threatens hard, nor do I know how to prevent the course of justice, except by paying the money myself, which, as I have been at some expences lately, previous to my intended marriage, is not so easy to be done. And then my steward talks of driving for the rent:* it is certain he knows his duty; for I never trouble myself with affairs of that nature. Yet still I could wish to serve you, and even to have you and your daughter present at my marriage, which is shortly to be solemnized with Miss Wilmot; it is even the request of my charming Arabella herself, whom I hope you will not refuse.'

'Mr. Thornhill,' replied I, 'hear me once for all: as to your marriage with any but my daughter, that I never will consent to; and though your friendship could raise me to a throne, or your resentment sink me to the grave, yet would I despise both. Thou hast once wofully, irreparably, deceived me. I reposed my heart upon thine honour, and have found its baseness. Never more, therefore, expect friendship from me. Go, and possess what fortune has given thee, beauty, riches, health, and pleasure. Go, and leave me to want, infamy, disease, and sorrow. Yet humbled as I am, shall my heart still vindicate its dignity, and though thou hast my forgiveness, thou shalt ever have my contempt.'

'If so,' returned he, 'depend upon it you shall feel the effects of this insolence, and we shall shortly see which is the fittest object of scorn, you or me.'—Upon which he departed abruptly.

My wife and son, who were present at this interview, seemed terrified with the apprehension. My daughters also, finding that he was gone, came out to be informed of the result of our conference, which, when known, alarmed them not less than the rest. But as to myself, I disregarded the utmost stretch of his malevolence: he had already struck the blow, and now I stood prepared to repel every new effort. Like one of those instruments used in the art of war, which, however thrown, still presents a point to receive the enemy.*

We soon, however, found that he had not threatened in vain; for the very next morning his steward came to demand my annual rent, which, by the train of accidents already related, I was unable to pay. The consequence of my incapacity was his driving my cattle that evening, and their being appraised and sold the next day for less than half their value. My wife and children now therefore entreated me to comply upon any terms, rather than incur certain destruction. They even begged me to admit his visits once more, and used all their little eloquence to paint the calamities I was going to endure. The terrors of a prison, in so rigorous a season as the present, with the danger that threatened my health from the late accident that happened by the fire. But I continued inflexible.

'Why, my treasures,' cried I, 'why will you thus attempt to persuade me to the thing that is not right! My duty has taught me to forgive him; but my conscience will not permit me to approve. Would you have me applaud to the world what my heart must internally condemn? Would you have me tamely sit down and flatter our infamous betrayer; and to avoid a prison continually suffer the more galling bonds of mental confinement! No, never. If we are to be taken from this abode, only let us hold to the right, and wherever we are thrown, we can still retire to a charming apartment, when we can look round our own hearts with intrepidity and with pleasure!'

In this manner we spent that evening. Early the next morning, as the snow had fallen in great abundance in the night, my son was employed in clearing it away, and opening a passage before the door. He had not been thus engaged long, when he came running in, with looks all pale, to tell us that two strangers, whom he knew to be officers of justice, were making towards the house.

Just as he spoke they came in, and approaching the bed where I lay, after previously informing me of their employment and business, made me their prisoner, bidding me prepare to go with them to the county gaol, which was eleven miles off.

'My friends,' said I, 'this is severe weather on which you have come to take me to a prison; and it is particularly unfortunate at this time, as one of my arms has lately been burnt in a terrible manner, and it has thrown me into a slight fever, and I want cloaths to cover me, and I am now too weak and old to walk far in such deep snow: but if it must be so—'

I then turned to my wife and children, and directed them to get together what few things were left us, and to prepare immediately for leaving this place. I entreated them to be expeditious, and desired my son to assist his elder sister, who, from a consciousness that she was the cause of all our calamities, was fallen, and had lost anguish in insensibility. I encouraged my wife, who, pale and trembling, clasped our affrighted little ones in her arms, that clung to her bosom in silence, dreading to look round at the strangers. In the mean time my youngest daughter prepared for our departure, and as she received several hints to use dispatch, in about an hour we were ready to depart.

CHAPTER XXV

No situation, however wretched it seems, but has some sort of comfort attending it

WE set forward from this peaceful neighbourhood, and walked on slowly. My eldest daughter being enfeebled by a slow fever, which had begun for some days to undermine her constitution, one of the officers, who had an horse, kindly took her behind him; for even these men cannot entirely divest themselves of humanity. My son led one of the little ones by the hand, and my wife the other, while I leaned upon my youngest girl, whose tears fell not for her own but my distresses.

We were now got from my late dwelling about two miles, when we saw a crowd running and shouting behind us, consisting of about fifty of my poorest parishioners. These, with dreadful imprecations, soon seized upon the two officers of justice, and swearing they would never see their minister go to gaol while they had a drop of blood to shed in his defence, were going to use them with great severity. The consequence might have been fatal, had I not immediately interposed, and with some difficulty rescued the officers from the hands of the enraged multitude. My children, who looked upon my delivery now as certain, appeared transported with joy, and were incapable of containing their raptures. But they were soon undeceived, upon hearing me address the poor deluded people, who came, as they imagined, to do me service.

'What! my friends,' cried I, 'and is this the way you love me! Is this the manner you obey the instructions I have given you from the pulpit! Thus to fly in the face of justice, and bring down ruin on yourselves and me! Which is your ring-leader? Shew me the man that has thus seduced you. As sure as he lives he shall feel my resentment. Alas! my dear deluded flock, return back to the duty you owe to God, to your country, and to me. I shall yet perhaps one day see you in greater felicity here, and contribute to make your lives more happy. But let it at least be my comfort when I pen my fold for immortality, that not one here shall be wanting.'

They now seemed all repentance, and melting into tears, came one after the other to bid me farewell. I shook each tenderly by the hand, and leaving them my blessing, proceeded forward without meeting any farther interruption. Some hours before night we reached the town, or rather village; for it consisted but of a few mean houses, having lost all its former opulence, and retaining no marks of its ancient superiority but the gaol.

Upon entering, we put up at an inn, where we had such refreshments as could most readily be procured, and I supped with my family with my usual chearfulness. After seeing them properly accommodated for that night, I next attended the sheriff's officers to the prison, which had formerly been built for the purposes of war, and consisted of one large apartment, strongly grated, and paved with stone, common to both felons and debtors at certain hours in the four and twenty. Besides this, every prisoner had a separate cell, where he was locked in for the night.

I expected upon my entrance to find nothing but lamentations, and various sounds of misery; but it was very different. The prisoners seemed all employed in one common design, that of forgetting thought in merriment or clamour. I was apprized of the usual perquisite required upon these occasions, and immediately complied with the demand, though the little money I had was very near being all exhausted. This was immediately sent away for liquor, and the whole prison soon was filled with riot, laughter, and prophaneness.

'How,' cried I to myself, 'shall men so very wicked be chearful, and shall I be melancholy! I feel only the same confinement with them, and I think I have more reason to be happy.'

With such reflections I laboured to become chearful; but chearfulness was never yet produced by effort, which is itself painful. As I was sitting therefore in a corner of the gaol, in a pensive posture, one of my fellow prisoners came up, and sitting by me, entered into conversation. It was my constant rule in life never to avoid the conversation of any man who seemed to desire it: for if good, I might profit by his instruction; if bad, he might be assisted by mine. I found this to be a knowing man, of strong unlettered sense; but a thorough knowledge of the world, as it is called, or, more properly speaking, of human nature on the wrong side. He asked me if I had taken care to provide myself with a bed, which was a circumstance I had never once attended to.*

'That's unfortunate,' cried he, 'as you are allowed here nothing but straw, and your apartment is very large and cold. However you seem to be something of a gentleman, and as I have been one myself in my time, part of my bed-cloaths are heartily at your service.'

I thanked him, professing my surprize at finding such humanity in a gaol in misfortunes; adding, to let him see that I was a scholar, 'That the sage ancient seemed to understand the value of company in affliction, when he said, Ton kosman aire, ei dos ton etairon,* and in fact,' continued I, 'what is the World if it affords only solitude?'

'You talk of the world, Sir,' returned my fellow prisoner; '*the world is in its dotage, and yet the cosmogony or creation of the world has puzzled the philosophers of every age. What a medly of opinions have they not broached upon the creation of the world. Sanconiathon, Manetho, Berosus, and Ocellus Lucanus have all attempted it in vain. The latter has these words, Anarchon ara kai atelutaion to pan, which implies*'—'I ask pardon, Sir,' cried I, 'for interrupting so much learning; but I think I have heard all this before. Have I not had the pleasure of once seeing you at Welbridge* fair, and is not your name Ephraim Jenkinson?' At this demand he only sighed. 'I suppose you must recollect,' resumed I, 'one Doctor Primrose, from whom you bought a horse.'

He now at once recollected me; for the gloominess of the place and the approaching night had prevented his distinguishing my features before.—'Yes, Sir,' returned Mr. Jenkinson, 'I remember you perfectly well; I bought an horse, but forgot to pay for him. Your neighbour Flamborough is the only prosecutor I am any way afraid of at the next assizes: for he intends to swear positively against me as a coiner.* I am heartily sorry, Sir, I ever deceived you, or indeed any man; for you see,' continued he, shewing his shackles, 'what my tricks have brought me to.'

'Well, sir,' replied I, 'your kindness in offering me assistance, when you could expect no return, shall be repaid with my endeavours to soften or totally suppress Mr. Flamborough's evidence, and I will send my son to him for that purpose the first opportunity; nor do I in the least doubt but he will comply with my request, and as to my evidence, you need be under no uneasiness about that.'

'Well, sir,' cried he, 'all the return I can make shall be yours. You shall have more than half my bed-cloaths to night, and I'll take care to stand your friend in the prison, where I think I have some influence.'

I thanked him, and could not avoid being surprised at the present youthful change in his aspect; for at the time I had seen him before he appeared at least sixty.—'Sir,' answered he, 'you are little acquainted with the world; I had at that time false hair, and have learnt the art of counterfeiting every age from seventeen to seventy. Ah sir, had I but bestowed half the pains in learning a trade, that I have in learning to be a scoundrel, I might have been a rich man at this day. But rogue as I am, still I may be your friend, and that perhaps when you least expect it.'

We were now prevented from further conversation, by the arrival of the gaoler's servants, who came to call over the prisoners names, and lock up for the night. A fellow also, with a bundle of straw for my bed attended, who led me along a dark narrow passage into a room paved like the common prison, and in one corner of this I spread my bed, and the cloaths given me by my fellow prisoner; which done, my conductor, who was civil enough, bade me a good-night. After my usual meditations, and having praised my heavenly corrector, I laid myself down and slept with the utmost tranquility till morning.

CHAPTER XXVI

*A reformation in the gaol. To make laws complete, they
should reward as well as punish*

THE next morning early I was awakened by my family, whom I
found in tears at my bed-side. The gloomy strength of every
thing about us, it seems, had daunted them. I gently rebuked
their sorrow, assuring them I had never slept with greater tranquility, and next enquired after my eldest daughter, who was not
among them. They informed me that yesterday's uneasiness and
fatigue had encreased her fever, and it was judged proper to leave
her behind. My next care was to send my son to procure a room
or two to lodge the family in, as near the prison as conveniently
could be found. He obeyed; but could only find one apartment,
which was hired at a small expence, for his mother and sisters, the
gaoler with humanity consenting to let him and his two little
brothers lie in the prison with me. A bed was therefore prepared
for them in a corner of the room, which I thought answered very
conveniently. I was willing however previously to know whether
my little children chose to lie in a place which seemed to fright
them upon entrance.

'Well,' cried I, 'my good boys, how do you like your bed? I
hope you are not afraid to lie in this room, dark as it appears.'

'No, papa,' says Dick, 'I am not afraid to lie any where where
you are.'

'And I,' says Bill, who was yet but four years old, 'love every
place best that my papa is in.'

After this, I allotted to each of the family what they were to do.
My daughter was particularly directed to watch her declining
sister's health; my wife was to attend me; my little boys were to
read to me: 'And as for you, my son,' continued I, 'it is by the
labour of your hands we must all hope to be supported. Your
wages, as a day-labourer, will be full sufficient, with proper frugality, to maintain us all, and comfortably too. Thou art now
sixteen years old, and hast strength, and it was given thee, my

son, for very useful purposes; for it must save from famine your helpless parents and family. Prepare then this evening to look out for work against to-morrow, and bring home every night what money you earn, for our support.'

Having thus instructed him, and settled the rest, I walked down to the common prison, where I could enjoy more air and room. But I was not long there when the execrations, lewdness, and brutality that invaded me on every side, drove me back to my apartment again. Here I sate for some time, pondering upon the strange infatuation of wretches, who finding all mankind in open arms against them, were labouring to make themselves a future and a tremendous enemy.

Their insensibility excited my highest compassion, and blotted my own uneasiness from my mind. It even appeared a duty incumbent upon me to attempt to reclaim them. I resolved therefore once more to return, and in spite of their contempt to give them my advice, and conquer them by perseverance. Going therefore among them again, I informed Mr. Jenkinson of my design, at which he laughed heartily, but communicated it to the rest. The proposal was received with the greatest good-humour, as it promised to afford a new fund of entertainment to persons who had now no other resource for mirth, but what could be derived from ridicule or debauchery.

I therefore read them a portion of the service with a loud unaffected voice, and found my audience perfectly merry upon the occasion. Lewd whispers, groans of contrition burlesqued, winking and coughing, alternately excited laughter. However, I continued with my natural solemnity to read on, sensible that what I did might amend some, but could itself receive no contamination from any.

After reading, I entered upon my exhortation, which was rather calculated at first to amuse them than to reprove. I previously observed, that no other motive but their welfare could induce me to this; that I was their fellow prisoner, and now got nothing by preaching. I was sorry, I said, to hear them so very prophane; because they got nothing by it, but might lose a great deal: 'For be assured, my friends,' cried I, 'for you are my friends, however the world may disclaim your friendship, though you swore twelve thousand oaths in a day, it would not put one penny in your purse. Then what signifies calling every moment upon the devil, and courting his friendship, since you find how scurvily he uses you. He has given you nothing here, you find, but a mouthful of oaths and an empty belly; and by the best accounts I have of him, he will give you nothing that's good hereafter.

'If used ill in our dealings with one man, we naturally go elsewhere. Were it not worth your while then, just to try how you may like the usage of another master, who gives you fair promises at least to come to him. Surely, my Friends, of all stupidity in the world, his must be greatest, who, after robbing an house, runs to the thieftakers for protection. And yet how are you more wise? You are all seeking comfort from one that has already betrayed you, applying to a more malicious being than any thieftaker of them all; for they only decoy, and then hang you; but he decoys and hangs, and what is worst of all, will not let you loose after the hangman has done.'

When I had concluded, I received the compliments of my audience, some of whom came and shook me by the hand, swearing that I was a very honest fellow, and that they desired my further acquaintance. I therefore promised to repeat my lecture next day, and actually conceived some hopes of making a reformation here; for it had ever been my opinion, that no man was past the hour of amendment, every heart lying open to the shafts of reproof, if the archer could but take a proper aim. When I had thus satisfied my mind, I went back to my apartment, where my wife had prepared a frugal meal, while Mr. Jenkinson begged leave to add his dinner to ours, and partake of the pleasure, as he was kind enough to express it, of my conversation. He had not yet seen my family, for as they came to my apartment by a door in the narrow passage, already described, by this means they avoided the common prison. Jenkinson at the first interview therefore seemed not a little struck with the beauty of my youngest daughter, which her pensive air contributed to heighten, and my little ones did not pass unnoticed.

'Alas, Doctor,' cried he, 'these children are too handsome and too good for such a place as this!'

'Why, Mr. Jenkinson,' replied I, 'thank heaven my children are pretty tolerable in morals, and if they be good, it matters little for the rest.'

'I fancy, sir,' returned my fellow prisoner, 'that it must give you great comfort to have this little family about you.'

'A comfort, Mr. Jenkinson,' replied I, 'yes it is indeed a comfort, and I would not be without them for all the world; for they can make a dungeon seem a palace. There is but one way in this life of wounding my happiness, and that is by injuring them.'

'I am afraid then, sir,' cried he, 'that I am in some measure culpable; for I think I see here (looking at my son Moses) one that I have injured, and by whom I wish to be forgiven.'

My son immediately recollected his voice and features, though he had before seen him in disguise, and taking him by the hand, with a smile forgave him. 'Yet,' continued he, 'I can't help wondering at what you could see in my face, to think me a proper mark for deception.'

'My dear sir,' returned the other, 'it was not your face, but your white stockings and the black ribband in your hair, that allured me. But no disparagement to your parts, I have deceived wiser men than you in my time; and yet, with all my tricks, the blockheads have been too many for me at last.'

'I suppose,' cried my son, 'that the narrative of such a life as yours must be extremely instructive and amusing.'

'Not much of either,' returned Mr. Jenkinson. 'Those relations which describe the tricks and vices only of mankind, by increasing our suspicion in life, retard our success. The traveller that distrusts every person he meets, and turns back upon the appearance of every man that looks like a robber, seldom arrives in time at his journey's end.

'Indeed I think from my own experience, that the knowing one is the silliest fellow under the sun. I was thought cunning from my very childhood; when but seven years old the ladies would say that I was a perfect little man; at fourteen I knew the world, cocked my hat, and loved the ladies; at twenty, though I was perfectly honest, yet every one thought me so cunning, that not one would trust me. Thus I was at last obliged to turn sharper in my own defence,* and have lived ever since, my head throbbing with schemes to deceive, and my heart palpitating with fear of detection.

'I used often to laugh at your honest simple neighbour Flamborough, and one way or another generally cheated him once a year. Yet still the honest man went forward without suspicion, and grew rich, while I still continued tricksy and cunning, and was poor, without the consolation of being honest.

'However,' continued he, 'let me know your case, and what has brought you here; perhaps though I have not skill to avoid a gaol myself, I may extricate my friends.'

In compliance with his curiosity, I informed him of the whole train of accidents and follies that had plunged me into my present troubles, and my utter inability to get free.

After hearing my story, and pausing some minutes, he slapt his forehead, as if he had hit upon something material, and took his leave, saying he would try what could be done.

CHAPTER XXVII

The same subject continued

THE next morning I communicated to my wife and children the scheme I had planned of reforming the prisoners, which they received with universal disapprobation, alledging the impossibility and impropriety of it; adding, that my endeavours would no way contribute to their amendment, but might probably disgrace my calling.

'Excuse me,' returned I, 'these people, however fallen, are still men, and that is a very good title to my affections. Good council rejected returns to enrich the giver's bosom; and though the instruction I communicate may not mend them, yet it will assuredly mend myself. If these wretches, my children, were princes, there would be thousands ready to offer their ministry;

but, in my opinion, the heart that is buried in a dungeon is as precious as that seated upon a throne. Yes, my treasures, if I can mend them I will; perhaps they will not all despise me. Perhaps I may catch up even one from the gulph, and that will be great gain; for is there upon earth a gem so precious as the human soul?'

Thus saying, I left them, and descended to the common prison, where I found the prisoners very merry, expecting my arrival; and each prepared with some gaol trick to play upon the doctor. Thus, as I was going to begin, one turned my wig awry, as if by accident, and then asked my pardon. A second, who stood at some distance, had a knack of spitting through his teeth, which fell in showers upon my book. A third would cry amen in such an affected tone as gave the rest great delight. A fourth had slily picked my pocket of my spectacles. But there was one whose trick gave more universal pleasure than all the rest; for observing the manner in which I had disposed my books on the table before me, he very dextrously displaced one of them, and put an obscene jest-book of his own in the place. However I took no notice of all that this mischievous groupe of little beings could do; but went on, perfectly sensible that what was ridiculous in my attempt, would excite mirth only the first or second time, while what was serious would be permanent. My design succeeded, and in less than six days some were penitent, and all attentive.

It was now that I applauded my perseverance and address, at thus giving sensibility to wretches divested of every moral feeling, and now began to think of doing them temporal services also, by rendering their situation somewhat more comfortable. Their time had hitherto been divided between famine and excess, tumultous riot and bitter repining. Their only employment was quarrelling among each other, playing at cribbage, and cutting tobacco stoppers.* From this last mode of idle industry I took the hint of setting such as chose to work at cutting pegs for tobacconists and shoemakers,* the proper wood being bought by a general subscription, and when manufactured, sold by my appointment; so that each earned something every day: a trifle indeed, but sufficient to maintain him.

I did not stop here, but instituted fines for the punishment of immorality, and rewards for peculiar industry. Thus in less than a fortnight I had formed them into something social and humane, and had the pleasure of regarding myself as a legislator, who had brought men from their native ferocity into friendship and obedience.

And it were highly to be wished, that legislative power would thus direct the law rather to reformation than severity. That it would seem convinced that the work of eradicating crimes is not by making punishments familiar, but formidable. Then instead of our present prisons, which find or make men guilty, which enclose wretches for the commission of one crime, and return them, if returned alive, fitted for the perpetration of thousands; we should see, as in other parts of Europe, places of penitence and solitude, where the accused might be attended by such as could give them repentance if guilty, or new motives to virtue if innocent. And this, but not the increasing punishments, is the way to mend a state: nor can I avoid even questioning the validity of that right which social combinations have assumed of capitally punishing offences of a slight nature. In cases of murder their right is obvious, as it is the duty of us all, from the law of self-defence, to cut off that man who has shewn a disregard for the life of another. Against such, all nature arises in arms; but it is not so against him who steals my property. Natural law gives me no right to take away his life, as by that the horse he steals is as much his property as mine. If then I have any right, it must be from a compact made between us, that he who deprives the other of his horse shall die. But this is a false compact; because no man has a right to barter his life, no more than to take it away, as it is not his own. And beside, the compact is inadequate, and would be set aside even in a court of modern equity, as there is a great penalty for a very trifling convenience, since it is far better that two men should live, than that one man should ride. But a compact that is false between two men, is equally so between an hundred, or an hundred thousand; for as ten millions of circles can never make a square, so the united voice of myriads cannot lend the smallest foundation to falsehood. It is thus that reason speaks, and untutored nature says the same thing. Savages that are directed by natural law alone are very tender of the lives of each other; they seldom shed blood but to retaliate former cruelty.

Our Saxon ancestors, fierce as they were in war, had but few executions in times of peace; and in all commencing governments that have the print of nature still strong upon them, scarce any crime is held capital.

It is among the citizens of a refined community that penal laws, which are in the hands of the rich, are laid upon the poor. Government, while it grows older, seems to acquire the moroseness of age; and as if our property were become dearer in proportion as it increased, as if the more enormous our wealth, the more extensive our fears, all our possessions are paled up with new edicts every day, and hung round with gibbets to scare every invader.

I cannot tell whether it is from the number of our penal laws, or the licentiousness of our people, that this country should shew more convicts in a year, than half the dominions of Europe united. Perhaps it is owing to both; for they mutually produce each other. When by indiscriminate penal laws a nation beholds the same punishment affixed to dissimilar degrees of guilt, from perceiving no distinction in the penalty, the people are led to lose all sense of distinction in the crime, and this distinction is the bulwark of all morality: thus the multitude of laws produce new vices, and new vices call for fresh restraints.

It were to be wished then that power, instead of contriving new laws to punish vice, instead of drawing hard the cords of society till a convulsion come to burst them, instead of cutting away wretches as useless, before we have tried their utility, instead of converting correction into vengeance, it were to be wished that we tried the restrictive arts of government, and made law the protector, but not the tyrant of the people. We should then find that creatures, whose souls are held as dross, only wanted the hand of a refiner; we should then find that wretches, now stuck up for long tortures, lest luxury should feel a momentary pang, might, if properly treated, serve to sinew the state in times of danger; that, as their faces are like ours, their hearts are so too;

that few minds are so base as that perseverance cannot amend; that a man may see his last crime without dying for it; and that very little blood will serve to cement our security.

CHAPTER XXVIII

Happiness and misery rather the result of prudence than of virtue in this life. Temporal evils or felicities being regarded by heaven as things merely in themselves trifling and unworthy its care in the distribution

I HAD now been confined more than a fortnight, but had not since my arrival been visited by my dear Olivia, and I greatly longed to see her. Having communicated my wishes to my wife, the next morning the poor girl entered my apartment, leaning on her sister's arm. The change which I saw in her countenance struck me. The numberless graces that once resided there were now fled, and the hand of death seemed to have molded every feature to alarm me. Her temples were sunk, her forehead was tense, and a fatal paleness sate upon her cheek.

'I am glad to see thee, my dear,' cried I; 'but why this dejection Livy? I hope, my love, you have too great a regard for me, to permit disappointment thus to undermine a life which I prize as my own. Be chearful child, and we yet may see happier days.'

'You have ever, sir,' replied she, 'been kind to me, and it adds to my pain that I shall never have an opportunity of sharing that happiness you promise. Happiness, I fear, is no longer reserved for me here; and I long to be rid of a place where I have only found distress. Indeed, sir, I wish you would make a proper submission to Mr. Thornhill; it may, in some measure, induce him to pity you, and it will give me relief in dying.'

'Never, child,' replied I, 'never will I be brought to acknowledge my daughter a prostitute; for tho' the world may look upon your offence with scorn, let it be mine to regard it as a mark of credulity, not of guilt. My dear, I am no way miserable in this place, however dismal it may seem, and be assured that while you continue to bless me by living, he shall never have my consent to make you more wretched by marrying another.'

After the departure of my daughter, my fellow prisoner, who was by at this interview, sensibly enough expostulated upon my obstinacy, in refusing a submission, which promised to give me freedom. He observed, that the rest of my family was not to be sacrificed to the peace of one child alone, and she the only one who had offended me. 'Beside,' added he, 'I don't know if it be just thus to obstruct the union of man and wife, which you do at present, by refusing to consent to a match which you cannot hinder, but may render unhappy.'

'Sir,' replied I, 'you are unacquainted with the man that oppresses us. I am very sensible that no submission I can make could procure me liberty even for an hour. I am told that even in this very room a debtor of his, no later than last year, died for want. But though my submission and approbation could transfer me from hence, to the most beautiful apartment he is possessed of; yet I would grant neither, as something whispers me that it would be giving a sanction to adultery. While my daughter lives, no other marriage of his shall ever be legal in my eye. Were she removed, indeed, I should be the basest of men, from any resentment of my own, to attempt putting asunder those who wish for an union. No, villain as he is, I should then wish him married, to prevent the consequences of his future debaucheries. But now should I not be the most cruel of all fathers, to sign an Instrument which must send my child to the grave, merely to avoid a prison myself; and thus to escape one pang, break my child's heart with a thousand?'

He acquiesced in the justice of this answer, but could not avoid observing, that he feared my daughter's life was already too much wasted to keep me long a prisoner. 'However', continued he, 'though you refuse to submit to the nephew, I hope you have no objections to laying your case before the uncle, who has the first character in the kingdom for every thing that is just and good. I would advise you to send him a letter by the post, intimating all his nephew's ill usage, and my life for it that in three days you shall have an answer.' I thank'd him for the hint, and instantly set about complying; but I wanted paper, and unluckily all our money had been laid out that morning in provisions, however he supplied me.

For the three ensuing days I was in a state of anxiety, to know what reception my letter might meet with; but in the mean time was frequently solicited by my wife to submit to any conditions rather than remain here, and every hour received repeated accounts of the decline of my daughter's health. The third day and the fourth arrived, but I received no answer to my letter: the complaints of a stranger against a favourite nephew, were no way likely to succeed; so that these hopes soon vanished like all my former. My mind, however, still supported itself though confinement and bad air began to make a visible alteration in my health, and my arm that had suffered in the fire, grew worse. My children however sate by me, and while I was stretched on my straw, read to me by turns, or listened and wept at my instructions. But my daughter's health declined faster than mine; every message from her contributed to encrease my apprehensions and pain. The fifth morning after I had written the letter which was sent to sir William Thornhill, I was alarmed with an account that she was speechless. Now it was, that confinement was truly painful to me; my soul was bursting from its prison to be near the pillow of my child, to comfort, to strengthen her, to receive her last wishes, and teach her soul the way to heaven! Another account came. She was expiring, and yet I was debarred the small comfort of weeping by her. My fellow prisoner, some time after, came with the last account. He bade me be patient. She was dead!—The next morning he returned, and found me with my two little ones, now my only companions, who were using all their innocent efforts to comfort me. They entreated to read to me, and bade me not to cry, for I was now too old to weep. 'And is not my sister an angel, now, pappa,' cried the eldest, 'and why then are you sorry for her? I wish I were an angel out of this frightful place, if my pappa were with me.' 'Yes,' added my youngest darling, 'Heaven, where my sister is, is a finer place than this, and there are none but good people there, and the people here are very bad.'

Mr. Jenkinson interupted their harmless prattle, by observing that now my daughter was no more, I should seriously think of the rest of my family, and attempt to save my own life, which was every day declining, for want of necessaries and wholesome air. He added, that it was now incumbent on me to sacrifice any pride or resentment of my own, to the welfare of those who depended on me for support; and that I was now, both by reason and justice, obliged to try to reconcile my landlord.

'Heaven be praised,' replied I, 'there is no pride left me now, I should detest my own heart if I saw either pride or resentment lurking there. On the contrary, as my oppressor has been once my parishoner, I hope one day to present him up an unpolluted soul at the eternal tribunal. No, sir, I have no resentment now, and though he has taken from me what I held dearer than all his treasures, though he has wrung my heart, for I am sick almost to fainting, very sick, my fellow prisoner, yet that shall never inspire me with vengeance. I am now willing to approve his marriage, and if this submission can do him any pleasure, let him know, that if I have done him any injury, I am sorry for it.' Mr. Jenkinson took pen and ink, and wrote down my submission nearly as I have exprest it, to which I signed my name. My son was employed to carry the letter to Mr. Thornhill, who was then at his seat in the country. He went, and in about six hours returned with a verbal answer. He had some difficulty, he said, to get a sight of his landlord, as the servants were insolent and suspicious; but he accidentally saw him as he was going out upon business, preparing for his marriage, which was to be in three days. He continued to inform us, that he stept up in the humblest manner, and delivered the letter, which, when Mr. Thornhill had read, he said that all submission was now too late and unnecessary; that he had heard of our application to his uncle, which met with the contempt it deserved; and as for the rest, that all future applications should be directed to his attorney, not to him. He observed, however, that as he had a very good opinion of the discretion of the two young ladies, they might have been the most agreeable intercessors.

'Well, sir,' said I to my fellow prisoner, 'you now discover the temper of the man that oppresses me. He can at once be facetious and cruel; but let him use me as he will, I shall soon be free, in spite of all his bolts to restrain me. I am now drawing towards an abode that looks brighter as I approach it: this expectation cheers my afflictions, and though I leave an helpless family of orphans behind me, yet they will not be utterly forsaken; some friend, perhaps, will be found to assist them for the sake of their poor father, and some may charitably relieve them for the sake of their heavenly father.'

Just as I spoke, my wife, whom I had not seen that day before, appeared with looks of terror, and making efforts, but unable to speak. 'Why, my love,' cried I, 'why will you thus encrease my afflictions by your own, what though no submissions can turn our severe master, tho' he has doomed me to die in this place of wretchedness, and though we have lost a darling child, yet still you will find comfort in your other children when I shall be no more.' 'We have indeed lost,' returned she, 'a darling child. My Sophia, my dearest, is gone, snatched from us, carried off by ruffians!'

'How, madam,' cried my fellow prisoner, 'miss Sophia carried off by villains, sure it cannot be?'

She could only answer with a fixed look and a flood of tears. But one of the prisoners wives, who was present, and came in with her, gave us a more distinct account: she informed us that as my wife, my daughter, and herself, were taking a walk together on the great road a little way out of the village, a post-chaise and pair drove up to them and instantly stopt. Upon which, a well drest man, but not Mr. Thornhill, stepping out, clasped my daughter round the waist, and forcing her in, bid the postilion drive on, so that they were out of sight in a moment.

'Now,' cried I, 'the sum of my misery is made up, nor is it in the power of any thing on earth to give me another pang. What! not one left! not to leave me one! the monster! the child that was next my heart! she had the beauty of an angel, and almost the wisdom of an angel. But support that woman, nor let her fall. Not to leave me one!'—'Alas! my husband,' said my wife, 'you seem to want comfort even more than I. Our distresses are great; but I could bear this and more, if I saw you but easy. They may take away my children and all the world, if they leave me but you.'

My Son, who was present, endeavoured to moderate our grief; he bade us take comfort, for he hoped that we might still have reason to be thankful.—'My child,' cried I, 'look round the world, and see if there be any happiness left me now. Is not every ray of comfort shut out; while all our bright prospects only lie beyond the grave!'—'My dear father,' returned he, 'I hope there is still something that will give you an interval of satisfaction; for I have a letter from my brother George'—'What of him, child,' interrupted I, 'does he know of our misery. I hope my boy is exempt from any part of what his wretched family suffers?'— 'Yes, sir,' returned he, 'he is perfectly gay, chearful, and happy. His letter brings nothing but good news; he is the favourite of his colonel, who promises to procure him the very next lieutenancy that becomes vacant!'

'And are you sure of all this,' cried my wife, 'are you sure that nothing ill has befallen my boy?'—'Nothing indeed, madam,' returned my son, 'you shall see the letter, which will give you the highest pleasure; and if any thing can procure you comfort, I am sure that will.' 'But are you sure,' still repeated she, 'that the letter is from himself, and that he is really so happy?'—'Yes, Madam,' replied he, 'it is certainly his, and he will one day be the credit and the support of our family!'—'Then I thank providence,' cried she, 'that my last letter to him has miscarried.' 'Yes, my dear,' continued she, turning to me, 'I will now confess that though the hand of heaven is sore upon us in other instances, it has been favourable here. By the last letter I wrote my son, which was in the bitterness of anger, I desired him, upon his mother's blessing, and if he had the heart of a man, to see justice done his father and sister, and avenge our cause. But thanks be to him that directs all things, it has miscarried, and I am at rest.' 'Woman,' cried I, 'thou hast done very ill, and at another time my reproaches might have been more severe. Oh! what a tremendous gulph hast thou escaped, that would have buried both thee and him in endless ruin. Providence, indeed, has here been kinder to us than we to ourselves. It has reserved that son to be the father and protector of my children when I shall be away. How unjustly did I complain of being stript of every comfort, when still I hear that he is happy and insensible of our afflictions; still kept in reserve to support his widowed mother, and to protect his brothers and sisters. But what sisters has he left, he has no sisters now, they are all gone, robbed from me, and I am undone.'—'Father,' interrupted my son, 'I beg you will give me leave to read this letter, I know it will please you.' Upon which, with my permission, he read as follows:

Honoured Sir,

I have called off my imagination a few moments from the pleasures that surround me, to fix it upon objects that are still more pleasing, the dear little fire-side at home. My fancy draws that harmless groupe as listening to every line of this with great composure. I view those faces with delight which never felt the deforming hand of ambition or distress! But whatever your happiness may be at home, I am sure it will be some addition to it, to hear that I am perfectly pleased with my situation, and every way happy here.

Our regiment is countermanded and is not to leave the kingdom; the colonel, who professes himself my friend, takes me with him to all companies where he is acquainted, and after my first visit I generally find myself received with encreased respect upon repeating it. I danced last night with Lady G——, and could I forget you know whom, I might be perhaps successful. But it is my fate still to remember others, while I am myself forgotten by most of my absent friends, and in this number, I fear, Sir, that I must consider you; for I have long expected the pleasure of a letter from home to no purpose. Olivia and Sophia too, promised to write, but seem to have forgotten me. Tell them they are two arrant little baggages, and that I am this moment in a most violent passion with them: yet still, I know not how, tho' I want to bluster a little, my heart is respondent only to softer emotions. Then tell them, sir, that after all, I love them affectionately, and be assured of my ever remaining

Your dutiful son.

'In all our miseries,' cried I, 'what thanks have we not to return, that one at least of our family is exempted from what we suffer. Heaven be his guard, and keep my boy thus happy to be the supporter of his widowed mother, and the father of these two babes, which is all the patrimony I can now bequeath him. May he keep their innocence from the temptations of want, and be their conductor in the paths of honour.' I had scarce said these words, when a noise, like that of a tumult, seemed to proceed from the prison below; it died away soon after, and a clanking of fetters was heard along the passage that led to my apartment. The keeper of the prison entered, holding a man all bloody, wounded and fettered with the heaviest irons. I looked with compassion on the wretch as he approached me, but with horror when I found it was my own son.—'My George! My George! and do I behold thee thus. Wounded! Fettered! Is this thy happiness! Is this the manner you return to me! O that this sight could break my heart at once and let me die!'

'Where, Sir, is your fortitude,' returned my son with an intrepid voice. 'I must suffer, my life is forfeited, and let them take it.'

I tried to restrain my passions for a few minutes in silence, but I thought I should have died with the effort—'O my boy, my heart weeps to behold thee thus, and I cannot, cannot help it. In the moment that I thought thee blest, and prayed for thy safety, to behold thee thus again! Chained, wounded. And yet the death of the youthful is happy. But I am old, a very old man, and have lived to see this day. To see my children all untimely falling about me, while I continue a wretched survivor in the midst of ruin! May all the curses that ever sunk a soul fall heavy upon the murderer of my children. May he live, like me, to see—'

'Hold, Sir,' replied my son, 'or I shall blush for thee. How, Sir, forgetful of your age, your holy calling, thus to arrogate the justice of heaven, and fling those curses upward that must soon descend to crush thy own grey head with destruction! No, Sir, let it be your care now to fit me for that vile death I must shortly suffer, to arm me with hope and resolution, to give me courage to drink of that bitterness which must shortly be my portion.'

'My child, you must not die: I am sure no offence of thine can deserve so vile a punishment. My George could never be guilty of any crime to make his ancestors ashamed of him.'

'Mine, Sir,' returned my son, 'is, I fear, an unpardonable one. When I received my mother's letter from home, I immediately came down, determined to punish the betrayer of our honour, and sent him an order to meet me, which he answered, not in person, but by his dispatching four of his domestics to seize me. I wounded one who first assaulted me, and I fear desperately, but the rest made me their prisoner. The coward is determined to put the law in execution against me, the proofs are undeniable, I have sent a challenge, and as I am the first transgressor upon the statute,* I see no hopes of pardon. But you have often charmed me with your lessons of fortitude, let me now, Sir, find them in your example.'

'And, my son, you shall find them. I am now raised above this world, and all the pleasures it can produce. From this moment I break from my heart all the ties that held it down to earth, and will prepare to fit us both for eternity. Yes, my son, I will point out the way, and my soul shall guide yours in the ascent, for we will take our flight together. I now see and am convinced you can expect no pardon here, and I can only exhort you to seek it at that greatest tribunal where we both shall shortly answer. But let us not be niggardly in our exhortation, but let all our fellow prisoners have a share: good gaoler let them be permitted to stand here, while I attempt to improve them.' Thus saying, I made an effort to rise from my straw, but wanted strength, and was able only to recline against the wall. The prisoners assembled according to my directions, for they loved to hear my council, my son and his mother supported me on either side, I looked and saw that none were wanting, and then addressed them with the following exhortation.

CHAPTER XXIX

*The equal dealings of providence demonstrated with regard
to the happy and the miserable here below. That from the
nature of pleasure and pain, the wretched must be repaid
the balance of their sufferings in the life hereafter*

MY friends, my children, and fellow sufferers, when I reflect on
the distribution of good and evil here below, I find that much has
been given man to enjoy, yet still more to suffer.* Though we
should examine the whole world, we shall not find one man so
happy as to have nothing left to wish for; but we daily see thousands who by suicide shew us they have nothing left to hope. In
this life then it appears that we cannot be entirely blest; but yet we
may be completely miserable!

Why man should thus feel pain, why our wretchedness should
be requisite in the formation of universal felicity, why, when all
other systems are made perfect by the perfection of their subordinate parts, the great system should require for its perfection,
parts that are not only subordinate to others, but imperfect in
themselves? These are questions that never can be explained, and
might be useless if known. On this subject providence has thought
fit to elude our curiosity, satisfied with granting us motives to
consolation.

In this situation, man has called in the friendly assistance of
philosophy, and heaven seeing the incapacity of that to console
him, has given him the aid of religion. The consolations of philosophy are very amusing, but often fallacious. It tells us that life is
filled with comforts, if we will but enjoy them; and on the other
hand, that though we unavoidably have miseries here, life is short,
and they will soon be over. Thus do these consolations destroy
each other; for if life is a place of comfort, its shortness must be
misery, and if it be long, our griefs are protracted. Thus philosophy is weak; but religion comforts in an higher strain. Man
is here, it tells us, fitting up his mind, and preparing it for another
abode. When the good man leaves the body and is all a glorious

mind, he will find he has been making himself a heaven of happiness here, while the wretch that has been maimed and contaminated by his vices, shrinks from his body with terror, and finds that he has anticipated the vengeance of heaven. To religion then we must hold in every circumstance of life for our truest comfort; for if already we are happy, it is a pleasure to think that we can make that happiness unending, and if we are miserable, it is very consoling to think that there is a place of rest. Thus to the fortunate religion holds out a continuance of bliss, to the wretched a change from pain.

But though religion is very kind to all men, it has promised peculiar rewards to the unhappy; the sick, the naked, the houseless, the heavy-laden, and the prisoner, have ever most frequent promises in our sacred law. The author of our religion every where professes himself the wretch's friend, and unlike the false ones of this world, bestows all his caresses upon the forlorn. The unthinking have censured this as partiality, as a preference without merit to deserve it. But they never reflect that it is not in the power even of heaven itself to make the offer of unceasing felicity as great a gift to the happy as to the miserable. To the first eternity is but a single blessing, since at most it but encreases what they already possess. To the latter it is a double advantage; for it diminishes their pain here, and rewards them with heavenly bliss hereafter.

But providence is in another respect kinder to the poor than the rich; for as it thus makes the life after death more desirable, so it smooths the passage there. The wretched have had a long familiarity with every face of terror. The man of sorrow lays himself quietly down, without possessions to regret, and but few ties to stop his departure: he feels only nature's pang in the final separation, and this is no way greater than he has often fainted under before; for after a certain degree of pain, every new breach that death opens in the constitution, nature kindly covers with insensibility.

Thus providence has given the wretched two advantages over the happy in this life, greater felicity in dying, and in heaven all that superiority of pleasure which arises from contrasted enjoyment.

And this superiority, my friends, is no small advantage, and seems to be one of the pleasures of the poor man in the parable,* for though he was already in heaven, and felt all the raptures it could give, yet it was mentioned as an addition to his happiness, that he had once been wretched and now was comforted, that he had known what it was to be miserable, and now felt what it was to be happy.

Thus, my friends, you see religion does what philosophy could never do: it shews the equal dealings of heaven to the happy and the unhappy, and levels all human enjoyments to nearly the same standard. It gives to both rich and poor the same happiness hereafter, and equal hopes to aspire after it; but if the rich have the advantage of enjoying pleasure here, the poor have the endless satisfaction of knowing what it was once to be miserable, when crowned with endless felicity hereafter; and even though this should be called a small advantage, yet being an eternal one, it must make up by duration what the temporal happiness of the great may have exceeded by intenseness.

These are therefore the consolations which the wretched have peculiar to themselves, and in which they are above the rest of mankind; in other respects they are below them. They who would know the miseries of the poor must see life and endure it. To declaim on the temporal advantages they enjoy, is only repeating what none either believe or practise. The men who have the necessaries of living are not poor, and they who want them must be miserable. Yes, my friends, we must be miserable. No vain efforts of a refined imagination can sooth the wants of nature, can give elastic sweetness to the dank vapour of a dungeon, or ease to the throbbings of a broken heart. Let the philosopher from his couch of softness tell us that we can resist all these. Alas! the effort by which we resist them is still the greatest pain! Death is slight, and any man may sustain it; but torments are dreadful, and these no man can endure.

To us then, my friends, the promises of happiness in heaven should be peculiarly dear; for if our reward be in this life alone, we are then indeed of all men the most miserable. When I look round these gloomy walls, made to terrify, as well as to confine us;

this light that only serves to shew the horrors of the place, those shackles that tyranny has imposed, or crime made necessary; when I survey these emaciated looks, and hear those groans, O my friends, what a glorious exchange would heaven be for these. To fly through regions unconfined as air, to bask in the sunshine of eternal bliss, to carrol over endless hymns of praise, to have no master to threaten or insult us, but the form of goodness himself for ever in our eyes, when I think of these things, death becomes the messenger of very glad tidings; when I think of these things, his sharpest arrow becomes the staff of my support; when I think of these things, what is there in life worth having; when I think of these things, what is there that should not be spurned away: kings in their palaces should groan for such advantages; but we, humbled as we are, should yearn for them.

And shall these things be ours? Ours they will certainly be if we but try for them; and what is a comfort, we are shut out from many temptations that would retard our pursuit. Only let us try for them, and they will certainly be ours, and what is still a comfort, shortly too; for if we look back on past life, it appears but a very short span, and whatever we may think of the rest of life, it will yet be found of less duration; as we grow older, the days seem to grow shorter, and our intimacy with time, ever lessens the perception of his stay. Then let us take comfort now, for we shall soon be at our journey's end; we shall soon lay down the heavy burthen laid by heaven upon us, and though death, the only friend of the wretched, for a little while mocks the weary traveller with the view, and like his horizon, still flies before him; yet the time will certainly and shortly come, when we shall cease from our toil; when the luxurious great ones of the world shall no more tread us to the earth; when we shall think with pleasure on our sufferings below; when we shall be surrounded with all our friends, or such as deserved our friendship; when our bliss shall be unutterable, and still, to crown all, unending.

CHAPTER XXX

*Happier prospects begin to appear. Let us be inflexible, and
fortune will at last change in our favour*

WHEN I had thus finished and my audience was retired, the
gaoler, who was one of the most humane of his profession, hoped
I would not be displeased, as what he did was but his duty,
observing that he must be obliged to remove my son into a
stronger cell, but that he should be permitted to revisit me every
morning. I thanked him for his clemency, and grasping my boy's
hand, bade him farewell, and be mindful of the great duty that
was before him.

I again, therefore laid me down, and one of my little ones sate
by my beside reading, when Mr. Jenkinson entering, informed me
that there was news of my daughter; for that she was seen by a
person about two hours before in a strange gentleman's company,
and that they had stopt at a neighbouring village for refreshment,
and seemed as if returning to town. He had scarce delivered this
news, when the gaoler came with looks of haste and pleasure, to
inform me, that my daughter was found. Moses came running in
a moment after, crying out that his sister Sophy was below and
coming up with our old friend Mr. Burchell.

Just as he delivered this news my dearest girl entered, and with
looks almost wild with pleasure, ran to kiss me in a transport of
affection. Her mother's tears and silence also shewed her pleasure.—'Here, pappa,' cried the charming girl, 'here is the brave
man to whom I owe my delivery; to this gentleman's intrepidity I
am indebted for my happiness and safety—' A kiss from Mr.
Burchell, whose pleasure seemed even greater than hers, interrupted what she was going to add.

'Ah, Mr. Burchell,' cried I, 'this is but a wretched habitation
you now find us in; and we are now very different from what
you last saw us. You were ever our friend: we have long discovered
our errors with regard to you, and repented of our ingratitude.
After the vile usage you then received at my hands, I am almost

ashamed to behold your face; yet I hope you'll forgive me, as I was deceived by a base ungenerous wretch, who, under the mask of friendship, has undone me.'

'It is impossible,' replied Mr. Burchell, 'that I should forgive you, as you never deserved my resentment. I partly saw your delusion then, and as it was out of my power to restrain, I could only pity it!'

'It was ever my conjecture,' cried I, 'that your mind was noble; but now I find it so. But tell me, my dear child, how hast thou been relieved, or who the ruffians were who carried thee away?'

'Indeed, Sir,' replied she, 'as to the villain who brought me off, I am yet ignorant. For as my mamma and I were walking out, he came behind us, and almost before I could call for help, forced me into the post-chaise, and in an instant the horses drove away. I met several on the road, to whom I cried out for assistance; but they disregarded my entreaties. In the mean time the ruffian himself used every art to hinder me from crying out: he flattered and threatened by turns, and swore that if I continued but silent, he intended no harm. In the mean time I had broken the canvas that he had drawn up, and whom should I perceive at some distance but your old friend Mr. Burchell, walking along with his usual swiftness, with the great stick for which we used so much to ridicule him. As soon as we came within hearing, I called out to him by name, and entreated his help. I repeated my exclamations several times, upon which, with a very loud voice, he bid the postillion stop; but the boy took no notice, but drove on with still greater speed. I now thought he could never overtake us, when in less than a minute I saw Mr. Burchell come running up by the side of the horses, and with one blow knock the postillion to the ground. The horses when he was fallen soon stopt of themselves, and the ruffians stepping out, with oaths and menaces drew his sword, and ordered him at his peril to retire; but Mr. Burchell running up, shivered his sword to pieces, and then pursued him for near a quarter of a mile; but he made his escape. I was at this time come out myself, willing to assist my deliverer; but he soon returned to me in triumph. The postillion, who was recovered, was going to make his escape too; but Mr. Burchell ordered him at his peril to mount again, and drive back to town. Finding it impossible to resist, he reluctantly complied, though the wound he had received seemed, to me at least, to be dangerous. He continued to complain of the pain as we drove along, so that he at last excited Mr. Burchell's compassion, who, at my request, exchanged him for another at an inn where we called on our return.'

'Welcome then,' cried I, 'my child, and thou her gallant deliverer, a thousand welcomes. Though our chear is but wretched, yet our hearts are ready to receive you. And now, Mr. Burchell, as you have delivered my girl, if you think her a recompence she is yours, if you can stoop to an alliance with a family so poor as mine, take her, obtain her consent, as I know you have her heart, and you have mine. And let me tell you, Sir, that I give you no small treasure, she has been celebrated for beauty it is true, but that is not my meaning, I give you up a treasure in her mind.'

'But I suppose, Sir,' cried Mr. Burchell, 'that you are apprized of my circumstances, and of my incapacity to support her as she deserves?'

'If your present objection,' replied I, 'be meant as an evasion of my offer, I desist: but I know no man so worthy to deserve her as you; and if I could give her thousands, and thousands sought her from me, yet my honest brave Burchell should be my dearest choice.'

To all this his silence alone seemed to give a mortifying refusal, and without the least reply to my offer, he demanded if we could not be furnished with refreshments from the next inn, to which being answered in the affirmative, he ordered them to send in the best dinner that could be provided upon such short notice. He bespoke also a dozen of their best wine; and some cordials for me. Adding, with a smile, that he would stretch a little for once, and tho' in a prison, asserted he was never better disposed to be merry. The waiter soon made his appearance with preparations for dinner, a table was lent us by the gaoler, who seemed remarkably assiduous, the wine was disposed in order, and two very well-drest dishes were brought in.

My daughter had not yet heard of her poor brother's melancholy situation, and we all seemed unwilling to damp her chearfulness by the relation. But it was in vain that I attempted to appear chearful, the circumstances of my unfortunate son broke through all efforts to dissemble; so that I was at last obliged to damp our mirth by relating his misfortunes, and wishing that he might be permitted to share with us in this little interval of satisfaction. After my guests were recovered from the consternation my account had produced, I requested also that Mr. Jenkinson, a fellow prisoner, might be admitted, and the gaoler granted my request with an air of unusual submission. The clanking of my son's irons was no sooner heard along the passage, than his sister ran impatiently to meet him; while Mr. Burchell, in the mean time, asked me if my son's name were George, to which replying in the affirmative, he still continued silent. As soon as my boy entered the room, I could perceive he regarded Mr. Burchell with a look of astonishment and reverence. 'Come on,' cried I, 'my son, though we are fallen very low, yet providence has been pleased to grant us some small relaxation from pain. Thy sister is restored to us, and there is her deliverer: to that brave man it is that I am indebted for yet having a daughter, give him, my boy, the hand of friendship, he deserves our warmest gratitude.'

My son seemed all this while regardless of what I said, and still continued fixed at respectful distance.—'My dear brother,' cried his sister, 'why don't you thank my good deliverer; the brave should ever love each other.'

He still continued his silence and astonishment, till our guest at last perceived himself to be known, and assuming all his native dignity, desired my son to come forward. Never before had I seen any thing so truly majestic as the air he assumed upon this occasion. The greatest object in the universe, says a certain philosopher,* is a good man struggling with adversity; yet there is still a greater, which is the good man that comes to relieve it. After he had regarded my son for some time with a superior air, 'I again find,' said he, 'unthinking boy, that the same crime—' But here he was interrupted by one of the gaoler's servants, who came to inform us that a person of distinction, who had driven into town with a chariot and several attendants, sent his respects to the gentlemen that was with us, and begged to know when he should think proper to be waited upon.—'Bid the fellow wait,' cried our guest, 'till I shall have leisure to receive him;' and then turning to my son, 'I again find, Sir,' proceeded he, 'that you are guilty of the same offence for which you once had my reproof, and for which the law is now preparing its justest punishments. You imagine, perhaps, that a contempt for your own life, gives you a right to take that of another: but where, Sir, is the difference between a duelist who hazards a life of no value, and the murderer who acts with greater security? Is it any diminution of the game-ster's fraud when he alledges that he has staked a counter?'*

'Alas, Sir,' cried I, 'whoever you are, pity the poor misguided creature; for what he has done was in obedience to a deluded mother, who in the bitterness of her resentment required him upon her blessing to avenge her quarrel. Here, Sir, is the letter, which will serve to convince you of her imprudence and diminish his guilt.'

He took the letter, and hastily read it over. 'This,' says he, 'though not a perfect excuse, is such a palliation of his fault, as induces me to forgive him. And now, Sir,' continued he, kindly taking my son by the hand, 'I see you are surprised at finding me here; but I have often visited prisons upon occasions less interest-ing. I am now come to see justice done a worthy man, for whom I have the most sincere esteem. I have long been a disguised specta-tor of thy father's benevolence. I have at his little dwelling enjoyed respect uncontaminated by flattery, and have received that happiness that courts could not give, from the amusing sim-plicity around his fire-side. My nephew has been apprized of my intentions of coming here, and I find is arrived; it would be wronging him and you to condemn him without examination: if there be injury, there shall be redress; and this I may say without boasting, that none have ever taxed the injustice of Sir William Thornhill.'*

We now found the personage whom we had so long entertained as an harmless amusing companion was no other than the cele-brated Sir William Thornhill, to whose virtues and singularities scarce any were strangers. The poor Mr. Burchell was in reality a man of large fortune and great interest, to whom senates listened with applause, and whom party heard with conviction; who was the friend of his country, but loyal to his king. My poor wife recollecting her former familiarity, seemed to shrink with apprehension; but Sophia, who a few moments before thought him her own, now perceiving the immense distance to which he was removed by fortune, was unable to conceal her tears.

'Ah, Sir,' cried my wife, with a piteous aspect, 'how is it possible that I can ever have your forgiveness; the slights you received from me the last time I had the honour of seeing you at our house, and the jokes which I audaciously threw out, these jokes, Sir, I fear can never be forgiven.'

'My dear good lady,' returned he with a smile, 'if you had your joke, I had my answer: I'll leave it to all the company if mine were not as good as yours. To say the truth, I know no body whom I am disposed to be angry with at present but the fellow who so frighted my little girl here. I had not even time to examine the rascal's person so as to describe him in an advertisement. Can you tell me, Sophia, my dear, whether you should know him again?'

'Indeed, Sir,' replied she, 'I can't be positive; yet now I recollect he had a large mark over one of his eye-brows.' 'I ask pardon, madam,' interrupted Jenkinson, who was by, 'but be so good as to inform me if the fellow wore his own red hair?'—'Yes, I think so,' cried Sophia.—'And did your honour,' continued he, turning to Sir William, 'observe the length of his legs?'—'I can't be sure of their length,' cried the Baronet, 'but I am convinced of their swiftness; for he outran me, which is what I thought few men in the kingdom could have done.'—'Please your honour,' cried Jenkinson, 'I know the man: it is certainly the same; the best runner in England; he has beaten Pinwire of Newcastle,* Timothy Baxter is his name, I know him perfectly, and the very place of his retreat this moment. If your honour will bid Mr. Gaoler let two of his men go with me, I'll engage to produce him to you in an hour at farthest.' Upon this the gaoler was called, who instantly appearing, Sir William demanded if he knew him. 'Yes, please your honour,' reply'd the gaoler, 'I know Sir William Thornhill well, and every body that knows any thing of him, will desire to know more of him.'—'Well then,' said the Baronet, 'my request is, that you will permit this man and two of your servants to go upon a message by my authority, and as I am in the commission of the peace, I undertake to secure you.'—'Your promise is sufficient,' replied the other, 'and you may at a minute's warning send them over England whenever your honour thinks fit.'

In pursuance of the gaoler's compliance, Jenkinson was dispatched in search of Timothy Baxter, while we were amused with the assiduity of our youngest boy Bill, who had just come in and climbed up to Sir William's neck in order to kiss him. His mother was immediately going to chastise his familiarity, but the worthy man prevented her; and taking the child, all ragged as he was, upon his knee, 'What, Bill, you chubby rogue,' cried he, 'do you remember your old friend Burchell; and Dick too, my honest veteran, are you here, you shall find I have not forgot you.' So saying, he gave each a large piece of gingerbread, which the poor fellows eat very heartily, as they had got that morning but a very scanty breakfast.

We now sate down to dinner, which was almost cold; but previously, my arm still continuing painful, Sir William wrote a prescription, for he had made the study of physic his amusement, and was more than moderately skilled in the profession: this being sent to an apothecary who lived in the place, my arm was dressed, and I found almost instantaneous relief. We were waited upon at dinner by the gaoler himself, who was willing to do our guest all the honour in his power. But before we had well dined, another message was brought from his nephew, desiring permission to appear, in order to vindicate his innocence and honour, with which request the Baronet complied, and desired Mr. Thornhill to be introduced.

CHAPTER XXXI

Former benevolence now repaid with unexpected interest

MR. Thornhill made his entrance with a smile, which he seldom wanted, and was going to embrace his uncle, which the other repulsed with an air of disdain. 'No fawning, Sir, at present,' cried the Baronet, with a look of severity, 'the only way to my heart is by the road of honour; but here I only see complicated instances of falsehood, cowardice, and oppression. How is it, Sir, that this poor man, for whom I know you professed a friendship, is used thus hardly? His daughter vilely seduced, as a recompence for his hospitality, and he himself thrown into a prison perhaps but for resenting the insult? His son too, whom you feared to face as a man—'

'Is it possible, Sir,' interrupted his nephew, 'that my uncle could object that as a crime which his repeated instructions alone have persuaded me to avoid.'

'Your rebuke,' cried Sir William, 'is just; you have acted in this instance prudently and well, though not quite as your father would have done: my brother indeed was the soul of honour; but thou—yes you have acted in this instance perfectly right, and it has my warmest approbation.'

'And I hope,' said his nephew, 'that the rest of my conduct will not be found to deserve censure. I appeared, Sir, with this gentleman's daughter at some places of public amusement; thus what was levity, scandal called by a harsher name, and it was reported that I had debauched her. I waited on her father in person, willing to clear the thing to his satisfaction, and he received me only with insult and abuse. As for the rest, with regard to his being here, my attorney and steward can best inform you, as I commit the management of business entirely to them. If he has contracted debts and is unwilling or even unable to pay them, it is their business to proceed in this manner, and I see no hardship or injustice in pursuing the most legal means of redress.'

'If this,' cried Sir William, 'be as you have stated it, there is nothing unpardonable in your offence, and though your conduct might have been more generous in not suffering this gentleman to be oppressed by subordinate tyranny, yet it has been at least equitable.'*

'He cannot contradict a single particular,' replied the 'Squire, 'I defy him to do so, and several of my servants are ready to attest what I say. Thus, Sir,' continued he, finding that I was silent, for in fact I could not contradict him, 'thus, Sir, my own innocence is vindicated; but though at your entreaty I am ready to forgive this gentleman every other offence, yet his attempts to lessen me in your esteem, excite a resentment that I cannot govern. And this too at a time when his son was actually preparing to take away my life; this, I say, was such guilt, that I am determined to let the law take its course. I have here the challenge that was sent me and two witnesses to prove it; one of my servants has been wounded dangerously, and even though my uncle himself should dissuade me, which I know he will not, yet I will see public justice done, and he shall suffer for it.'

'Thou monster,' cried my wife, 'hast thou not had vengeance enough already, but must my poor boy feel thy cruelty. I hope that good Sir William will protect us, for my son is as innocent as a child; I am sure he is, and never did harm to man.'

'Madam,' replied the good man, 'your wishes for his safety are not greater than mine; but I am sorry to find his guilt too plain; and if my nephew persists—' But the appearance of Jenkinson and the gaoler's two servants now called off our attention, who entered, haling in a tall man, very genteelly drest, and answering the description already given of the ruffian who had carried off my daughter—'Here,' cried Jenkinson, pulling him in, 'here we have him, and if ever there was a candidate for Tyburn,* this is one.'

The moment Mr. Thornhill perceived the prisoner, and Jenkinson, who had him in custody, he seemed to shrink back with terror. His face became pale with conscious guilt, and he would have withdrawn; but Jenkinson, who perceived his design, stopt him—'What, 'Squire,' cried he, 'are you ashamed of your two old acquaintances, Jenkinson and Baxter: but this is the way that all great men forget their friends, though I am resolved we will not forget you. Our prisoner, please your honour,' continued he, turning to Sir William, 'has already confessed all. This is the gentleman reported to be so dangerously wounded: He declares that it was Mr. Thornhill who first put him upon this affair, that he gave him the cloaths he now wears to appear like a gentleman, and furnished him with the post-chaise. The plan was laid between them that he should carry off the young lady to a place of safety, and that there he should threaten and terrify her; but Mr. Thornhill was to come in in the mean time, as if by accident, to her rescue, and that they should fight awhile and then he was to run off, by which Mr. Thornhill would have the better opportunity of gaining her affections himself under the character of her defender.'

Sir William remembered the coat to have been frequently worn by his nephew, and all the rest the prisoner himself confirmed by a more circumstantial account; concluding, that Mr. Thornhill had often declared to him that he was in love with both sisters at the same time.

'Heavens,' cried Sir William, 'what a viper have I been fostering in my bosom! And so fond of public justice too as he seemed to be. But he shall have it; secure him, Mr. Gaoler—yet hold, I fear there is not legal evidence to detain him.'

Upon this, Mr. Thornhill, with the utmost humility, entreated that two such abandoned wretches might not be admitted as evidences against him, but that his servants should be examined.— 'Your servants,' replied Sir William, 'wretch, call them yours no longer: but come let us hear what those fellows have to say, let his butler be called.'

When the butler was introduced, he soon perceived by his former master's looks that all his power was now over. 'Tell me,' cried Sir William sternly, 'have you ever seen your master and that fellow drest up in his cloaths in company together?' 'Yes, please your honour,' cried the butler, 'a thousand times: he was the man that always brought him his ladies.'—'How,' interrupted young Mr. Thornhill, 'this to my face!'—'Yes,' replied the butler, 'or to any man's face. To tell you a truth, Master Thornhill, I never either loved you or liked you, and I don't care if I tell you now a piece of my mind.'—'Now then,' cried Jenkinson, 'tell his honour whether you know any thing of me.'—'I can't say,' replied the butler, 'that I know much good of you. The night that gentleman's daughter was deluded to our house, you were one of them.'—'So then,' cried Sir William, 'I find you have brought a very fine witness to prove your innocence: thou stain to humanity! to associate with such wretches!' (But continuing his examination) 'You tell me, Mr. Butler, that this was the person who brought him this old gentleman's daughter.'—'No, please your honour,' replied the butler, 'he did not bring her, for the 'Squire himself undertook that business; but he brought the priest that pretended to marry them.'—'It is but too true,' cried Jenkinson, 'I cannot deny it, that was the employment assigned me, and I confess it to my confusion.'

'Good heavens!' exclaimed the Baronet, 'how every new discovery of his villainy alarms me. All his guilt is now too plain, and I find his present prosecution was dictated by tyranny, cowardice and revenge; at my request, Mr. Gaoler, set this young officer, now your prisoner, free, and trust to me for the consequences. I'll make it my business to set the affair in a proper light to my friend the magistrate who has committed him. But where is the unfortunate young lady herself: let her appear to confront this wretch, I long to know by what arts he has seduced her honour. Entreat her to come in. Where is she?'

'Ah, Sir,' said I, 'that question stings me to the heart: I was once indeed happy in a daughter, but her miseries—' Another interruption here prevented me; for who should make her appearance but Miss Arabella Wilmot, who was next day to have been married to Mr. Thornhill. Nothing could equal her surprize at seeing Sir William and his nephew here before her; for her arrival was quite accidental. It happened that she and the old gentleman her father were passing through the town, on their way to her aunt's, who had insisted that her nuptials with Mr. Thornhill should be consummated at her house; but stopping for refreshment, they put up at an inn at the other end of the town. It was there from the window that the young lady happened to observe one of my little boys playing in the street, and instantly sending a footman to bring the child to her, she learnt from him some account of our misfortunes; but was still kept ignorant of young Mr. Thornhill's being the cause. Though her father made several remonstrances on the impropriety of going to a prison to visit us, yet they were ineffectual; she desired the child to conduct her, which he did, and it was thus she surprised us at a juncture so unexpected.

Nor can I go on, without a reflection on those accidental meetings, which, though they happen every day, seldom excite our surprize but upon some extraordinary occasion. To what a fortuitous concurrence do we not owe every pleasure and convenience of our lives. How many seeming accidents must unite before we can be cloathed or fed. The peasant must be disposed to labour, the shower must fall, the wind fill the merchant's sail, or numbers must want the usual supply.

We all continued silent for some moments, while my charming pupil, which was the name I generally gave this young lady, united in her looks compassion and astonishment, which gave new finishings to her beauty. 'Indeed, my dear Mr. Thornhill,' cried she to the 'Squire, who she supposed was come here to succour and not to oppress us, 'I take it a little unkindly that you should come here without me, or never inform me of the situation of a family so dear to us both: you know I should take as much pleasure in contributing to the relief of my reverend old master here, whom I shall ever esteem, as you can. But I find that, like your uncle, you take a pleasure in doing good in secret.'

'He find pleasure in doing good!' cried Sir William, interrupting her. 'No, my dear, his pleasures are as base as he is. You see in him, madam, as complete a villain as ever disgraced humanity. A wretch, who after having deluded this poor man's daughter, after plotting against the innocence of her sister, has thrown the father into prison, and the eldest son into fetters, because he had courage to face his betrayer. And give me leave, madam, now to congratulate you upon an escape from the embraces of such a monster.'

'O goodness,' cried the lovely girl, 'how have I been deceived! Mr. Thornhill informed me for certain that this gentleman's eldest son, Captain Primrose, was gone off to America with his new-married lady.'

'My sweetest miss,' cried my wife, 'he has told you nothing but falsehoods. My son George never left the kingdom, nor never was married. Tho' you have forsaken him, he has always loved you too well to think of any body else; and I have heard him say he would die a batchellor for your sake.' She then proceeded to expatiate upon the sincerity of her son's passion, she set his duel with Mr. Thornhill in a proper light, from thence she made a rapid digression to the 'Squire's debaucheries, his pretended marriages, and ended with a most insulting picture of his cowardice.

'Good heavens!' cried Miss Wilmot, 'how very near have I been to the brink of ruin! But how great is my pleasure to have escaped it! Ten thousand falsehoods has this gentleman told me! He had at last art enough to persuade me that my promise to the only man I esteemed was no longer binding, since he had been unfaithful. By his falsehoods I was taught to detest one equally brave and generous!'

But by this time my son was freed from the incumbrances of justice, as the person supposed to be wounded was detected to be an impostor. Mr. Jenkinson also, who had acted as his valet de chambre, had dressed up his hair, and furnished him with whatever was necessary to make a genteel appearance. He now therefore entered, handsomely drest in his regimentals, and, without vanity, (for I am above it) he appeared as handsome a fellow as ever wore a military dress. As he entered, he made Miss Wilmot a modest and distant bow, for he was not as yet acquainted with the change which the eloquence of his mother had wrought in his favour. But no decorums could restrain the impatience of his blushing mistress to be forgiven. Her tears, her looks, all contributed to discover the real sensations of her heart for having forgotten her former promise and having suffered herself to be deluded by an impostor. My son appeared amazed at her condescension, and could scarce believe it real.—'Sure, madam,' cried he, 'this is but delusion! I can never have merited this! To be blest thus is to be too happy.'—'No, Sir,' replied she, 'I have been deceived, basely deceived, else nothing could have ever made me unjust to my promise. You know my friendship, you have long known it; but forget what I have done, and as you once had my warmest vows of constancy, you shall now have them repeated; and be assured that if your Arabella cannot be yours, she shall never be another's.'— 'And no other's you shall be,' cried Sir William, 'if I have any influence with your father.'

This hint was sufficient for my son Moses, who immediately flew to the inn where the old gentleman was, to inform him of every circumstance that had happened. But in the mean time the 'Squire perceiving that he was on every side undone, now finding that no hopes were left from flattery or dissimulation, concluded that his wisest way would be to turn and face his pursuers. Thus laying aside all shame, he appeared the open hardy villain. 'I find then,' cried he, 'that I am to expect no justice here; but I am resolved it shall be done me. You shall know, Sir,' turning to Sir William, 'I am no longer a poor dependant upon your favours. I scorn them. Nothing can keep Miss Wilmot's fortune from me, which, I thank her father's assiduity, is pretty large. The articles, and a bond for her fortune, are signed, and safe in my possession.* It was her fortune, not her person, that induced me to wish for this match, and possessed of the one, let who will take the other.'

This was an alarming blow, Sir William was sensible of the justice of his claims, for he had been instrumental in drawing up the marriage articles himself. Miss Wilmot therefore perceiving that her fortune was irretrievably lost, turning to my son, she asked if the loss of fortune could lessen her value to him. 'Though fortune,' said she, 'is out of my power, at least I have my hand to give.'

'And that, madam,' cried her real lover, 'was indeed all that you ever had to give; at least all that I ever thought worth the acceptance. And now I protest, my Arabella, by all that's happy, your want of fortune this moment encreases my pleasure, as it serves to convince my sweet girl of my sincerity.'

Mr. Wilmot now entering, he seemed not a little pleased at the danger his daughter had just escaped, and readily consented to a dissolution of the match. But finding that her fortune, which was secured to Mr. Thornhill by bond, would not be given up, nothing could exceed his disappointment. He now saw that his money must all go to enrich one who had no fortune of his own. He could bear his being a rascal; but to want an equivalent to his daughter's fortune was wormwood. He sate therefore for some minutes employed in the most mortifying speculations, till Sir William attempted to lessen his anxiety.—'I must confess, Sir,' cried he, 'that your present disappointment does not entirely displease me. Your immoderate passion for wealth is now justly punished. But tho' the young lady cannot be rich, she has still a competence sufficient to give content. Here you see an honest young soldier, who is willing to take her without fortune; they have long loved each other, and for the friendship I bear his father, my interest shall not be wanting in his promotion. Leave then that ambition which disappoints you, and for once admit that happiness which courts your acceptance.'

'Sir William,' replied the old gentleman, 'be assured I never yet forced her inclinations, nor will I now. If she still continues to love this young gentleman, let her have him with all my heart. There is still, thank heaven, some fortune left, and your promise will make it something more. Only let my old friend here (meaning me) give me a promise of settling six thousand pounds upon my girl, if ever he should come to his fortune, and I am ready this night to be the first to join them together.'

As it now remained with me to make the young couple happy, I readily gave a promise of making the settlement he required, which, to one who had such little expectations as I, was no great favour. We had now therefore the satisfaction of seeing them fly into each other's arms in a transport. 'After all my misfortunes,' cried my son George, 'to be thus rewarded! Sure this is more than I could ever have presumed to hope for. To be possessed of all that's good, and after such an interval of pain! My warmest wishes could never rise so high!'—'Yes, my George,' returned his lovely bride, 'now let the wretch take my fortune; since you are happy without it so am I. O what an exchange have I made from the basest of men to the dearest best!—Let him enjoy our fortune, I now can be happy even in indigence.'—'And I promise you,' cried the 'Squire, with a malicious grin, 'that I shall be very happy with what you despise.'—'Hold, hold, Sir,' cried Jenkinson, 'there are two words to that bargain. As for that lady's fortune, Sir, you shall never touch a single stiver* of it. Pray your honour,' continued he to Sir William, 'can the 'Squire have this lady's fortune if he be married to another?' —'How can you make such a simple demand,' replied the Baronet, 'undoubtedly he cannot.'—'I am sorry for that,' cried Jenkinson; 'for as this gentleman and I have been old fellow sporters, I have a friendship for him. But I must declare, well as I love him, that his contract is not worth a tobacco stopper,* for he is married already.'—'You lie, like a rascal,' returned the 'Squire, who seemed rouzed by this insult, 'I never was legally married to any woman.'—'Indeed, begging your honour's pardon,' replied the other, 'you were; and I hope you will shew a proper return of friendship to your own honest Jenkinson, who brings you a wife, and if the company restrains their curiosity a few minutes, they shall see her.'—So saying he went off with his usual celerity, and left us all unable to form any probable conjecture as to his design.—'Ay let him go,' cried the 'Squire, 'whatever else I may have done I defy him there. I am too old now to be frightened with squibs.'*

'I am surprised,' said the Baronet, 'what the fellow can intend by this. Some low piece of humour I suppose!'—'Perhaps, Sir,' replied I, 'he may have a more serious meaning. For when we reflect on the various schemes this gentleman has laid to seduce innocence, perhaps some one more artful than the rest has been found able to deceive him. When we consider what numbers he has ruined, how many parents now feel with anguish the infamy and the contamination which he has brought into their families, it would not surprise me if some one of them—Amazement! Do I see my lost daughter! Do I hold her! It is, it is my life, my happiness. I thought thee lost, my Olivia, yet still I hold thee—and still thou shalt live to bless me.'—The warmest transports of the fondest lover were not greater than mine when I saw him introduce my child, and held my daughter in my arms, whose silence only spoke her raptures. 'And art thou returned to me, my darling,' cried I, 'to be my comfort in age!'—'That she is,' cried Jenkinson, 'and make much of her, for she is your own honourable child, and as honest a woman as any in the whole room, let the other be who she will. And as for you 'Squire, as sure as you stand there this young lady is your lawful wedded wife. And to convince you that I speak nothing but truth, here is the licence by which you were married together.'—So saying, he put the licence into the Baronet's hands, who read it, and found it perfect in every respect. 'And now, gentlemen,' continued he, 'I find you are surprised at all this; but a few words will explain the difficulty. That there 'Squire of renown, for whom I have a great friendship, but that's between ourselves, has often employed me in doing odd little things for him. Among the rest, he commissioned me to procure him a false licence and a false priest, in order to deceive this young lady. But as I was very much his friend, what did I do but went and got a true licence and a true priest, and married them both as fast as the cloth could make them. Perhaps you'll think it was generosity that made me do all this. But no. To my shame I confess it, my only design was to keep the licence and let the 'Squire know that I could prove it upon him whenever I thought proper, and so make him come down whenever I wanted money.' A burst of pleasure now seemed to fill the whole apartment; our joy reached even to the common room, where the prisoners themselves sympathized,

> *And shook their chains*
> *In transport and rude harmony.**

Happiness was expanded upon every face, and even Olivia's cheek seemed flushed with pleasure. To be thus restored to reputation, to friends and fortune at once, was a rapture sufficient to stop the progress of decay and restore former health and vivacity. But perhaps among all there was not one who felt sincerer pleasure than I. Still holding the dear-loved child in my arms, I asked my heart if these transports were not delusion. 'How could you,' cried I, turning to Mr. Jenkinson, 'how could you add to my miseries by the story of her death! But it matters not, my pleasure at finding her again, is more than a recompence for the pain.'

'As to your question,' replied Jenkinson, 'that is easily answered. I thought the only probable means of freeing you from prison, was by submitting to the 'Squire, and consenting to his marriage with the other young lady. But these you had vowed never to grant while your daughter was living, there was therefore no other method to bring things to bear but by persuading you that she was dead. I prevailed on your wife to join in the deceit, and we have not had a fit opportunity of undeceiving you till now.'

In the whole assembly now there only appeared two faces that did not glow with transport. Mr. Thornhill's assurance had entirely forsaken him: he now saw the gulph of infamy and want before him, and trembled to take the plunge. He therefore fell on his knees before his uncle, and in a voice of piercing misery implored compassion. Sir William was going to spurn him away, but at my request he raised him, and after pausing a few moments, 'Thy vices, crimes, and ingratitude,' cried he, 'deserve no tenderness; yet thou shalt not be entirely forsaken, a bare competence shall be supplied, to support the wants of life, but not its follies. This young lady, thy wife, shall be put in possession of a third part of that fortune which once was thine, and from her tenderness alone thou art to expect any extraordinary supplies for the future.' He was going to express his gratitude for such kindness in a set speech; but the Baronet prevented him by bidding him not aggravate his meanness, which was already but too apparent. He ordered him at the same time to be gone, and from all his former domestics to chuse one such as he should think proper, which was all that should be granted to attend him.

As soon as he left us, Sir William very politely stept up to his new niece with a smile, and wished her joy. His example was followed by Miss Wilmot and her father; my wife too kissed her daughter with much affection, as, to use her own expression, she was now made an honest woman of.* Sophia and Moses followed in turn, and even our benefactor Jenkinson desired to be admitted to that honour. Our satisfaction seemed scarce capable of increase. Sir William, whose greatest pleasure was in doing good, now looked round with a countenance open as the sun, and saw nothing but joy in the looks of all except that of my daughter Sophia, who, for some reasons we could not comprehend, did not seem perfectly satisfied. 'I think now,' cried he, with a smile, 'that all the company, except one or two, seem perfectly happy. There only remains an act of justice for me to do. You are sensible, Sir,' continued he, turning to me, 'of the obligations we both owe Mr. Jenkinson. And it is but just we should both reward him for it. Miss Sophia will, I am sure, make him very happy, and he shall have from me five hundred pounds as her fortune, and upon this I am sure they can live very comfortably together. Come, Miss Sophia, what say you to this match of my making? Will you have him?'—My poor girl seemed almost sinking into her mother's arms at the hideous proposal.—'Have him, Sir!' cried she faintly. 'No, Sir, never.'—'What,' cried he again, 'not have Mr. Jenkinson, your benefactor, an handsome young fellow, with five hundred pounds and good expectations!'—'I beg, Sir,' returned she, scarce able to speak, 'that you'll desist, and not make me so very wretched.'—'Was ever such obstinacy known,' cried he again, 'to refuse a man whom the family has such infinite obligations to, who has preserved your sister, and who has five hundred pounds! What not have him!'—'No, Sir, never,' replied she, angrily, 'I'd sooner die first.'—'If that be the case then,' cried he, 'if you will not have him—I think I must have you myself.' And so saying, he caught her to his breast with ardour. 'My loveliest, my most sensible of girls,' cried he, 'how could you ever think your own Burchell could deceive you, or that Sir William Thornhill could ever cease to admire a mistress that loved him for himself alone? I have for some years sought for a woman, who a stranger to my fortune could think that I had merit as a man. After having tried in vain, even amongst the pert and the ugly, how great at last must be my rapture to have made a conquest over such sense and such heavenly beauty.' Then turning to Jenkinson, 'As I cannot, Sir, part with this young lady myself, for she has taken a fancy to the cut of my face, all the recompence I can make is to give you her fortune, and you may call upon my steward to-morrow for five hundred pounds.' Thus we had all our compliments to repeat, and Lady Thornhill underwent the same round of ceremony that her sister had done before. In the mean time Sir William's gentleman appeared to tell us that the equipages were ready to carry us to the inn, where every thing was prepared for our reception. My wife and I led the van, and left those gloomy mansions of sorrow. The generous Baronet ordered forty pounds to be distributed among the prisoners, and Mr. Wilmot, induced by his example, gave half that sum. We were received below by the shouts of the villagers, and I saw and shook by the hand two or three of my honest parishioners, who were among the number. They attended us to our inn, where a sumptuous entertainment was provided, and coarser provisions distributed in great quantities among the populace.

After supper, as my spirits were exhausted by the alternation of pleasure and pain which they had sustained during the day, I asked permission to withdraw, and leaving the company in the midst of their mirth, as soon as I found myself alone, I poured out my heart in gratitude to the giver of joy as well as of sorrow, and then slept undisturbed till morning.

CHAPTER XXXII

The Conclusion

THE next morning as soon as I awaked I found my eldest son sitting by my bedside, who came to encrease my joy with another turn of fortune in my favour. First having released me from the settlement that I had made the day before in his favour, he let me know that my merchant who had failed in town was arrested at Antwerp, and there had given up effects to a much greater amount than what was due to his creditors. My boy's generosity pleased me almost as much as this unlooked for good fortune. But I had some doubts whether I ought in justice to accept his offer. While I was pondering upon this, Sir William entered the room, to whom I communicated my doubts. His opinion was, that as my son was already possessed of a very affluent fortune by his marriage, I might accept his offer without any hesitation. His business, however, was to inform me that as he had the night before sent for the licences, and expected them every hour, he hoped that I would not refuse my assistance in making all the company happy that morning. A footman entered while we were speaking, to tell us that the messenger was returned, and as I was by this time ready, I went down, where I found the whole company as merry as affluence and innocence could make them. However, as they were now preparing for a very solemn ceremony, their laughter entirely displeased me. I told them of the grave, becoming and sublime deportment they should assume upon this mystical occasion, and read them two homilies and a thesis of my own composing, in order to prepare them. Yet they still seemed perfectly refractory and ungovernable. Even as we were going along to church, to which I led the way, all gravity had quite forsaken them, and I was often tempted to turn back in indignation. In church a new dilemma arose, which promised no easy solution. This was, which couple should be married first; my son's bride warmly insisted, that Lady Thornhill, (that was to be) should take the lead; but this the other refused with equal ardour, protesting she would not be guilty of such rudeness for the world. The argument was supported for some time between both with equal obstinacy and good breeding. But as I stood all this time with my book ready, I was at last quite tired of the contest, and shutting it, 'I perceive,' cried I, 'that none of you have a mind to be married, and I think we had as good go back again; for I suppose there will be no business done here to-day.'—This at once reduced them to reason. The Baronet and his Lady were first married, and then my son and his lovely partner.

I had previously that morning given orders that a coach should be sent for my honest neighbour Flamborough and his family, by which means, upon our return to the inn, we had the pleasure of finding the two Miss Flamboroughs alighted before us. Mr. Jenkinson gave his hand to the eldest, and my son Moses led up the other; (and I have since found that he has taken a real liking to the girl, and my consent and bounty he shall have whenever he thinks proper to demand them.) We were no sooner returned to the inn, but numbers of my parishioners, hearing of my success, came to congratulate me, but among the rest were those who rose to rescue me, and whom I formerly rebuked with such sharpness. I told the story to Sir William, my son-in-law, who went out and reproved them with great severity; but finding them quite disheartened by his harsh reproof, he gave them half a guinea a piece to drink his health and raise their dejected spirits.

Soon after this we were called to a very genteel entertainment, which was drest by Mr. Thornhill's cook. And it may not be improper to observe with respect to that gentleman, that he now resides in quality of companion at a relation's house, being very well liked and seldom sitting at the side-table, except when there is no room at the other; for they make no stranger of him. His time is pretty much taken up in keeping his relation, who is a little melancholy, in spirits, and in learning to blow the French-horn. My eldest daughter, however, still remembers him with regret; and she has even told me, though I make a great secret of it, that when he reforms she may be brought to relent. But to return, for I am not apt to digress thus, when we were to sit down to dinner our ceremonies were going to be renewed. The question was whether my eldest daughter, as being a matron, should not sit above the two young brides, but the debate was cut short by my son George, who proposed, that the company should sit indiscriminately, every gentleman by his lady. This was received with great approbation by all, excepting my wife, who I could perceive was not perfectly satisfied, as she expected to have had the pleasure of sitting at the head of the table and carving all the meat for all the company. But notwithstanding this, it is impossible to describe our good humour. I can't say whether we had more wit amongst us now than usual; but I am certain we had more laughing, which answered the end as well. One jest I particularly remember, old Mr. Wilmot drinking to Moses, whose head was turned another way, my son replied, 'Madam, I thank you.' Upon which the old gentleman, winking upon the rest of the company, observed that he was thinking of his mistress. At which jest I thought the two miss Flamboroughs would have died with laughing. As soon as dinner was over, according to my old custom, I requested that the table might be taken away, to have the pleasure of seeing all my family assembled once more by a chearful fire-side. My two little ones sat upon each knee, the rest of the company by their partners. I had nothing now on this side of the grave to wish for, all my cares were over, my pleasure was unspeakable. It now only remained that my gratitude in good fortune should exceed my former submission in adversity.

EXPLANATORY NOTES

Abbreviations

Collected Letters	*The Collected Letters of Oliver Goldsmith*, ed. Katherine C. Balderston (Cambridge: Cambridge University Press, 1928)
Collected Works	*Collected Works of Oliver Goldsmith*, ed. Arthur Friedman, 5 vols. (Oxford: Clarendon Press, 1966)
Doughty	*The Vicar of Wakefield*, ed. with introd. and notes by Oswald Doughty (London: Scholartis Press, 1928)
Johnson	Samuel Johnson, *Dictionary of the English Language*, 4th edn. revised by the author (London: W. Strahan, J. and F. Rivington, 1773)
Lonsdale	*The Poems of Gray, Collins and Goldsmith*, ed. Roger Lonsdale (London: Longman, 1969) (the poetry of Goldsmith appears on pp. 567–769)
OED	*Oxford English Dictionary* (2nd edn., Oxford: Oxford University Press, 1989)
Oxford DNB	Colin Matthew and Brian Harrison (eds.), *Oxford Dictionary of National Biography* (Oxford: Oxford University Press, 2004)
Percy Memoir	Thomas Percy, 'The Life of Dr. Oliver Goldsmith', in *The Miscellaneous Works of Oliver Goldsmith, M.B.* (London, 1801), vol. i

Some of the Explanatory Notes are drawn from Friedman's 1981 World's Classics edition without further attribution.

title page: *Wakefield*: in the *Collected Works*, iv. 13, Friedman had observed that the title of the novel may have been suggested by a poem in the *Annual Register* (1759), 452–4, entitled 'On the Vicar of W——d'. The poem itself bears no relation—except by way of contrast—to the contents of the novel; it is satirical of the miserliness of the vicar, whose character is clearly indicated in the first two couplets:

> The vicar's rich, his income clear,
> Exceeds eight hundred pounds a year.
> Yet weeping want goes by the door,
> Or knocks unheard—the vicar's poor.

title page: *Sperate miseri, cavete fælices*: 'Hope, ye miserable ones; ye happy ones, fear'. Goldsmith's epigraph is taken from the penultimate sentence of Robert Burton's *Anatomy of Melancholy* (1621).

3 *ADVERTISEMENT*: the remarks offered here regarding the standards expected in 'this age of opulence and refinement' are echoed in the actual text of the novel by those of Mr Burchell on 'the reputation of books' and the 'greatness of their beauties', p. 67.

9 *migrations from the blue bed to the brown*: the language used by the Vicar to describe the couple's domestic 'migrations' is drawn from Goldsmith's own life. Goldsmith had playfully complained in a letter to his friend and brother-in-law Daniel Hodson, in December 1757, that the arrival of his much younger brother Charles in London late in 1757 had brought him no real news of his Irish relations: 'Some friends, he tells me, are still lean but very rich, other very fat but still very poor[.] Nay all the news I hear from you, is that you and Mrs. Hodson [Goldsmith's older sister, Catherine] sally out to visits among the neighbours, and sometimes make a migration from the blue bed to the brown' (*Collected Letters*, 30).

Our cousins . . . without any help from the Herald's office: the Herald's Office was the office of the royal corporation, the Herald's College or College of Arms, which had been founded in 1483. In addition to exercising jurisdiction in matters armorial, and granting Armorial bearings, the Office proved pedigrees. A 'remove' was 'a degree in descent or consanguinity' (this example cited in *OED*).

10 *pathetic*: used here specifically in the sense of 'producing an effect upon the emotions; moving, stirring, affecting' (*OED*).

the famous story of Count Abensberg: Friedman, in the *Collected Works*, iv. 20, successfully traced the source for this story in Louise Moreri's *Le Grand Dictionnaire historique* (Amsterdam, 1740), ii. 163. Moreri had included in his history the tale of Bébon, Baron of Abensburg, in Bavaria, who arrived at the court of the Emperor Henri II accompanied by all thirty of his sons. Astounded by the appearance of so many people, the Emperor asked the Baron why he was surrounded by such a numerous assembly. Bébon responded that he had only brought his male children and their servants so that he might have the opportunity to make a 'present' of them to the Emperor. The Emperor was so charmed by the handsome appearance of the entire company, Moreri wrote, that 'he embraced each of them in turn, and promised to look upon them as his own, and always to keep them close to his heart'.

11 *two romantic names in the family*: Friedman, in the *Collected Works* (iii. 177), notes another instance of possible self-referentiality in Goldsmith's writings here, observing that in his essay on the coronation of George III included in the *Public Ledger* for 24 September 1761, Goldsmith had given the wife of the common-councilman the name *Grizzle*. On the Vicar's suggestion that the naming of his two daughters was influenced by the fact that his wife had been reading too much romantic fiction, see Introduction p. xxxvi.

handsome is that handsome does: a proverbial expression dating at least as far back as 1659 (in his note in the original Oxford World's Classics edition of the novel, p. 199, Friedman traces it to 'at least 1670'); earlier variations of the same sentiment—e.g. 'goodly is he that goodly doth'—can be found in texts dating from the late sixteenth century.

Hebe: in Greek mythology, the daughter of Zeus and Hera, and cup-bearer of the Gods. Her name—which means, almost literally, 'beautiful youth'—remained, despite its classical origins, fashionable among the writers of popular songs and ballads.

ribbands: throughout Goldsmith's work 'ribband' is used for 'ribbon', which here refers specifically to those kinds of silk and satin ribbons used by women in the period as items of ornamentation.

12 *one of the learned professions*: traditionally, George's study at Oxford would have prepared him, if not for the Church, then for later employment in the fields of medicine, law, and science or academic scholarship.

credulous: used here not in the negative sense of 'over-ready to believe' or 'apt to believe on weak or insufficient grounds', but rather to mean simply 'disposed to believe' or free from guile (*OED*).

my living . . . thirty-five pounds a year: cf. Goldsmith's description of the local vicar of a rural parish in his popular poem *The Deserted Village* (1770), ii. 41–4, in which the vicar is described as being '. . . to all the country dear, | and passing rich with forty pounds a year; | Remote from towns he ran his godly race, | Nor e'er had changed, nor wished to change, his place . . .' (*Collected Works*, iv. 293). Lonsdale (p. 682) notes that the village preacher of Goldsmith's poem has 'inevitably' been identified with Goldsmith's father, the Revd Charles Goldsmith, and with his brother, the Revd Henry Goldsmith, 'both of whom held the living of Kilkenny West near Lissoy'.

I made over to the orphans and widows of the clergy of our diocese: in the first (March 1766) edition of Goldsmith's novel, this passage reads 'I gave to the orphans and widows of our diocese'. This change from 'gave' to 'made over' in the second edition suggests that Goldsmith wanted deliberately to emphasize that the income from his living had not so much been freely offered to the poor of the parish, but had rather actually been made over or transferred by the Vicar into the hands of trustees, from whom he could no longer claim it back.

I also set a resolution of keeping no curate: a curate was 'a clergyman engaged for a stipend or salary . . . to perform ministerial duties in the parish as a deputy or assistant of the incumbent' (*OED*). The Vicar wishes to emphasize that he had made a point of dispatching with any assistance in fulfilling his duties in the parish.

I maintained with Whiston: William Whiston (1667–1752) was a mathematician, a natural philosopher, a clergyman, a proponent of primitive Christianity, and a student and sometime friend of Sir Isaac Newton. He published over 120 separate books on a wide range of subjects including geology, mathematics, astronomy, and philosophy, and played an important role in the earliest attempts to determine longitude at sea. The *Oxford DNB* notes that Whiston was 'a vigorous opponent of both deism and unbelief on the one hand, and high-church orthodoxy on the other' who sought to maintain a middle ground 'between what to him were two extremes'. Goldsmith focuses on the extent to which Dr Primrose has adopted Whiston's principles of monogamy. Whiston had argued in his 1749 autobiography: '*Paul* and the Apostolic Constitutions agree, and above four Centuries concur with them, that neither a *Bishop*, a *Presbyter*, nor a *Deacon*, ought to be more than the *Husband of one Wife*; or to be more than once married, altho' neither the modern Churches, nor Baptists, have always observed this Rule of Primitive Christianity' (*Memoirs of the Life and Writings of Mr. William Whiston* (London, 1749), 467). Whiston himself remained happily married for over fifty years. See Stephen D. Snobelen, 'William Whiston', in the *Oxford DNB*, lviii. 502–6.

13 *a complexion so transparent*: a disposition or temperament so 'candid' or 'open'.

14 *to prevent the ladies leaving us*: it was traditional in the period even in provincial towns for women to withdraw to the drawing room or the parlour following midday dinner. After an hour or occasionally a little less the women usually ordered their tea to be served, at which time they also called for the men to finish their drinking and to come and join them.

forfeits: 'in certain games, an article (usually something carried on the person) which a player gives up by way of penalty for making some mistake, and which he afterwards redeems by performing some ludicrous task' (*OED*).

a two-penny hit: a stake or bet amounting to twopence; in other words, the Vicar even when wagering with his old friend at backgammon plays for only the most modest of amounts.

fling a quatre . . . threw deuce ace: he wanted to throw a total of four with the two dice, but threw a two and a one (or perhaps two aces).

courting a fourth wife: of a clergyman's taking a fourth wife Whiston says: 'This is a Piece of Licentiousness, and a Contradiction to the Laws of the *New Testament* plainly intolerable' (*Memoirs*, 468).

15 *a statute of bankruptcy*: the Bankruptcy Laws, first instituted in England in the fifteenth century, were originally directed against fraudulent traders, who, much like the 'merchant' in town (i.e., his agent) into whose hands the Vicar has placed his money, could potentially 'run off' with the property of their creditors.

young lady's fortune secure: the 'fortune' that Arabella Wilmot brought to the marriage would immediately, upon the couple's exchange of vows, become the property of her husband. See also p. 161 and note.

one virtue . . . which was prudence: one of the four so-called pagan virtues: Prudence, Temperance, Fortitude, and Justice. Combined with the

Christian virtues of Faith, Hope, and Love, they together formed the traditional seven virtues.

16 *a small Cure*: a curacy or living: 'a parish or other sphere of spiritual ministration; a "charge" ' (*OED*).

enjoy my principles without molestation: see sixth note to p. 12. Friedman maintained that it had not been made adequately clear why the Vicar should resign his living of £35 a year at Wakefield to take a cure of £15 a year. The Vicar's remark here about enjoying his 'principles without molestation' and his reference in Chapter XIV to 'the Whistonian controversy, the last pamphlet, the archdeacon's reply, and the hard measure that was dealt me', Friedman argued, suggest that in an earlier version of Chapter II the Vicar left Wakefield to escape persecution for his principles.

the same horse that was given him by the good bishop Jewel, this staff: Richard Hooker (1554–1600) was a theologian, philosopher, and preacher. The story referred to here is found in the account of Hooker's departure from Bishop Jewel in Isaak Walton's *The Life of Mr. Richard Hooker* (first pub. 1665): 'at the Bishop's parting with him, the Bishop gave him good counsel, and his benediction, but forgot to give him money; which when the Bishop had considered, he sent a servant in all haste to call Richard back to him; and at Richard's return, the Bishop said to him, "Richard, I sent for you back to lend you a horse, which hath carried me many a mile, and, I thank God, with much ease:" and presently delivered into his hand a walking-staff, with which he had travelled through many parts of Germany' (*Lives* (Oxford, 1805), i. 244).

17 *his seed begging their bread*: this passage is quoted verbatim from Psalm 37: 25.

throwing him naked into the amphitheatre of life: a similar phrase is used in the history of the Man in Black in Goldsmith's *Citizen of the World*, letter 27: 'I resembled, upon my first entrance into the busy and insidious world, one of those gladiators who were exposed without armour in the amphitheatre at Rome' (*Collected Works*, ii. 114).

18 *paid three guineas to our beadle . . . whipped though the town for dog-stealing*: in a small village community such as the one in which the Vicar has paused on his way to his new living, the beadle would have been the officer who acted in the capacity of a constable; he would likewise have been responsible within the local parish for the administration of justice. The infamous Black Act of 1723 had made many offences related to poaching capital crimes—i.e., crimes punishable by death. Beadles were obliged by the statute law of England to arrest even vagrants. Male beggars and vagrants would have been subject to public whipping and removal and—more likely than not—imprisonment at hard labour for as long as seven days; petty thievery was to remain punishable by public whipping until 1820.

18 *cloaths that once were laced*: the clothes of gentlemen—particularly their
coats—were frequently ornamented with high quality gold or silver lace;
linen fabrics of cotton, silk, and wool, could also be embroidered and
trimmed with inwrought patterns of different colours.

Mr. Burchell, our new companion: Goldsmith may have taken such names
in the novel as 'Burchell' and 'Arnold' from Frances Sheridan's *Memoirs
of Miss Sidney Bidulph* (1761). In that novel, the marriage of the title
character to Orlando Faulkland is forestalled by the revelation of his
previous attachment to the former Miss Burchell. Sidney Bidulph
accepts instead the proposals of a Mr Arnold.

19 *he carried benevolence to an excess*: the danger of excessive benevolence is a
constant theme in Goldsmith's writings. See *Collected Works*, v. 3.

Physicians tell us of a disorder . . . this gentleman felt in his mind: Sir William
Thornhill is represented here as possessing a degree of non-verbal sensibility more usually reserved for the female heroines of popular novels of
sentiment. The description not only underscores the intimate alliance
that was thought to connect the moral sense with the physical body and
its 'exquisite' sensations in a healthy individual, but draws attention to
the possibility that an otherwise commendable inclination towards
benevolence could lead in some cases to the development of a 'sickly
sensibility of the miseries of others'.

20 *I forgot what I was going to observe*: Mr Burchell's momentary confusion
here, as he falls into the first-person singular, is the first of many indica-
tions that he is himself Sir William Thornhill.

21 *the polite*: used here to refer to 'the refined' or 'the sophisticated' and
urbane.

religiously cracked nuts on Michaelmas eve: one of the customs associated
with the feast of St Michael the Archangel or Michaelmas Day (29
September) was that of picking hazelnuts; in some rural parishes the
evening prior to Michaelmas Day, i.e. Michaelmas Eve, took on the name
of Nut Crack Night, on which occasion harvested nuts were carried into
the church to be broken open. Also associated with Michaelmas were the
festivities surrounding the many hiring and livestock fairs that took place
at this time of the year. The rituals Goldsmith here connects to the other
feast days and holidays mentioned are more obviously maintained in
some form in contemporary society.

In his essay 'The Revolution in Low Life', first printed in June 1762,
Goldsmith had written of the inhabitants of a village some fifty
miles from London: 'They were merry at Christmas and mournful in
Lent, got drunk on St. George's-day, and religiously cracked nuts on
Michaelmas-eve' (*Collected Works*, iii. 195).

22 *my little enclosures*: the consequences of the enclosure of open land in the
Hanoverian period—by which procedure open or 'common' fields were
'enclosed' or marked off with a boundary as private property—are of

some significance elsewhere in Goldsmith's work, particularly with regard to his 1770 poem *The Deserted Village* (on which, see Lonsdale, 67–74).

The little republic to which I gave laws: in the dedication to *A Discourse on Inequality* (1754), Jean-Jacques Rousseau defined a republic as 'a state where every individual being acquainted with each other, neither the dark manoeuvres of vice nor the modesty of virtue [is] concealed from public gaze or judgement' (Rousseau, *A Discourse on Inequality*, trans. Maurice Cranston (Harmondsworth: Penguin, 1984), 57). It has been argued convincingly that Primrose's description of his family as 'a little republic' is entirely in keeping with Goldsmith's own political views as they are expressed elsewhere in the novel (esp. Chapter XIX) and in his history writing more generally. See James P. Carson, ' "The Little Republic" of the Family: Goldsmith's Politics of Nostalgia', *Eighteenth-Century Fiction*, 16/2 (2004), 173–96.

23 *the blind piper*: a generic reference to an itinerant musician, although Iain Dall Mackay (1656?–1754) was hereditary piper to Sir Kenneth MacKenzie of Gairloch, and a composer famously known under the names 'Iain Dall' (Blind John) and 'Am Piopare Dall' (or the Blind Piper).

Johnny Armstrong's last good night, or the cruelty of Barbara Allen: both traditional English ballads. 'Barbara Allan' and 'Johnny Armstrong's Last Good Night', like the equally familiar 'Sir Patrick Spens', are variations on the 'good night' or popular funeral lament.

my sumptuary edicts: a sumptuary edict could refer to 'any law regulating expenditure', but was used most frequently with reference to any such law that looked to prevent the spending of money 'with a view to restraining excess in food, dress, equipage, etc.' (*OED*).

bugles and catgut: a bugle is 'a tube-shaped glass bead, usually black, used to ornament wearing apparel' (*OED*). Shining beads of black glass of this kind were popular in the period, although considered by some to be slightly common or vulgar. Catgut is 'a kind of coarse thick-ribbed cotton stuff' (*OED*); it had often formerly been used as stiffening, although the 'cord' or 'corduroy' of the sort referred to in this instance, from the French *corde du roy*, could refer to ribbed fabrics of any material, including such 'fancy' stuff as velveteen, crêpe, and even silks.

her crimson paduasoy: a strong, rich, silk fabric, usually slightly corded or embossed, popular in the eighteenth and nineteenth centuries; Deborah Primrose's 'passion' for her crimson paduasoy betrays a degree of vulgarity.

pomatum . . . patched: pomatum was a scented ointment, frequently of the sort used for application to the skin or, as in this instance, the dressing of the hair. Patched: it was fashionable among women in the period to apply small pieces of black silk or court-plasters to the face, so as to hide any blemishes, or, more usually, to show off the delicacy of their complexions by contrast.

24 *pinkings*: elaborately decorated cloth or leather.

flouncing and shredding: a flounce was 'an ornamental appendage to the skirt of a lady's dress, consisting of a strip gathered and sewed on by its upper edge around the skirt, and left hanging and waving'; to 'shred' one's clothing was to trim it 'with shreds of gold lace' (*OED*).

the nakedness of the indigent world may be cloathed from the trimmings of the vain: cf. [William Penn,] *Some Fruits of Solitude*, 7th edn. (London: Assigns of J. Sowle, 1718), 32: 'Excess in *Apparel* is another *costly* Folly: The very Trimming of the vain World would *cloath* all the *naked* one.'

25 *centaury*: also known in England as common or lesser centaury, and so-called because its medicinal properties were said first to have been discovered by the centaur Chiron, of Hellenic mythology; the plant was sometimes compared by herbalists to oregano, marjoram, and St John's Wort.

vacant: meaning in this instance not 'vacuous' but 'free from preoccupation' (*OED*).

was going to salute my daughters: i.e., made as if to embrace and then to kiss them.

disproportioned acquaintances: friendships between individuals so widely separated by social class.

26 *Dryden*: John Dryden (1631–1700), pre-eminent poet and dramatist of the Restoration period.

the satisfaction of being laughed at: in the first edition of the novel, this passage continued: 'for he always ascribed to his wit that laughter which was lavished at his simplicity'. It has been suggested that this was omitted in subsequent editions 'because . . . Goldsmith found it was used against himself' (see e.g. Doughty, 'Introduction', p. xxvii).

we sate down with a blank: i.e. gambled unsuccessfully; participated in the lottery but did not win the prize.

28 *an halfpenny whistle:* a small musical toy, pierced with six holes and usually made of tin, to be had for the price of a penny or less, usually from passing peddlers.

the history of Patient Grissel, the adventures of Catskin, and then Fair Rosamond's bower: in *A Collection of Old Ballads*, i (3rd edn., 1727), are to be found 'An Excellent Ballad of a Noble Marquis and Patient Grissel' (pp. 252–60) and 'a Lamentable Ballad of Fair Rosamond, King Henry the Second's Concubine' (pp. 11–17). Both are likewise mentioned in John Gay's *The Shepherd's Week* (1714). The 'adventures of Catskin' is probably the ballad entitled *The Wandering Young Gentlewoman; or, Catskin* or *The Catskin's Garland*. Austin Dobson noted the latter to have been reprinted in Bell's *Ballads of the Peasantry* (1857), 115. (Dobson, *The Life and Writings of Oliver Goldsmith* (London, n.d. [1888?]), 115).

the beast retires to his shelter . . . he that came to save it: the Vicar's language here recalls passages from the New Testament, including Matthew 8: 20 and Luke 4: 58.

29 *an after-growth of hay*: the second growth, harvested toward the latter end of the year.

the bagnio pander: a pimp in a brothel; Johnson's definition observes that a pander could more generally refer to 'an agent for the lust or ill designs of another'.

30 *the attempts of a rustic to flay Marsyas . . . stript off by another*: in classical mythology, the satyr Marsyas, having picked up the flutes first invented and then discarded by Athena, grew so proficient in his ability that he challenged Apollo to a contest. Apollo agreed to the challenge. His divine skill having assured his success in the match, Apollo subsequently had Marsyas flayed alive. The tale is a variation of that which more often pits Apollo against Pan in a contest judged by King Midas.

lightsome: 'permeated with light; well-lighted, bright, illumined' (*OED*).

making a wash: 'a liquid cosmetic for the complexion'. This example is cited in *OED*.

31 *feeder*: Goldsmith's critics have disagreed as to exactly what the word means in this context. It is clear, since the 'chaplain and feeder' here are synonymous with the 'couple of friends' who arrive with Thornhill, that 'feeder' is not being used simply as another term for the parson. Thornhill's 'feeder'—according to contemporary usage—is likely to have been the huntsman in charge of feeding his hounds; others have noted, however, that Johnson rather confusingly defines the word not only as 'one that gives food', but also as 'one that eats'. In the *Collected Works*, Friedman further entertains the possibility, however, that the designation is used here to identify the individual in question as Thornhill's tutor; to call someone a 'feeder' could be a humorous way of referring to the manner in which they 'crammed' their charges with learning.

under the clock at St. Dunstan's: the famous clock outside the old church of St Dunstan's in the West, in London, had since the late seventeenth century been a place of popular resort, and one of the more famous sights of the capital.

lawn sleeves: sleeves made of 'lawn', a fabric of fine linen, resembling cambric, that was used for the sleeves of bishops, and was consequently a mark of the dignity or office of a bishop.

an imposition: in this sense, a levy or a tax, but also perhaps a pun by the Squire on use of the word in its more proper ecclesiastical sense of the laying on of hands in blessing or confirmation.

smoaked him: to 'smoak' or 'smoke' was, according to Johnson, 'to smell out'; 'to find out'. The Squire, in other words, has instantly understood Moses' purpose, and has decided to pretend to entertain the boy's desire to engage him in a learned disputation.

34 *free-thinkers*: generally speaking, individuals who refused 'to submit [their] reason to the control of authority in matters of religious belief' (*OED*).

the disputes between Thwackum and Square: cf. Henry Fielding's *The History of Tom Jones* (1749), particularly bk. III, chs. iii, viii, ix; bk. IV, ch. iv; and bk. V, ch. viii. As John Bender and Simon Stern note: 'the contrast between Square's and Thwackum's precepts is the contrast between rational religion, or deism, based in the law of nature, versus revealed religion based in the authority of Scripture'. See Henry Fielding, *Tom Jones*, ed. Bender and Stern (Oxford: Oxford World's Classics, 1998), 879.

the controversy between Robinson Crusoe and Friday the savage: after having rescued Friday from his enemies, Crusoe sets up to instruct him in the Christian religion, with decidedly mixed results. Crusoe, confessing his own confusion on doctrinal matters, decides finally to settle with such 'plain Instruction' as 'sufficiently serv'd to the enlightening [of] this Savage Creature'. See Daniel Defoe, *Robinson Crusoe*, ed. J. Donald Crowley (Oxford: Oxford World's Classics, 1998), 221.

Religious courtship: Olivia had clearly not paid attention to the subtitle of this work by Daniel Defoe (1722): *Being Historical Discourses on the Necessity of Marrying Religious Husbands and Wives only*.

35 *the two lovers, so sweetly described by Mr. Gay*: the story is told in a letter from John Gay to Mr F.——, dated 9 August 1718, in *The Correspondence of Alexander Pope*, ed. George Sherburne (Oxford: Clarendon Press, 1956), i. 482–3. The reference here appears to be particularly to the verse epitaph in the letter, which Gay says was furnished by himself and Pope:

> When Eastern lovers feed the funeral fire;
> On the same pile the faithful fair expire;
> Here pitying Heaven that virtue mutual found,
> And blasted both, that it might neither wound.
> Hearts so sincere, th'Almighty saw well pleas'd,
> Sent his own lightening, and the Victims seiz'd.

the Acis and Galatea of Ovid: a reference to the myth recounted by the Roman poet in *Metamorphoses*, 13. 738 ff. Acis was a Sicilian shepherd beloved of the sea nymph Galatea, who was crushed to death by his rival, the cyclops Polyphemus. Acis was transformed by the gods into a stream that rises from a fountain on Mount Etna.

without carrying on the sense: Mr Burchell's protestations regarding contemporary English poetry were maintained by Goldsmith himself. See *Collected Works*, iv. 46 n. 3.

A BALLAD: in 1765 a few copies of this poem were printed with the title *Edwin and Angelina. A Ballad. By Mr. Goldsmith. Printed for the Amusement of the Countess of Northumberland*. Lonsdale speculates that the poem was written perhaps as early as 1761, and 'may well have been included in the MS. of *Vicar* which [Goldsmith] sold in the autumn of 1762'. For a full critical text and the circumstances of the poem's composition see *Collected Works*, iv. 191 ff. and Lonsdale, 596–8.

41 *women of very great distinction and fashion from town*: the two women reveal themselves in the coarse vulgarity of their conversation, and later demonstrate by the duplicity of their conduct, to be 'abandoned women of the town' (p. 109). Goldsmith must be given some credit for advancing the currency of the word Blarney—in the sense of 'smoothly flattering or cajoling talk'—in colloquial English; his is the first example cited of the use of the term in that sense in *OED*.

The second of the two names used by Goldsmith here—Miss Carolina Wilelmina Amelia Skeggs, the full length of which, the Vicar later confesses, so delights him as he writes it (p. 49)—finds its origins in letter 55 of Goldsmith's *Citizen of the World* (first published in the *Public Ledger* for Friday, 1 August 1760). In that letter, Lien Chi Altangi mentions a 'sweet pretty creature' by the name of Carolina Wilhelmina Amelia Tibbs, a name which itself derives from the names of Queen Wilhelmina Caroline, wife of George II, and of Princess Amelia, his second daughter. See *Collected Works*, ii. 230.

42 *top-knots*: bows or ribbons tied and used as ornaments in the hair.

the jig ... round-about ... country dances: the reference to 'country dances' here is understandably somewhat confusing for modern readers. The daughters of the Vicar's neighbour Flamborough would be familiar with such native dances as they had grown up with in their rural community—dances that would often be practised in the open air, and would have included the familiar steps of a jig or a simple round dance, like the 'round-about' mentioned in the passage. What the Vicar in this instance characterizes as 'country dances' were in fact those that followed the more complex minuet and other similar forms from France, and which remained popular among the fashionable classes throughout the eighteenth century. The assistance of both pocket book guides as well as the instruction of formal dancing masters were available to those young people who had not had the opportunity to learn the latest steps at venues such as Vauxhall or Ranelagh.

chit: used here by the Vicar in an uncharacteristic sense to refer affectionately to his own daughter.

by the living jingo, she was all of a muck of sweat: for the level of usage suggested here, cf. the *Spectator*, 217 (8 November 1711), where a correspondent complains of a lack of '*Delicacy*' in 'a young Creature'; 'After our Return from a Walk the other Day, she threw her self in an Elbow Chair, and professed before a large Company, that *she was all over in a Sweat*.' Goldsmith's use of the vulgar and intensified 'by the *living jingo*' as a vigorous form of asseveration in this passage is cited in *OED* as one of the first appearances of that phrase in English.

the musical glasses: concerts on musical glasses had been given in London earlier in the eighteenth century, although 1761 seems to have been the year of their greatest popularity (the various notes were produced by rubbing the rims of glasses filled with different amounts of water). See Alec Hyatt King's article 'Musical Glasses' in Stanley Sadie (ed.), *The New Grove Dictionary of Music* (2nd edn., London Macmillan, 2001), xvii. 471–3.

43 *a single winter in town*: the winter would have constituted for the Vicar's daughters the necessary exposure of a social 'season'—'the period of the year during which [London] was most frequented for business, fashion, or amusement; . . . the time (now May to July) when the fashionable world . . . assembled in town' (*OED*).

coup de main: a martial metaphor, meaning literally, 'stroke of hand': 'a sudden and vigorous attack, for the purpose of instantaneously capturing a position' (*OED*).

45 *gauzes . . . catgut*: gauze here means any relatively transparent garment of silk, linen, or cotton; on catgut see note to p. 23.

a Nabob: a nawab; in extended use, 'a wealthy, influential, or powerful landowner or other person, esp. one with an extravagantly luxurious lifestyle; . . . any wealthy or high-ranking foreigner' (*OED*).

46 *they saw rings in the candle, purses bounced from the fire*: the Vicar's daughters and his wife misinterpret their dreams and everyday occurrences according to the rituals of rural superstition. The *Connoisseur* for 13 March 1755, in an article on 'Country Superstitions', notes a 'purse' to be 'a round cinder, as opposed to a hollow oblong one, which betokens a coffin'. The detection of 'rings' circling the flame of a candle was likewise taken to be a harbinger of some vague and undesignated future event. Cf. the *Universal Spectator* (3rd edn., 1756), ii. 175: 'She never has any Thing befals her, without some fore-notice or other; she . . . is forewarn'd of Deaths by the bursting of Coffins out of the Fire; Purses too from the same Element promise Money; and her Candle brings her Letters constantly before the Post.'

47 *scrubs*: 'mean insignificant fellow[s], person[s] of little account or poor appearance' (*OED*). For this usage, see also Henry Fielding, *Tom Jones*, bk. VIII, ch. iv: 'He is an arrant scrub, I assure you.'

blowzed and red with walking . . . winners at a smock race: to look 'blowzy' or 'blowzed' was to be high coloured or reddened by sunburn and exposure; a 'smock race' was a race run by women or girls in which a smock was the prize, although it may also have connoted a race or contest of some sort that was undertaken by women *in* their smocks.

48 *pillion*: a light saddle used by women—in this instance, the Vicar's wife, Deborah—when riding a horse.

Michaelmas eve happening on the next day: although it is doubtful that Goldsmith would have paid attention to such a detail, Michaelmas eve

(28 September) fell on Monday ('the next day') in 1761, when he was probably engaged in writing the novel.

lamb's-wool: 'a drink consisting of hot ale mixed with the pulp of roasted apples, and sugared and spiced' (*OED*).

Hot cockles: 'a rustic game in which one player lay face downwards, or knelt down with his eyes covered, and being struck on the back by the others in turn, guessed who struck him' (*OED*).

49 *prolocutor*: this formal or legal term signifies 'one who speaks for another or others' (*OED*); a spokesperson. The Vicar appears to adopt such formal language in misplaced deference to the sudden appearance of the family's 'two great acquaintances from town'.

50 *a sound*: a swoon (the reading of the first edition).

would cry out fudge . . . damped the rising spirit of the conversation: 'fudge', according to Eric Partridge's *A Dictionary of Slang and Unconventional English*, rev. Eric Beale (London, 1984), signified 'a lie, nonsense'; the exclamation alerts any listener to Mr Burchell's considered opinion that the conversation between Miss Skeggs and the Peeress is a calculated deception.

the Lady's Magazine: Goldsmith contributed to this magazine in 1760 and 1761; indeed, he was—disguised as the 'Honourable Mrs. Caroline Stanhope'—for a time its editor.

51 *plain-work*: 'plain needlework or sewing, as distinct from fancy work or embroidery' (*OED*).

breadstitch . . . pink, point . . . cut paper: 'breadstitch', properly 'brede-stitch', in which 'brede' means 'braid', was sewing work that involved some kind of interweaving, braiding, or embroidery; to 'pink' waas to 'Ornament (cloth, leather, or the like), by cutting or punching eyelet-holes, figures, letters, &c.'; to 'point' was to 'Fasten or lace with tagged points or laces' (*OED*); and to 'cut paper' was to fashion paper into elaborate designs or patterns.

53 *higgles*: strives 'for petty advantage in bargaining' (*OED*), i.e., haggles.

brushing his buckles, and cocking his hat with pins: the buckles referred to here are likely to be shoe-buckles or knee-buckles; to cock one's hat, according to Johnson, meant 'to set up the hat with an air of petulance and pertness'; Moses' sisters have been pinning his hat so that it sits at a jaunty angle on one side of his head.

thunder and lightening: 'a cloth, apparently of glaring colours', also 'applied to articles of apparel of a "loud" or "flashy" style, or combining two strongly contrasted colours' (*OED*; the Vicar's observation that the coat is still being worn by his son, 'though grown too short' suggests that its slightly gaudy colouring might have been more appropriate to a child than to a young man 16 years of age.

54 *gosling green*: 'a pale, yellowish green' (*OED*).

54 *a pennyworth of gingerbread each . . . give them by letters at a time*: small
portions of gingerbread would typically be formed in the shapes of men,
animals, and letters of the alphabet.

boxes, in which they might keep wafers, snuff, patches, or even money: the
word 'box' was only gradually extended since about 1700 to include, as it
does here, 'cases of larger size, made to hold merchandise and personal
property . . . understood to be four-sided and of wood' (*OED*).

a weesel skin purse: a purse probably made from the brown summer coat of
the European ermine or stoat-weasel.

55 *I'll warrant we'll never see him sell his hen of a rainy day*: a proverbial
expression going back at least to 1639. Stephen Coote notes its inclusion
in James Kelly's 1721 collection of *Scottish Proverbs* as 'You will part
with nothing to your disadvantage, for a hen looks ill on a rainy day'.
See *The Vicar of Wakefield*, ed. Stephen Coote (Harmondsworth:
Penguin, 1986), 206.

shagreen: this word, denoting a kind of untanned leather with a rough,
granular surface, was common in the period, although it appears, perhaps
because of its suggestions of artful delicacy or fastidious and appealingly
colourful protection, almost to have a totemic value in the sentimental
novels of the eighteenth century.

56 *A murrain take such trumpery*: i.e. 'a pox upon such rubbish'; a 'murrain'
was, even in the eighteenth century, a rather archaic word for 'plague' or
'disease'.

a prowling sharper: a wandering rogue; used here and elsewhere in the text
to connote various types of swindlers and con-artists.

58 *I stood neuter*: to 'stand neuter' was 'to remain neutral' or to 'declare
neutrality'.

60 *a spavin . . . a windgall . . . the botts . . . a blind, spavined, galled hack*: all
afflictions, obviously, that would render the Vicar's 'poor animal' an
unpromising sale. A 'spavin' is 'a hard bony tumour or excrescence
formed at the union of the splint-bone and the shank in a horse's leg, and
produced by inflammation of the cartilage uniting those bones'; a wind-
gall is 'A soft tumour on either side of a horse's leg just above the fetlock';
'botts' or 'bots' is 'a parasitical worm or maggot . . . inhabiting the digest-
ive organs of the horse' (*OED*).

St. Gregory, upon good works, professes himself to be of the same opinion:
possibly a reference to a passage in the fifth *Theological Oration* of
St Gregory Nazianzen, in which the 'number of witnesses' required for
testification is discussed with reference to John 1: 8. Included in the
Greek Anthology—excerpts from which helped to form the basis for
most schoolchildren's knowledge of Greek—St Gregory Nazianzen
would have been an author with whom Goldsmith was familiar.

61 *my last pamphlet, the archdeacon's reply, and the hard measure that was dealt*

me: these allusions make no sense in the present state of the novel. See note to p. 16, above.

62 *all human doctrines*: all doctrines relating to secular—as opposed to divine—matters.

Sanconiathon, Manetho, Berosus: the first a Phoenician, the second an Egyptian, the third a Chaldean, whose writings on the history and culture of their respective countries are largely lost.

Anarchon ara kai arelutaion to pan: Friedman suggests this phrase is a reference to Ocellus Lucanus, *De universi natura*, 1. 2. Jenkinson's understanding of the Greek here—to suggest that 'things have neither beginning nor end'—is roughly correct.

ek to biblion kubernetes: Friedman comments that the words appear twice in Galen: *De libris propriis*, 5 and *De compositione medicamentorum per genera*, 3. 2. Judging from the slightly mangled Greek, however, the quotations here appear to have come from a popular book of adages, and not directly from the ancients. If Jenkinson is indeed referring to Galen (AD 129–216) in his subsequent assertion that 'books will never teach the world', he would then appear to be alluding to Galen's methodology, as expressed in his writing on ancient medicine. Galen stressed the need for experiment and practical observation, and chastised those who based their practice on a priori arguments and established hypotheses.

63 *a thirty pound note*: banknotes had been issued in the mid-century to the value of £100 and even £1,000, although it would yet have been unusual to encounter notes of even £10 or £15 in such an environment. Jenkinson's associate Abraham has (supposedly) offered as much as a silver half-crown—itself worth two and a half shillings—to anyone who could change the £30 note for him, but has still met with no success.

the great scarcity of silver: at the time of the novel's action, there would have been several denominations of silver coin (e.g., crown, half-crown, shilling, sixpence) in circulation, and the shortage of such currency was a common and even chronic hindrance. A letter in *Lloyd's Evening Post* for 22–5 January 1762 offers a remedy for the 'scarcity of silver coin'; the *Gazetteer* for 28 August 1762 says, 'The distress of mankind, from the great scarcity of silver, grows every day more insupportable'; the *Gentleman's Magazine* had observed three years earlier, in March 1759, that 'people who have numbers of workmen to pay frequently give 10s in £100 to supply themselves with silver coin'.

a draught upon him, payable at sight: instead of paying the Vicar in cash, Jenkinson has given him a formal, written order for payment of the money that is due to him that has been addressed to Solomon Flamborough; according to such a 'draught' or 'draft', Primrose should now be able to 'draw on' Flamborough as an individual who holds funds that have been set aside or are available for this purpose. He rightly admits within a very short period of time that it was foolish of him to have taken such a draft 'from a stranger'.

65 *a letter-case*: such private letter-cases or letter books, in which an individual could keep, for their own reference, copies of any correspondence sent as well as materials for writing any new letters, or items such as visiting cards or covers, were relatively common in the period.

66 *we shall have some rain by the shooting of my corns*: see a letter on country superstitions in the *Connoisseur*, 59 (13 March 1755): 'my aunt assured us it would be wet, she knew very well by the shooting of her corns'.

67 *a jest book*: collections in which amusing jokes or diverting stories were gathered and made available to the reader as his or her own bons mots were common; the material in some such collections could be bawdy.

An honest man is the noblest work of God: from Alexander Pope's *An Essay on Man* (1733–4), iv. 248: 'An honest man's the noblest work of God.' Burchell is somewhat unusual in so vigorously criticizing Pope's line as 'hackney'd'; he is admittedly suggesting that the maxim was only a slip on Pope's part, one that was, as he puts it, 'very unworthy' of a man of such genius.

tame correct paintings of the Flemish school ... sublime animations of the Roman pencil: Mr Burchell evinces the common preference of the era. As Jeremy Black has observed: 'Renaissance and later Italian paintings were valued greatly in Britain, where they were regarded as the best example of their art. ... The Italian school of painting was considered superior to the Dutch school.' See Jeremy Black, *The British Abroad: The Grand Tour in the Eighteenth Century* (London: Sutton Publishing, 1992), 261.

68 *Don't you know ... hang you all up at his door*: a great many new laws in the 1700s—collectively dubbed the 'Bloody Code' by some historians—would have looked upon the Primrose family's treatment of Mr Burchell's letter-case as a property crime potentially meriting the death penalty. The local 'justice' whose authority Mr Burchell invokes in this passage would have been the justice of the peace, whose office was charged with preserving the peace and apprehending and charging criminals. Ironically, the reader learns later in Goldsmith's novel that this same office is held by no one other than Sir William Thornhill—alias 'Mr Burchell'—himself (see p. 154).

69 *piquet*: (or picquet), 'a card game played by two persons with a pack of 32 cards (the low cards from the two to the six being excluded), in which points are scored on various groups or combinations of cards, and on tricks' (*OED*). The Vicar clearly considers piquet an appropriate game to be taught to his daughters.

sharp: used here to mean both rugged and quick-witted.

70 *well knit*: a term sometimes used by viticulturists and wine enthusiasts to describe the nature of a wine's palate or taste; a wine can be described as

'well knit' or 'well integrated' with reference to its structure or coherence, as opposed to 'disjointed', 'unstructured', or even 'flabby'.

a limner: a picture-maker or, as here, more specifically, an itinerant painter of portraits.

drawn with seven oranges: the orange was occasionally used in such depictions as a symbol of fertility.

one large historical family piece: the Vicar's desire that he and his family be depicted as 'independent historical figures' in 'one large historical piece' in fact results in a picture that is close to catastrophic in its wildly anachronistic depiction of discord and thematic incompatibility. As it stands completed, the oversized family portrait not only includes the inexplicable depiction of the Vicar's wife, as Venus, being presented by her husband with his (in this instance, in particular) radically inappropriate books on monogamy and the Whistonian controversy, but the equally arbitrary inclusion of the disconnected figures of Olivia, represented as an Amazon (see note, below), Sophia, as a shepherdess, and a nondescript Moses. The intrusion of the Squire as Alexander the Great (a historical figure whose rapacious desire for conquest can at least be connected with his own character in the novel) only suggests how foolish the family will prove to have been in permitting him to stand in a position of such intimacy in their household.

71 *a stomacher*: 'an ornamental covering for the chest (often covered with jewels) worn by women under the lacing of the bodice' (*OED*).

Amazon: in classical mythology, Amazons were a band of female warriors that lived on the edges of the known world.

a green joseph, richly laced with gold: a 'joseph'—so called in allusion to the coat worn by the patriarch Joseph in Genesis 41: 48–57—was 'a long cloak, worn chiefly by women in the eighteenth century when riding, and on other occasions; it was buttoned all the way down the front and had a small cape' (*OED*).

encomiums: panegyrics or praises.

Crusoe's long-boat, too large to be removed: the Vicar recalls a famous incident in Defoe's *Robinson Crusoe* (1719). Having been stranded on his island for three years, Crusoe decides to craft a boat for himself. He embarks upon his undertaking 'the most like a Fool, that ever Man did, who had any of his Sense awake'. Only after he has spent close to half a year on the project does Crusoe pause to calculate that it would take him a further ten to twelve years to dig the canal necessary to bring the boat (uphill) to the water. From this episode, Crusoe observes that he has learned a lesson with regard to 'the Folly of beginning a Work before we count the Cost; and before we judge rightly of our own Strength to go through with it'. See Defoe, *Robinson Crusoe*, ed. Crowley, 126–7.

a reel in a bottle: like the more familiar ship in a bottle; an object 'too large to be removed' from the container in which it has been placed.

72 *warm*: used here and in the discussion regarding farmer Williams that follows in the sense of 'comfortably off, well to do; rich, affluent' (*OED*).

76 *Death and the Lady*: an old ballad. Note the portrait of Goldsmith by Joshua Reynolds, in which he links the title with that of the two other ballads referred to in the novel (see p. 23 and note): 'His favourite songs were *Johnny Armstrong*, *Barbara Allen*, and *Death and the Lady*. In singing the last he endeavoured to humour the dialogue by looking very fierce and speaking in rough voice for Death, which he suddenly changed when he came to the lady's part, putting on what he fancied to be a lady-like sweetness of countenance with a thin, shrill voice' (*Portraits by Sir Joshua Reynolds*, ed. F. W. Hilles (London: Heinemann, 1952), 50).

the Dying Swan: the song is given in *The Musical Miscellany; being a Collection of Choice Songs* (1729–31), i. 110–12.

An ELEGY on the Death of a Mad Dog: Lonsdale speculates that this poem was originally written 'between the summer of 1760 and the autumn of 1762' during the early part of which period London 'was seized with something of a panic about mad-dog bites' which Goldsmith derided in his 'Chinese Letters' and reprinted as letters 29, 68, 69, and 75 of his *Citizen of the World* (1762). Noting that the context of the novel makes it clear that the *Elegy* was 'once again satirizing contemporary elegies', Londsale likewise notes that Goldsmith was particularly imitating for three stanzas (as he done throughout the earlier 'An Elegy on that Glory of her Sex, Mrs Mary Blaze') lines included in the French poet La Monnoye's *Menagiana* (3rd edn. 1715) and *Poésies* (1716), the hero of which is 'le fameux la Galisse, homme imaginaire', and in which the last line of each verse stanza deflates the banality of the lines that have preceded it. See Lonsdale, 593–5.

77 *Grograms*: by placing this family name alongside those of 'Blenkinsop' and 'Huginson', Goldsmith appears pointedly to wish to draw attention to the fact that Deborah Primrose's maiden name also designates 'a coarse fabric of silk, of mohair and wool, or of these mixed with silk; often stiffened with gum' (*OED*). The fourth name here—Marjoram—of course recollects the aromatic herb, the leaves of which are used in cooking.

Put the glass to your brother, Moses: i.e., raise your glass in a toast.

78 *Ranelagh*: one of the two most fashionable pleasure gardens in London in the Hanoverian era, the other being Vauxhall. Ranelagh was opened in Chelsea in 1742, and continued until its closure in 1803 to attract a distinctly more 'aristocratic' crowd than its counterpart on the south side of the Thames. Both pleasure gardens remained, for many, venues notorious for sexual assignations; even 'respectable' women were to some degree aware of the extent to which they were putting themselves on display when they paced around Ranelagh's rotunda. It is a testament either to the Vicar's complete innocence or to his complete folly that he

declares that 'there is not a place in the world where advice [regarding courtship and marriage] can be given with so much propriety as there'. In no circumstances would it be at all appropriate for him to praise Ranelagh, as he does here, as 'an excellent market' for potential wives.

Colin meets Dolly ... to get married as fast as they can: an anonymous popular 'Ranelagh song' of this sort entitled 'Colin and Dolly' was included in the first volume of *Clio and Euterpe, or British Harmony*, published in London by Henry Roberts in 1758. The ballad narrative recounted by Moses here, however, more precisely recalls lines such as John Cunningham's 'Holiday Gown', a version of which would be published in Newcastle in 1771.

Fontarabia: perhaps the allusion here is to the manner of securing husbands at Fontarabia employed by the girls operating the boats on 'the river of Andaye', described by the Comtesse d'Aulnoy in *The Ingenious and Diverting Letters of the Lady——Travels into Spain* (2nd edn. 1692; repr. London, 1899), 22: 'When they are willing to marry, they go to Mass at Fontarabia, which is the nearest Town to 'em; and there the young Men come to chuse 'em Wives to their Humour.'

all the ladies of the Continent would come over: Peter Heylyn wrote of England: 'it is acknowledged the *Paradise of Women*. And it is a common by-word among the *Italians*, that if *there were a Bridge built over the Narrow Sea, all the Women of* Europe *would run into* ENGLAND' (*Cosmography, in Four Books: Containing the Chorography and History of the Whole World* (London, 1670), 296–7). See also Edward Chamberlayne, *Angliae Notitia; or, The Present State of England* (London, 1671), i. 316.

79 *a post chaise*: a travelling carriage, further noted in the *OED* usually to have 'a closed body', and capable of seating as many as four individuals. The driver or postilion usually rode on one of the horses.

81 *followed them to the races*: race meetings were held all across the country in the eighteenth century, but the most celebrated racing took place at Newmarket in Cambridgeshire, where, by the middle of the century, the Jockey Club framed the rules for racing that were eventually adopted throughout England.

82 *the philanthropic bookseller in St. Paul's church-yard*: Goldsmith's friend and publisher, John Newbery (1713–67). See J. Rose, 'John Newbery', in J. F. Bracken and J. Silver (eds.), *The British literary Book Trade, 1700–1820*, Dictionary of Literary Biography series, 154 (1995), 216–28; Charles Welsh, *A bookseller of the last century, being some account of the life of John Newbery* (London, 1885).

the history of one Mr. Thomas Trip: 'Thomas Tripp's History of Birds and Beasts, 6d.' appears in a list of children's books advertised by Newberry in the *Public Ledger* for 28 December 1761.

Deuterogamists: 'one who marries a second time, or who upholds second marriages'. This is the only example cited in *OED*.

83 *the Drydens and Otways of the day*: the dramatists admired by the Vicar—
John Dryden (1631–1700) and Thomas Otway (1625–85)—are dismissed
by the player as old-fashioned. Dryden had dominated the theatrical
world of the Restoration and late seventeenth century with tragedies such
as *Tyrannic Love* (1669), *Aurung Zebe* (1675), and *All For Love* (1677).
Otway's two masterpieces, *The Orphan* (1680) and *Venice Preserved* (1682)
were to remain stock pieces (in spite of what the player says here of his
work being 'quite out of fashion') well into the nineteenth century.

Row ... Fletcher ... Johnson: Nicholas Rowe (1674–1718) enjoyed
tremendous success in the early years of the century with his tragedies
The Fair Penitent (1703) and *Jane Shore* (1715); John Fletcher (along with
his frequent writing partner, Francis Beaumont) and Ben Jonson were
both among those popular dramatists whose work rivalled Shakespeare
on the early sixteenth-century stage.

84 *Congreve and Farquhar ... our modern dialect is much more natural*:
William Congreve (1670–1729) and George Farquhar (1677–1707),
whose often elaborately 'witty' comedies had been the popular products
of the late seventeenth-century stage.

85 *in an easy deshabille*: i.e., 'dishabille', from the French *en déshabillé*, meaning 'the state of being partly undressed, or dressed in a negligent or
careless style; undress' (*OED*).

Monitor ... Auditor: weekly periodical essays concerned with politics.
The *Monitor* was founded by Alderman Beckford in 1755, and was
opposed to the government of Lord Bute; the *Auditor*, founded seven
years later by Arthur Murphy, was also in opposition to Bute. Friedman
observes that the fact that the *Auditor* was published regularly only
from 10 June 1762 until 16 May 1763 would suggest time limits for the
composition or revision of this passage.

The Daily ... the White-hall Evening: the newspapers mentioned are
the *Daily Advertiser*, the *Public Advertiser*, the *Public Ledger* (to which
Goldsmith contributed in 1760 and 1761), the *London Chronicle*, the
London Evening Post, and the *Whitehall Evening-Post*.

the two reviews: the *Monthly Review*, to which Goldsmith contributed in
1757 and 1758, and the *Critical Review*, to which he contributed in 1759
and 1760.

by all my coal mines in Cornwall: the fact that his host twice swears by this
oath should have alerted even the Vicar to his duplicity. Cornwall was
well known for the mining not of coal, but of tin.

anotherguess manner: in another way, or a different manner of behaving.

86 *Levellers*: originally, a party among Cromwell's soldiers who wished to
level to an equality all distinctions of rank and property. By 1755,
Johnson could confidently extend the term to refer to any individual
'who destroys superiority' or who 'endeavours to bring all to the same
state of equality'.

87 *a Cartesian system, each orb with a vortex of its own*: according to the 'Cartesian System' or the theory of vortices advanced by the French philosopher René Descartes (1596–1650) to account for the formation of and movement within the universe, space was filled with particles of subtle matter in various states, all of which matter was endowed with a rotary motion postulated as spinning around the sun.

88 *in his family a tyrant*: parallels for most of the political ideas in the Vicar's long speech can be found in Goldsmith's writings of 1760–2.

89 *Wilkinson*: the name is probably intended to suggest John Wilkes, to whose political principles Wilkinson's bear a resemblance.

lie down to be saddled with wooden shoes: wooden shoes were in the eighteenth century 'popularly taken as typical of the miserable condition of the French peasantry' (*OED*).

90 *garden . . . decorated in the modern manner*: i.e., in the less formal and even 'expressive' and 'natural' manner of such landscape architects as Charles Bridgeman, William Kent, and—in the period in which Goldsmith was writing—Lancelot 'Capability' Brown.

near three years absent: the Vicar's assertion that his son George has been absent from the family for nearly three years is at odds with the chronology implied by the rest of the novel, according to which the narrative has by this point moved, roughly, only from spring to early winter.

the Fair Penitent . . . the part of Horatio: Horatio is the friend of one of the central male characters, Altamont, in Nicholas Rowe's notorious 'she-tragedy', first acted at Lincoln's Inn Fields in 1703. *The Fair Penitent* was one of the most popular plays of the century, and Goldsmith might with confidence have expected his readers to draw some possible connections with Rowe's heroine, Calista, who is seduced by the man she loves (Lothario) before being abandoned and forced to marry another (Altamont).

92 *usher at an academy*: taken by many to be a reminiscence of Goldsmith's own experience as a tutor in Dr Milner's school for nonconformists in Peckham in 1756, and again in 1758.

93 *an anodyne necklace*: the Anodyne Necklace, for the relief of teething infants, was sold—curiously enough—'In LONG-ACRE, At Mr. *Burchell's*, at the ANODYNE NECKLACE' (see, for example, the *Public Advertiser* for 6 July 1761). Friedman, apparently working on the notion that an 'anodyne' was a drug or medicine that soothed or assuaged pain, suggested that perhaps here 'an anodyne necklace' is used as slang for a hangman's halter, which would at least bring misfortune to an end. The oath used by George's cousin here may similarly indicate a willingness sooner to succumb to the dubious nostrums and remedies of a 'quack' doctor than ever resume teaching in a school.

honest jogg trot men: straightforward men who go about their work in a humdrum or perfunctory manner.

94 *Propertius*: Sextus Propertius (50–16 BCE), with Ovid, one of the best known of the classical amatory and elegiac poets.

   a Creolian . . . from Jamaica: an obsolete form of 'Creole', the name by which the British referred to 'a person born and naturalized in the West Indies, but of European or of African descent' (*OED*). The name did not carry any reference to skin tone or colour, but was used rather to distinguish those who were born in Europe or Africa from the aboriginal peoples.

   a dedication fee: the fee paid to or asked by a writer for having a work dedicated to a particular subscriber.

95 *Philautos, Philalethes, Philelutheros, and Philanthropos*: pseudonyms supposedly used by writers, meaning—respectively—Lover of Self, of Truth, of Other, and of Mankind. Cf. the preface to *Essays by Mr. Goldsmith* (1765): 'If there be a pride in multiplied editions, I have seen some of my labours sixteen times reprinted, and claimed by different parents as their own. I have seen them . . . signed at the end with the names of Philautos, Philalethes, Philelutheros, and Philanthropos' (*Collected Works*, iii. 1).

96 *My business was to attend him at auctions . . . assist him at tattering a kip*: it was fashionable for otherwise idle loungers of the upper class to pass the morning attending auctions. To 'tatter' meant to tear down or reduce to tatters, and a 'kip' was slang for a brothel, hence George has assisted Thornhill in 'tearing down a brothel' and generally helping to make mischief when he 'had a mind for a frolic'.

97 *her bully and a sharper*: 'bully' was another term for 'the "gallant" or protector of a prostitute; one who lives by protecting prostitutes'.

98 *I found myself alone at his lordship's gate*: Friedman, in *Collected Works* (iv. 114), notes that A. Lytton Sells identified the source of the conclusion to this episode in the first paper of Marivaux's *Le Spectateur français*.

   nature . . . thrown by into her lumber room: 'lumber' was sometimes used as slang in the period for 'a house or room . . . where stolen property is hidden; a house used by criminals' (*OED*).

   Mr. Cripse's office: Friedman noted that a Mr Crisp actually conducted an employment office in London: 'Wanted for North-America, a great Number of Tradesmen, such as House-Carpenters, Joyners, Masons, . . . and a great Number of young Women with their Friends Consent. . . . Enquire at Crisp's Office behind St. Lawrence's Church, near Guildhall'. (*Public Advertiser*, 28 September 1761). Perhaps Goldsmith was willing to make free with Crisp's character because in the first part of 1762, at about the time when Goldsmith was probably writing the novel, Crisp was in trouble with the law: 'A few Days since Elizabeth Webb, a Girl of about Fifteen Years of Age, applying to an Office kept by one *Crisp* for a Service, was by him seduced, kidnapt, and put on board the Elizabeth lying at Gravesend, in Order for her Transportation to America; and

Yesterday he being taken before the Right Hon. The Lord Mayor, was by his Lordship committed to the Poultry Compter [the prison at Poultry Street, in the City].—It was said by some Girls present, that *he*, not content with depriving them of their Liberty, used his utmost Efforts, by Promise of Money, &c. to seduce their Virtue' (*Public Advertiser*, 29 April 1762).

100 *Louvain*: the university at Louvain, in what was then the Duchy of Brabant, was established in 1425 by John IV of the House of Burgundy and Pope Martin V. George's experiences and disappointment at Louvain are in line with a decline in the reputation of the university in this period, when its programme of study and scholarship was perceived to be out-of-date.

like Æsop and his basket of bread: Herodotus informs us in his *Histories* (2. 134) that the historical Aesop was a slave who lived in the middle of the sixth century BCE. One of the many fables attributed to him tells the story of an occasion on which his master, a merchant, intended to undertake a journey. Having requested that he might carry the lightest burden, Aesop took up the basket of bread. The other servants, at first scornfully pointing out that the basket he had chosen was the heaviest of them all, were later compelled to acknowledge the fabulist's ingenuity when— having distributed the bread equally among the servants for dinner and then their later supper—they realized that Aesop's burden had all but disappeared, while their own seemed to grow heavier with each step.

101 *I resolved to go forward*: George's wanderings bear some close resemblances to Goldsmith's own tour of the Continent on foot in 1755. The nature and extent of the resemblances is confused, however, by the fact that some of Goldsmith's earliest biographers put some of George's exact words into Goldsmith's mouth as things he said about himself.

intaglios: 'figure[s] or design[s] incised or engraved; cutting[s] or engraving[s] in stone or other hard material' (*OED*).

connoscento: i.e. cognoscente, 'one who knows a subject thoroughly; a connoisseur: chiefly in reference to the fine arts' (*OED*).

102 *Pietro Perugino*: Italian painter (1446–1524) whose work was particularly admired by a 'cultivated' eighteenth-century audience.

105 *an ensign's commission in one of the regiments that was going to the West Indies*: Mr Thornhill has purchased for George Primrose a commission in the armed forces on the basis of a payment of £100; the Vicar has promised to advance the remaining £200. The practice of selling commissions in the service in this manner continued until as late as 1871 (see W. Fortescue, *A History of the British Army* (London: Macmillan and Co., 1899), i. 316 ff.).

106 *thy brave grandfather . . . to die with Lord Falkland*: Lucius Carey, second Viscount Falkland (b. 1609/10) was killed in action in 1643, when fighting for the royalist cause at the battle of Newbury. If George's grandfather

died with him, and if the time of the action of the novel is supposed to be about 1761 or 1762 (the time the work was probably written), then the Vicar would have to be considerably over 100 years old.

107 *the house is going out of the windows*: proverbial phrase, meaning that everything is falling into confusion.

with a sassarara: alternatively, 'with a siseray', meaning 'with a vengeance'; promptly, suddenly. This example is cited in *OED*.

110 *you shall inform against him to-morrow*: to 'inform' on someone in this sense meant to accuse them of a crime or wrongdoing; i.e., to act as an informant to the law.

114 *ninety nine persons who have supported a course of undeviating rectitude*: Goldsmith's biblical references are to Matthew 18: 12–14 and Luke 15: 4–7, both of which relate versions of the parable of the lost sheep.

119 *WHEN lovely woman stoops to folly*: reprinted in Lonsdale as 'Song from *The Vicar of Wakefield*', where the editor notes that the lines were 'presumably written before the autumn of 1762 when the MS of *Vicar* was sold to Newberry'. Lonsdale also comments that Austin Dobson, in his *Complete Poetical Works* (Oxford, 1906), had 'objected to "the impropriety, and even inhumanity" of making the wretched girl sing such a song but [Goldsmith] and his audience, like the Primrose family, enjoyed the mood of soothing melancholy which it induced'. See Lonsdale, 595–6.

120 *my steward talks of driving for the rent*: i.e., the officer who manages Thornhill's lands and household has been obliged to put pressure on the Vicar for prompt payment of the rent owed to the Squire.

121 *Like one of those instruments . . . presents a point to receive the enemy*: the Vicar compares his defiant attitude to that of a projectile missile used in war as a kind of weapon—such as a heavy metal ball or chuck—that is designed so as to be 'pointed' or dangerously studded in such a manner as to harm the enemy, regardless of the attitude in which it strikes.

125 *He asked me if I had taken care to provide myself with a bed . . . never once attended to*: prisoners in the Vicar's position would actually have been compelled to pay extra for any amenities when imprisoned. Such payment extended not only to a bed or to any food and drink beyond the simplest penny-loaf of bread and water, but to such items as sheets, candles, coals, and also to the privilege of entertaining any visitors.

Ton kosman aire, ei dos ton etairon; roughly, 'Take the world, and with it you are given a companion'.

Welbridge: apparently a place of Goldsmith's own invention.

126 *a coiner*: a counterfeiter.

131 *turn sharper in my own defence*: Jenkinson claims that he was compelled to become a 'sharper'—a rogue and a swindler—only because people, judging him from his appearance, insisted that he must have been one in the first place.

132 *cribbage . . . tobacco stoppers*: cribbage is 'a game at cards, played by two, three, or four persons, with a complete pack of 52 cards, five (or six) of which are dealt to each player, and a board with sixty-one holes on which the points are scored by means of pegs; a characteristic feature being the "crib", consisting of cards thrown out from each player's hand, and belonging to the dealer' (*OED*). Ironically, of course, given the context here, 'cribbage' also referred to anything that had been 'cribbed' or stolen. Tobacco stoppers are instruments used for tamping down loose tobacco in the bowl of a pipe, to be smoked.

cutting pegs for tobacconists and shoemakers: the Vicar sets his fellow prisoners to work fashioning the small pins of wood used by tobacconists and their customers to tamp tobacco into pipes or, later, cigarettes with series of light taps. Shoemakers used a slightly different sort of peg to fasten the 'uppers' of a shoe to the sole, or to fasten the 'lifts'—the layers of leather used to form the heel—to each other.

143 *the first transgressor upon the statute*: such a statute is apparently a complete invention on the part of Goldsmith. A challenge to fight was found to be a misdemeanour, punishable with fine and imprisonment, only in 1851. See Earl Jowitt and Clifford Walsh (eds.), *The Dictionary of English Law* (London, 1959), i. 399.

144 *much has been given man to enjoy, yet still more to* suffer: Friedman draws attention in *Collected Works* (iv. 160) to the similarity between the Vicar's sentiments here and those expressed in chapter XI of Johnson's *Rasselas*: 'The Europeans, answered Imlac, are less unhappy than we, but they are not happy. Human life is everywhere a state in which much is to be endured, and little to be enjoyed.'

146 *the poor man in the parable*: the parable of Lazarus, as it is told in Luke 16: 20–5.

151 *says a certain philosopher*: Seneca, in his short ethical treatise *De Providentia* (On Providence), 2.6. One of ten such treatises, the work maintains that it is impossible for a good man truly to suffer in the hands of evil. Goldsmith's library—at the time of his death—contained a complete set of the works of Seneca.

152 *staked a counter*: a counter was 'an imitation coin of brass or inferior metal; a token used to represent real coin' (*OED*). Hence 'to stake a counter' meant to make a wager with a counterfeit coin, to undertake a gamble with nothing 'at stake'.

Sir William Thornhill: Oswald Doughty calls attention to the possible identification of Sir William Thornhill as Sir George Savile, MP for the county of York—an identification first made by Edward Ford in his article 'Names and Characters in *The Vicar of Wakefield*', *National Review* (May 1883). Sir George Savile (1726–84), the eighth baronet Savile, was a politician. His main estate was at Rufford, Nottinghamshire, but, like his father, he pursued his parliamentary career in Yorkshire, where his seat was at Thornhill, near Dewsbury. He was best known for speaking out in favour of respecting the wishes of the voters in the matter of John Wilkes and the contested Middlesex election in 1769, and for his fierce opposition to the punitive measures directed against the American colonies beginning in 1774. See John Cannon, 'Savile, Sir George, eighth baronet (1726–1784)', in the *Oxford DNB*, xlix. 107–9.

153 *Pinwire of Newcastle*: an athletically superior individual apparently of Goldsmith's own invention, although his name—further suggestive of the 'lengthy' legs commented on by Sophia and the extremely lean physique suitable for pre-eminence in activities such as sprinting and running—recalls the descriptive nicknames often bestowed on those who dominated other sports in the period, such as those of the prizefighters Benjamin ('Big Ben') Bryan or Brain, Bill ('the Tinman') Hooper, or the otherwise unidentified 'Fighting Grenadier' who was defeated by Brain in Bloomsbury in 1786.

156 *equitable*: fair or technically in accordance with equity, if not exactly just or—as Sir William puts it—'generous'.

a candidate for Tyburn: someone likely to be hanged.

161 *The articles, and a bond for her fortune, are signed, and safe in my possession*: i.e., the articles of marriage. The development in the mid-eighteenth century—signalled most notably by Lord Hardwicke's Marriage Act in 1753—of parliamentary civil laws that transferred the authority governing the regulations of marriage to the central government, although primarily concerned with the outlawing of clandestine marriages as well as marriages entered into without parental consent by persons under the age of 21, in fact helped to give husbands even greater control of their wives' properties. Squire Thornhill, as his uncle immediately acknowledges, would consequently, under those stricter laws governing marriage settlements in the period, legally already have secured for himself the entirety of Miss Wilmot's 'large fortune'.

163 *stiver*: used generally to refer to any small coin of little value; a small quantity of anything, a 'bit'; 'not a stiver' means 'not one single bit'.

a tobacco stopper: see note to p. 132.

squibs: the term squib was occasionally used in the mid-eighteenth century to signify 'a mean, insignificant, or paltry fellow' (*OED*), although it more commonly referred to any firework or small explosive device that terminated in a slight or annoying rather than dangerous explosion. In either case, Thornhill means to signify that he is beyond such petty tricks.

164 *And shook their chains | In transport and rude harmony*: from William Congreve's tragedy, *The Mourning Bride* (1697), Act I, scene ii.

165 *made an honest woman of*: Judith Siefring (ed.), *Oxford Dictionary of Idioms* (Oxford: Oxford University Press, 2004), s.v. 'honest', notes that the phrase *make an honest woman of* was already, by this time, 'dated and

humorous', and meant to marry a woman, 'especially to avoid scandal if she is pregnant'. For the level of usage of this phrase see Fielding, *The History of Tom Jones*, bk. XV, ch. viii: 'Miss Nancy was, in vulgar language, made an honest woman'; Richardson, *The History of Sir Charles Grandison* (5th edn., 1766), iv. 251: 'The Lord grant . . . that he may be. . . obliged to make a ruined girl an *honest woman*, as they phrase it in LANCASHIRE.'

The Oxford World's Classics Website

www.worldsclassics.co.uk

- Browse the full range of Oxford World's Classics online

- Sign up for our monthly e-alert to receive information on new titles

- Read extracts from the Introductions

- Listen to our editors and translators talk about the world's greatest literature with our Oxford World's Classics audio guides

- Join the conversation, follow us on Twitter at OWC_Oxford

- Teachers and lecturers can order inspection copies quickly and simply via our website

www.worldsclassics.co.uk

American Literature

British and Irish Literature

Children's Literature

Classics and Ancient Literature

Colonial Literature

Eastern Literature

European Literature

Gothic Literature

History

Medieval Literature

Oxford English Drama

Poetry

Philosophy

Politics

Religion

The Oxford Shakespeare

A complete list of Oxford World's Classics, including Authors in Context, Oxford English Drama, and the Oxford Shakespeare, is available in the UK from the Marketing Services Department, Oxford University Press, Great Clarendon Street, Oxford OX2 6DP, or visit the website at www.oup.com/uk/worldsclassics.

In the USA, visit www.oup.com/us/owc for a complete title list.

Oxford World's Classics are available from all good bookshops. In case of difficulty, customers in the UK should contact Oxford University Press Bookshop, 116 High Street, Oxford OX1 4BR.

	Late Victorian Gothic Tales
JANE AUSTEN	Emma
	Mansfield Park
	Persuasion
	Pride and Prejudice
	Selected Letters
	Sense and Sensibility
MRS BEETON	Book of Household Management
MARY ELIZABETH BRADDON	Lady Audley's Secret
ANNE BRONTË	The Tenant of Wildfell Hall
CHARLOTTE BRONTË	Jane Eyre
	Shirley
	Villette
EMILY BRONTË	Wuthering Heights
ROBERT BROWNING	The Major Works
JOHN CLARE	The Major Works
SAMUEL TAYLOR COLERIDGE	The Major Works
WILKIE COLLINS	The Moonstone
	No Name
	The Woman in White
CHARLES DARWIN	The Origin of Species
THOMAS DE QUINCEY	The Confessions of an English Opium-Eater
	On Murder
CHARLES DICKENS	The Adventures of Oliver Twist
	Barnaby Rudge
	Bleak House
	David Copperfield
	Great Expectations
	Nicholas Nickleby
	The Old Curiosity Shop
	Our Mutual Friend
	The Pickwick Papers

WALTER SCOTT	Rob Roy
MARY SHELLEY	Frankenstein The Last Man
ROBERT LOUIS STEVENSON	Strange Case of Dr Jekyll and Mr Hyde and Other Tales Treasure Island
BRAM STOKER	Dracula
JOHN SUTHERLAND	So You Think You Know Jane Austen? So You Think You Know Thomas Hardy?
WILLIAM MAKEPEACE THACKERAY	Vanity Fair
OSCAR WILDE	The Importance of Being Earnest and Other Plays The Major Works The Picture of Dorian Gray
ELLEN WOOD	East Lynne
DOROTHY WORDSWORTH	The Grasmere and Alfoxden Journals
WILLIAM WORDSWORTH	The Major Works

D. H. LAWRENCE | The Rainbow
Sons and Lovers
The White Peacock
The Widowing of Mrs Holroyd and Other Plays
Women in Love

KATHERINE MANSFIELD | Selected Stories

MARIE STOPES | Married Love

ROBERT TRESSELL | The Ragged Trousered Philanthropists

VIRGINIA WOOLF | Between the Acts
Flush
Jacob's Room
Mrs Dalloway
The Mark on the Wall and Other Short Fiction
Night and Day
Orlando: A Biography
A Room of One's Own and Three Guineas
To the Lighthouse
The Voyage Out
The Waves
The Years

W. B. YEATS | The Major Works

	Travel Writing 1700–1830
	Women's Writing 1778–1838
WILLIAM BECKFORD	Vathek
JAMES BOSWELL	Life of Johnson
FRANCES BURNEY	Camilla
	Cecilia
	Evelina
	The Wanderer
LORD CHESTERFIELD	Lord Chesterfield's Letters
JOHN CLELAND	Memoirs of a Woman of Pleasure
DANIEL DEFOE	A Journal of the Plague Year
	Moll Flanders
	Robinson Crusoe
	Roxana
HENRY FIELDING	Jonathan Wild
	Joseph Andrews and Shamela
	Tom Jones
WILLIAM GODWIN	Caleb Williams
OLIVER GOLDSMITH	The Vicar of Wakefield
MARY HAYS	Memoirs of Emma Courtney
ELIZABETH INCHBALD	A Simple Story
SAMUEL JOHNSON	The History of Rasselas
	The Major Works
CHARLOTTE LENNOX	The Female Quixote
MATTHEW LEWIS	Journal of a West India Proprietor
	The Monk
HENRY MACKENZIE	The Man of Feeling

ALEXANDER POPE	Selected Poetry
ANN RADCLIFFE	The Italian
	The Mysteries of Udolpho
	The Romance of the Forest
	A Sicilian Romance
CLARA REEVE	The Old English Baron
SAMUEL RICHARDSON	Pamela
RICHARD BRINSLEY SHERIDAN	The School for Scandal and Other Plays
TOBIAS SMOLLETT	The Adventures of Roderick Random
	The Expedition of Humphry Clinker
LAURENCE STERNE	The Life and Opinions of Tristram Shandy, Gentleman
	A Sentimental Journey
JONATHAN SWIFT	Gulliver's Travels
	Major Works
	A Tale of a Tub and Other Works
JOHN VANBRUGH	The Relapse and Other Plays
HORACE WALPOLE	The Castle of Otranto
MARY WOLLSTONECRAFT	Mary and The Wrongs of Woman
	A Vindication of the Rights of Woman

An Anthology of Elizabethan Prose Fiction

An Anthology of Seventeenth-Century Fiction

Early Modern Women's Writing

Three Early Modern Utopias (Utopia; New Atlantis; The Isle of Pines)

FRANCIS BACON   **Essays**
The Major Works

APHRA BEHN   **Oroonoko and Other Writings**
The Rover and Other Plays

JOHN BUNYAN   **Grace Abounding**
The Pilgrim's Progress

JOHN DONNE   **The Major Works**
Selected Poetry

BEN JONSON   **The Alchemist and Other Plays**
The Devil is an Ass and Other Plays
Five Plays

JOHN MILTON   **The Major Works**
Paradise Lost
Selected Poetry

SIR PHILIP SIDNEY   **The Old Arcadia**
The Major Works

IZAAK WALTON   **The Compleat Angler**